A TIME BETWEEN

A Novel

SHIRLEY STRESHINSKY

A TIME BETWEEN

A Novel

TURNER

TURNER PUBLISHING
200 4th Avenue North, Suite 950
Nashville, Tennessee 37219

445 Park Avenue, 9th Floor
New York, New York 10022

www.turnerpublishing.com

A Time Between

Published simultaneously in Canada by General Publishing Co. Limited, Toronto.
The author gratefully acknowledges permission from the following sources to reprint
material in their control: Norma Millay (Ellis), Literary Executor, for lines from "Eel-
grass" by Edna St. Vincent Millay in Collected Poems published by Harper & Row.

Copyright 1921, 1943 by Edna St. Vincent Millay.
Warner Bros. Inc. for lines from "Ain't We Got Fun" © 1921(Renewed) by Warner
Bros. Inc. and "Silv'ry Moon" © 1929 (Renewed) by Warner Bros. Inc.
All rights reserved.

Library of Congress Cataloging in Publication Data
Streshinsky, Shirley.
A time between / Shirley Streshinsky.
pages cm
ISBN 978-1-61858-023-8 (pbk.)
1. Women journalists--Fiction. 2. Irish--United States--Fiction. 3. United States--
History--1919-1933--Fiction. I. Title.
PS3569.T6928T5 2013
813'.54--dc23
2012040325
Cover by Gina Binkley
Designed by Glen M. Edelstein
Printed in the United States of America
13 14 15 16 17 18 0 9 8 7 6 5 4 3 2 1

ACKNOWLEDGMENTS

IT IS IMPORTANT to begin by thanking Diane Reverand, the editor of this book, who from the very beginning was excited about San Francisco in the 1920s and the extraordinary women who were part of that time and place. Diane's own extraordinary skills have been mainstays in the writing of this book.

I want also to thank two veteran San Francisco newspapermen who were especially generous with their time, and who shared their memories of San Francisco in the 1920s with me. Eugene Block began his newspaper career in 1908 and served as city editor under the legendary Fremont Older. Stuart Rasmussen, librarian at the *San Francisco Examiner*, was a young man in the 1920s, but his memory of the era is keen.

Several very good friends must be thanked: newsman Ben Bagdikian, long a Washington correspondent and now professor of journalism at the University of California at Berkeley; David Johnston, reporter for the *San Francisco Examiner* and his wife, photographer Janet Fries, who went to the fights with me; San Francisco lawyers Ken Jones and John Vlahos; Ingrid and Ralph Schultheis, who always do whatever needs doing; and Marge and Leon Markel, longtime San Franciscans who charmed me with their stories. I need also to thank my brother, Harry Gaghen, who helped me with the Montana research, and my cousin, Joyce Eastin, who made my Sacramento probings so much easier.

The librarians in the newspaper room at the Oakland Public Library were particularly helpful, as were those who staff the San Francisco Historical Society and the Bancroft Library in Berkeley. The librarians at the Kensington Public Library deserve a special round of applause.

Two who did library time with me are Mark and Maria Streshinsky, and their father was my coconspirator in all of this. I cannot thank those three enough.

When a work of fiction includes historical material, as this one does, the reader is often hard put to separate fact from fiction. To ease this dilemma, I would like to say that while all of the major characters in this book are fictional, two were suggested by real people: Sanford Curtin, by San Francisco editor Fremont Older, and Agnes Marchant, by an Oakland woman named Anita Whitney. Even so, only the most general outlines of their lives coincide with my characters'. Curtin and Marchant are inventions.

Real historical figures do appear in this book, and occasionally they do make speeches. Whenever that happens, I have tried always to make them speak in character. For example, Alice Roosevelt Longworth is quoted as having called President Harding a "slob."

One historical error is purposeful. The movie *Greed* was filmed in 1921, not 1923 as I have it here. If there are other errors, they are mine.

Shirley Streshinsky

For Ted

It was an era of lawless and disorderly defense of law and order, of unconstitutional defense of the Constitution, of suspicion and civil conflict—in a very literal sense, a reign of terror.

—Frederick Lewis Allen, *Only Yesterday, An Informal History of the 1920's*

In the meantime
In between time
Ain't we got fun?

A TIME BETWEEN

PROLOGUE

San Francisco
November 11, 1927

ODD MEMORIES and random shards of conversation work their way into my thoughts in the early hours of morning. I wake at four or at five, too excited to sleep. It has been this way for weeks.

This morning something Faith said in passing kept at me. Provoked, I suppose, by someone she was photographing, she had complained, "People don't listen. They become so absorbed in what they have to say that they never hear what you are telling them."

She is right. People don't listen. I didn't listen. I heard the words but not the silences between them. I missed the important inflections, the small hesitations, the peripheral details. I missed the nuances where the truth so often hides.

I should have heard but I didn't.

Today is Armistice Day. The war ended nine years ago. There will be a parade down Market Street. There will be bunting and flags flying and veterans marching in uniform, the wide hats and the winding puttees. There will be speeches about the Great War and how the Yanks came and how they stayed until it was over, over there.

As if it were over. As if we weren't a generation crippled, in one way or another, by the war.

Too restless to sleep, I pace about my flat, exhilarated by the prospect of a new day. I want to hurry the sun, to lift it from behind the East Bay hills. I tread lightly, not to disturb those sleeping in the flat below. Yet wanting them to be up, to be alive with me, to get on with the day.

We are to sail on the *Ile de France*. First to the American cemetery at Romagne-sous-Montfaucon. A pilgrimage, an end to old sorrows. Then on to Paris for an interview with Aristide Briand, the minister of foreign affairs. And to Germany with a letter of introduction to Hermann Muller, who will be the Chancellor if the Socialists win in the May elections. Europe is in economic chaos; France has devalued the franc; Hindenburg has repudiated Germany's responsibility for the War; there is so much to understand before I can write with any authority.

I am to be special correspondent for six West Coast newspapers, including my own, the *San Francisco Times*. To mark the tenth anniversary of the war, I have been assigned to travel through Europe to talk to the people and their leaders, and to write about what is happening and try to predict what lies ahead. "The American people want to be reassured that there will never be another war," the Boss told me. "We hope you will be able to give those assurances."

I pick up a fossilized sand dollar from the table near my bed and hold it in the palm of my hand. The photograph I keep next to it was taken the day Agnes found the fossil and gave it to me. It is not a posed picture. My brother and I had walked down the beach together and had paused, locked in conversation, leaning into the wind with the ocean stretched to infinity behind us, his head bent to mine. Faith made that photograph the first time we went to

Willow Camp together—Agnes and Sara, Clive and Faith. And Riordan. October, 1921. To celebrate my twenty-seventh birthday and Agnes's fifty-first. *Before.* I am like those San Franciscans who define time in terms of before or after the 1906 quake, which must have created some intrinsic division in their lives.

I study the fossil and the photograph, both frozen in time. I look out of my kitchen window and see that the sun is lighting the fingers of fog that have drifted from the Bay into the deep recesses of the city. The floorboards of the Victorian flat creak, as if to signal some diurnal change.

Right now, Lennie, the newsboy who has a stand on the corner of Fifth and Mission, will be waiting for the first edition. Lennie, who isn't a boy at all, though he was when his legs were blown off at Chateau-Thierry.

Lennie won't be marching in the parade today.

Nor will Riordan.

On my way to work I will stop at the Laurel Hill Cemetery to take flowers to Babe, who fell in another war.

Strange, how one circle closes just as another, wider circle opens. When I spoke to Faith of the war and of circles closing, she said that perhaps they weren't circles at all, but only seemed so if viewed from above, or in hindsight. If we look at them from another angle, she suggested, they might prove to be spirals, ever rising, ever widening.

I said I found that to be a frightening prospect—no circle ever closing, no war to end all wars. And she said that maybe all we could ever be certain of was movement, and change.

I think now that she is right about that, too.

There are times when, late in the afternoon before the fog rolls back through the Golden Gate, a luminous yellow light catches, permeates, holds. For the time that it lasts, which is not long, the whole world is bathed in radiant light. I saw it for the first time not long after I arrived in San Francisco in the summer of 1920. It seemed to me to be an illusion, too beautiful to be real. I did not know, then, what it was to be real.

I know now that nothing was as it seemed. Perhaps nothing ever is. What I must do is go back, thread through all that has happened, make translations of a sort—in light of what I know now that I did not know then. Now and then. Before and after. Circles and spirals.

ONE

ANNIE FARRELL stood looking down at some papers spread out before her on the press table, oblivious of the commotion all around her in the Sacramento County Courthouse. She shifted, bent over to pencil some notation on one of the papers and seemed scarcely to notice as the principals—the jealous husband, his wife, the minister—entered the courtroom. The women crowded into seats all around me stirred and craned to get a look at them. I watched Annie Farrell.

It was late in the winter of my first year out of high school. The trial promised to be sensational enough to draw reporters from as far as Los Angeles. The minister of the largest Methodist congregation in the city had been sued by his secretary's husband, the manager of the Savoy Theater, for alienation of his wife's affections. In a complaint filed in Superior Court, the theater manager accused the minister of making "violent love"—those were the words in the complaint—to the manager's wife. He said he would still have her affections "but for the malevolent, conniving, lustful and lecherous pastor and his prurient carnal desire."

Lecherous preachers and carnal desires—normally forbidden subjects—were suddenly, by virtue of justice and the law, entertainment of a high order. Since people love to see the lofty fall from grace, the old courthouse was overrun the first morning of the trial by women pushing for a good seat. I was there too, having decided to forgo the shorthand and typing I was supposed to be learning at the business academy.

Most of the newspapers in northern California sent reporters. Annie Farrell came from the *San Francisco Times*. A murmur of awe sifted through the crowd: "The *Times* is here." It gave the trial added stature. Annie Farrell was known as a "sob sister," a reporter who concentrates on the human aspects of a story, who writes about the people behind the headlines. Most sob sisters larded their stories with sentimentality, making them mawkish and maudlin. Annie Farrell never did, I suspected because she had been trained by Sanford Curtin. She had moved with him from the *Bulletin* to the *Times*. I had been reading Annie Farrell's stories ever since I came to California. What I liked about them was their sparseness. With a few straightforward sentences she could make you see someone with perfect clarity or understand what was important.

I was surprised at how small she was. She had a strong jaw that kept her from being pretty. She was wearing a severely tailored suit with a ruffled waist, a careful feminine touch. I noted that her skirt was shorter than most of those in the courtroom, and wider at the hemline so she could walk more easily. But what held my attention was something else, something more difficult to describe. It was that she seemed somehow to belong at the press table with all the men. She was at ease in the stately courtroom, and with the ritual. It was a wonder to me, to see a woman nodding and speaking familiarly with the men who shared the table with her, seeming so competent in these surroundings.

I watched how she sat, her back straight and her hands folded on her lap until she needed to make notes. She would take up her pen and write steadily, concentrating so hard she wasn't aware of the reporter next to her who was reading what she wrote. Whenever there were delays in the court proceedings she would study one of the principals—the accused or the accuser or their mates, and then the slightest little furrow would appear between her eyes, and she would pick up the pen again and write steadily.

I watched as she watched the Savoy manager in his belted Norfolk jacket and natty bow tie. Every now and then he would tip back in his chair and, preening, run his hands through his wavy hair. They were small hands, soft and repulsive. He seemed to be having too good a time, I thought, and I wondered what Annie Farrell was writing.

A few days later I found out. "The husband," she wrote in the *Times*, "has cast himself as the wronged party in this domestic tragicomedy. He tips his chair frequently to give his audience a better view of his profile. He makes comments to his lawyers, loud enough to carry to the first rows of spectators, much as an actor would deliver a soliloquy. Then he smiles in the direction of those townspeople who have crowded into the courtroom, some of them Methodists from the accused's congregation. For a man who has introduced so many acts in his capacity as manager of the Savoy Theater, he seems to enjoy being at stage center at last, playing a leading role in his own life's drama. All the while his wife, a pale young woman whose hands will not be still, sits in a seat that is equidistant from her husband and her employer, and stares at the floor. As each sordid detail is read into the record, she seems visibly to shrink until it seems possible that soon she may vanish altogether."

I returned to Howe's Academy with a renewed vigor that amazed my instructors. I knew, now, how I was going to use those typing and shorthand skills. I was going to be a newspaper reporter.

In a few weeks I finished my course, scoring well in speed and accuracy and poorly in neatness. That weekend I announced to my grandparents that I planned to become a reporter in the manner of Annie Farrell. Grandmother raised her sun-browned hand to her head and said, "Oh, my goodness, Hallie," so I knew how much I had shocked her, since she almost never called me by my given name, which had been my mother's. Grandfather didn't say anything at all, which was not surprising. But the light was in his eyes. Near the end of the following day he asked if I would like for him to talk to a friend of his who published a weekly paper in the next county.

It wasn't until I pulled out my valise and put it on the bed that had been my mother's, in the room that had been hers, that a wave of sorrow welled in me. I had come to this room six years ago, filled with pain and hurt and an aching loss. And those two good people, who had loved my mother, had loved me as well. *Home*, I thought: *This is my home. I am leaving home.*

Grandmother appeared in the doorway, wiping her hands on her apron. "So, girl," she said, "you're going off to write stories that will bring a tear to the eye, are you?"

I grinned at her and answered, "Yes, I am. Hallie Duer, Sob Sister. How do you like that?"

There was, we both knew, a certain irony to the idea.

I did not cry when my mother died on a Sunday and I did not cry when my father ended his own life the Thursday after. I did not cry even when Grandmother Duer decided that my brother should stay on in Chicago with her while I was to be sent to California to live with my mother's parents. Nor did I cry at Union Station when my brother said good-bye to me, though for a terrible moment I was afraid that he might break our pact and cry. He grasped me hard by the shoulders and told me he would come and get me just as soon as he could, and I tried to act as if I believed him because I knew he wanted me to.

Grandmother Duer had kissed me coolly on one cheek and then the other. I understood that she would take comfort in my tears, but I would not shed them. The year was 1906. My brother Clive was fifteen, I was twelve. At nine-thirty on a Sunday morning I climbed onto the Overland Limited, took my seat and watched out the window as Iowa and Nebraska, Wyoming and Utah and Nevada rolled by. I watched as the rain streaked against the window. Throughout the night black drops of rain pelted the windows like all the dark tears inside me, locked hard against the world. I watched as we passed through the lonely plains, the monotony broken by little towns huddled around stands of dusty trees. On the fourth day we reached the mountains, the Sierra Nevada. Cold seeped up through the floorboards as we climbed higher and higher in the mountains, but I didn't feel the cold. All I felt was the tears blowing inside of me, pelting and hurting so that I feared I might drown.

I tried never to sleep. Whenever I drowsed off, I could feel tears rising, moving up into my throat and mouth and nose so that I couldn't breathe. I would wake and sit up straight in the dark, rolling and rocking through the land, and I would breathe in careful measures. Sometimes I would wake and for an instant believe that if I could only concentrate hard enough I could will it not to have happened, I could will them back. . . .

Then the train dropped down the western slope and into the Sacramento Valley, arriving at the great Gothic station in Sacramento at five-thirty in the afternoon. My grandparents were waiting.

My grandparents lived on a small farm on the edge of town, next to a woods. The house sat at the end of a lane lined by a double row of royal palms. It was possible, I soon discovered, to climb out the window of my room, which had been my mother's, onto a limb of oak tree, and down to the ground. I did this secretly for some time, until Grandmother happened to see me one day. I discovered she didn't mind in the least.

My grandparents seemed not to mind much that I did. I was treated with great courtesy and an absentminded kindness. They made no demands. Though little seemed expected of me, I had the feeling they were watching me from a distance at times.

I assigned myself some chores—gathering eggs for Grandmother, which meant climbing into the hayloft in search of hidden nests. I went for the mail every day, walking the half-mile to the row of boxes at the crossroads, almost always finding one of the magazines or newspapers Grandfather subscribed to. In all, eighteen magazines and six newspapers came to the farm, and Grandfather read them all.

Sometimes I pumped water for the horses or went blackberry picking with Grandmother into the far gullies, careful always to take along a rattlesnake stick made from an old broom handle.

Grandmother gave me careful instructions: "Swish that stick ahead of you in the grass and make a commotion to let them know you're coming. Most of the time a rattler will get out of your way. They're defenders, not attackers. But if you surprise one of them, well, girl, you're just going to have to face up to it. You can't give in to fears. Rattlers will teach you that. You're going to have to kill it. Either settle that in your head or never go out of the house, not in these parts."

Those first weeks I explored the farm and the countryside that bounded it. I found a magnolia tree in the pasture south of the farm, and climbed high into the branches to pick the largest blossoms. Grandmother loved flowers, and I wanted to take her the biggest, most perfect blooms I could find.

On the way back I stopped to rest on one of the stone fences Grandmother told me the Chinese had built back in the Gold Rush days.

I heard the sound—dry, like wind drumming on hot air—and I knew it was there before I saw it, coiled on the rocky ledge . . . its heart-shaped head was waving and its neck was arched and moving, moving. I jumped as it struck. It hit the folds of my dress, then it pulled back, its tongue flickering, ready . . . my grip tightened on my broomstick . . . the head waved, arched, struck and I brought the stick down. I beat at it, flailing at first . . . then I aimed. I hit and

I hit again, I hit it until it did not move but only lay there on the rocky ledge. I looked at it until the throbbing inside of me exploded and I could feel my legs go weak. Then I picked up Grandmother's magnolia blossoms and moved, my heart pounding, toward home.

Grandfather brought it back to the barnyard and draped it over the fence.

"Big fella," Grandmother said, shielding her eyes.

"Big and young," Grandfather allowed, "Crotalus—a Pacific rattler." Then he asked, "How old are you now, Hallie?"

"Twelve," I answered.

"Twelve and what?" he wanted to know.

"Twelve and nine months?" I said.

"And how many days?"

I had to stop and figure. "Twelve and nine and eleven."

"Go look in the barn," he told me. "See what you see nailed to a wall in the old tack room. You'll have to poke behind where the harnesses are hanging."

The barn was dim and dusty in the afternoon light, and smelled of straw and dung, rich and earthy. I blew away some of the cobwebs from the old harnesses and I found it: the dusty remains of a snakeskin, tacked to the wall, and a small board on which was carved: *Henrietta Lanier, aged 13 years, 3 months, 2 days, killed this rattler on August 5, 1882. It was 4 feet, 2 inches long.*

I walked back out into the sunlight, blinked and asked: "How long is mine?"

"Four-feet-nine," Grandfather said, and then I saw something in his eyes that I hadn't seen before—a flicker of motion, light . . . and surprise, and something else, something I didn't understand but liked. I wanted to make it happen again. At that moment, Grandmother tucked her arm around my shoulders and said, "Scares me silly, those creatures . . . just sends terrible shivers through me."

I let myself lean against her and I said, "Me too." We all laughed then. I hadn't laughed in a very long time, and it felt nice.

Over the following months and years I subscribed to *Scribner's* and *The Atlantic Monthly* and, for some reason, *Hotel Management*. Grandfather read these as well as his own, and sometimes we would trade articles back and forth until after a while it came to seem as if we were having long discussions. In fact, Grandfather was not a talkative man, but whenever he spoke he always said something that was worth hearing.

In the spring of my first year in high school, the *San Francisco Bulletin* fired its famous editor, Sanford Curtin, because he was "too chummy with labor, anarchists and Bolshevists and low life." He was promptly hired by the rival *San Francisco Times*, where he wrote an editorial explaining the kind of freedom he felt a newspaper editor needed. Grandfather cleared his throat and read aloud: "For me, freedom has always meant the chance for an honest, frank discussion of the ideas of other people. It seems to me that a newspaper ought to represent the wishes and interests and experiences of people—it ought to reflect their follies and their crimes, their fears as well as their hopes, their weaknesses as well as their heroic efforts. A newspaper that is allowed this freedom can be a force for progress; even more, it can be an instrument to create a kindly, happy environment."

Grandfather cancelled our subscription to the *Bulletin* and I copied Mr. Curtin's editorial in my best hand and put it on the wall in my room.

There was a library of sorts in the house, an eclectic selection that lined two whole walls of our front hall. The books were mildewed and the mice had nibbled on some of the bindings. One set offered three-page synopses of the major works of the world's great authors. From Louisa May Alcott to Homer, from Ibsen to Zola. I read them all.

On rainy winter days the front entry was my haven. I would

curl in a big chair, cover myself with one of Grandmother's afghans, and read or write letters to my brother.

For the first few years, I wrote him every week without fail. He wrote me each Monday, the only day of the week when Grandmother Duer had to be away, tending to details of the business Grandfather, and father after him, had left.

By 1910 I was attending Sacramento High School, while Clive was enrolled at the University of Chicago in the school of civil engineering, taking courses in architectural design. I was pleased for him, and pleased with myself for helping him get there, but I had paid a price for it.

Grandmother Duer had been set on Clive's taking a liberal-arts degree, as our father had, and then going into the family business.

"Dear Clive," I had written, "I have your last letter in which you seem determined to go against your own best interests and do what Grandmother has decided you should do. Think! For as long as I have known you, and that is forever for me, you have wanted to build things. When we were little, you drew pictures of buildings. I remember Mother saying she was sure you'd grow up either to be a carpenter or a designer of great buildings. It is your life, Clive. Your career. Grandmother can't live it for you, and you mustn't let her. Give her all the arguments you have given me in your letters. Convince her. I'll stand behind you, I promise!"

That was when I discovered that Grandmother Duer read my letters. I was to have returned to Chicago that summer for my first visit with my brother in two years. Grandmother Duer wrote to say that "unforeseen events" had made my visit impossible.

The day her letter arrived I sat in my room long past dusk and wished that I could cry. I needed to see Clive, to be with him. I thought that if only we could be together even for a little while, I wouldn't need to feel so afraid . . . of the rain against the window, spattering in the wind . . . inside of me, rising. With Clive, I was certain, I could feel the way I had once felt . . . lighter, able to laugh more easily. I missed him, his lopsided grin, the way he would rap on my door and poke his head in and say, "Anyone home here?" and I would know he wanted to go off exploring.

"I'll be Livingstone and you be Stanley," Clive would say. Or: "I'll be Peary and you be Cook." We would roam the neighborhoods around Grandmother's big house on the North Side of Chicago, and sometimes we would forget the time and have to run, to get back before dark. Occasionally we got caught and there was an awful row. Once, Father had been waiting for us in the great foyer, pacing, angry and worried. He was about to reprimand us when Grandmother Duer came flying in from the library; in her high scratching voice she called us "wild animals." Father turned from us to her, and he said, "Perhaps you would rather we moved out, Mother?" He said it in a quiet voice; Father said everything in a quiet voice. Grandmother looked at him, turned and sailed out again. Then Father took each of us by the hand and led us upstairs, to his and Mother's rooms, and Mother had laughed and said, "So, the explorers return!"

In my California summers, when the valley heat was oppressive, we lived on the screened porch and in the yard. I spent most of my time in a hammock slung between two walnut trees. Oranges in Grandfather's little orchard were allowed to ripen on the tree and that made them supremely sweet. I would pick several and squeeze the warm sweet juice into my mouth and turn the pages of my book with sticky fingers.

I missed Clive, but I was not lonely. What I did feel sometimes, lying in the hammock with the summer heat pressing on me, was a yearning so vast and swelling that it seemed at times it would burst out of me and flutter about like some great bird beating its wings. There was something I wanted to do, had to do, but I didn't know what. It was as if I was waiting; the air would be still, the only sound leaves rustling high in the tree, and I would listen as hard as I could. I listened and I waited, wanting to know.

And then the heat would be broken by the rain. I would watch it come, silver sheets moving across the fields, across the pastures, moving closer and closer and then breaking on us. I wanted to run into the rain, to dash through those silver sheets and into the fields. I wanted to run and run until my lungs ached and my heart raced. I did not want to have to wait.

But I did wait. My somnolent existence in the dusty Sacramento Valley continued, my grandparents moving about the periphery of my life, good and easy and kind.

Clive wrote that he wanted to study at the Ecole des Beaux-Arts in Paris. "It is what I would most like to do. I've worked hard to learn a passable French. (I hide my French books in the back of my closet, but I think G. knows; she has a penchant for ferreting out my secret vices.) Even while I dream of Paris, however, I know it is not likely. G. holds the purse-strings tightly. She has begun to talk of her 'failing' health, and I suspect it is in anticipation of my request. Now you are thinking, 'Why do you put up with it, brother?' And you are right. I shouldn't complain if I am not going to take action. Still, if I give an ultimatum I might find myself out on the sidewalk with neither a penny nor a job. First, I say, the job. Not to appear too heartless, I should also add that Grandmother is an old woman, and quite alone in the world except for you and me."

I read the letter, crumpled it into a ball and flung it from me, causing Grandmother to start. Too angry to explain, I pushed out of the door and headed for the woods, to walk and think. The struggle had finally broken through to the surface.

That evening I wrote: "I have just today received your letter in which you speak of the future, and say 'Grandmother is an old woman, quite alone in the world except for you and me.' Those are your words exactly—'except for you and me.'

"Forgive me if this letter rambles, but I do have a point to make. Do you remember when we would return late from our exploring 'expeditions' to find Father pacing, worried and cross with us? Mother would only laugh and say something to let us know she hadn't minded, which is why I suppose we always had the courage to go again. But Grandmother would be livid. Her face would be all red and mottled and her eyes flashing. I remember so clearly! I also remember she told Father we were 'wild animals, allowed to prowl the streets.'

"I knew Father was worried that we might get hurt or be lost. I know, now, that Mother had always been an explorer herself. (You can't imagine the stories I've heard; one of the old uncles told me they used to call Mother their 'Will-o'-the-wisp' because she seemed able to appear and disappear at will.) But Grandmother Duer's anger, I never could understand it.

"Do you remember—I'm certain I must have told you—that every now and then someone brings a wounded fawn, or a raccoon or once, even, a wild piglet to Grandmother? She cares for them and when they are well, she always sends them back to the woods, to what she calls 'their right life.' *Their* life, Clive. No matter how attached she might get to one—and she does—she always sends it back to the wild.

"Grandmother Duer *is* all alone. Except for you, not me. And that was her choice. You know how I longed to stay, how you begged her not to send me away, how much it hurt. Still hurts, after all these years. You're my brother, and my best friend in the world, but I haven't even been allowed to come and see you, nor you me. Grandmother Duer wants to keep you locked up in that big cage of a house in Chicago. She's not going to let you find your 'right life' if she can help it. I know it, Clive. You're going to have to break out. When you're ready, if you need an explorer to help, I'll be here. Just say the word. Your loving sister, Stanley." (Clive would remember that Stanley had been sent by the *New York Herald* to find Livingstone.)

The postscript I added was calculated: "You need never fear that anyone here reads your letters. Grandfather believes that privacy is, or should be, a Constitutional Right."

Clive answered soon enough, at length, saying the same thing several different ways: *You're right, but be patient with me.* It left me feeling unsettled, dissatisfied.

Clive did not go to Paris, and my high school years ended as uneventfully as they had begun, with me waiting.

I think it was not until graduation that I understood how my classmates' plans differed from my own. I envied them for knowing what they wanted, what they would do with their lives. I envied them because they did not seem to be waiting. Some were to marry and settle down on farms of their own, or in town. Others would go to teachers' college in San Jose or to work in their fathers' feed store or the bank. All I knew was what I didn't want to do.

I did not particularly want to go to business school, but I enrolled at Howe's Academy anyway, to learn to take shorthand and to type. It would give me something to do while I figured out how I was going to support myself.

That much I did know: I would work. I would not marry.

TWO

MY FIRST JOB was as secretary and office manager of the *Amador County News*, a weekly serving the little communities huddled into the foothills of the Sierra. Within a month of my arrival, one of the paper's two reporters left without notice and I was allowed to do his work so long as I finished my office chores and didn't require any additional pay. I accepted gladly, asking only that my name appear on the front-page stories I wrote.

Lucky for me, the other reporter was a good editor. I would turn in my copy, study what he did with it, and after a while I learned how to put a newspaper story together.

At first I traveled the dirt back roads by horseback. When the state began to build hard roads, I asked Grandfather to lend me the money to buy a Model T.

"Never thought to see you here, Henry," Abe Peterson, who sold farm machinery and Fords and was hard of hearing, shouted at Grandfather, who objected to noise of any sort.

"It's for my grandgirl here," Grandfather answered, refusing to raise his voice.

Abe heard. "Ain't she kinda small for this thing?" he bellowed. Turning to me he added, "No offense, honey, but I doubt you can handle—"

"Don't doubt it, Abe," Grandfather interrupted. "Now, if you'll just show her how to run that machine and give her one of those licenses, we won't take any more of your time."

It took me all of that day to learn to set the spark and throttle levers, grab hard onto the crank and slip my finger through the loop that controls the choke, then pull the loop with a mighty tug until the engine roared to life.

"I've got it," I would shout to Grandmother, who stood watching from the porch. Then I jumped onto the running board to move the spark and throttle to the proper position and, if all went well, I could crawl into the driver's seat, release the hand brake and shove my foot against the low speed pedal. I lurched off, down the lane, whooping . . . a surge of excitement rising in me . . . *I was commanding this machine* . . . I released my left foot and felt the Ford careen into high gear.

"I'm flying!" I called back to Grandmother, who by then had her apron over her head, sure that I would crash.

There were plenty of Model T's on Sacramento streets. A few of the boys who had graduated with me had them by now, but I never failed to make heads turn when I drove into town.

"I figured it was true!" Billy Homans, who had been in my class, shouted out to me on I Street one day. "When somebody told me Hallie got herself a T, I said, 'She surely would!'"

Clive wrote, "When Grandmother saw the photo of you beside your Model T she said, 'Hallie looks like a flower, but it seems to me she's as tough as a weed.'"

Whenever I rumbled down back country roads where motor-cars didn't often stray, farm folks would come out to look. More than once I had to ask an obliging farmer to bring his team to pull me out of a ditch or mudhole.

I traveled those back roads for three years, getting to know the

towns and the people who lived in them. I wrote about their troubles and I wrote about their joys. I learned to listen, not only to
what they said, but to pick up what they weren't saying. I wrote
about the night the Erlfelds' house burned to the ground, and how
the family was taken in by neighbors and fed and clothed until a
new house could be built for them. I wrote about the child who fell
down the old Jupiter mine shaft and how he was pulled out after
thirteen long, cold hours. (That story came close to costing me
some frostbitten toes.) By the time I had published enough stories
to go looking for a bigger paper, it was 1916 and we were at war.
An American expeditionary force had left for France, several of the
Sacramento Union reporters in its ranks.

I was twenty-two when I went to work at the *Union*, but I told
them I was twenty-five. (I looked sixteen.) My first assignment, to
my chagrin, was on the women's page, where I was to write household hints and social notes.

The war came to us over the wire services, the Associated Press
machine clicking out the strange-sounding names . . . *Chateau-
Thierry, the Marne, Belleau Wood, the Meuse-Argonne offense* . . . Soon
enough the casualty lists came clicking over the wires. We would
watch, in silence, as the names of local boys were transcribed. Then
a picture would be collected and run in the paper edged in black:
a solemn-faced boy in the stiff-collared uniform, dead in France.

I followed the war news, spent as much time as I could learning
how to cover the political news that came out of the state capital,
and tried to resign myself to be content with the few stories I was
allowed to cover—a school-board meeting or an interview with the
owner of a department store about his new sign.

I started going out to the Hamlin track on Sunday afternoons.
Billy Homans and some of the other Model T owners in town had
taken to racing their machines on a makeshift track. Naturally, the
boys taunted me to join them. And naturally, after a while, I had
to give it a try. To my surprise, I liked it. To their surprise, I was
good enough to make most of them eat my dust. When one of the

editors heard about it, he had me do the motoring news that appeared in the Sunday paper.

Then it was 1918 and the war was over. The boys paraded down Fifth Avenue in New York in their tunics and Sam Browne belts, and down K Street in Sacramento, where they were cheered by the Daughters of the Golden West and the survivors from the Old Soldiers' Home, their frail bodies pulled to attention. Bands played "Over There" and car horns sounded and school children, let out for the day, straggled alongside the marching men, oblivious of anything but the excitement of the flag-waving, drumrolling march.

The uniforms were packed in camphor and stored in tin trunks in a far corner of the barn loft, and the boys who had gone to France came back to the farm or got jobs in town selling tractors or insurance or Chevrolets, or they did nothing at all. There was an awful silence then, as quiet and as thick as the tule fog that lay close over the valley that winter.

People listened politely as President Wilson talked about a League of Nations, but it was over. They knew there was trouble in the land—trouble with Bolsheviks and anarchists and the colored and the Jews. But the war was over, and most of the good people of the Sacramento Valley turned their attention to other things.

Radios. And aeroplanes. Moving pictures and motorcars and boxing matches. The world was changing; the war was won and now it was time to look ahead.

Only one *Union* reporter returned to the paper, so I was told I could stay on. He came back to the City Hall beat I had been coveting. I couldn't complain. Still, a steady diet of recipes and wedding stories was not enough to sustain me. I hungered for more substantial fare. I tried to remember how Annie Farrell had made me feel that day, five years before, in the courthouse . . . I began to see how foolish I had been, to think I could do what Annie was doing. I couldn't even move onto the front page of the Sacramento *Union*. . . .

I walked over to the courthouse and sat alone in the big room where the trial had been. It was steamy hot; a fan was whirring somewhere in the building. The windows were open and I could hear the soft clacking of a palm tree outside as the fronds brushed against each other in the warm breeze. I tried to think of Annie, but my mind kept wandering. I brushed away a horsefly, sailing in great lazy loops around me, when it came too close.

My mind wandered to a story that had appeared in the paper that day, about a couple out on Route 4 whose boy had died of pneumonia. The child was ten years old and so badly retarded he could scarcely walk or talk. He had become sick and, according to the story, his parents had chosen to let him die. They admitted it to the doctor who signed the death certificate. There was some talk of prosecution. Child neglect was mentioned.

Something about that story troubled me. After work that day I drove out to the farm to talk to the parents of the dead boy. I found the mother in the kitchen; she looked worn, the way a lot of farm women do who have been worked too hard. And she was older than I had expected her to be. At first she made small, unfinished gestures with her hands, as if she didn't know where to start. You could see the hurt in her eyes. She brought me a glass of lemonade and we sat on the front porch. I plucked a blowing cottonwood plume from the air. She smiled and said, "Billy used to like me to catch them for him." Then she started talking about her boy, talking as if she could say what she had been wanting to say all along, had there been anyone to listen.

"He never was right, you know," she told me, "not from his first poor breath." Her voice was soft and sad, and as worn as the faded handkerchief she twisted. "It got harder for him, the older he got. You could see the little fella trying, struggling to do something he just never was going to be able to do. And it got harder for us too. He was our late child . . . we didn't expect him, after raisin' up three grown boys and all, but we took him as God's grace."

She stopped and pushed her fingertips into her eyes as if to stop the flow of tears. After a moment she went on, "Last year my man got sick, real sick. And he could see how hard it was, me taking care of him and the boy, too. Billy was getting too big for me. And his pa, well . . . his pa said to him, 'Sonny, how's your ma to get on when I'm gone?' Being sick scared him so, don't you see? Well, the boy didn't know what he meant, but I did. And that's when we figured what we had to do. We said the next time the boy took sick, we wouldn't try to keep him. We'd just let him go while we were both here to help. And, God willing, he'd go without pain and suffering."

She stopped then, gazing out over the farmyard, not seeing. I waited. Finally she went on, with a small wave of her hand, as if to stir the heavy air. "That's what happened," she said with a sigh. "He took sick last Monday a week, and we made him as comfortable as we could, but we didn't go for the doc. We stayed with Billy all the while, taking turns so if he waked and was scared, we'd be there. We sat with him like that for six days and five nights, poor thing. We sang a little, and we held him and told him we'd be along soon enough. He went real easy, just slipped away."

Her voice was small and dry and I had to lean close to hear before the sounds scattered in the summer air. For a while we sat in silence, my hand over hers. She tried to smile, and I tried to smile back. When I asked if I might speak to the boy's father, she said, "He just can't . . . words about Billy just seem to stick in his craw . . ." I did talk to the couple's sons and to their minister and their neighbors. Then I wrote my story and left it on Hal Lugas, the city editor's, desk.

An hour later he called me in. His face was flushed. He slammed his fist so hard his inkwell jumped and splattered.

"This had better be the first and the last time you ever give yourself an assignment," he said with what, for him, was controlled rage. "I give the assignments around here, is that understood?"

I nodded.

"I was going to throw it out," he went on, "but I made myself read it over again." I paused. "I've decided to run it, to show you I can overlook something as reprehensible to me as insubordination. But I don't expect this to happen again, understood?"

"Yes," I said, backing out of his office, biting my lip to keep from smiling.

My story ran the next day on page two, and the public response was immediate. People telephoned to say "those poor folks have suffered enough." Some came into the office, others wrote. One by one, the *Union* reporters stopped by my desk to say "good job." One even told me, "You didn't leave a dry eye in Sacramento County."

Hal Lugas, the city editor, said nothing at all, but after that he would let me do a story on my own now and then. Invariably, these would run under a head that said, "A woman's look behind the headlines." I didn't know what being a woman had to do with it, but I didn't argue. It was better than a constant diet of social notes and recipes.

My working life was stymied and my social life was fast becoming limited to a few old high school friends and an occasional Saturday night out, dancing at one of the roadhouses with an outdoor platform under a great oak tree. The new men who came to work at the state capital seemed most interested in grappling in the backseats of their Oaklands or Chevrolets. After a time, I found myself turning down almost all invitations.

A letter from Clive arrived every week, as always. He stayed on in Grandmother's house, having taken a position in an architectural firm which, as it turned out, Grandfather Duer had financed many years ago. Although Clive didn't linger on the details, it was clear that Grandmother had arranged the position. Our letters were filled with the details of our lives, the books we read, laments about our social calendars. We no longer talked about visits. And yet I settled down, each week, to Clive's letter with what amounted to a dependency. I looked forward to it, needed it, and when, once or twice, he missed writing, I felt all the old anger and pain well up, and a sense of desolation would engulf me.

On October 7, 1919, I was twenty-five. Officially, a spinster. My friends would now cease trying to find me a mate and content themselves with feeling sorry for me. I was relieved to be able to settle into a single life.

The Volstead Act became law in January of 1920, putting every saloon in Sacramento—and the rest of the country—out of business. In a way, it was to put me out of business in Sacramento too.

Quite a few of the saloons became soft-drink parlors. You could buy an Orange Crush or a Coca-Cola or, with a city license, a "nonintoxicating" alcoholic beverage, which meant the alcohol content was minuscule. In fact, no one was fooled by the change of name. Already, two members of the police force had been found in an alley outside one of the parlors, stone drunk.

One day in March of that first year of Prohibition I was sifting through the minutes of the City Council meeting, expecting little, when I came upon what seemed an innocuous notation: "The city manager has authorized two special operatives to visit the soft-drink parlors in the city." Reading on, I discovered that these two "operatives" had teamed with three federal agents to make a series of raids. The only name given was the federal agent in charge, one M. M. Griffin. Armed with search warrants, the agents had found liquor in some form—"vinous, spirituous, malt, cereal or mixed non-intoxicating" in each of the parlors. Most of the time it was jackass brandy, made palatable by mixing with Orange Crush or Coca-Cola.

I found M. M. Griffin in a small, unmarked office on the third floor of a downtown office building. I knocked tentatively on the glass window.

"Come on in," a cheerful, high-pitched voice called out. I thought it must be a secretary. In fact, it was Griffin himself, sitting all alone behind a large desk. Lined up before him were a number of mason jars, each with a label, each containing a pale liquid.

When he stood to greet me, he seemed to hop off his chair.

He was short and chubby, with tiny hands and tiny feet. I was reminded of the little people I had met the week before when I did a story about Lord John Sanger's Circus, encamped in the Southern Pacific yards.

"Miss Duer, you say? Of the *Union*? Of course I'll talk to you, I'll be delighted to talk to you." With the palm of his hand he smoothed a few strands of hair which were plastered, sideways, across his bald head.

"I know about the raids on the city's soft-drink parlors," I started, hoping to catch him off guard by getting straight to the point. "Before we do a story, I want to ask you a few questions."

"Certainly, certainly," he surprised me by saying. He was beaming at me with an almost cherubic expression. "Ask away."

Pacing myself, I began to get the background information: when the raids had taken place, where, how much illegal brew had been confiscated (it was, as it happened, lined up before me on his desk), how they went about building a case. Then I asked, "Will there be more raids?"

He picked up one of the mason jars and said, "This one tests out at fifty-three percent alcohol," wrinkling his nose, "vile stuff." And then he asked, "Why don't you come along on our next raid?"

I was dumbstruck.

"Do you mean it?" I blurted, and wanted to bite my tongue. It would be a mistake to let him know how anxious I was to go. My mind was racing. Hal Lugas would have my head. I shouldn't even be here. Dear Lord, what now?

"When?" I asked the little agent.

"Tonight." He smiled winningly.

I swallowed; my mouth was dry. *Careful*, I said to myself, and walked to the window. I straightened my back and pretended to stretch a bit, so he wouldn't think me nervous. It was too good to miss. Too good.

"Where?" I asked, adding, "I mean, where should we meet?"

"Right here," he came back. "Be here at eleven tonight and you can go along." He said it as if he were my favorite uncle, offering me a chance to go fishing.

I felt myself nodding. I wet my lips. "Good," I said, moving toward the door. "Fine, but . . ." I was about to say that I would have to talk to my editor, that he might send another reporter, when Griffin raised one of his soft little hands as if to bestow his benediction.

"One thing," he said. "Not one word between now and tonight—not to your mother, not to your editor, not to anyone. This is all very *secret*, you know." He smiled again.

"But—" I started.

"Sorry, Miss Hallie," he came back, "not even your editor. It's you or nobody." In spite of the smile, I understood that he meant it. I had a vague feeling that he had understood my blunder, but I couldn't be certain.

I shook my head and said I'd be there. In fact, I had no idea what I would do. None at all.

The reporter who had sent me to get the City Council notes was annoyed with me for being late. "I've been waiting for an hour," he said petulantly. I stared at him. *Of course, that was it—a way out.* I handed him my notebook, in which I had jotted down, word for word, the report of the raids. He would see it and do what I had done—go looking for Griffin. These were the first raids in Sacramento; it was big news; it would certainly make the front page. I began to feel hopeful. I would keep my word to Griffin, and keep my job as well.

"Here they are," I said, loud and slow. "Read it all," I tried to warn him.

Then I watched as he looked over my notes, typed out his story and called the copyboy. Something inside of me groaned. *He hadn't seen it.* The story would be buried on an inside page, and by the time the city editor saw it, it would be too late.

At five minutes before eleven I parked my car near Capitol Park. It was two blocks to Griffin's office. My stomach was churning . . .

there was still time . . . I didn't have to show up . . . I stood at the entrance to the building, staring at the door handle. It would be locked! Of course, and then I could leave because the building was locked. I lifted my hand, paused . . . pushed. The door was open.

I walked through it. I was going on the raid. I was committed, even if it meant the end of me on the *Sacramento Union*.

I found Griffin where I had left him that morning, a cigar clamped between his teeth, his smile in place. He waved me through a door I had not even noticed that morning, to an inner room. Four men in dark business suits were carefully handling an assortment of weapons, including several sawed-off shotguns.

"Boys, meet Miss Hallie Duer of the *Union*," Griffin said jovially. The "boys" nodded, blinked at me. "She's going along for the ride tonight, so see she don't get hurt." To me he said: "The boys are a little gun-shy about names."

I nodded. In fact, I knew two of them. They were uncles of one of my high school friends, men with reputations as ne'er-do-wells.

"Got the warrants, Fred?" Griffin asked.

Fred patted his pocket.

"Then let's mount up. Miss Duer, you ride with me in the lead car." He grasped my elbow with an amazingly firm grip, guiding me toward a big six-cylinder Cadillac.

I took a deep breath and told myself to be calm. We moved slowly down Tenth Street. It had rained earlier in the evening and now the electric lights were reflected in the wet streets. One of Grandmother's sayings slipped into my thoughts: "A ship in port is safe, but that's not where ships are meant to be." We passed Levinson's Book Shop, where Grandfather and I had spent long hours, but it did not seem familiar. Nothing seemed familiar now. I was in strange waters; possibly I was beyond my depth.

"Turn on J Street," Griffin told the driver. We moved silently through the streets, casting shadows. No one spoke. I was aware only of the sounds of the motor and the shifting of weapons.

When we pulled to a halt on J Street, Griffin said, "Stay behind me, sister," and for a moment I had a wild urge to giggle at the idea of the little man protecting me.

The attack was orchestrated: Fred slammed open the door, the others rushed in. There was a rumble of movement, then words sharp and angry. Suddenly a girl with white-blond hair stood blocking the way. "Dump it," she shouted to someone behind her, her hard eyes on Griffin.

The man called Clyde bolted over the bar and with one hand grabbed a small dark man while with the other he retrieved a pitcher, the contents of which the man had been trying to pour down a hole in the wall.

Someone pushed for the door, slamming me into a corner. Two of the agents blocked each entrance, while Griffin's men ransacked the bar. A barrage of words filled the air and for a moment I was afraid I had lost the ability to understand. Then I realized they weren't speaking English.

Over it all, the young woman with the hard face was shouting at Griffin: 'They're Mohammedans, you dumb little shit. Mohammedans don't drink, even a stupid ass like you should know that."

Griffin was staring at her, his cigar clenched, the smile in place and his face frozen in an attitude of disgust. He motioned me to come closer, without ever taking his eyes from her.

"This here is Miss Babe Conlon, make sure you get the name right for the papers," he said. "Miss Conlon here is one of our city's finer types, a real high liver." He was using me as a threat. I knew it, and so did Babe Conlon.

She turned to look at me, a long, lazy, insolent look. Then she turned back to Griffin and said, "Tell your little newspaper dolly that's Conlon with a C." She turned her back on him then and slowly walked away. The little man exhaled. "Whore," he said. My face was burning, I could feel it. But I also felt a surge of admiration for Babe Conlon. *She hadn't given in to him.* When he reached to take my elbow, it was all I could do to keep from shrinking from his touch.

Babe Conlon had the last word that day. As the agents left with their samples, she stood at the door, her hand on her hip. As Griffin passed with me in tow, I heard her whisper, "So long, you little prick."

As we climbed into the Cadillac, one of the men muttered, "Black bastards." Griffin hissed, "Watch your language, boys, there's a lady present."

It was two o'clock by the time the fourth and last raid of the night was finished, at the Fairview Hotel. Agents had found jackass brandy in each place.

I was in the newspaper office by seven the next morning, typing from the handwritten notes I had made. The story was finished by nine. I read it over. It was good, but that probably wouldn't matter. It was better than anything that had appeared in the *Union* for months. A scoop, I was sure of it.

When Hal Lugas came in at nine-thirty, it was waiting on his desk. At nine-forty he bellowed my name.

"Close the door and sit down," he said, tight-lipped.

I did.

"What the hell . . ." he began, waving the pages of the story in the air.

"It's—" I started.

"Don't say anything," he came back. He was right. There was nothing for me to say.

"You've gone too damned far this time, missy. I let you off once. Hell! I not only let you off, I helped you—and this is the thanks I get. What do you think? Because you're a girl I ought to say, 'Why, yes, little miss'? That's what's wrong with women on newspapers. They want to be treated like little princesses. You knew the rules, miss. And you broke them. I'll be damned if I'm going to play favorites just because you wear a skirt. And then go off on something dangerous like that—I guess you used your feminine wiles to get this Griffin fellow to take you along, is that how you did it? Pouted and smiled and acted like some little dolly?"

I could feel the blood drain from my face; again, *some little dolly*. I stood because if I didn't I knew I would faint, slumped over in the chair. If I stood I could will myself not to faint. I concentrated on my breathing. *If you faint he will be right. You cannot. You will not faint*. I could feel the blood pump back, the anger abate. It was over and I was all right. I thought about Babe Conlon—the stony set of her face. I lifted my chin as she had and straightened my spine and looked him in the eyes, as she had Griffin last night. Lugas had been leaning over his desk, shouting at me, but now he stopped and sat down, his own face more coldly arranged.

"Now, listen to this and listen carefully," he said, "I'm going to tell you what you can do if you want to stay on this newspaper." He paused, as if waiting for me to say something. When I didn't, he went on: "You've stumbled into a front-page story—a beat, I'll be the first to admit. I don't think you have any idea what a big story this is, the first raids in town. Jack shouldn't have sent you to get those City Council notes, but since you did that much for him you can go a step farther. Give him this story and all your notes so he can rewrite it in time for the first edition."

I looked at him. *Dumb shit*. I wished I had the courage to say it. What I said was, "Or?"

It had a similar effect. A vein in his forehead seemed ready to pop. He rasped, "Or you can get out, right now."

Stupid ass. My throat closed, I couldn't say it, no matter how much I wanted. "If the story runs at all, it runs under my name," I told him, walking out of his office and the length of the city room, careful not to reach out to steady myself, my face arranged, I hoped, so that nothing showed. I stopped at my desk long enough to collect my notes. Then I left the *Union*.

I found Babe Conlon about an hour after the paper had hit the stands with a banner head and the story I had written, my swan song on the *Union*, my name in bold print. She was sitting on the back porch of an old wooden building on K Street, dressed in a loose flowered wrapper, sipping coffee and reading the paper.

"You're the chippie who wrote this trash," she said in a friendly voice. Her eyes weren't hard now. She was younger than I had thought her to be. Not much older than I. She waved at a dilapidated chair across from her. "I notice you didn't spell my name at all." She grinned.

I shook my head. Suddenly I felt hot and tired and shaky.

"So what do you want?" she asked.

"Something," I answered dully, trying to remember. She knew something I needed to know, but I couldn't seem to get it straight in my mind. What she had said to Griffin, that was part of it. Or maybe not. Maybe it was how she said it, or why. Something.

"Hey, kid," she said, suddenly standing, "hold on." She felt my forehead. "When did you eat?"

I shook my head and said, "I'm sorry."

"For what?" she wanted to know. "Wait here."

She returned with a piece of cracker bread and some cheese, which she cut into small pieces and handed me, one by one, nodding as I chewed and swallowed. I felt a sudden surge of gratitude and I wanted to thank her, but I didn't know how.

"There," she said, "the color is back in your face. Trouble with girls like you, with all that natural high color, when you lose it you look awful." She patted me on the shoulder and sat down again with her coffee cup and her paper.

"I really am sorry," I said. "It's been a bad day."

"Not to mention a bad night," she added. "My friends the Singhs—they run that soda parlor that was raided last night—they've lost their living. Mason Griffin saw to that."

"But they found liquor—" I started.

"Sure they did. One lousy pint of jackass brandy, which every soft-drink parlor in this city carries. If you can't give an occasional slug of brandy in an Orange Crush to some of these folks, you don't stay in business. Mr. Singh is caught, either which way. But even if the jackass brandy hadn't been there, they would have found some."

I tried to think about that, but I couldn't seem to put the parts of it together. Finally I asked, "Why did you say my story was trash?"

Babe Conlon looked at me and sighed. "Look, kid, I'm sorry. It's just that Griffin used you, like he uses everybody. He wanted you to write that story just the way you wrote it. He probably handpicked you, I wouldn't be surprised. And you did it. The only thing you didn't do that he wanted was put me out in print, so I'd have to leave town or get hounded by the local cops."

I felt sick now in a different way. *She was right. I should have known.* But something else nagged at me, something else was wrong, and I couldn't put my finger on it. My stomach was churning and I felt clammy and hot, but I needed to know what it was that I had missed.

"Is it graft? Is that it?" I asked.

She shook her head and snorted. "Hah! Graft would be easy. You can understand greed—at least I can. No, it's not greed with Griffin. Never has been. He don't care two hoots about money."

"What, then?" I asked.

"He told you he chooses the places to raid 'by the luck of the draw.' That's a lie. Take a look at the names of the owners of the places he raided last night. Singh, Donato, Levy, Lincoln. That last one—Lincoln—think he's any relation to the President?"

I smiled wanly. "I don't think so," I said. "He's a Negro." "I would have bet on it," Babe Conlon answered caustically.

I stared at her, remembering the words: *black bastards.*

"I'd also be willing to bet," she went on, "that the next time there's a cross burning, one of the burners will be wearing a little fat sheet—and underneath, he'll be wearing his little fat grin."

I slept for fourteen hours, waking before light and pulling on my boots to take a long trek through the spring-green countryside, walking to try to sort out what had happened, what I must do. *A ship in port is safe, but that's not where ships are meant to be.* Still, I hadn't been seaworthy; I hadn't known enough. I had been used, and the idea sickened me. It didn't help to read the stories the *Union* ran in the following days, front-page articles on Mason Griffin's crack team of Prohibition agents, with the growing lists of his victims' names . . .

I took refuge in Grandfather's comfortable silence and Grandmother's gentle presence. I slept late, I walked, I read. And I thought. If I was going to be a reporter, I would have to learn to question motives, to be skeptical, to look for answers where no one else had thought to look. At first I tried not to think of Mason Griffin. Then I thought of him a great deal. *Make a commotion,* Grandmother had said. *Most of the time they'll get out of your way. But the times they don't, well, you're just going to have to face up to them.*

One morning, on the hall table where I would be sure to see it first thing, I found a scrapbook in which had been pasted every bylined story I had written. Puzzled, I carried it into the kitchen, where I found Grandmother peeling apples and Grandfather, sitting across from her at the table, cracking walnuts.

"What is this?" I asked.

"I'm sending that off to Sanford Curtin," Grandfather answered.

I sat down and stared at him. I couldn't think what to say.

"Isn't that where you would like to work, dear?" Grandmother asked. "On the *Times*?"

"I don't know . . . I'm not. . ." I started, wanting to explain my confusion, wanting to tell them that I was no longer sure . . .

"You're ready," Grandfather said. "The last time I showed him your writings, he said to give you six more months. It's been that and some."

I stared at him, this little man with the pink face and white mustache. "You've already spoken to him?" I whispered.

Grandfather pursed his lips and nodded almost imperceptibly.

"On the telephone," Grandmother said proudly.

"On the telephone," I repeated, knowing how much he disliked the instrument. I sat, stupefied, and looked at the two of them. Grandmother never missed a cut on the apple peel as it spiraled off in one long loop. And Grandfather concentrated on the walnuts he was cracking.

THREE

THAT WINTER THE rains were late. By June the hills that separate the Sacramento Valley from the coast remained an astonishing shade of green, soft and so smoothly rounded that I wanted
to reach out and caress their velvet contours, petting them as one
might a cat. I drove west on the narrow road that cuts up and
over each of the hills in turn, moving through undulating grasses,
scattered here and there with sprays of orange poppies. A spring
breeze caught the wisps of my hair and blew them across my eyes.
I had pushed most of my hair under a boy's cap, one with a crown
full enough to hold it all, and I wore a cotton duster which reached
almost to my ankles.

By August, when the dry season is firmly established, the
valley heat would have parched this sea of grass, draining it of color,
turning it a tawny gold—so that a lion might lie up there in the
tall grasses and never be seen. Then, with the valley simmering in
ninety-degree heat, the change in temperature as the first hill was
negotiated would be almost imperceptible. It would not be until
the third, or perhaps the fourth, was topped that the cool air from
the ocean would wrap around, erasing the oppressive memory of

the valley heat. San Francisco Bay would be there, spreading out below, blue and glinting bright in the sun, while behind lay the valley and all the somnolent summers when I had waited.

On this June day in 1920 I drove from Sacramento to Vallejo, a town that clings to the northern edge of Suisun Bay, where I caught a car ferry to the other side, then on to Berkeley to take the ferry that would deliver me to the terminal at the foot of Market Street in San Francisco.

In Berkeley I stopped at a grocery store to buy some cheese and fruit for my lunch. At the waterfront, I sat for a long time looking at San Francisco across the bay, sprawling low and white on its peninsula like some impossible kingdom, its hills covered with buildings. The day was bright with a brisk wind which sent a spray over the bow of the ferry. I held hard to the railing as we approached the city. The bay was alive with ferries and freighters and lumber schooners and tugs and, sprinkled like butterflies among them, sailboats. And I was part of it, in the middle. I wanted to laugh, it was so good.

In the distance I could see Alcatraz, small and desolate, and beyond it Angel Island, covered with trees and brush. I thought of Mr. Chen, the orchardist who helped Grandfather. Mr. Chen had been held on Angel Island for a year and four months. He called it "Devil Island." It was not a good place, Mr. Chen had said. I shivered; there was so much here to see, so much to do.

Sanford Curtin had written that he would see me at eleven o'clock on the morning of June 16 *if that time is convenient . . .*

I took a room at the Mary Elizabeth Inn on Bush Street, a great Victorian mansion that had survived the fire to be converted into a boardinghouse for young women, most of whom came to the city in search of jobs in the shops or in offices. It was clean and shabbily respectable, with dusty cretonne draperies and the kinds of mismatched furniture peculiar to transient places.

A pale, freckled girl hovered about the office as I registered. As soon as I had been assigned a room and given the list of house rules, the girl stepped forward. "I'm Sue," she said, whistling out the S. "I'll be happy to show you around."

She pulled my satchel from my hand and, beckoning me to follow, proceeded to talk me up to my second-floor room. She said she worked in the business office of the White House, a large department store.

She pushed ahead into my room, the words flowing at a rapid rate—all sibilance and spit—she raised my window, inspected the drawers in my chiffonier. I looked down on Bush Street at the traffic—automobiles and buggies mixed together. I wanted to be out there, walking, feeling what the city was like. I wanted to be free of this girl who was gushing words like some uncapped well.

"You will have to excuse me," I said abruptly. She left in a sputter of S's, on the way out pushing past another young woman passing in the hallway. We stood together, watching Sue's departure. This new girl had the most delicate face I had ever seen—small, heart-shaped, with eyes that were deep brown and which seemed almost to be outlined in black ink. Her dark hair had been pulled into a disheveled coif on top of her head, and she was wearing an ordinary shirtwaist and skirt, except that, draped over one shoulder and caught into her belt was a Spanish shawl of black silk, embroidered with bright green peacocks. The long fringes of the shawl swayed with her every move. The effect was almost exotic. I realized I was staring.

She looked back at me, her face stoic. "I see you've met Sister Sue," she said, whistling out the S's, mocking Sue.

I laughed, and so did she. Then I knew why I had thought *almost* exotic. This girl was too good-humored to be truly exotic.

"I'm Faith Moore," she told me, shifting a large portfolio she was carrying so that she could put out her right hand to shake mine, firmly. I had never shaken hands with a woman before. I couldn't think of what to say, except, "I'm Hallie. Hallie Duer."

"Well, Hallie," she went on, "I wish I were going to be around to give you a proper welcome, but I'm moving out. I've found a little cottage on Telegraph Hill and I'll be leaving tomorrow." Her tone was triumphant.

"Telegraph Hill," I said. "I'm afraid I don't even know where that is."

"You'll find out soon enough," she told me. "It's one of the nicest hills in the city, at least I think so—and it's almost entirely Italian. Wonderful garlic smells . . . spaghetti, osso bucco . . ."

I wished her the best of luck and closed the door. For a while I sat on the bed, trying to sort out these first impressions. I had met one girl I didn't want to know and one I did.

I had come to San Francisco a few days early to learn my way around and to buy some new clothes . . . just in case Mr. Curtin decided to hire me.

The next day, equipped with a map of the city, I drove from the Embarcadero out to Ocean Beach, then up Twin Peaks, where you could see all of the city and the bay spread out below. I explored the outlying areas beyond Van Ness Avenue, untouched by the 1906 fire—and the new core of the city, that part of downtown that had been rebuilt and was now a fine, modern place, the fussy old monstrosities built by the railroad barons having been replaced by functional buildings with clean lines. In my mind I began making plans for Clive to come west. He would have to see this city—the movement, the excitement. You took your life in your hands when you crossed Market Street, the main thoroughfare with its four streetcar lines. Newsboys shouted out the headlines, dandies with flowers in their lapels strutted in front of restaurants with names like "The Ritz Old Poodle."

The day before my interview I went to the City of Paris and selected a navy serge suit, belted and tailored, a white georgette waist, stockings and shoes to match. I tried on the costume in a dressing room that was larger, and much more elegant, than my bedroom at home. The skirt was smooth over my hips, the waist small and snug. *Yes*, I thought. *You look all right.*

The shopgirl who had helped me find my size knocked at the door. When I opened it, she stood staring. Then she blurted, "Oh my, you're so pretty!"

I could never think what to say when people told me that. I was not, I knew, pretty in the usual sense—I look younger than I am, I have no curves to speak of, my hair is too thick and too straight, my face too full of color, my mouth rather wider than most.

"Thank you," I finally managed.

The confidence my new suit gave me evaporated at the door of the *Times* office. "Mr. Curtin's over there," a girl at the front desk told me, tossing her head in the direction of the city room, where perhaps thirty desks were arranged, more or less in rows. Some had telephones standing on them, most had typewriters, all were littered. In a far corner, in a glass cubicle, I could see a man sitting at a desk. Since he was the only man in the big room at the moment, I decided he would have to be Sanford Curtin.

He ignored my first knock, though the door was open. I felt peculiar, standing there trying to get his attention. It was not at all as I had imagined, this first meeting. I knocked again, feeling a small shaking anger welling up to mix with my embarrassment. Sanford Curtin was a famous editor. He wasn't supposed to work in a cluttered glass cubicle in the corner of the city room.

"Yes?" he growled, as if to shake me off.

"Mr. Curtin?" I ventured, furious that my voice cracked.

He did look up then, annoyed.

"I'm Hallie Duer," I told him. "You wrote that you would see me at eleven this morning."

He frowned. His fierce expression was accentuated by a sharp nose and receding hairline. He looked rather like a hawk. He did not remember our appointment, I was sure.

I wanted to retreat, to disappear. My throat was dry, but I made a last effort. "I've been working on the *Sacramento Union* . . ." I began.

He stared even harder, and then he whooped, "That's right!" as if I had given a correct answer. He was smiling then and inviting me in, moving around his desk to clear a stack of papers from a chair so that I might sit. My legs felt weak; I was glad to sit down.

He was very tall, more than six feet in height, and as fastidiously tailored as his office was cluttered. *Contradictions,* I thought. It was, I would learn, the one word that best defined this man.

"How old are you?" he wanted to know.

"Twenty-six," I answered, "in October."

He shook his head, and pretended to be chastened. "I thought you were some schoolgirl who had wandered in here by mistake," he said, and then, noticing my wince, added, "Forgive me, Miss Duer. I can see I've been neither very original nor very kind." He smiled then, a disarmingly boyish smile for a man of his years, and added, "Remind me to say that to you again in ten years' time; then, I promise, you'll take it as a compliment."

I smiled back at him and felt unreasonably happy with the idea that in ten years' time he might still know me.

For the next hour or so he talked to me, in detail, about the stories I had written—asking questions, taking his time. I had a sense of people coming and going in the city room; he seemed oblivious of them. I think I have never had anyone listen so carefully to what I was saying. Sometimes the questions he asked were trivial, sometimes pointed. He especially wanted to know why I had decided to go into a field dominated by men. I told him about seeing Annie Farrell in Sacramento.

"Oh, yes—Annie," he said with a theatrical sigh. "I suppose you know she has left us? Just couldn't resist William Randolph Hearst's siren call." He accentuated his rival's name, rolling out all three of them.

Tilting forward in his chair, he added quietly, "Little Billy Hearst is able to pay a great deal more than the *Times* can pay. I suppose you know that, young lady?"

I wanted a job on the *Times* more than I had ever wanted anything; I suspected he knew it; I suspected he was testing me.

I said, "I'm not interested in working for Mr. Hearst or for the

Chronicle or the *Call* or the *Tribune*. I'm interested in working for the *Times*. I made fifteen dollars a week on the *Union*, but I lived at home. I will need twenty dollars to start, at the very least." I did not avoid his glance; he looked at me for quite a long while, turning a cigar around and around in his fingers. Then he smiled, as if he had just thought of something.

"You realize," he said, "that we are simply speculating here. I'm afraid I don't have an opening at the moment. But say we do have a place sometime in the future . . . how much would you expect to earn after, say, a two-month training period?"

There was no job. I wasn't going to go to work for the *Times*, and I didn't fully understand his question, or the reason for it.

I was saved from having to answer by a man who put his head in the door and said, "Trouble, Boss. Had a call from John over at the courthouse. He says the state's waived rebuttal in the Dempsey case—caught everybody by surprise. It's going to the jury on direct evidence. They've called a recess, then Judge Dooling will instruct the jury—and McCoy is nowhere in sight."

Curtin was on his feet. "Damnation!" he exploded. "It's past noon—where the hell is he?"

The man in the door shrugged. They looked at each other and Curtin asked, "Does anybody know where he drinks these days?"

"Hard to say," the man answered. "All his old watering holes were closed, nobody's sure where the new ones are."

I kept my seat and was silent; I could see that Curtin's mind was racing. "Damn," he said again under his breath. Remembering me, he added, "Sorry, miss." Then, having addressed me, he stared.

"What do you know about the Dempsey trial?" he asked.

I took a deep breath. "That Mr. Dempsey—the boxing champion—is being tried in federal court for being a slacker." I hesitated, then decided I should be more precise. ". . . a draft evader, that is," I continued. "He was excused from the Army because he said he had to support his wife and his parents, and he was supposed to be doing war work in the shipyards—in Seattle, I think—

to fulfill his obligation. He was brought to trial because his wife, who is now his former wife . . . Maxine Dempsey . . . said that he didn't support her at all and that he didn't work in the shipyards either, except for having his picture taken there for the papers now and then."

"Good enough," Curtin said. "If you can get over to Seventh and Mission—Judge Maurice Dooling's courtroom—before he charges the jury, and get the story in time to make the afternoon paper, you've got a job on the *Times*."

My mouth went dry, my hands clammy. I suppose I must have been staring, because he added, ". . . at seventeen-fifty a week to start."

On my way out I repeated, ". . . to start," and the editor shook his head and grinned.

I half-ran, half-trotted the four blocks to the courthouse, pushing my way past horse-drawn buggies and bicycles and automobiles, keeping my eye out for a taxicab that might get me there faster. I was too excited, too much in a hurry to stand and wait for a streetcar or a taxi. I darted past peddlers and ignored the remarks of a small knot of draymen gathered on a corner eating their lunches out of pails.

I pushed open the heavy door of the courtroom and stood for a moment to get my bearings. The judge's bench was empty; I was in time. It was the most elaborate courtroom I had ever seen, with Italianate statues and stained-glass windows and the high gleam of polished wood.

As purposefully as I could, I made my way up the aisle and headed for the one empty seat at the press table. Letting myself past the bar, I could feel some eyes turn toward me. Four of the five men at the table looked at me with a cold passivity. "Sorry, sis," the fifth man said. "This table is for the press."

"I know," I answered, sitting down.

He leaned closer to me and said in a slightly tougher tone, "That's Red McCoy's place and he'll be along, so scoot."

"I'm filling in for McCoy," I explained, not looking at him but opening the pad I had thought to tuck in my bag that morning.

"Since when?" another man asked, leaning across the table.

I looked up at him. "Since half an hour ago," I replied, careful to keep my voice even, "when Sanford Curtin asked me to."

They looked at each other then, and someone said, "Sounds like Curtin." And someone else added, "McCoy's probably got a snoutful."

Then Jack Dempsey entered the courtroom and they forgot about me.

A collective murmur rose from the crowd. Flanked by lawyers, the world's champion made his way to the defendant's table. Jack Dempsey, even in an ordinary business suit, did not look like an ordinary man. There was something tightly wound about him, something held back, removed. His face was a tough, leathery mahogany color—as if he had been too long in the wind and the sun. He was, perhaps, the best-known man in the country. And yet I think I have never seen anyone so ill-at-ease, and working so hard to hide it. He was scowling, concentrating. A few of the reporters tried to get his attention, but he ignored them. He didn't want to be here, that much was clear.

Next to Dempsey, fussy in a belted suit, was a dapper little man I figured to be Doc Kearns, his manager. On the other side was his lawyer, leafing through a sheaf of papers. I would need to get his name. I needed to get so much information . . . the thought of all that I did not know, and would need to learn before I could write the story, made my stomach churn.

"All rise," the court crier intoned as the judge entered. Light streamed through a skylight decorated with stained glass, so that rays of colored light shimmered about the room.

Sitting behind the prosecutor's table, set apart, was a woman with a small, tight face—a gauntness sharpened by splashes of color from the skylight. Reds and blues played across her face. She was, I guessed, the former Mrs. Dempsey. I watched her carefully; she had fixed her gaze to the right of the judge's bench. She seemed furtive, out of place. Dempsey did not look at her. Neither belonged here in this classical setting with its highly polished wood and stained glass and court criers intoning old rituals. But Dempsey wasn't afraid, and she was.

After some minutes of shuffling paper, the judge began his charge to the jury. "The question is," Judge Dooling said, "in its basic aspect, whether or not Jack Dempsey sought to evade military service by falsely answering certain points in the questionnaire, and whether or not, if false statements were made, these were made willfully and knowingly . . ."

I wrote that Jack Dempsey said he had to support his parents and the woman who was then his wife, the same woman who had sworn in this court that she had earned her own living, had supported herself. The judge paused, looked over his glasses and into Maxine Dempsey's eyes and said, "Proof that Maxine Dempsey has been engaged in practicing prostitution is not to be regarded as proof that she was working. Prostitution is not to be classed as work."

I read what I had written, looked up and caught the eye of the reporter sitting next to me. He grinned.

I whispered, "Did he really say that?"

The other reporters were looking at me now, waiting to see what I was going to do.

The jury adjourned, the reporters stood, stretching, waiting. "Does this mean what I think it means?" I asked, unbelieving still.

"What do you think it means?" one of the men asked.

"That since prostitution isn't work, Maxine must have been supported by her husband?"

Several of them grinned, and one said, "You catch on fast, kid."

"Not fast enough," I groaned. "I'll never catch up enough to write this story."

"Look, kid," a middle-aged man with fading blond hair said, "we've got maybe ten minutes before the jury comes back. What do you need to know?"

I breathed a sigh of relief. "Everything," I said. "To begin, who is his defense lawyer?"

"Gavin McNab," the blond man told me. "A Scotsman, and about the best legal mind in the state. He handled Mary Pickford's divorce from Owen Moore. Charlie Thomas is the poor bastard—sorry, miss—who had to do the state's case."

"So you think they'll find him not guilty?" I asked.

All of them snorted. "Not guilty of what?" one laughed.

"Of being a slacker," I said.

He laughed again. "Of course he's guilty. Whoever heard of a boxing champion fighting for love of country?"

"But they'll find him not guilty anyway?" I insisted.

"The only question is, how long will it take?" another answered, and a third put in, "I'll wager fifteen minutes." The others quickly put in their bets.

"It doesn't seem quite fair," I said, and when they looked at me I added, "She does it for money, doesn't she?"

There was an instant of silence, then a wild whoop of laughter from the four reporters.

"What's your name, kid?" the man from the *Examiner* said, smiling broadly.

"Hallie," I answered, "Hallie Duer."

"And you're working for the *Times*?"

"If I get this story," I answered, and was about to ask another question when the jury came in. It took them precisely ten minutes to find Dempsey not guilty. I pushed my way into the crowd around the champion and found myself being pressed by the momentum of the crowd against the lawyer McNab. I tried to hold back, but it was no good, the pressure was too great.

"Watch out," McNab called. "You boys are about to squash this pretty little girl." He had his arm around me then and passed me along to Dempsey—in whose protective orbit I suddenly found myself.

Dempsey did not know what to make of me, clearly. I watched

a flicker of doubt pass over his face, and then he took my pad and pencil from my hands and wrote in a cramped little hand, "The best of everything. Your friend, Jack Dempsey."

All this while, the reporters were shouting questions at him. "How does it feel, Mr. Dempsey?" they asked.

"I'm the happiest boy in the world," he answered, passing my notebook back to me. In print, those words would sound innocent, even wholesome. In fact, they had a cynical ring.

"What do you think of your former wife now?" I asked. Suddenly there was silence. Dempsey looked down at me, surprised. His eyes narrowed, became wary.

"It feels good to get out from under a charge like that," he said, staring at me. "Now I can start square and not feel that people are thinking that I tried to get out of doing my duty." And then he repeated, "I'm the happiest boy in the world."

"Why did the ex-Mrs. Dempsey accuse you?" I asked. "Do you know?"

Gavin McNab stepped forward, but Dempsey raised his hand. Suddenly no one was asking any questions. Dempsey looked at me, and I thought to myself: *This is how he does it, he scares his opponents to death.* Somewhere, very close to the surface, was a pool of black rage. He picked me up and sat me on the bar. The silence was growing; I had to shatter it. "Did you ever really work in a shipyard?" I asked. "Or did you just have your picture taken there, like Maxine says?"

I felt, rather than heard, a collective intake of breath. My eyes never left Dempsey's; if they had, I knew I would be lost.

He blinked then, and said, "The war is over." Turning away from me, he went on, "Now, I want you all to come and see me fight. That's what I do, boys. I fight." He paused for a dramatic moment, then turned to me and added, ". . . and girls." Everyone laughed then, but no one left. They wanted to see what he was going to do with me. I was curious, too. I had a peculiar, detached feeling, as if I was floating above it all, looking on. Mr. McNab finally said in a jovial tone meant to lighten, "Why don't we let the little lady from the *Times* down from her perch, Jack?"

"From the *Times*?" Dempsey said, frowning. "Red McCoy writes for the *Times*. Where's Red?"

"Drunk," somebody shouted.

"Yeah, well," Dempsey rejoined, "wait till he hears what they sent in his place."

I'd been keyed up and now it spilled over. Willing my voice not to quiver, I spat: "You don't have the slightest notion *what they sent in his place*, Dempsey. And even if you did, it wouldn't be any of your damned business." I said this as low and slow and menacing as Babe Conlon would have, adding, "If you haven't anything more original to say than your 'Happy Boy' speech, I think I'll go find your ex-bride and see what she thinks about this whole sorry affair."

I jumped down then, but I wasn't nimble enough to keep my skirts from pulling up past my knees. The men whooped and laughed, but I didn't care. I had served notice on Jack Dempsey— and on the rest of them too—that I wasn't going to play the schoolgirl to their he-man. I didn't much like having to prove that I was tough, but it looked as if it was going to be necessary. At that moment I knew I would do whatever was necessary, if it meant I could get this story . . . if it meant I could stay.

I found Maxine Dempsey sitting on a marble bench in the hallway. People were giving her wide range; she had become a pariah. I sat down next to her. She glanced at me without registering any interest.

"Mrs. Dempsey, I'm Hallie Duer from the *Times*," I said. "Would you mind talking to me for a bit?"

"I'd mind less over a drink," she answered. "I don't suppose you'd know where to find one?"

"I'm sorry," I said, and I was. If going to a saloon would help, I'd do it.

"It's okay," she answered, her voice as lifeless as her eyes. "Ask."

"Why did you push this suit? Why did you want your former husband to be convicted of draft evasion?"

She blinked a few times, and I remembered how the red lights had played on her face in the courtroom. Now she seemed paste white.

"I was sore at him, that's all. Jack's okay."

"Okay?" I repeated, surprised. "I don't understand. If you're not really angry with him, why bring a charge like that?"

"I was broke," she answered. "Still am, busted. Nada. Nothin'. Bastards won't pay."

"You mean Dempsey?" I asked. "Did you tell him you'd drop the suit if he would pay?"

She looked at me as if I were excessively stupid. "Nah. Not Jack. He's always paid up." She stood then, abruptly. "'Scuse me," she said. The reporters were spilling into the hall now, having left Dempsey. She spotted one of them, a wiry little man in a green checkered jacket, and ran after him. As I stood watching, the reporter from the *Examiner* came up to me.

"Some couple, eh?" he said, nodding toward the disappearing Maxine and the reporter.

"Who is he?" I asked.

"Prentiss of the *Herald*. He's the one who broke the story. If you've been reading his columns, he's had the inside track with the ex-Mrs. D. from the beginning. She told all, claiming to have written proof. The 'written proof' never materialized, however. But her big mouth—and his columns—forced the state to bring suit. You know the rest."

"That's what she meant, then, about the money."

"What?" he asked.

"She said she was broke, and that they wouldn't pay."

"I'll just bet," he laughed. "She didn't come up with hard evidence, and Prentiss wouldn't give her a cent." As we walked down the long marble hallway together, he asked, "What did you think of Dempsey?"

I looked at him, wary, but he wasn't laughing at me. "I don't know," I answered.

"Do you want to know what he thinks of you?" he asked.

I shrugged. "Why not?"

"He said, 'The kid's no fool, and she's probably got a wicked right.'"

It took me an hour to read the clips on Dempsey from the library, and another hour to write my story. I put it in, all of it: Judge Dooling's amazing charge to the jury, Dempsey's practiced little speech about being "the happiest boy in the world," his refusal to answer questions by pretending they hadn't been asked, Maxine's plaintive excuse that she had been "sore" at Jack. I ended with the observation that in the underworld of prostitution and prizefighting, honor and dignity and patriotism were not particularly indigenous. That survival matters more, that in the end, perhaps, justice had been done.

I sat at McCoy's desk to type out my story. He had surfaced, I was told, long enough to hear that someone else had covered for him, and then he disappeared again. As each page was typed, the copyboy took it to the copy desk, where it was marked for minor corrections and a few additions. I made them and sent it in to Mr. Curtin, as he requested. As the deadline drew near, the momentum picked up in the newsroom. You could feel the tension as typewriters clattered, copyboys scurried. It was exciting, the most exciting thing I had ever done; the words came easily . . . I would have to stay now, I would have to.

The story appeared in McCoy's column, "The Real McCoy," which started on the front page and jumped to sports. At the bottom of the column, in italics, was the notation: *Today's column by Hallie Duer.*

I finished at two-thirty; at three-thirty-five Sanford Curtin called me into his office and said, "Welcome to the *Times*, Hallie."

FOUR

RED MCCOY did not come into the office the next day or the next. Four days later an office boy emptied his desk and I was told it was to be mine. I learned from Gwen, who operated the telephone switchboard and the office grapevine as well, that McCoy's real name was Harry McConaughey, that he was a great hulk of a man with a large heart and a large thirst, and that after missing the Dempsey verdict he had gone on a three-day binge. Some of his buddies found him, passed out in an alley in North Beach, which had the greatest concentration of speakeasies in the city. When McCoy finally sobered up, Mr. Curtin helped convince him it was time to go up to his brother-in-law's farm in Oregon to take the cure. "Red's a city boy," Gwen had explained in her rasping contralto, "born South of the Slot—South of Market, that is—hates the country and fresh air and trees. Figures he's doing penance."

"Will Mr. Curtin take him back?" I asked, and Gwen answered, "Do flowers bloom in the spring?" She told me there was nothing the Boss, as she called him, loved better than a reformed drunk, unless it was a reformed crook. "They get out of prison and head straight for the *Times*," she rasped. "He's got a soft spot in his head for sinners."

I thought she was telling tales, but in fact she wasn't. Sanford Curtin was a tough editor, intolerant of dishonesty or corruption. He was a crusader, a reformer, a champion of the poor. But there was nothing sentimental or self-righteous about him; perhaps most important, he was a forgiving man. There were times, I was told, when he exasperated his friends and admirers—which took in the whole of the newsroom—by turning the other cheek, going out of his way to help an old enemy. Not only did he put Boss Ruef in prison, but also he worked to get him out, claiming that he had become a "scapegoat," that others who were equally guilty had gone free. And when he did get him out of prison, he found him a job and a place to stay.

Red McCoy, I learned, was also a favorite in the newsroom. As the head of the sports desk, a florid man called "Ham," told me, "Red's a good boy—the bottle's his only weakness. But give me a drunk over a Bible-thumper any day."

I got McCoy's address from Gwen, who had orders to send him a package of *Times*'s once each week. I wrote to say that while, for me, the Dempsey story had been a stroke of luck, I felt badly that it had to be at his expense. The reply came in a big, scrawling hand: "Dear Miss Hallie: Glad to hear some good came of the Dempsey trial. I read your story and it was top of the card. You did me a favor covering for me and I thank you. The way I see it, it was good luck for us both. Sincerely, Harry McConaughey."

After that first, exhilarating day I was turned over to Irma Albright, the publisher's sister, who wrote a society column under the sobriquet "Lady Teasley," and Jessamyn Weaver, the household-sciences editor. Miss Albright was small and precise, with such an excess of nervous energy that she spent much of her time walking up and down through the city room, clucking at the disarray. Hers was the only neat desk in sight, and the only one with a vase of carefully arranged flowers on it. Fastidiously dressed, she

was never without a large hat, and the hat always matched perfectly whichever costume she was wearing.

Jessamyn—"Jess," as she said I must call her—never appeared
in anything so elegant as Miss Albright's costumes. As often as
not, she would forget the belt to a dress, or wear brown stockings
with a gray suit. It didn't take long to discover that Jess considered
Miss Albright a dilettante because she was financially independent
and thus didn't have to work. Miss Albright, on the other hand,
considered herself superior because, as she said at least once every
day, "I work by choice, not necessity."

Amazingly, the two got on well together most of the time. And
aside from Mr. Curtin, Jess was the only one who dared call Miss
Albright "Irma."

The two were to share me as an assistant.

"That's trouble," Gwen predicted. Gwen's predictions were
legend; she was almost never wrong. The two women editors were
warring over possession of me before the week was out, under
cover of a strained politeness.

"Oh, my dear, no," Society would say to Household Sciences,
"I am quite sure you've had Hallie for your four hours. She's mine
now." She would laugh then, a strained trilly little laugh, and Jess
would sigh and say in a hurt tone, "Well, all right, I suppose, but . . ."

My days were occupied with recipes for prune-and-potato
cake, trimming Lady Teasley's effusive prose and trying to keep
both women happy.

Early on I managed to offend the society editor by deleting
a sentence that read: "It has been proven, time and time again,
that more joy is gotten out of life when doing for others." When
she asked me please to explain how I could possibly object to that
sentiment, I told her I questioned if any such thing had ever been
proven. Her feathers ruffled, she flew into Mr. Curtin's office
and the whole city room heard his reaction: "Drivel, Irma! Pure,
undiluted drivel." It took me several days to get back into her
good graces.

I told myself to be patient. I was on the *Times*. I was working with Mr. Curtin—though I was beginning to wonder if I would ever know him well enough to call him "Boss." But I could wait; there was plenty of time now.

One Friday I was leafing through a stack of photographs of young women to select those to run in the Sunday society section, along with the announcements of their engagements. Two of the photos caught my attention. In each, the girl was casually posed— almost as if she had been sitting chatting with a friend. Each was looking directly into the camera in a rather intimate way. They were very different from the usual studio photographs. Curious, I turned them over and on the back was lettered: "Photograph by Faith Moore Studio, 111 Market Street, San Francisco."

Faith Moore. The girl I had met my first day in San Francisco had been named Faith Moore. And she had been carrying a large portfolio; I wondered if it could be . . . At lunchtime I decided to stroll down Market Street to see. It was a bright day, the summer fog had lifted at eleven and office people were coming into the street to absorb the sunshine.

Number 111 Market was a small building tucked between two larger ones. I walked up one floor, to the door that said "Portrait Studio" and in smaller letters "Faith Moore." I rang the bell on the counter.

She came through the doorway wiping her hands and smiling as she would to a prospective customer. She was wearing an elaborately embroidered peasant blouse of a soft, shiny fabric and she had a magenta scarf wound around her hair so that only her face showed. She looked like pictures I had seen of Gypsies; I felt drab and dull in my tailored suit.

"We met about six weeks ago," I reminded her, "at the Mary Elizabeth residence club."

"Yes we did!" she said, recognition and pleasure registering on her face at the same moment. "You're Hallie Duer—I read your story on Dempsey and I wanted to tell you I liked it, but I thought you wouldn't remember me."

We laughed then, and I told her about coming upon her photographs and how much I liked them. She pressed her lips together and grinned in a pixie way, so I knew she was pleased. Words seemed to come spilling out of me—I heard myself telling her about the Dempsey story, and how Society and Household Sciences were fighting over me. And she told me about opening the studio, and how her roommate knows a lot of society people who were starting to come to her for their portraits. She interrupted herself to say, "I don't have anybody coming for the next hour, and it is beautiful outside. If you can wait a minute while I do something in the darkroom, we could get a sandwich and walk down to the Ferry Building."

I used those few minutes to study the photographs on the wall, portraits of women and children, all with that same revealing quality.

We chattered away that day like magpies, and I went back to work thinking that in all of my life I had never met anyone to whom I had so much to say.

We met often after that, for a sandwich sometimes and even, now and then when we felt daring, for dinner. She knew a lot of cheap restaurants in North Beach, near her cottage on Telegraph Hill. She shared the cottage with an art student named Sybil, a young woman from a well-to-do family. I visited the cottage—built to house refugees after the 1906 quake—often. Although Faith never complained, it was clear that Sybil did not share any of the household chores. Her things were scattered everywhere, with the exception of the little closed-in back porch which served as Faith's room. It was immaculate, the bed covered with a double-wedding-ring quilt, the windows looking out onto a tangle of morning glories.

We talked about everything, Faith and I—politics, the Harding administration, her work and mine. The portrait studio, she told me, was a way to make a living so she could do the kind of photography she wanted to do—photos taken on the street, not posed but from life, to show how people lived.

The photographer she most admired was a man named Lewis Hine, who had done a series of photographs of children laboring in sweatshops and on the streets of New York, photos that had helped get new child-labor laws passed. She wanted to have that kind of influence, to point up the evils of society. When she spoke, her eyes, which were dark to begin with, became darker still. I envied her—for her convictions, for knowing what she wanted to do and setting out to find a way. She made me aware of my own aimlessness. I didn't want to be writing about debutante balls or cauliflower salads. As usual, I only knew what I didn't want to do.

Since coming to San Francisco I had stored my Model T in a public garage a few blocks from the residence club. For selfish reasons, I had kept quiet about it. If the girls knew I had a machine, I would become popular, I was afraid.

Faith could hardly believe her eyes the first time I appeared in front of the cottage in the T. She clapped her hands over her mouth, her eyes sparkling. "Of course," she said then. "Of course you *would* drive an automobile. You look perfectly right sitting up there in the driver's seat, all ready to go. Perfect!" We started our Sunday trips that day, piling her camera equipment in the car and exploring the far reaches of the bay region. If I was able to take Saturday off, we decided, Faith would close her shop and we would drive all the way to Half Moon Bay on the coast south of San Francisco. It happened soon enough. We made our way along a narrow ribbon of road that had been cut into the Santa Cruz mountainsides, winding up one and down another, and up again until we could see the crescent of coastline that included Half Moon Bay, with the hidden coves that had made it a rumrunner's paradise.

We checked into the Palace Miramar Hotel, a fine shingled building that seemed to blend into the dunes. When we left San Francisco the sun had been out, but when we arrived a warm summer fog had wrapped the beach in a fine, gauzy white.

"No photographs today," Faith said. "Let's put on our gum boots and take a hike on the beach." We walked farther than we had intended, ending at the kind of deserted beach that seemed likely to attract smugglers. We gathered driftwood to make a little fire, for cheerfulness more than anything. When the fire was blazing, we sat back to enjoy it.

Faith wanted to know if I had ever been to Coney Island. It struck me as an odd sort of question, since she knew I had never been east of Chicago.

"Have you?" I asked.

"My mother and father took me there once," she started, "when I was about six years old. I can still remember. We took a train out from the city and had dinner at a little Italian place with a garden and an umbrella to shade against the sun. It was green and red and white, the umbrella. I remember so much about that day—distinct, precise things, like the color of the Italian ice my father bought me."

I was surprised; she had never mentioned her father. "What else do you remember about him?"

"Ummm," she said, poking in the fire with a stick, "he left not long after that day. We never saw him again. Mostly, I remember the Italian ice."

I thought about it for a while. "There were just the two of you, then? Your mother and you?"

She nodded. "It wasn't so bad, really—at least not for me. It was hard for Mother. She had a job in a hat factory and she used to bring me bits of ribbons and lace and feathers. I'd put them together in a kind of bouquet sometimes, and she got it into her mind that I was artistic. So she sent me to art school at the Cooper Union. That's where I discovered photography."

We were quiet for a while, thinking our own thoughts. After a time I said, "My father abandoned us, too."

Faith looked, at me curiously. "I thought you told me he died," she said.

"He did," I answered. The words were coiled tight inside of me, but I wanted them out. "He put a bullet through his brain. He was too selfish—or scared—to live without her."

59

"Your mother?"

I nodded. My throat was getting tight. I tried to swallow to keep it from closing.

"How did she die?" Faith wanted to know.

"Boating accident," I answered. "On the lake." I seemed able to speak in simple sentences only. "A lark. The ride was a lark. It was how she was."

Faith was looking at me searchingly now. "Was she alone?"

I shook my head. "Me. I was there."

"In the boat? Just the two of you?"

I nodded. "Mother said, 'Let's take a boat ride, just us.' She was wearing a long white dress . . ." The words were coming now, I could feel them rising inside of me. ". . . and petticoats, lots of petticoats, and a big hat. Father had taken Clive somewhere, I don't remember where . . . and we were at the lake where they rent rowboats . . . and the man at the window said, 'Going out alone, ma'am?' And Mother said, 'Oh, no, I'm going with my friend here.' We were laughing, and rowing, and then it got dark. It had been bright and then it got dark, fast. The wind came up. Mother started singing . . . 'Row, row, row your boat!' . . . we tried to get back, but the waves . . . we couldn't, the wind whipped up the waves . . . the boat turned over, I couldn't breathe. She held me up . . . her fingers pressing under my arms . . . 'Hang on, Hal,' she kept saying, 'don't be afraid.' I don't know how long she held me up, a long time. They saw us from shore . . . a man swam out with a rope around him and took me . . . and when he went back for her . . . she was gone."

I was trembling, my teeth chattering uncontrollably so that I couldn't say any more. Faith put her arm around me and pulled me tight against her. She didn't say anything for a while, and then she said, "Such a hurtful memory, Hallie."

"No," I tried to explain, needing to make her understand, "I think about her, the way she was then . . . how brave she was, not letting me give up. Not giving up."

We sat for a long time, studying the fire and the sea beyond, waiting. Faith gave me time; then she asked what needed to be asked: "Your father—what happened?"

I heard myself tell her in a voice that seemed disconnected, remote: "They found Mother on Thursday. Father went to where they had taken her . . . her body . . . and he never came back. He drove out to the country, left his carriage near a woods, walked into a stand of alder trees and shot himself through the head." I found a handkerchief in my pocket and blew my nose; then I went on: "Grandmother Duer was . . . well, he was her only child, it had been just the two of them since Grandfather died when my father was a small boy . . . and she went wild when they told her. Clive and I were upstairs, but we could hear. She said it was Mother's fault, that Mother had been spiteful and stupid to go out in the boat. And she said I was just like her, that I even looked like her and she wanted someone to take me away so she wouldn't have to see me. I understand now that it was the grief, the shock, but at the time . . ."

"You were only a child," Faith said, "and you'd just lost your mother and your father. Dear God."

I took a deep breath. "Anyway, people would tell me that I must always remember how much my father must have loved my mother, to have done what he did. I suppose they thought it would be comforting. It wasn't, not at all. I don't think that he killed himself out of love. I think it was out of fear. If he had loved her well enough, he wouldn't have deserted us. Mother never would have, I know that."

Faith looked at me, her head tipped to one side to avoid a stream of smoke that was blowing from the fire. "What is 'well enough'?" she asked.

I took a deep breath of the salt air and the smoke, and tried to find the answer. "Something larger," I finally said, "love that isn't all tight and close and limited. I guess I wanted to love—and to be loved—the way you love the ocean or the air . . . or an idea that you know is important. . ." I took another breath and managed to laugh. "I've never quite been able to say all of that out loud before," I told her; then I added stiffly, "Thank you."

"What for?" she wanted to know.

"For making it possible for me to talk," I answered.

We sat quietly for a time, until she said: "Isn't it strange, how few people there are in this world you can talk to—I mean, the kind who seem to be able to turn some key inside of you and unlock all those words that are backed up, stored inside, threatening to strangle, all those things you thought you'd never be able to say?"

"The Italian-ice memories?" I asked, and she nodded and began to bury the fire with the sand.

On the long walk back I felt, somehow, lighter; something that had been tight and hard in my chest was gone.

I spent as little time at the residence club as I could. Until Mr. Curtin decided to raise my salary, I wouldn't be able to afford a place of my own. Faith wanted me to move into the cottage, and had gone so far as to ask Sybil to take the little porch so that Faith and I could share the larger bedroom, but the idea did not appeal to Sybil, who pointed out that she was cramped for space as it was. She was right; the cottage was too small for three people.

The women at the residence hall felt me to be unfriendly, they resented my preference for privacy and they were suspicious of a woman who worked on a newspaper. It did not, as one girl put it at dinner one evening, "seem very feminine." They could not just let me be. I think I became something of a challenge to them. Possibly they took a perverse pleasure in asking me to join them, just to see what my excuse would be. Saturday was the big date night. Usually a group of the girls would go to one of the city's several ballrooms and come home all flushed with excitement.

One Saturday, empty of excuses, I agreed to go along. Their

reaction was a mixture of surprise and disappointment. A girl named Nina told me I was going to have a swell time and that when I saw all the fun I'd been missing I'd thank them for not giving up on me. While we were getting ready somebody wound up the Victrola and put on "Ain't We Got Fun," the current hit tune. *Times are hard and getting harder . . . still we have fun . . . There's nothing surer, the rich get rich and the poor get . . . children. In the meantime, in between time . . .* Through the hallways you could hear them singing along, happy that it was Saturday night and they were going out, *Ain't we got fun.*

We left at seven-thirty, en masse—a jumble of silk stockings and flowered dresses and talcum powder, our hats perfectly positioned on our heads. We caught a cable car down to Market, then walked to Fifth to the Woolworth's store, where we would meet several of the girls when they got off at eight. I was surprised to find, already there, a dozen or so young men waiting alongside a bank of automobiles, a few Model T's among them. The boys gathered round us. They knew most of the girls in our group, introductions were called out.

A tall boy with a shock of wet hair introduced himself to me as Roger. I tried to catch his last name, but before I could ask, Nina quickly took my arm and said to him, "This is Hallie, she lives at the Mary Elizabeth."

"A Mary Liz girl, huh?" Roger asked, as if he and Mary Liz were old chums. He had a sharp Adam's apple that was, unfortunately, at my eye level, and his manner was so studied that I had to bite my lip to keep from laughing. Everything the girls around me were babbling struck me as foolish. *Don't be such an almighty snob*, I told myself. And then I accepted Roger's offer of a ride to the Trianon Ballroom near Van Ness.

At the window I opened my purse to get the money for the ticket, and felt Nina's elbow in my ribs. "Put that away," she muttered under her breath. "Girls don't pay."

"Why not?" I asked out loud.

"Because girls get in free," she whispered, even more urgently, embarrassed by my ignorance.

I allowed myself a small groan. *We're the bait*, I thought. "Do we get a roll of tickets?" I asked Nina, who threw me a scathing glance. I thought about Babe Conlon then; Babe would think we were a bunch of amateurs, and she would be right.

In the first hour or two I must have danced with nine or ten young men. They smelled of strong soap and toilet water and they danced, most of them, with a concentration so intense it overwhelmed any idea of grace or rhythm. They talked about other ballrooms, other dance bands, other fabulous nights on the town. I was beginning to believe the night would never end when Roger appeared and asked if I would like to go for a ride with him in his Model T.

He put his hand on the small of my back in a proprietary way that I didn't like, but I was so happy to be leaving, I didn't pull away. On the sidewalk I paused to take a deep breath of cool air, glad to put the noise and the heat of sweaty bodies behind me, and then I swung into the passenger seat of the T without waiting for Roger to help me.

It took him three tries to get the car to turn over; I could have helped by adjusting the spark and throttle, but I knew it wouldn't be good form, not with Roger. He was too proud of himself, giving added flourishes to every maneuver, some of which were perfectly simple. I sat there motionless, feeling as dumb as I was acting.

He drove west on Market, then turned to make the long, winding trip to the top of Twin Peaks. It was a clear, bright night and I had never seen the city so sparkling. The lights of Market Street cut a bright swath all the way to the Ferry Building. Across the bay you could see scattered lights in the hills of Oakland. I wrapped my arms around me and looked over it all and felt, once more, a rising sense of excitement—of something about to happen, of being almost there . . .

When Roger touched my elbow I jumped, startled.

"Sorry," he muttered, "I didn't mean to scare you."

I was about to apologize—for a moment I had forgotten him—and then I noticed that he was carrying a blanket. Roger was craftier than I had thought.

"Why don't we sit for a spell," he said.

"I don't think so," I answered with what I hoped was the right mix of polite coolness. "I just want to look for a while, and then I'd like to go home."

"Just like that?" he said.

I thought of all the Rogers I had pushed away in Sacramento and I was sorry I had allowed myself to get in this situation again.

"Yes, Roger, just like that," I said. "I appreciate the ride and the lovely view. I've never seen the city from this point at night, and it is a treat."

"What is this, anyway?" he said, annoyed. "I thought when you said you'd leave the dance early—"

"You thought what?" I cut in, letting my voice go razor cold.

He became peevish: "I thought you'd be nicer."

Nicer. My God!

"I have been nice, Roger. And so have you, so far, and I'd very much like to keep it that way. So let's go now. You don't have to drive me to the residence club, just take me to Market Street and I can catch a streetcar, then you can go back to the dance."

"Go back?" he exploded, as if I had suggested something outrageous. "That's a good one." His Adam's apple was working, moving sharply up and down. He sputtered, "If you want to go home, be my guest. Nobody's stopping you." He looked as if he had just had a winning idea. "You're so all fired up to leave," he said, waving his arm magnanimously, "drive yourself. I'm not ready to go just yet." To show he meant it, he turned his back to me and began walking away.

I watched him, thinking *you impossible ass*, not knowing if I meant him or me. Anger welled up in me. Should I call to him to stop, to come back, please to take me home? No. No. *Keep going*, I said under my breath, *just keep moving, Roger.*

When he was about forty feet away, I moved as quietly as I could to set the levers. I gave it a hard crank, *one chance is all I would get* . . . the engine roared to life, and I was behind the wheel before Roger had time to think what was happening. He stood staring at me . . . I released the pedal and the car jumped forward at the same moment that Roger did . . . he was running . . . I had to get enough speed to outrun him . . . I threw myself against the wheel and made a wide arc, putting him on the far side. I could see his face straining now, twisted with anger and surprise . . . but I had the speed, now I was in control.

"Stop!" he screamed. "What the hell. . ."

"What you told me to do," I shouted. "If you want a ride, jump in."

I slowed alongside him enough to allow him to tumble into the passenger seat, then I jerked forward to unsettle him so he couldn't grab the wheel. I let it out then, slamming down the hill, taking the curves as fast and as sharp as I could without losing control. It was a new road, wide and smooth and not anywhere near as bad as the roads I'd raced on in Sacramento. I glanced over at Roger. He was hanging on with both hands, frozen. *He thinks I've never driven before,* I realized.

"Hold on," I shouted, and swerved to make it seem worse than it was. He screamed and crouched low in the seat, his hands over his face. Embarrassed for him, I let up. After a while he straightened up and sat silently until we reached Market.

At the first opportunity, I pulled over to the side and told him in my best Babe Conlon manner, "The next time you decide to strand a girl up there, make sure she can't drive." Then I ran for the streetcar.

I had planned to warn the others about Roger, but suddenly I was a pariah at the Mary Elizabeth. Nobody would talk to me. A meeting was called for the next evening, which meant it was of some urgency, since meetings were usually held on Wednesday nights. It started with a lecture on what was considered "proper feminine behavior." I was on trial, it seemed, though no formal charges were made, and it took me a while to figure out that Roger had managed to accuse me of taking *him* for a ride, then stealing his car. "Whatever happened on Twin Peaks is your personal business," Sue hissed out, puffed up with self-importance, "but certainly you must know that by agreeing to go up there at night alone with a young man, you compromised yourself and the good name of the Mary Elizabeth."

After four or five others had made long, rambling statements which more or less hinted that some s-s-sin, as Sue whistled out, had been committed, I was asked if I had anything to say in my defense.

I looked at the faces—young and set and self-righteous—and knew that nothing I would say could change their minds.

"No," I said.

A vote was taken, and it was democratically decided to ask me to leave the Mary Elizabeth.

I moved into the cottage with Faith and Sybil, sleeping on a cot in the living room while I looked for a place I could afford. I found a room in a private home, but Faith said it would be impossible, pointing out so many drawbacks that I had to agree with her. I kept looking, but Faith urged me to take my time, not to rush.

One night at dinner, the three of us squeezed around the little dining table, I said, "I really am making a nuisance of myself, crowding both of you. I have to move out, and I've decided—"

Faith's face fell. Sybil saw it, sighed and interrupted me, "Mum's been after me to go to Europe with her, and I've been thinking it's a good idea. I could study in Paris for a while and—"

This time it was Faith who interrupted: "That's wonderful, Sybil," she bubbled. "You'll absolutely love Paris."

We were amazed at the spaciousness of the cottage when Sybil removed her things. We spent several Sundays scrubbing and cleaning and polishing. We put new curtains on the little porch, which was to be my room, and photographs on the walls, and when we were finished it looked neat and orderly and bright.

We sat in the middle of the newly polished floor feeling happy with our labors and pleased with how everything had worked out.

"Wait one small moment," Faith said, bobbing up and running out to the little shed behind the cottage. She reappeared with a dark bottle, which she held high. "Gift of Mr. Maggiore," she said proudly. "Actually, a payment for a photograph of Baby Maggiore. One bottle of the real thing—homemade red wine!"

We toasted Sybil and her mum, we toasted Roger and his Model T, we toasted Sister Sue and the girls of the Mary Elizabeth. When the bottle was almost empty Faith stood, raised her glass and, weaving a little, said, "And here's to Babe Conlon and to s-s-s-sin."

FIVE

I FELT HAPPY. It was easy to talk and easy to laugh. Even the
silences were easy between us. We would come tumbling out of
the cottage before eight each morning, tucking our hair up with
our tortoiseshell combs . . . always a little late, always a bit breathless, rushing down the steep Filbert Street hill, trying not to topple
headfirst . . . laughing as we cut across Washington Square, getting
our shoes wet in the grass, out of breath as we jumped onto the
streetcar and one of the regulars called out, "They made it again!"

After work I joined the crowd heading down Market Street
toward the Ferry Building. Faith would be waiting at the corner of
California and we would start talking at once. There was always so
much to say, so many details of the day to be shared. We made our
way home again, all the while learning to read each other's moods,
knowing when it was right to talk and when it was best to be silent.
For the first time in as long as I could remember, I felt in step—the
way you feel when marching along in a parade, music drumming,
everything fresh and moving. I was part of something—Faith, the
cottage, San Francisco, the *Times*.

September arrived, warm and bright, dispelling the summer fogs. The city settled into its own season of warmth. On those days when the heat would linger past sunset, every window would be open in the tall wooden apartment buildings that climbed the hills. The smell of garlic would drift out onto the summer air, and someone would call to us in the dialect of Milan or Naples or Bologna as we labored up the hill, Faith and I, carrying bags from Panelli's grocery—brown eggs and bread still warm against my stomach—and we would call back *"Buon giorno"* or *"Come vanno le cose?"* Then, delighted at our stumbling attempts, someone would lean out of a window and tell us, in a glorious mix of Italian and English, what a pleasure we were for their eyes to see, how good for their ears to hear us laugh.

We knew that in reality they felt sorry for us—considering us too pale, too thin and too old for marriage. Once or twice a week we would come home to find a dish on our sideboard—lasagna or a cioppino or scallopini—and a child would be posted in our kitchen, waiting patiently to tell us, in the English his mother couldn't manage, what it was, how it was to be heated and, most important of all, that we were to eat every bite.

We always did. One evening as I finished my cannelloni I said contentedly, "I eat and I eat and I never get fat so I suppose I'll never find a husband."

Faith looked at me, scowling.

I waited. Finally I prodded. "Yes?"

She sighed. "I don't know," she started, "maybe it is too late. I suppose it worries me."

"Let me guess," I tried to joke, "is the 'it' that worries you anything to do with marriage?"

The look she gave me said that I was not to treat the subject lightly. In as compassionate a tone as I could muster, I asked, "Are you trying to say that you're worried you will never marry?"

"Aren't you?" she asked, her usually firm voice cracking.

I concentrated on cutting myself a slice of the rough Italian bread, thinking, concentrating. "I'm not sure *how* I feel about it," I said—because she was waiting, watching me. "Have you ever been . . . ever cared . . . for anyone that much?"

Faith nodded. "In New York," she said. "It's one of the reasons I left. It was too soon. I mean, I was too young and my mother said he was too much like my father . . ." She paused. ". . . he was older than me, quite a lot older."

While we waited for the water to heat so we could wash our supper dishes, we chatted about this and that—a socialite she had photographed that day, a woman with a nose she said was shaped like a summer squash, and about my ill-fated suggestion that we test in our own kitchens the recipes we planned to run in the paper. I washed, submerging the plates in the hot, soapy water, then swirling them in the cold-water rinse before positioning them on the drainboard. Faith polished a green ceramic bowl, waiting and thinking, both of us knowing that we would return to the subject of marriage. It was there now, between us, waiting.

I wiped off the oilcloth that served as a splashboard and said, "It's warm out, why don't we climb to the top of the hill? The kids are still playing there, you can hear them."

The crest of Telegraph Hill was covered with scrub bushes and straggly eucalyptus trees. A game of hide-and-seek was under way; we carefully avoided giving away the positions of two little girls, curled together behind a large rock as the seeker counted . . . *ventotto, ventinove, trenta . . . here I come, ready or not.*

In the days of the clipper ships, a man was posted on this hill to telegraph the arrival of a ship through the Golden Gate to downtown merchants. Now the hill was the purview of the children and those of us hardy enough to climb the rough stairs to the top for a view of the city and the bay, everything spread out below so that you felt removed. Things seemed clearer on the hill.

We found a ledge away from the game and sat watching a freighter make its way through the Gate and move slowly toward the wharves. "You asked if I want to marry," I started, not looking at Faith but letting my eyes follow the freighter. "The thing is, I don't even know what it feels like to be . . . I started to say 'in love,' but those words stick in my throat. Certainly what the girls at the Mary Elizabeth called 'love' is not what I consider a particularly attractive feeling. I guess I'm trying to say that the word itself is so imprecise . . . and also that I don't know how it feels to care that much for someone, some man. I've never had it happen to me, and that bothers me quite a lot because sometimes I think it might mean that something is missing in me. . . ." The words began to pour from me, thoughts I had never quite completed, and once started, I couldn't seem to stop. "Once, maybe more than that but once at least, I was with someone I thought I might be able to care for if I could just get to know him . . . there seemed some depth . . . In the beginning we might be dancing and I would feel this strange, warm tremor—a kind of quivering sensation—that was only partly physical."

I paused, trying to think, to sort things out. When I didn't go on, Faith coaxed, "And?"

I sighed. "Nothing. It didn't happen. I got to know him and he seemed just . . . well, empty. Shallow. I don't know! I don't mean dull, but something that I had wanted to be there wasn't. Another time, for some reason or other we just never got to know each other. He started talking about marriage and having children, and I was only twenty and had just started learning what I needed to know about newspapers . . . and after that, I think I stopped looking. It seemed too complicating . . . I don't know." I didn't know, and it made me angry with myself. I turned away to hide it, concentrating on the freighter, now almost lost in the gathering dusk.

"The lights are going on," Faith said in a voice meant to bring me back. I turned to look at her. The hill was catching the last light and it gave her face the cast of cool marble. "You're talking about loving someone, and I know what you mean," she said, "the lovely, swelling feeling . . . and the disappointments. But I think what has been on my mind more than love is children. The thing is, I can't imagine what it would be like not to have children. I want to feel a child growing in my body . . . I want to be a mother. I don't want to miss it, Hal."

I tucked her arm in mine and we sat close together on the ledge, watching the lights of the ferryboats move about on the black of the bay.

"I'm going to be twenty-seven next month, you're twenty-eight," I said. "Is that so very old? Does that make us spinsters?"

"I think we still have a little time left," Faith said, pressing my arm.

Suddenly I knew what she had been trying to tell me.

"You've met someone," I blurted. "Who?"

"Thayer Gerson," she answered.

"Oh, my," I said, surprised. "The artist?"

"The fifty-one-year-old artist," she answered.

Thayer Gerson was one of the city's most successful sculptors. His name appeared regularly in the cultural sections of the newspapers. He was on the art commission and had achieved a small international reputation. I also knew, from the society editor at the paper, that he was seldom without a benefactress, usually an elderly widow who was active in the social set. Miss Albright dismissed him as a parvenu, but then, she was no judge of character. I was certain that if Faith cared for him enough to consider marriage, there would be substance to the man.

"Does he make little tremors skittle up your spine?" I teased.

Faith, quite serious, said, "Something like that. He really is a very exciting man to be with—filled with ideas, and intense about his work. Do you think he's too old?"

"For what?" I asked, making her laugh.

"What has age to do with it?" I went on. "Besides, I don't think I could picture you with anyone very young, I'm not sure why. . ."

She answered my next question before I could ask it: "He's divorced. There are two children, girls—in the teens now."

We sat for a while longer, saying little. When finally we made our way back to the cottage it was dark. We snagged our skirts on the bushes, and managed to get our hands dirty from clinging to the rocks on the path down.

At the *Times* that fall I continued to be the cause of squabbles between Domestic Science and Society. I was removed from the struggle in a peculiar way. Both women were satisfied with my efforts, but neither felt as if she had enough of my time. It was the city editor, Gene Bolten, who was caught in their crossfire. Almost daily they wrangled with him over the division of my labors. Finally, on the day the rains began in mid-November, his patience gave out.

No sooner had Gene appeared at the city desk, positioning himself across from two of the rewrite men, ready to tackle the day's assignments, than Miss Albright came whispering up to him. Gene was a small, gray, unassuming man. His appearance belied his phenomenal news sense and, in a city where a scoop was all-important, an amazing tenacity. No one stayed with a story longer than Gene, or went to greater lengths to be first on the street—which meant first at Lotta's fountain—with a story. On at least one occasion, rumor had it, Gene had kept a prime source hidden at his home for a week, to ensure the scoop for the *Times*. On this particular morning, Gene was in the first, nervous stages of pursuing a scoop, and not in a mood to grapple with Miss Albright. Had Jess, of Household Sciences, not entered the fray at that moment, it might have passed. But she came barreling down on the two of them, clucking her "my dears" and "my goodnesses" like some preposterous old hen, and Gene threw up his hands and even raised his voice. "That's all," he said, and the two of them, stunned by this remarkable show of displeasure, retreated.

After a time the Boss came in, and within minutes Gene entered the cubicle and closed the door, an ominous signal. I watched all of this from the newsroom, glancing up from the story I was supposed to be rewriting about one Mills College graduate visiting another in Santa Monica. It was very much like watching a silent movie. The Boss and Gene spoke earnestly, the city editor raised his hands, palms up, in an expression of anguish, the Boss lit one of his five-cent Owls and pondered. A few minutes passed in this fashion; then the Boss walked to the door and motioned to Miss Albright. She fluttered into the cubicle, the door was closed. She sat, then stood. The Boss talked, more movement with arms flying, standing up and sitting down. The door opened again, Curtin summoned Jess. She moved ponderously into the smoke-filled cubicle. Both men were puffing away, a signal of their displeasure, an announcement that they were not making concessions on the basis of sex. The women did not notice. Miss Albright coughed, waved her hand in front of her face. More words, some hand-wringing. The smoke created a haze, it became difficult to see clearly. Finally it was over and the actors filed out. No one was smiling.

And then I was summoned, and Ham. The Boss wasted no time. "Hallie's on sports now, Ham. Starting today."

Ham was struck dumb. "Whaduyamean?" he mumbled.

"I mean," the editor said, glowering, "that you have been ragging me for someone ever since Harry left—well, Hallie's the one."

"But what will I do with her?" Ham asked plaintively.

"Put her to work," the Boss exploded. "Let her do rewrite, the wires. Hallie can spell better than any of your boys, and her grammar is better too."

"But," Ham whined, "she don't know the lingo."

"Then teach her the lingo," the Boss boomed.

I learned the lingo. Learned the difference between a left hook and a right cross, between a puncher and a boxer, learned the intricacies of a combination. I could not, however, convince Ham to let me go to a match to see for myself. "The fights," he would say, "is no place for nice girls."

"What would you say," I baited him once, "if I told you I wasn't a nice girl?"

"I'd say," he came back, tapping my shoulder with the fingers which held his omnipresent cigar, "you wasn't telling the truth."

So I stayed in the office, made Ham's verbs match his subjects and cleaned up the other sportswriters' copy. After a while, when I didn't wilt under their barrage of clumsy jokes and earthy humor, they gave up and accepted me. That was when I started my campaign in earnest. I was determined to get out on the street working as a legman, getting the stories as they happened. I wanted a beat—city hall, police, I'd even have settled for the hotels. Failing that, I wanted to cover a sporting event of some kind. "A tennis match," I would beg, "a golf game. Anything!"

And Ham would make his standard joke about croquet and leave me at the rewrite desk.

I never knew what time I would be able to leave the city room. If some big sports story were breaking, I might have to stay until seven or eight in the evening. When this happened, Faith would often come to the newspaper and wait with me, and we would have sandwiches and coffee at the rewrite desk. More often, she would go over to Thayer Gerson's studio in the Montgomery Building. His working hours started at about three in the afternoon and often went long into the night. He was working on a large commission, Faith explained, and would be unable to see anyone at all until it was finished. It was, I realized, her way of explaining why she had not yet introduced him to me.

I met Thayer Gerson for the first time a few weeks before Christmas, at a party in his studio in the Montgomery Building, a great old brick structure catacombed with studios, some small and a few, like Thayer's, enormous.

His annual Christmas party was an Event, covered by all of the newspapers, usually in the society columns because so many art patrons attended. This year the studio was decorated like a winter wonderland, with tree branches painted white crowding the rafters. A dance floor was fashioned to look like an ice pond, and a full orchestra—in white tie and tails—played. The guests came in formal attire; it was Thayer Gerson's habit to wear a costume.

I stood at the door watching—trying to catch a glimpse of Faith, wanting to have a few moments to take it all in, to become accustomed. The studio was filled with the scent of fresh-cut pine boughs. A mirrored sphere turned slowly overhead, scattering colored lights over the dancers . . . a rainbow of colors sparkled off the bugle beads that covered elegant silk ballgowns and diamond necklaces that flashed as couples danced by. The women wore satins and silks and trailed egret feathers and trains. Then, a flash of outrageous color as a man in a Spanish bullfighter's suit of lights swept by. He would be one of the artists. It was the juxtaposition of bohemian artists and conventional San Francisco society that gave this fete its flamboyant reputation.

An attendant appeared and asked if he might take my cape. I slipped out of it warily; my new white silk gown had a lower neckline than I had ever worn before; I felt exposed. I fingered the pearls that circled my neck, and tried not to seem ill-at-ease. "It is not the sort of ball that requires an escort," Faith had said. Even so, I wished I were with someone. It would be nice to dance under the lights, to be part of the sparkling movement. . . .

The orchestra began to play "Avalon" and I must have been swaying to the music because I leaned into a small woman who was wearing a paisley turban with a beautifully simple brocade gown trimmed in fur. She must, I said to myself, be very rich. To her I said, "I *am* sorry," and put out my hand to steady her.

"Don't be," she laughed, "but I daresay a pretty girl like you could find a much nicer dancing partner!" She had lively dark eyes—young eyes, though she was not young. She would not have been handsome as a girl, but she was handsome now. Something about her gave me confidence; suddenly feeling expansive, I asked if she could point out our host.

"You mean Gerson of the North Woods?" she said drily. "He's

the one over there in the red shirt and bushy beard—his way of pretending to thumb his nose at the whole thing."

I was about to ask what she meant by "pretending" when I saw Faith on the far side of the dance floor, her face flushed with excitement, trying to thread through the crowd to reach me.

I waved and, excusing myself, went to meet Faith. When I had left for work that morning, she had still been fretting over what she would wear to the ball. In the short time I had known Faith, she had never once decided on what to wear more than an hour before putting it on, and then always added a scarf or a tie or some colorful embellishment at the last moment.

The dress she was wearing now was, I realized, a combination of three patterns I had seen in one of the Paris fashion magazines Faith had brought home. It was made of the sheerest pale yellow *peau d'ange,* was loosely gathered, having the appearance of being cut on the bias, with a hemline that was longer in the back than the front. The dress was held in place by silk ties in graduated shades of orange and red. On Faith, it was perfect.

"I don't know how you do it," I told her, squeezing her hand. "You look magnificent, you really do!"

"I'm probably the only one in the room wearing a made-over nightgown," she whispered in my ear. "But look at you, Hal! You look preposterously virginal in that dress. Everybody's staring . . . all these rich men, watch out."

All the while she was pulling me through a thicket of people (some did turn to look at us) toward a little knot of well-wishers gathered around the host.

Thayer Gerson was a big man with a studied presence. He stood very straight, his legs planted firmly on the floor as if he actually were a woodsman surveying a forest, as if all the others in their elegant clothes and costumes were decidedly out of place. The impression he gave was that only Thayer Gerson was dressed properly.

"So, the famous Hallie has arrived at last," he said before Faith could introduce me. Taking both of my hands in his, he said, "Let's have a look at you."

Everybody stepped back, as if to observe. I could feel myself beginning to flush; I wanted to pull my hands back to cover my bare neck. I wanted not to be the center of attention. There was something slow and sure and calculating about the way Thayer Gerson was looking at me; I wasn't prepared, I couldn't think what to say. Then, without a word, he tucked my hand in his arm and led me off. I glanced back at Faith, who only shrugged and smiled a little, as if to say *"one never knows with great men."*

I stood in the corner of the studio, positioned there by Thayer Gerson. My back was against a large branch of ponderosa pine, and the needles pricked my bare skin.

"Faith told me you were lovely to look at," he said, an insinuating tone in his voice. "She was right. You are." He stared at me openly, coldly.

"The problem is," he went on, "Faith looks at you as a photographer would—she sees only the surfaces, the smooth skin, the good bone structure. I see you somewhat differently. An artist looks for what lies under the skin. An artist looks for something more essential . . . Now, when I look at you I see steel, something hard. Sharp. Isn't that right?" He was taunting. I took a step back, into the needles. "I think you are hard as nails, Miss Hallie Duer. I think you could chew Faith up and spit her out at will. In fact," he said, his voice lowered, "you strike me as a very pretty version of my friend Gertrude Stein. Not in looks, of course. You should know this: I don't intend to let Faith become your Alice Toklas."

A pain shot up through my chest and took my breath. I no longer felt the needles piercing the thin stuff of my dress. When I got my breath, I could not think what to say. Words, disconnected, flooded into my head and I couldn't bring them into any order. My cheeks were burning, my mouth dry.

"My conclusions," he went on, seeing that I was unable to speak, "are drawn totally from what Faith has told me about you, and that is quite a lot. More than you know, certainly." Someone approached us and he waved him off. "Faith thinks you are some kind of wonder, full of piss and vinegar. Well, I think you're something else, as I've said, and I'm going to tell Faith that you are the worst thing that could have happened to her."

I felt my hand opening and closing . . . if I had my stick, I thought, I would have brought it down on him, on his leering face and flickering eyes. I would have hit him with it again and again and again, until someone stopped me or he was dead.

I pushed my way through the crowd, stumbling, seeing nothing. The band was playing, but I didn't hear. I walked out of the studio and into the street, not stopping to put on my coat but walking as fast as I could, my heart pumping. I could hear myself making small noises, little gasps. Suddenly my stomach surged. I leaned into an alleyway and everything came up: I retched until I was empty. Weak and drained, my mouth sour from the taste, I leaned against the building to rest.

A long gray Pierce-Arrow drew up alongside the alley and stopped. A small face in a turban appeared at the rear window and ordered, "Get in, my dear, I'll take you home."

I sank into the plush seat and took the handkerchief she handed me to wipe my mouth.

"Just tell me where you live," she said. "You don't have to say anything else."

I don't know how long I sat in the darkened living room of the cottage sipping cold water to rid myself of the bad taste, thinking what I would say to Faith when she returned. I knew I had to sort out everything—what had been said, what it meant. I lay back on my bed, still in my party dress, and when I awakened it was light and a blanket was over me. Faith was sitting in the little chair by my bed, her eyes rimmed in red. "Do you know what happened?" I asked.

She bit her lip and nodded. *But did she know?* I couldn't be sure.

"He doesn't—" I started.

"I know," she broke in, her voice small and anguished. "He's wrong. I try to tell him how wrong he is, Hallie . . . if you could just see the other side to him—if only he would let you. I am sorry, so sorry . . . I thought if he could just see you and talk to you it would . . ."

"He never gave me a chance," I said.

"I know that," she whispered, "I know . . . he has this idea about newspaperwomen, how they are. It's wrong, but . . ."

But . . . So that is what he told her, I thought. That he didn't like me because I was a reporter, and women reporters are tough and hard. It was as if he had looped a rope around her, had taken one end in his own grip and thrown me the other, then pushed me over the side of a cliff.

I decided I would hold on; I would not tug the rope, but I would not let go either. Thayer Gerson had something in mind: I would wait to see what it was. "Faith," I said, making myself smile as if everything were going to be fine, "let's try not to worry. Some sleep, and we'll both feel a lot better."

The following week I decided to go home for Christmas. We would have two days off, since Christmas fell on a Saturday.

I took the overnight riverboat to Sacramento, leaving the fog and the pall cast by Thayer Gerson behind me. My old room seemed smaller, my grandparents older. I helped Grandmother separate milk in the creamery off the kitchen, and went with Grandfather to gather the manzanita for our Christmas Eve fire.

Then I pulled on some gum boots and set off to walk the familiar paths through the woods, clambering over the old stone fences and across pastures. It was dusk by the time I returned, my cheeks and my fingers cold. Grandfather had the fire going, a warm mug of mulled wine ready for me.

"This is the first time you've shared your bootleg wine with me, Grandfather," I teased.

"There's a reason," Grandmother said, almost shyly.

We stood there, the three of us, in the old parlor, and suddenly

I realized there *was* a reason. Grandfather cleared his throat and lifted his cup.

"To you, Hallie," he toasted. He took a sip, then went on: "It's been fourteen years now since you came to us. Your grandmother and I thought we'd never seen such a woebegone little thing as you were, that day at the train station. Your mama had been such a bright, happy child. But you were just so filled with woe. So lonely for your brother, and for those who had gone . . ." His eyes filled with tears, Grandmother patted his arm, and I wanted to touch him but I was afraid to move, afraid he wouldn't be able to go on. He wiped his eyes with an old red handkerchief and continued: "We didn't know what to do with you, Hallie. Except to let you be. You always seemed to have to tackle things that were harder than what anybody else tackled. When you told us you were set on newspapering—well, that's a hard life for a man, let alone a woman. You know there were plenty of skeptics. You've shown them, girl. You've made us proud. All we can tell you is how proud your mama would have been of you, too."

I looked at them, my sweet good grandparents, and finally, finally, I found the words to tell them all that they meant to me, to thank them for all they had given me. When I left the next day, we held hands tightly, the three of us. They waved until the ferry was out of sight; even then, I could close my eyes and see them standing there, the two of them, together on the dock.

I stood on the top deck, looking out at the shoreline, more gray than green in the winter haze . . . *they were proud of me, my mother would have been proud.*

My mother. Clive. Mother and Father, Clive and me. Clive and me.

There had always been a slow ache inside of me for my brother; if I hadn't felt it so much these past months, I knew it was because of Faith. I had Faith to talk to, Faith to listen, to question, to understand. The way it would have been, and should have been, with Clive. If only Grandmother Duer hadn't held on to him so tightly, hadn't pushed me away so totally.

Clive was twenty-nine years old, and still living in that monstrous old house with that grasping old lady. I had to think about him, and soon. If I didn't, it would be too late for us. I couldn't let him slip away, vanish from my life. He had been my mainstay all these years. If I lost him, I would lose those years we had been together, the four of us. I needed Clive's memories to sustain my own. Without him, there was no way I could be certain it had ever happened, any of it. . . .

Oh God, I thought, gripping the cold handrail, listen to yourself . . . I, I, I . . . Is that all that matters? What about Clive, trapped by Grandmother Duer, too kind ever to leave her, just as Father had been too kind. Clive had written to me once that he understood Father better, having lived the life Father had once lived with Grandmother. I had been sent away, and it had hurt, but now I knew I had been the lucky one. Those two dear souls I had just left on the dock . . . they had taken a woebegone little girl in. Now I needed to help my brother. He had to be made to see how exciting the world is, how wrong it is to deny himself. I would have to take action, do something, I would have to *insist*, fight if need be.

As sometimes happens, events were even then under way that would bring the issue to the surface. Clive had been working for the architectural firm of Rogers and Callam for nine years, ever since he graduated from the University of Chicago. Grandfather Duer had financed the firm for the elder Mr. Rogers, and Grandmother had secured the position for Clive even before he graduated. Mr. Rogers Junior now ran the firm.

In February Clive wrote: "There have been some uncomfortable moments of late. I learned only recently that Grandmother has been inviting the elder Mr. Rogers to tea for months, and he continued to send his regrets until Christmas, when for some reason (perhaps the spirit of the season?) he capitulated. The first

I knew of the invitation was in the form of a summary declaration from Grandmother that I was to appear at four sharp on the afternoon of the twenty-third of December for tea. (She had taken the liberty of sending a note to my supervisor, arranging that I should be let out early that day.) I could only guess—and hope I was wrong—as to her motives. I was not wrong. You know, I believe, how formidable Grandmother can be, and poor Mr. Rogers the elder, who is rather feeble now, was no match for her. Scarcely had he a chance to sip his tea than she launched her attack, demanding an explanation for my lack of status in the firm.

"I tried to stop her, with my usual success—which is to say, none. But the Old Gentleman must have known what was coming, because he was prepared. She gave him no choice but to say what, clearly, he had wished to avoid: that I am not ready to assume more responsibility in the firm, in the opinion of his son, who is now in full charge of the business. You would think that even Grandmother would understand that anyone 'not ready' after nine years was probably never going to be. The peculiar thing about this, Hallie, is that in a way Mr. Rogers is right. By 'not ready' he didn't mean not capable. He meant, and has said as much to me, that I resist those responsibilities. And I do. What I want to do is just what I am doing. I am a very good draftsman. The work pleases me and it pleases my employer. It has taken me a long time to admit this to myself, and now to admit it to you makes it seem a declaration. I simply am not ambitious. Is that so very wrong, do you think?

"I cannot tell Grandmother. She will never accept it. Instead, she convinces herself that I am being 'humiliated' by the Rogerses, father and son. I think the truth is that she feels I humiliate her. After Father's death, all I heard was what 'high hopes' she had for me. I wonder if she had those same 'high hopes' for Father?

"I am going to have to make a decision, and probably I am going to have to change jobs. The atmosphere is strained in the office. (The Rogerses do owe Grandfather a debt of gratitude—and quite possibly a debt of cash, too, though Grandmother is close about her finances.) I know that Junior would be greatly relieved if

I simply removed myself. But before I decide, I would like to take a long overdue vacation trip west, to visit you and our grandparents. I would like to come in April, if that is agreeable with you."

That same day I posted a letter to Clive telling him to come, and to bring samples of his work. I suggested he might even consider asking Mr. Rogers Junior to write him a letter of recommendation.

Faith began to see less of Thayer Gerson. She did not say why, and I did not ask. We fell back into our old routine, coming and going together, spending Tuesday evenings washing our hair—warming rainwater on the gas ring, helping each other soap and rinse, and then we would sit before the fire in the Franklin stove and brush our hair dry, complaining all the while of the bother of it, the weight, the trials of keeping it coiled and neat and held in place with the tortoiseshell combs and pins. At least once each week Faith would threaten to have her fine, dark waist-length hair cut off, bobbed. "It is so perfectly silly," she would say, "to work so hard to keep it clean and nice, when all we do is pin it up so it looks short. Aesthetically," she would add, "the result is the same. Short and neat and tidy." I listened and laughed at her, knowing that it was not likely she would have it cut. Knowing, too, that Thayer thought her hair to be her finest feature.

On Saturdays we would treat ourselves to lunch at the Pig 'n Whistle or at John's Grill, or we would go to one of the Italian places in North Beach, where we joined our neighbors at long tables to eat huge portions of taglierini and homemade red wine in heavy coffee mugs—the restaurant owner lifting his eyebrows conspiratorially as he poured from a heavy earthenware jug. We still laughed together, Faith and I; and at the same time we were cautious, waiting.

Now and then we would be invited to a party on Saturday

night and sometimes we went. Occasionally Thayer Gerson would make an appearance at one of these parties, and Faith would greet him with such studied casualness that I could feel the tension between them. I guessed that it was his decision that they not see each other, but I could only feel it was a performance on his part, carefully staged. One day soon, I told myself, he is going to give a mighty jerk to the rope.

On Sunday morning we would get up very early, pack Faith's camera equipment into the Model T and explore some new part of town. There was so much to see, so many facets to this city, different cultures, surprises. One Sunday we would go to the docks, where freighters from all over the world would be loading or unloading, or we would drive out the Great Highway to Ocean Beach and then back again through either the Richmond district or the Sunset, recording on film the new houses that were sprouting—row upon row of them, neat little stucco bungalows with vaguely Spanish facades, one much like another, their occupants newly arrived from the Mission or South of Market.

Once, while driving aimlessly over the rutted roadways in an old section of town now encompassed by warehouses and ship-yards, we happened upon what at first seemed an illusion—a tiny little park that looked as if it had been transported from England. It was tucked between Second and Third streets, a self-contained little block of stone-fronted mansions, shabby now but clearly patrician in ancestry, crowded about an oval-shaped park. In all, we guessed, the park was some five hundred feet long and sev-enty-five feet wide, and in it were elm trees and some gnarled old rosebushes. We stood staring, as if at a chimera, when an elderly Japanese man emerged from one of the houses, walked slowly into the park to take a seat on a bench near a small willow tree. A while later, three drifters appeared and built a fire in an open barrel. Faith began to take photographs, recording the details of this remarkable little park, so out of time and place.

In the newspaper's library I learned that it was called South

Park, that it had been designed and built in the city's earliest days by an Englishman named George Gordon, homesick for London. It was said that Gordon had even imported English sparrows to make it seem more like home. Once, South Park had vied with Rincon Hill as the most fashionable address in town. Now Rincon Hill was leveled, and South Park was tucked away in the city's attic, out of sight and mind.

Fascinated, I spent my lunch hour at the city library, where I learned that Gordon's wife was a heavy drinker, and when their infant daughter was born, the mother fed her spoonfuls of spirits until the child, too, was addicted. It was a sordid story and I wondered how much truth there was to it, after so many years and so many tellings.

By Tuesday, Faith had printed a dozen photographs of the square, including one with the three vagrants huddled around the open fire, a once-elegant stone mansion in the background. It was a haunting picture. I did not wash my hair that night. Instead, I stayed up long past midnight working on a story to go with those pictures. By eight the next morning, an oversize envelope holding photographs and the story was on the city editor's desk.

Sometime that afternoon I looked up from a rewrite of a golf story to see Gene waving at me. "The Boss wants to see you," he said noncommittally.

"Hallie, I like this," he told me as I walked through the door. "It's time we ran a story on old South Park. I'd just about forgotten about that fine old place. The photographs are just right. Isn't Faith Moore the one who does all those society portraits?"

"She does those society portraits so she can afford to take these on Sundays," I told him.

He looked up and asked, "The story—did you do that on Sunday?"

"On Tuesday night. . . I wasn't sure how you would feel about my doing stories on my own. At the *Union*—"

"I know about the *Union*," he interrupted. "Hal Lugas told me how brassy you were, nosing out stories on your own. That's why I hired you, and I've been waiting to see what you were going to do."

"But . . ." I said, feeling weak and silly. "But the Dempsey trial, I thought . . ."

"You thought I hired you on a whim? My dear Hallie, I could have sent any one of the legmen to cover that trial. It just happened to be good timing, don't you see? I wouldn't have replaced Annie Farrell that haphazardly."

Replaced Annie Farrell! I sat down and stared at him.

He laughed. "Now that you're nosing out stories on your own, I have a hunch you are going to be a better reporter than Annie ever was. *Going to be* . . . remember that. You've still things to learn."

I stared at him until he started laughing, and then I laughed too. At that moment I knew why Sanford Curtin's reporters would work longer hours for fewer dollars than on any other paper in town. At the door I paused, turned back, and as soon as I had his attention said, "You didn't say how much you were going to pay for the story."

"Pay?" he answered, raising his eyebrows innocently. "Since Miss Moore isn't on staff, she'll be paid her usual per-picture rate."

"I didn't mean Miss Moore," I said, "I meant *me*. I wrote that story on my own time, and I'm still earning Sacramento wages."

He took his five-cent Owl cigar out of his mouth, held it poised in the air and said, "You learn fast, Miss Hallie Duer. Talk to Gene about it. Tell him I said to pay you by the column inch."

"One more thing," I said. "Can I call you 'Boss' now?"

He grinned boyishly. "You may call me whatever you wish, my dear, so long as it is complimentary."

In the next month I doubled my salary by writing articles on my own time, often with photographs done by Faith. The publisher of the paper, alarmed by this turn of events, suggested I be given a substantial raise and be allowed to do the stories during working hours. The raise was less than I had been earning on a column-inch rate, so I held out as long as I could—long enough to make them heave a sigh of relief when finally I did consent.

We did stories on the people who made their homes in the old streetcars which had been abandoned out by the beach, we spent more time on the docks and came to understand the depths of the longshoremen's plight. Then I hit on an idea that I was absolutely certain would create a stir—a series of articles on women who were professionals, who were successful first-rate practitioners in fields that were dominated by men. I wanted to talk to women lawyers, women judges, women doctors, women architects. I wanted to find out how they got there, what challenges they had to meet, what trials endure. I wanted to know what their lives were like . . . I wanted to know everything about these women, and I was certain our women readers would too.

Gene Bolten, the city editor, shrugged and said, "Why?"

"Why?" I repeated, amazed at his indifference. "Because women want to read about other women, that's why. And because working women are treated as if they didn't exist, as if they are abnormal or eccentric or odd. In fact, women have always worked, and most of them because they have to—either a husband died or they had to support a family, or they never married . . . And it may come as a considerable surprise to you, sir, but there are even women who work because they want to . . . and some of these women do a fine job, just fine! But they're treated as if they don't exist, by men. Yes. By men like you!"

Gene had been shaking his head for a few minutes, but I had been too wound up to stop and hear what he had to say.

"Hold on there," he finally managed to get in. "No need to get abusive, Hallie. Go ahead. Try one. We'll see how it goes, all right?"

I was out the door before he could change his mind. I knew exactly whom I wanted to see first, and I wasn't going to take a chance that she would turn me down by calling ahead. I meant to interview Julia Morgan, the architect.

I made my way across town, over Powell to Bush, where her offices were located, walking briskly so I wouldn't lose momentum. *Miss Morgan does not seek publicity, Miss Morgan prefers her work speak for itself, Miss Morgan is extremely busy.* I knew all that. It wasn't going to stop me.

"Is Miss Morgan expecting you?" the young woman asked.

"I certainly hope so," I answered brightly.

She hesitated only a moment. "I suppose you can go on up—top floor."

In the elevator I girded for the next obstacle: to convince Julia Morgan to talk to me.

It was a great open room flooded with daylight from the sky-lights above. Four or five men worked at drafting tables, bent to their task. Julia Morgan—it would have to be her—stood at the far end of the room, a small woman in a severely tailored black suit and white shirt, wearing steel-rimmed glasses which magnified her eyes, making them seem too large for her body. She was deep in conversation with another woman, not much larger than she, but softer, somehow, dressed in a suit of sky blue with a matching turban. Something about the woman seemed familiar.

They were studying a drawing spread out before them. I stood waiting, knowing I shouldn't interrupt them but not knowing how gracefully to withdraw. One or two of the draftsmen had looked up at me.

"Miss Duer," the woman in blue said, looking up. "What a nice surprise!"

Now embarrassment added to my confusion. It was the woman from the Christmas party. She knew my name, but I didn't know hers. "I have your handkerchief!" I blurted. "I didn't know . . ."

Julia Morgan looked from one to the other of us, puzzled.

"I'm so sorry to interrupt," I blundered on. "I had hoped to have a few words with Miss Morgan, but I can see . . ."

"I'm about to leave, my dear," the woman said. "Julia and I are just finished, so she is all yours. But first . . ." She was rummaging in her handbag. "Let me give you my card. You don't really need to return my handkerchief, but it would be a nice excuse to have you come visit."

I glanced at the name on the card. Miss Sara Hunt. "Thank you, Miss Hunt. I promise to come, and I will return your lovely handkerchief."

She turned her great warm eyes on me and said, "I expect you're the sort of person who keeps promises."

I could feel myself flushing with pleasure. There was something about Sara Hunt that made me want to please her; or perhaps I simply felt grateful that she had eased the way with Julia Morgan.

The architect was studying me, and waiting. Words did not come easy, I suspected. "Miss Morgan, I'm a newspaper reporter—for the *Times*," I began. "I am going to do a series of articles about women who are successful in fields that are normally the domain of men. I would like the first article to be about you. I hope you'll forgive my simply appearing like this, but I was afraid if I didn't you wouldn't see me."

She pursed her lips and said, "I see." With the barest motion of her hand, she signaled me to follow her. She moved so lightly I had the curious feeling that she was not touching the floor. It was hard not to compare her to Sara Hunt, who was about the same size and age, I guessed, but who wore lovely soft colors and seemed to reach out, take part, never to shrink away . . . *come to tea,* she had said as she left, an open invitation to Miss Morgan as well as me.

She motioned me to a chair in an office as unprepossessing as the woman herself, and said: "I remember the first time Sara invited me to tea. I remember how honored I felt."

I blinked. Could she have been reading my mind?

"I don't really know Miss Hunt," I felt compelled to say, "I've only met her once, and she was very kind to me."

"Sara Hunt is the kindest woman I've ever known," Julia Morgan said, "and of course, one of the finest portraitists in this country, though her work is less well known in San Francisco than in New York or Paris."

"Perhaps I should do an article about Miss Hunt," I said, "but I do want the first in this series to be about you. I know you are one of the most successful architects in the city. You are at the height of your career, and I am sure our readers would like to know how you got there."

She sat very straight in her chair, her fingertips grasping the edges of the desk as if to smooth the corners. I could tell that she was struggling to get the words right, to make me understand. "I do not want to seem difficult," she began, "but I simply do not feel I want to be singled out because I am a woman. I want to be judged on the merit of my work. I have never expected any concessions because I am a woman, and I don't believe I've been given any. I don't even like to be written about in the architectural journals— my fellow architects find that very strange, indeed."

I was prepared for that argument. "You tell me you've never been given any concessions because of your sex," I began, "and that is exactly why I want to do this series of articles. Because women aren't given any concessions, but all kinds of obstacles are put in their way. You have been able, somehow, to overcome those obstacles in your field. And if you could do it, other women can—if you are willing to tell them how. You must have made mistakes . . ."

"Oh my, well," she said, "I don't think mistakes can be avoided. In fact, I think mistakes are one of the best ways to learn."

"All right," I came back, "you tell me that you haven't been given any concessions, but that isn't exactly right, is it? Your first commission, I believe, was for the campanile at a women's college, Mills in Oakland. And I also know that women's clubs and the YWCA have come to you to design their buildings. And Mrs. Hearst—she has encouraged so many young women. You do a great deal of work for the Hearsts, I know. Can you honestly say that being a woman had nothing to do with their choice of you? Isn't this a case of women helping women?"

She frowned and two tiny furrows appeared between her eyes. Her fingers seemed to grip the desk more firmly. In the drafting room outside, someone dropped a metal rule and the sound reverberated, but Julia Morgan did not seem to hear it. I had disturbed her, I could tell.

"I'm sorry to be so blunt," I went on, "but I do honestly believe an article is important, especially to any young woman who has the courage to say 'I want to be an architect' and who is being told 'All you can try for is interior design because you're a woman.' And that is what women are told. I have a brother who is an architect in Chicago, and he wrote me a long letter once about several of his classmates, females, who were forced to drop engineering in favor of interior design. I think these women might take heart if they read that you were the first woman graduate of the Ecole des Beaux-Arts in Paris."

She stood and began to pace, her hands clasped firmly in front of her. She sighed. "I had hoped no one would ever put those arguments to me," she said.

"Then you agree to the interview?"

She smiled for the first time. "No, I submit to it."

In the next hour and a half, Julia Morgan described her work. The voice, which had seemed dry and sparse, took on a resonance. Before my eyes, Julia Morgan, austere in black suit and white shirt, came to life. When she talked of architecture, she was transformed. *Almost,* I thought, *a woman in love.*

"Architecture is the servant," she began, "life the master . . . The finest architect will answer both spiritual and physical needs of the people who will live or work in the building. The design of any building must be determined by the interior space. That is always the first consideration. And simplicity. Especially the simplicity of ordinary materials used in an elegant manner. And restraint."

She talked about her first meeting with a client, her assessment of his needs, how she tried to visualize those who would live in the building. The excitement of creating a place that would serve them well. The excitement spilled into the room; I could feel it, her need to make me understand. Now and then her hand would touch her hair and she would brush away a strand.

She was expansive about the people who, through the years, had helped her. She spoke haltingly about the obstacles, she made suggestions.

"Architecture, my work, fills my life," she said, choosing her words carefully. "There is little time for a private life."

I wanted to ask, "Is it enough?" I wanted to say, "A home, a family—did you want that?" But I couldn't. Julia Morgan had been passionate, had allowed me to glimpse something of what she felt about her work. She was, I understood, content. But I didn't understand how, or why.

"I hope we will meet again," I said as I left. She only smiled, and nodded.

I worked late into the night, writing and rewriting, straining to put on paper the quality of Julia Morgan, the intensity of feeling for the work she did. I wanted to convey the idea that Julia Morgan was an architect in spite of being a woman. The struggle was worth it, I wanted to say, one had only to listen to Julia Morgan to know that. At the same time, I realized, I was couching my sentences in ways that I thought would please Miss Morgan: using words with restraint, with a simplicity that was not unlike the woman herself.

"Julia Morgan is an architect," I began. "Not a woman architect. An architect. The buildings she designs are statements . . ."

I finished at three in the morning, read the story over twice and then, unable to sleep, pulled on a sweater and went to sit on the back stairs.

Julia Morgan and Sara Hunt. They knew something, each of them, that I did not know. They were . . . What? Content with their lives? Was that it? Julia Morgan, who had seemed so austere at first, but who was in fact so exuberant about her work, tracing with those small, capable hands, long lines on great white sheets of paper, *creating places to fill the physical and the spiritual needs . . .*

And Sara Hunt. What did I know about Sara Hunt? That she was rich, and kind. That she took chances, reached out. That she had eyes that looked into you and saw things. That she was plain to look at, and beautiful at the same time. I would telephone Sara Hunt tomorrow.

I had passed Sara Hunt's elegant *petit palais* at the crest of California Street on Nob Hill any number of times, admiring it without knowing who lived in the exquisite mansion. An English butler with a distinctly sour look on his face ushered me into the foyer, all Italianate pink marble, and with scarcely a word led me to a small parlor on the second floor.

I was just beginning to survey the paintings that hung on the walls—like everything else in this remarkable place, they were stunning, and highly personal. *Sara Hunt*, I said to myself, *holds nothing back*.

"Don't mind Weatherlee," she said, as if she'd only just left the room and we were continuing a conversation. "Rich Americans always hire English butlers because they're so wonderfully snobbish. Put us in our places, so to speak. And don't mind me either—I've been painting and I reek of it."

I smiled and held out the cellophane package which held her handkerchief. "I washed it twice," I told her.

"That was a dreadful night for you, I think," she said. "I noticed you leaving the party, and as I'm sure you realize, I followed you—I didn't think you'd had time to get sick on the rotten gin they were serving, so I figured you were terribly upset. I know your friend took you to meet Thayer—I was watching to see what would happen. I'm a terrible snoop, as I suppose you've gathered. At any rate, I know Thayer Gerson too well. But you are here for tea and I am not about to question you about that night. Tell me, instead, how you happen to be reporting for the *Times*. And then I'll tell you how much I liked the story you wrote about dear Julia."

I sank back into the goose-down softness of a settee upholstered in rose silk moire, and gave myself over to the talk and
the tea, lavishly flavored with a very good brandy. I talked about
myself, and asked about her painting, and said I would like to
know more about her work. She laughed and told me that in good
time she was certain I would know more about her feelings about
art than I would ever care to know, and gently, very gently, guided
the conversation back to Faith and Thayer Gerson.

"Have you ever been one of his benefactors?" I asked.

She laughed out loud and said, "Me? Never! Thayer Gerson is
a third-rate sculptor and a fourth-rate person. My opinion of him
is not shared by most of the cultural arbiters in this city, however.
Thayer has a strange appeal for certain women, especially those a
bit past their prime." She paused and looked at me searchingly. "I
suppose he also has a taste for young women, judging by his alliance with your friend . . . Faith, is it?"

The slight edge of disapproval in her voice made me wary. "My
friend Faith is an extraordinary photographer," I said, feeling it
somehow important to make Sara Hunt understand. "She really is
an artist. Her photographs seem to probe beneath the surface, to
tell you something about the people that you hadn't known—or
that you had known, but couldn't explain. And Faith is an intelli-
gent woman too, and good . . ." I blushed, realizing how hard I was
trying to convince Sara.

"You love your friend," she said.

It was the simplicity of the statement that jarred me. If she had
said anything else, anything, I would have turned away, deflected
it. But she said: *You love your friend*, and I heard myself choking out
the story of that night, and all that Thayer had said to me.

She listened, leaning forward slightly, saying nothing at all
until I had finished. She did not seem shocked, only saddened. She
lifted her hands slightly in the air, in a gesture that seemed to ask
for my full attention. "Listen to me now, Hallie," she began, "listen
to me not as Faith's friend, but as Hallie the reporter, the observer.

If Thayer Gerson has any real talent, it's for knowing how to draw blood. I don't know if it helps to know this, but he has done this sort of thing before, and to women far more vulnerable than you, my dear . . . women who are older, less self-assured, less able to protect themselves. I'm sorry to have to say that it is a standard gambit in the particularly venal game that Thayer plays."

"What do you mean, what game?" I asked.

"Whenever he's interested in a woman—for whatever reason, but with the women I happen to know it is money—the first thing he wants to do is get rid of her best friend, if she has one. If nothing else works, he accomplishes his objective by accusing the friend of having amorous designs on the woman. It is an efficient ploy."

"But why should he want to get rid of a friend?"

"Why? Because best friends tend to care enough to speak out, to take risks. But to be accused of having physical designs on someone who is your own sex—of being in love—well, most women can't deal with that. Not in this society." She paused then, and asked, "Why didn't you tell Faith what Thayer said to you?"

"How do you know I didn't?" I asked.

"Did you?"

"No. No, because if I had and Thayer said it wasn't so, that I had lied, I don't know which of us she would believe, and I didn't want to put her in that position. She loves him, so she needs to believe him. Even if she should believe me, I would always be the one who spoiled it for her, there might even be a residue of doubt. Anyway, it would damage our friendship. And that is what I'm trying to prevent."

Sara nodded as if satisfied. She lifted the brandy bottle in invitation. I declined. "If I have any more, my head will be swimming."

Setting it aside, she said very softly, "Would it be so terrible, Hallie, if what Gerson said were true?"

A worried look must have crossed my face, because she added, "No. I'm not . . . but I have some dear women friends who do love each other, physically as well as emotionally. I also happen to know

Miss Stein and Miss Toklas—Alice Toklas and I have been friends for many years—and I can tell you that their lives together are happier than if either were alone."

"Please," I said, "don't misunderstand. It's not that I am repulsed by the idea of women as lovers. At the same time—and I'm not certain I can explain this—Faith is the first truly close friend I've ever had. And that friendship has been right just the way it is—I can't think of anything that would make the way I feel about her any better. But Thayer Gerson, with his accusation, was denying that . . . he was saying that what we have is something less than what I want, and that is not true. It's as if he is trying to diminish me . . . I'm not being very clear."

"Yes you are," Sara said, "and I know just what you mean. I have a dear friend, you see . . . we've known each other since we were girls, and it is just as you have described. We've been through a great deal together; we are as close as sisters, closer I believe. I think I would seriously consider killing anyone who suggested our friendship is not chaste. I couldn't care more for her."

We sat in silence for a while, thinking our own thoughts. Then Sara stirred to say, "The article you wrote about Julia. I think that, after having read it, most people who met Julia would be surprised. The word picture you paint of her *is* Julia— you captured her exactly—but it is not the Julia most people ever see. If I painted her, it would be the same thing. People would look at the portrait, at the life in her, the animation, and say, 'But that doesn't look like Julia!' I suspect that if your friend Faith photographed her, she too would capture the Julia only a few of us seem privileged to see." She paused. "I hope you will join the ranks of the Julia admirers—there are only a few of us—who keep in touch with her. She tends to be such a little hermit, you know!"

"I would like that," I said at the door. "I really would. And I would like to see you again, too."

"Of course you will," she answered, holding my hand tightly.

"You're going to have to work to keep your friend Faith. You are going to have to be very smart. Don't play by his rules. You are doing fine so far, but take care. Come to me whenever you wish, if you think I can help. I will if I can." She touched my face with her hand, and I walked out into the brightness of California Street and lifted my face for the sun to warm.

SIX

"TODAY," Gwen called out as I passed the switchboard, "is going to be one very crazy Monday."

I stopped and waited as she took a call. When she had finished, she continued, ". . . crazy because Gene is on the trail of a scoop and because the Boss is quoting from something called Plutarch and because you have a very strange-sounding male person waiting to talk on your line."

I picked up the telephone on my desk. "Hi, kid," a high, rasping voice said, "I hear you want to see a fight."

I glanced over at Ham; this was probably another of the boys' practical jokes. "That's right," I answered cautiously, staring at Ham until he looked up at me.

"Well, come on out to the Colma Pavilion this afternoon, I'll be sparring with Big George. You can watch."

"Big George?" I said.

"Big George Godfrey," he answered.

"That's very generous of you," I told him, "and if I knew who you were I'd even thank you."

"I thought—" he began.

I stopped him with, "Look, I'm really very busy and while I know it is great sport to have a laugh at my expense, right now—"

"Okay," he said. "I thought maybe after putting the knock on you at the trial I could make it up, but if—"

"Trial?" I repeated. Then it flashed in my head.

"Dempsey?" I said aloud. "It *is* Dempsey, isn't it?" By now Ham had stopped chewing on his cigar and was staring at me.

There was a long pause on the other end of the line. "Look," I said, "I really am sorry. The boys here are great practical jokers, and it isn't often that anyone gets a call from Jack Dempsey, you know . . . but do you mean it, about my interviewing you?"

"Interview?" he said, a note of doubt in his voice. "No, I thought you might just want to watch me spar . . . but an interview, no, I don't—"

"I don't mean a regular interview, nothing like that," I put in. "Just a few minutes, a couple of questions, nothing embarrassing, I promise."

Ham looked as if he might swallow his cigar. His eyes were rolling. Everybody on the sports desk knew that Dempsey wasn't giving interviews.

"Please," I said, "just a few minutes, a very small exclusive."

Ham exploded in a fit of coughing. I waved him off. A kind of rough chortle sounded over the line. "Talk about giving an inch and taking a mile," Dempsey said. "Okay, come on out. Then we'll see."

I put the earpiece back into its cradle and stood there, my hands clasped. Then I was laughing. "I've got an exclusive with Jack Dempsey," I said, trying to keep some of the triumph out of my voice.

Whit Jones, who covered golf and tennis, said, "Maybe I should start wearing a skirt."

"You would look sweet," I told him, and was about to say more when Ham broke in to say, "I don't care what the hell my reporters wear as long as they know what they're doing, and from the looks of things, Hallie sure as hell knows."

Whit wasn't giving up so easily. "Kearns isn't going to like it, not at all," he said. "The only femmes Kearns can take are chippies—he's the one who put down the rule against interviews."

"But Kearns don't always speak for Dempsey," Ham said, "and if Dempsey said he'd do it, he will."

Fizz Bradley, the newspaper's artist, and I arrived at Colma Pavilion at about two. We figured Dempsey wouldn't sit still for photographs but that Fizz could make some quick sketches of the champion from the sidelines. The pavilion was a white frame structure badly in need of paint; it looked especially grim in the foggy afternoon light. Inside the pavilion, which was open to the air, a boxing ring padded with old bed quilts was surrounded by bleachers. An assortment of men milled around—fighters and trainers and hangers-on. The place smelled of liniment and old sweat and wasted dreams. It was as if I had entered a world in which women didn't exist. Some of the fighters wore very tight briefs, so abbreviated that you could see the bindings they wore as protection to their privates. In any other place I would have been embarrassed.

We found our way to Dempsey's training room, a small place bare except for some equipment, a table, two straight-backed chairs which had long ago lost their varnish. Dempsey was sitting on the table, dressed in a baggy pair of boxing shorts and an old sweater.

"Big George is going to be a little late," he said. "The doc has to take a look at him."

"Then there's time for us to talk?" I asked, breathlessly enough to cause him to grin.

Fizz excused himself (as I had asked him to if I had a chance to talk to Dempsey alone), saying he wanted to do some sketches of the pavilion.

"Tell me about your first fight," I said.

"You mean my first professional fight?" he asked.

"No," I said, "I mean your very first fight—the first time you ever hit somebody with your fists."

"Christ!" he said in something between a laugh and a snort. "I couldn't remember that."

"Then tell me about the first one you do remember," I pushed on.

His brown face cracked into a slow smile; he began to talk then, slowly at first and then more easily. He told me about the early years, fights with toughs, fights in barrooms, riding the rails from one no-account little western town to another, so hungry his stomach was numb, and going into a bar and offering to whup any man in the place. Bored, somebody would throw a nickel on the floor, and when it amounted to two bits, maybe four, some big country kid would step out, sure he could beat the skinny kid that just hopped off the freight. Some of them would be big guys, too. But he'd have to knock the holy bejesus out of them if he was going to eat, and he was hungry. He was always hungry.

"Is that how you learned to hit so hard, being hungry?" I asked.

"It's one way," he answered.

"Did you ever lose?" I asked.

"Not much," he answered.

A dapper little man appeared at the doorway and stood scowling until Dempsey looked at him.

"If you think you can pull yourself away," the man said caustically, "Big George's waiting for you."

"Come on, Miss Duer," Dempsey said, rising, ignoring the little man.

"Hallie," I told him. "My name's Hallie."

"Her name's Hallie," the little man mocked.

"Knock it off, Doc," Dempsey told him, and the man wheeled and left.

"Is that your manager?" I asked.

"The one and only," Dempsey told me, "and you don't want to meet him."

"Why not?" I asked.

"Because he breaks out in hives when he's in the presence of decent women."

I figured they had already had a few rounds on my account, and Dempsey was warning me to give Doc Kearns a wide range.

A very large Negro was in the ring, taller by an inch or so than Dempsey, and heavier, too. Big George Godfrey was Dempsey's favorite sparring partner. They moved about the ring like dancers, bobbing and swaying, watching each other with such intensity that you could feel the concentration. And then Dempsey moved, raining blows with such speed that I wasn't able to follow. I hadn't noticed that Kearns was standing alongside me until he said, "Watch this one coming up . . . there, a left to the body, a right, the followthrough . . . there, did you see it?"

"I think so," I answered, looking at him. His eyes were small and close-set and filled with contempt.

"You think so," he mocked. "Women don't think. Aren't supposed to. Aren't supposed to be out here either, this is off limits. And they especially aren't supposed to hang around my boys. Understand?" Having delivered his message, he wheeled and huffed away.

I turned back to the sparring; Kearns had been right about one thing—I needed to learn a lot more before I could write about a fight with any authority. I might know the lingo, but I didn't know the moves.

My exclusive ran the next day in all editions, starting on the front page and jumping to sports. We sold more papers than we had in two months, ever since Gene kept the secretary of the Board of Control and his affidavits stashed away in his home until he could break the story of a scandal in the state budget office. Scandals and sports exclusives sold papers; everybody knew that.

The city room was buzzing. "Good story, Hallie," someone would say. "Nice going." For the first hour or so I basked in it. Then I began to worry: What would Dempsey think? Once he started, he had talked so effortlessly. I wondered if he remembered that I was writing it all down, that what had been private was public now.

The call came a few minutes before five. I glanced up at Gwen and she mouthed: *It's him.* She would be listening in.

"Kid?" he said.

"Dempsey?" I answered.

"I saw your story."

"And?" I asked.

"And it's okay."

Okay wasn't enough for me. "Just okay?" I prodded. "I was worried that you might think . . ." I stopped, realizing that I didn't know just what it was that he might have thought, or why it should have worried me. I left my sentence hanging there, and Dempsey let the silence build.

Finally he said, "No, it's okay."

I decided to leave it at that. "Then do you think I could come to a real fight next time?"

"Sure. Why not?" he answered.

"From your corner?" I asked.

He laughed then, and I could see his brown face crack into a smile. Dempsey had not been bothered by the story and he was going to let me come in close to cover a fight. Now there was reason to celebrate. "Dempsey called," I said to Ham. "He liked the story."

Ham shifted his cigar in his mouth and looked at me sternly. "That's the last thing you got to care about, kid," he said. "It doesn't matter two hoots if Dempsey liked it. What matters is those stiffs on the street who buy papers. They're the ones you got to please, and don't forget it."

I went back to my desk and sat down, jolted. The Dempsey story had been a victory, or had it? It wasn't a boxing story but a feature. Doc Kearns had shown me that I didn't know enough to

write a boxing story. And yet I had just talked Dempsey into letting me have special access for his next fight. And, worst of all, I
had *needed* him to like the story I wrote . . . I had, and I knew that
was trouble.

The Boss was sitting in his office, his feet propped on his desk,
deep into a book. He waved me in, saying, "Listen to this, Hallie,"
and he read: "Anacharsis laughed at Solon for 'imagining the dis-
honest and covetousness of his countrymen could be restrained
by written laws, which were like spider's webs . . .' Spider's webs!
That's good, isn't it?"

I said yes, it was good. And yes, that Plutarch was indeed
amazing. And then I tried to explain to the Boss all of the doubts
the Dempsey story had raised in me.

He heard me out, and then he said: "You're right to ponder these
things, Hallie. Any reporter worth his . . . or her . . . salt does. Ham
was right about Dempsey, about how you can't care what he thinks.
But then again, if you alienate Dempsey right now, you're never going
to get another story out of him, and he's good for many more stories.
When I put you in sports, I had in mind you'd do feature articles when
the time came for you to get off rewrite. We've got plenty of boys who
are experts in whatever sport they're covering. What we don't have is
somebody who can give us some fresh insights. And I think we've got
a lot of readers who aren't expert, and might like some plain talk on
the sports page, some behind-the-scenes material." He was quiet for
a while then, thinking, and I didn't disturb him. "It's not enough for a
paper to be a business," he said, "so I'll have to disagree with Ham to
a certain extent when he says you have to write for the man with the
nickel in his pocket, the reader. A paper must also serve as a forum
for ideas, and it's the writer who delivers those ideas. You won't keep
readers very long if you don't give them some of what they want—but
you have to tell them what they need to know, too, and remind them
of their responsibilities."

He talked then of his current crusades, and some of his past
crusades, how he had been pushing for municipal ownership of the

water company, for a minimum wage and an eight-hour day for women, about the abolition of capital punishment.

"Yet, at the same time that we are giving them what they need, we are also covering murder trials and scandals. I don't fool myself. In a way we are pandering to prurient interests, by sensationalizing crime we are turning it into a form of entertainment. But in the end, I think, the writer must listen to his own conscience, must write what he needs to write . . . and must please himself that what he is writing is purposeful."

"The Dempsey story," I said haltingly, "I wanted to bring out the differences in the public's idea of Dempsey and the reality. I wanted to show what a desperate time he had as a young boy, the ugliness of the way he had to survive. I mean, Dempsey is a very straightforward man. He's not trying to hide a thing about his past. It's the fans who seem to want to turn him into something he isn't and never was. And they want to do it, it seems to me, to salve their own consciences—because they get such pleasure out of watching him use those lethal fists of his . . . I don't know if I'm making any sense, or if I've figured out anything at all . . . it just seems so hypocritical," I finished.

"Of course it is," he answered, "but that doesn't make Jack Dempsey a hypocrite. Or you—you don't have to tell them what they want to hear. You can make them listen to the truth. And if you are clear enough in your own mind, you can convince some of them. Not all, by any means. But even a few makes it worth it."

I was turning his words over in my mind as I walked into the cottage that night. I was curious to see what Faith would make of them. We had touched on this same subject before, when we were talking about photographs—how truth could be bent, how photographs could be made to lie. I was looking forward to having her help me sort it all out. Faith had a way of summarizing things, shifting issues into interesting juxtapositions.

She was in her bedroom with the door closed, which was unusual. I knocked.

She opened the door. On the bed was her valise. She was packing.

We sat at the kitchen table where we had talked so often, and she tried to explain: "Thayer came into the studio this morning. He was all disheveled, he looked as if he hadn't slept in a week. He said he hadn't been able to get me out of his mind, and that we had to settle things between us, somehow."

A burst of steam poured out of the kettle. I got up, turned off the gas ring and poured two cups of tea. Faith sat staring out of the window, waiting until I returned to my chair to continue. She took the tea mug in both hands—it was hot, and must have burned, but she held on to it—took a deep breath and said, "I know you don't like him."

I sat down, looked at her. She exhaled. "If only he wasn't so priggish about women doing 'men's' work, and if only you could see that side of him that so appeals to me! I wish . . ."

She stopped herself, and then she repeated the speech I guessed she had prepared. "He's asked me to go away with him for a few days, to talk things out. I said I would."

I started to say something, but she rushed on. "Oh, please try to understand, Hallie. I have to do this, I do." Her eyes were filling. I took the hot cup from her, clasped both her hands in mine, and held them, hard.

"I hope we will always be friends," I told her. "No matter what, I hope there will always be a way for us to be friends." She lifted my hand to her cheek, which was hot and wet with tears. "I do love you, Faith," I said. "I always will. Thayer should know that."

When she left, the cottage seemed so empty that I pulled on a sweater and climbed to the top of the hill. For the first time in as long as I could remember, I could feel tears inside of me, trapped, with no way to get out. I kicked a rock, and felt a surge of pain shoot up my leg.

Good, I thought. Let it hurt.

The next day I telephoned Sara Hunt and took the Powell Street cable up the hill to see her. She opened the door herself.

I had come to talk about Faith, but when I arrived, I knew I could not. Sara did not press me; on the telephone I had said only that I wanted to talk to her. We chatted for a while in the little parlor. I told her about my lunch with Julia Morgan, how she had insisted we go to the Garden Court because she admired the room so, how pleased she had been by the article. "She liked it well enough to allow an architectural magazine to reprint it," I said. "I can't believe, now, that when I first saw her that day I thought she was rather severe-looking . . . almost austere."

Sara laughed. "Yes, but isn't that true of most of us? Take Porter here"—she waved to introduce a tall young man who had appeared in the doorway. "Porter Reade, my godson, that is. To look at him, wouldn't you think, 'My, what a proper young man. Interested in his studies, so prompt, so studious.'"

The young man grinned; the banter, I realized, was how they got on. "Porter, this is Hallie Duer, who is a reporter on the *San Francisco Times*. She wrote the story on Julia Morgan."

He came into the room and collapsed on the settee next to Sara. "I liked it." He grinned. "I wish there were more editors like Sanford Curtin, so more stories like that could run."

Porter, I learned, was in his first year at the University of Berkeley, but seemed more interested in the labor movement on the San Francisco docks than in his studies, which was the reason for Sara's gentle prodding.

"Sara calls me a first-year radical," he said, smiling at his godmother with obvious affection. "Aunt Lena writes that she's coming up to check on my academic progress." They laughed together then, and Sara said, as if in explanation, "Porter's Aunt Lena is the good friend I told you about. And she, of all people, knows that Porter's progress won't be found in the classroom."

Porter could not for long stray from the topics that concerned him. We talked for an hour or more, about politics and politicians, about the people with power and the disenfranchised poor. Sara listened and nodded and sometimes put in a comment, but mostly she seemed to enjoy listening to the two of us. At one point I thought to ask, "Are we offending you, Sara—you are, after all, part of the 'power elite' we keep talking about."

Porter answered for her, pulling her to him in a casual hug. "Sara's the only benevolent capitalist I know. She handles her money responsibly. I keep check on her." He gave her a quick kiss on the forehead and she burst into pleased laughter.

I left the house on California Street feeling rested. I had been able to get away from everything that concerned me—notably Faith—for that time, and it was refreshing.

When I walked into the cottage, Faith was there. Her face was drawn and pale. "Are you all right?" I asked cautiously.

"I don't feel much like talking," she said in a voice drained of emotion. "I really am awfully tired, I'd like to get some sleep." I started to ask if she would like some tea, but she was already in her room and had closed the door. I wanted to knock, to ask what had happened, but I couldn't. I would have to wait.

She was sleeping still when I left for work the next morning, so I did not see her until evening.

I was in the kitchen, chopping cabbage for our supper, when she came in. Her long, beautiful dark hair was gone. She was wearing a new bob, cut close to her head like a cap, wisps of hair turned forward on her face. It might have looked pretty, had I not known that it was, in fact, a form of self-mutilation.

"Your Declaration of Independence?" I said.

"I don't know what you mean," she answered in a flat tone of voice. "I always said I was going to do it, and I did."

I was going to have to be careful, I knew that. Had I thought about it at all, I would also have realized that there was no way to be careful enough to avoid an eruption. It was coming; nothing could stop it.

It happened the next morning when I asked an innocuous question. "Do you have time to drop our shirtwaists at Ling Soo's?"

"Is there anything else you would like for me to do for you?" she snapped. "Make your bed, polish your shoes maybe?"

"What are you talking about?" I asked.

"I'm talking about all those things you want me to do for you," she bristled, ready to explode.

"You sound as if you've made some great sacrifices for me," I flung back at her. "Would you like to list them so I would know, too?"

"I'm here," she said, raising her voice. "I've made my decision and I'm staying. That's all."

I stared at her. Always slim, she now looked gaunt, her face drawn and pale, her eyes filled with pain. Unhappiness was etched in the lines about her mouth. I took a deep breath and sat down, folding my hands on the table before me. "Please sit down, Faith," I said softly. "It's time we cleared up a few things."

She looked frightened, and for a moment I thought she might bolt. "Now," I insisted, and she sat down.

"I've never asked you to make any kind of choice," I told her. "If you choose to stay on here, fine. But I don't think you should stay only because you feel I want you to. I'd be willing to leave, if you think you'd rather live by yourself, or with someone else."

She looked away, biting her lip to keep from crying. All my anger of a few moments before evaporated. She was miserable, and I could not be angry with her.

"You were with Thayer?" I asked.

She nodded, twisting her hands together.

"And he asked you to move out of the cottage and not see me?"

Again she nodded.

"And you said *no*," I went on. "Why?"

She looked at me. "Because we're friends," she said, "and that is important. But that's not all of it. I'd be lying if I said it was. I suppose I said no because I don't think he has the right to make that kind of demand, to put that kind of condition on marriage."

Something sad and heavy shifted inside of me. So. He was speaking of marriage. . . .

"Do you want to be married to Thayer?" I asked.

She looked out of the window. "Yes, yes I do," she said, studying the patterns the maple leaves made against the light. "There is so much about him that is right for me. He understands so much . . . my need to work, my abilities . . . he is so vibrant, so alive, when I'm with him I feel just . . ." She looked at me then, and went on, "He does love me, and he wants children . . . and everything would be right except for this irrational side to him that I don't understand . . ."

I put my hand over hers. "I haven't wanted this to happen, Faith. I don't like being part of the problem, and I've tried very hard not to make it worse for you. I hate seeing you so unhappy, believe me I do. But I have to tell you this—please, please don't let your hurt turn into anger against me. Remember that I'm not the one who is keeping you from Thayer. And I also have to say that I think you *should* be concerned about what you call his 'irrational' side."

She took a deep breath, as if to pull herself together. "I'll get the shirtwaists for Ling Soo," she said.

A day later I saw Sara again, and this time I told her all that had happened. She heard me out, shaking her head or making a small clucking noise, and finally she said, "I agree with you when you say you know that, sooner or later, it is going to happen—she will marry him. He's making a good living for himself now, he doesn't need to court rich women. And Faith is a fine choice—young and pretty, talented in a field of art that he sees as inferior to his own. He can even have a child to prove his virility. I hope you don't think me cruel, but I've known too many men like Thayer Gerson— seekers after power. My father was one. Every field has them, art as well as commerce. The wonder of it, to me, is that bright and talented women are attracted to these men." She sat silent for a time, thinking. I did not interrupt. Finally she said, "I think it is true to say that the power of a friend, even the closest of friends, is limited. Any true friendship is going to be tested. It may even go into eclipse for a time. But if it has a hard center to it—diamond hard—it will keep. And one day, or one year, it will flourish again. I hope you are a good friend to Faith, because I believe she is going to need a good friend."

Sara was wearing a smock over her dress, and with her large shining eyes, she looked like nothing so much as a soothsayer.

Gwen had called it "one crazy Monday." Tuesday, Wednesday and Thursday had been disordered as well, and by Friday I wanted nothing so much as a respite. Nothing more could happen, I thought. I was wrong.

About three that afternoon the last edition came out. My work for the day was done, and I was busy polishing a story I had written about a woman rancher in Solano County, for my series on women, when the Boss appeared in his doorway and scanned the newsroom.

"Hallie," he called to me, motioning me into his office. He handed me a copy of the last edition, just off the presses, and asked if I had read a story headlined "FATHER KILLS SON, THEN KILLS SELF." I skimmed the first paragraphs: The father, a thirty-two-year-old war veteran, had taken his little boy, who was only three, for a long walk in the morning, then they had returned home, where the father had put a gun to the child's head and killed him, and then he shot himself. The man's wife was in the hospital, giving birth to the couple's second child.

I looked up at the Boss and shook my head sadly.

"The war isn't over, not for a lot of those boys," he said, "but the thing that is on my mind right now is, they listed the young man's company in the AEF, and a friend of mine was the commander of that company and I know he's going to be mightily upset about this. I don't want him to read about it in the paper . . . I've been calling his law office, but he's in court today and there's no way to reach him. I'm wondering if you would do me the favor of going over to the Hall of Justice and find him and tell him—prepare him, I mean—could you do that?"

I nodded that I could. I didn't want to do it, but I would for the Boss.

"I'd go myself if I didn't have this blasted meeting," he said. "My friend—he's a tall fellow and good-looking, with a shock of brown hair. He walks with a limp—lost his kneecap in France. A good man."

I stood at the door while the courtroom emptied. The counsels were the last to leave, walking slowly up the aisle toward me, the short fat man talking while the tall man listened, nodding occasionally.

"Jim Riordan?" I asked.

He looked up, only mildly surprised.

"I'm Hallie Duer of the *Times*. Sanford Curtin sent me with a message. Is there someplace we can talk privately?"

The short, fat man cackled and said, "The Irish have all the luck."

Riordan dismissed him without saying a word; then he looked behind us as if he planned to talk in the empty courtroom. The bailiff called out that he would be locking up in a minute, and added respectfully, "Sorry, Mr. Riordan."

The halls were filled with people. Preoccupied with finding a place to talk, he said nothing. "Maybe you'd rather come back with me to my office?" he finally suggested.

"No," I said, too loudly. I couldn't let him go into the streets, where the newsboys would be shouting out the headlines. "There," I said, "behind the elevator—under the stairs."

He had to stoop to stand in the narrow space. He was looking at me now, grinning encouragingly. His face seemed all angles, sharp and clean.

"I'm sorry," I started, and then it spilled out all at once, in a rush. The air seemed to thicken, the space constrict. I watched his face drain of color, watched the cold white lines of a scar appear at his hairline. His knee must have collapsed, because he pitched forward and I could hear his head crack against the marble of the staircase. I braced my body against his to keep him from falling, and I held on to him. Behind us, in the hallway, two men had stopped to watch. I shouted at them to leave. Riordan was fighting to control his breathing; I could hear it coming in short, angry bursts. I propped myself against him, holding on to him, the wool of his jacket rough against my cheek. I could almost feel the struggle inside of him, and then I could feel the strength coming back. He braced himself with his arm then, and leaned back against the wall. I was watching his eyes, and when I knew that he could see me again, that he was in control, I left.

SEVEN

"RED MCCOY'S BACK," Gwen whispered, her hand over the speaker of her headset, "and he's looking grand!" She was smiling, which marked the homecoming of Harry McConaughey—also known as Red or "The Real McCoy"—as a singular event.

It had been nine months since the Dempsey trial and five months since Ham had received a letter from Harry that said: "I've cut about half the trees in Oregon and chopped them into neat little piles of firewood, enough to last that tight-assed brother-in-law of mine a hundred years. I haven't died of thirst, and I've lost maybe fifty pounds. But to answer your question—I figure I'll take a job on a weekly up here and if that goes and I have another try left in me, I'll be back—God and the Boss willing."

And now he *was* back, a big and bulky man wearing a wrinkled shirt, baggy trousers and a sheepish grin. It was the first time I had seen the city room come to a halt. Everyone crowded around him, clapping him on the back. You could see that he was pleased and embarrassed at once.

My first thought was: *I'm using his desk*, and I began frantically to clear out all the odds and ends I had accumulated in those nine months. Intent on this chore, I was bending over a bottom drawer when I heard Ham say, "Hallie, come up here and meet Red."

Looking up, I blurted, "I'm sorry about the desk, I would have been out if . . ."

He was embarrassed. "No, now," he said, "you stay right there—"

Ham broke in. "Cut it out, you two. We'll find Hallie another desk."

Harry started to object, but when he saw the look on Ham's face he laughed instead and said to me, "I thought you did a good job on the Dempsey feature. I'd sure like to hear how you got around Kearns on that one."

I smiled at him, relieved. Dempsey was a friend of Harry's, an important part of his beat—and just about the biggest story in sports.

"She did okay for a skirt," Ham jabbed.

"For an anybody," Harry came back, ready to defend me—until he saw that Ham was joking.

"The teasing comes with the territory," I told him, "and I've still a lot to learn about that territory. I'm hoping that when you have time—"

The arrival of Sanford Curtin interrupted me. The Boss went straight for Harry, arms open—the impeccably tailored editor embraced the bulk of Harry McConaughey and hugged him, saying, "Welcome home, son."

The whole of the city room applauded. It was a clear moment, uncluttered by sentimentality. Harry's eyes filled and tears slid down his cheeks. He took out his handkerchief and wiped his face while we all watched, approving.

In the next few weeks I learned why Harry had been so warmly welcomed. He was even-tempered, hardworking and funny, all at once. He wrote about sports because he was comfortable in that world, and because boxing, more than anything else, fascinated

him. In Harry's hands, a four-round match could become a meta-
phor for life.

He spoke with eloquence about fighters and what he called
"the fight game." I listened, rapt, which was surprising since I
found the idea of two men battering each other senseless for the
enjoyment of others to be repugnant, even obscene. I agreed with
those who felt boxing was no sport at all, that it appealed to man's
basest instincts, that it was barbaric, even.

Except: Jack Dempsey was the World's Champion, more
popular even, some said, than President Harding. A feature on
Dempsey was better than a scoop—for any reporter, but especially
for a woman reporter. I wanted that story, so I listened to Harry
and tried to learn.

"Bestial?" Harry would say. "I suppose boxing is bestial. Also
honest. Two men, four fists. Stripped to the essentials—shorts,
gloves. And the object is simple too. To hit and hurt. No complicated game rules to obscure the struggle, no teams, no balls, no
excuses, no pretense. Nobody says the object is to play the game
well, that winning doesn't matter. Nobody talks about *good sports-
manship*. Everybody knows Dempsey hits low when he can. That's
the way he fights, hard and sometimes dirty. In the fight game,
there aren't too many romantics."

Sometimes I would say, "Do you believe that, Harry?" And he
would grin at me, that funny lopsided grin of his, and we would
both laugh. It was an exercise, of course. An elaborate rationale.
He agreed with me, I was sure of it. Except, he took pleasure in
the fights. I knew that, too. But I didn't understand it, because I
had never been to a real fight—the sparring that day I watched
Dempsey didn't count. I didn't know the first thing about how to
cover a fight, and I was afraid my chance to do the Dempsey story
would come before I found out.

Harry laughed at me. "You've got plenty of time," he said. "Old
Doc Kearns isn't in any hurry to put Dempsey in the ring—he has
to make people believe the Carpentier fight really is the 'Fight of

the Century,' as he is calling it. Kearns and the New York promoter are going to string it out—and when it is set, it'll be in New York. There aren't enough people out here to make a million-dollar gate."

My face must have registered my disappointment, because Harry tried to comfort me by saying that it wouldn't be much of a fight anyway, that Dempsey would play around with the Frenchman for a few rounds, enough to get some action for the cameras, and then he would just politely finish him off.

"How can you be so sure?" I wanted to know, disappointed enough to sound angry.

"I can't," Harry answered. "That's the thing about boxing, you never can be sure. I guess that's why I want to be there too . . . though I could never want Carpentier to win. I don't like the man, I don't like the way he fights."

"I'm beginning to think I'll never know what you're talking about," I sighed.

"If you want," Harry said, "you can come along when I cover some local fights. I can show you better than I can tell you about them."

"I'd like to go along," I quickly answered.

"Matter of fact, Thelma told me to invite you out to the house. She thought you might like to meet the kids and all."

"I would," I said. "When?"

Startled by the suddenness of my acceptance, he stuttered, "Anytime . . . tomorrow if you want. It's corned-beef-and-cabbage night."

"Wonderful!" I said enthusiastically.

We gathered around the big table—Harry and Thelma and the four young McConaugheys—and ate corned beef and laughed and talked, sometimes everybody all at once. I enjoyed myself so obviously that I was given an open invitation: *Come again, come*

anytime, please come back . . . Harry looked on, smiling benevolently. It had been a long time since I had been part of such a noisy, happy crowd.

That evening was the first of many at the McConaugheys'. Thelma was as petite as Harry was bulky; she fussed over everyone like a small mother hen. The boys were large for their ages—which ranged between five and eleven—and good-natured, each with a thatch of red hair and a dusting of freckles. Every now and then Thelma would reach across the table to flick her napkin and sting a hand that had reached too far. There would be wild bursts of laughter from everyone but the culprit.

Thelma urged me to bring Faith along, and one night I did. On the way home she sighed. "That's the way I always imagined it should be—a home and a family, rowdy brothers and laughter and a real father and a real mother and people who seem to like each other."

"They're not without problems," I reminded her. "Harry was gone for nine long months, remember?"

"But he came back," Faith said, "and he isn't drinking now, and nine months is not the same as forever." I slipped my arm through hers as we climbed the long hill home, wrapped in a comfortable silence.

One evening after supper at the McConaugheys', Thelma and I were alone in the kitchen doing the dishes. She was, as usual, chattering away in time to the rhythm of the dishwashing. "Now that Harry's off the bottle," she said, sloshing a bowl with soapy water, "everything is going to be just fine, I can feel it. I've always had faith that my prayers would be answered, but then, you never do know when the Good Lord is listening, do you?" She rinsed the bowl, put it to drain on the board and continued, "You modern women are a wonder. Working as a reporter—you surely are brave to take on such a job as that. I suppose you'll think me old-fashioned, Hallie, but I'm glad Harry will be going to the fights with you. I don't think a woman should go to those places alone. Besides which, nobody knows as much about the fights as Harry does."

I stood, dishtowel in hand, smiling at her. "You are an extremely good woman, Thelma," I said.

Flustered, she sputtered, "Good? Oh no, not me. I just rear the boys and keep the house, and hope for the best, that's all."

"You talk about a 'modern woman,'" I interrupted her, "and about being brave . . . but who took over here when Harry was away?"

"Who?" she asked, as if I'd asked a puzzling question.

"Yes, who ran the house and took care of the boys and kept everything together so Harry had a home to come back to?"

She waved a hand in the air, as if to brush away some worrisome insect, and said, "Oh, well, but . . . it's not the same. I did what had to be done, I didn't go looking to have to take over. Everybody has problems. Praise be, ours seem to be over for now. Thanks to good friends and Mr. Curtin. He helped, you know. Without him, I'd of had to scrub floors."

"I didn't know," I told her. "I'm not surprised, but I think if you had to scrub floors, you would. And what you did—keeping your home together—was braver than anything I've ever done." I thought about Clive, and felt a sharp sting of regret . . . we *hadn't* fought hard enough, we had given in too easily.

She took my towel from me, hung it neatly on the rack to dry; then she patted my hand and said quietly, "I pray harm will never come your way, Hallie dear."

Sometimes Harry and I would go to the fights at the Dreamland Rink, where the press table was close enough to the floor of the ring for sweat to splatter out onto us, and once or twice a fighter would be knocked out of the ring and land in our laps, slick with sweat. Cigar smoke mingled with the smell of sweat and liniment; the air was fetid and ripe, punctuated by the thick slap of leather against skin. A long wail would rise from the gathered crowd, would gain momentum as the attack sharpened, as the blows fell, would burst into one loud roar as one man slumped under the rain of blows or lay sprawled out and unconscious on the mat. I could feel it in my throat, a tightness, primitive and hard. It knotted and I tried to swallow, but I couldn't. And sometimes, when it was over and my throat was sore (from shouting? was that why?), I would not be able to look at anyone, not even Harry, for fear of what I would see reflected.

Harry called it "a distillation of rage." I felt that rage and knew it was mine, knew that the men in the ring were playing out a dance of violence that belonged to us all, to me, to the roaring crowd that surged and bellowed and shouted when blood spilled. The violence was buried so deeply that most of us never felt it. I feared it, hated it, wanted it not to be. But it was there. The men in the ring had brought it to the surface—in themselves, in us, the onlookers.

I thought of the rattlesnake on the stone wall and how the blood had pounded in my ears, hot and throbbing. It was like that, at moments, at the fights. It would be that way always, I thought. In the boxing ring, on a field in Flanders. Whenever there was no choice but to fight.

I could not sleep after those first few fights. I would come back to the cottage and lie in my bed on the little porch, staring out into the night sky. My body would be tense, my jaw tight. Harry had been right: there was something to be learned at the fights. I was angry with myself, and shamed too—for having dismissed boxing so self-righteously, so easily, before I had made myself look at it. Before it had made me look into myself and see the hard truth. Hard and ugly, consuming, and enthralling.

After three of these sleepless, troubled nights I knew that if I intended to go to any more fights I would have to find a way to protect myself from the raw violence, from the way it touched me.

I would have liked to quit, but I couldn't. There was still the Dempsey story, but that wasn't all of it. I simply couldn't quit, not until I had seen it through, not until I knew enough to cover a fight.

As it happened, it would be Ham who would find a way for me. As a joke he gave me a copy of a book called *The Science of Boxing,* used at the university, he explained, to teach all the fancy young men. Ham had little respect for the science of any sport, and even less for university men. But I read the book cover to cover, and decided I would study the fights, each man's moves. I would become so engaged by the mechanical skills, I thought, that I would not be swept away by the emotions. I would become the dispassionate observer, removed from the frantic crowd.

To my surprise, it worked.

Sooner or later, Harry had said, you see everybody at the fights. Before the war, boxing had been considered vulgar; now the Prince of Wales was at ringside when Georges Carpentier dispatched Joe Beckett, the English champion, and George Bernard Shaw wrote about it. In America, the same was true. At the Dreamland Rink in San Francisco I met the mayor, James Rolph—called "Sunny Jim" by almost everybody. He was a dandy and something of a rogue, and that endeared him to San Franciscans. I began scanning the crowds. Once I was certain I had caught a glimpse of Babe Conlon. She had looked at me, her heavy lids lowered, a blink of recognition, but by the time I pushed to the other side of the ring she was gone.

Between fights one March night I sat looking idly over the crowd, trying to see through the yellow haze that hovered over the arena. I caught a glimpse of him—the Boss's friend. Leaning to the left, for a clearer view, I saw I was right, it was Jim Riordan. Everything had happened so quickly that afternoon. I had a general sense of him—his height, the thick hair, the sharp angles of his face. Now, in the crowded, noise-filled room, I could study him.

He was good-looking, I decided. Not in the usual way, there was nothing fine or delicate about his features. They were, in fact, somewhat rough. It was more in the way he smiled, the way he held himself, his expressions. His—*ease*. That was it. He must have come from his office because he was wearing a suit. He had taken off the jacket, so he sat in his vest and with his shirt sleeves rolled up. The men with him had taken their suit coats off too, but they looked less comfortable. One man leaned across another to say something to Riordan. He nodded, as if he agreed, and the man seemed pleased. It struck me that Riordan was the sort of man other men would want to please.

"They look like politicos from Sacramento," Harry said when I asked him about the group. "The tall guy on the right, that's Jimmy Riordan, a lawyer. The word is that he can go to Sacramento if he wants to."

"Do you know him?" I asked, trying to sound offhand.

"Jimmy? That I do," Harry answered, preoccupied with his fight card. "Thelma grew up on the same block as the Riordan boys— South of the Slot. The Irish part of town, you might say. She and Mary Margaret used to be best friends, but that was a ways back."

"Who is Mary Margaret?" I wanted to know.

"Jimmy's wife," he told me.

Jimmy's wife, I thought.

I watched him, his head tilted to one side, listening to one of the men. Suddenly he lifted his eyes and looked at me. He nodded slowly, and smiled. As if he knew I had been watching him. Flustered, I looked away. I was being foolish, silly and foolish. The rest of the evening I made an effort not to let my eyes move to where he was. Instead, I concentrated on listening to Harry and watching the action in the ring.

I drove Harry back to the newspaper office that night so he could write his story for the early edition. Mission Street was empty at that late hour. Lights reflected from the wet streets, and I was trying to think of a way to bring up the subject when Harry did it for me.

"I haven't seen Jimmy Riordan for a year or more," he started. "His family lived over on Shipley Street. . . good Irish Catholics, of course." He grinned. "You know why they call Market Street the Slot? Because of all the streetcar tracks. Living 'South of the

Slot' used to mean you were Catholic and Irish. Now most of the people Thelma and I went to school with have moved out of the old neighborhoods." He was talking easily and I didn't interrupt. "The Riordans graduated from St. Ignatius the same year Thelma graduated from St. Brigid's. Thelma and Jimmy's wife—she was Mary Margaret O'Dowd—were friends when they were girls. I was five years older, but I got caught in the Riordan twins' wake, too," he said, with a short, hard laugh.

"Twins?" I asked.

"Tom and Jimmy were the spitting image of each other," he went on. "Nobody could tell them apart—not even their ma if they didn't want her to. The Riordans knew how to handle themselves, I'll say that. All the mothers in the parish could tell you that the Riordan boys were going to make something of themselves while the rest of us were going to hell in a handbasket."

"You said 'were'—were the spitting image—what about the brother, Tom, was it?"

Harry opened and closed his big hands, spreading the fingers wide. "Jimmy left his brother and part of his own kneecap in some godforsaken woods in France. He never would talk about it. He came back and he wouldn't put on his uniform or march in any of the parades or have anything to do with the veterans' groups . . . Most of the old crowd were like Dempsey—we did what we had to do to stay out of it. None of us wanted to become cannon fodder. But we all envied Jimmy Riordan with his closed mouth and his limp."

"Do you ever see them?" I asked.

"Them?" Harry said. "Who?"

"Riordan and his wife."

He shook his head and began opening and closing his hands again. "See them? No. No . . . the war, something happened to Jimmy. When he came back he bought a house out in the Sunset for Mary Margaret and the kids, but as far as I know he doesn't live there. I think he stays in some hotel downtown. To tell the truth,

I don't know what Jimmy does with himself outside of work. I can tell you where Mary Margaret is every morning, though. She's back down in the old neighborhood at first light, scrubbing down the front steps of St. Patrick's on her hands and knees."

I raised my eyebrows in surprise. "Why?"

"When the war was on," Harry explained, "some of the mothers who had boys over the water—mostly the mothers who had come over from the Old Country—would scrub the church steps as a way of storing up favors in heaven. You know—I'll scrub your church steps, God, if you'll bring my boy home safe. The kind of thing simple old souls do. When Mary Margaret took to joining them, nobody knew what to make of it. She had always been a religious girl—Thelma says now she should have been a nun. Then the war was over and all the old women quit, but Mary Margaret just kept on scrubbing. It isn't an easy chore, either, I can tell you, having spent a couple of nights stone drunk on those steps myself, sick and miserable." He shook his head, remembering.

We rode in silence for a while, bouncing as we crossed over the streetcar tracks.

"The Boss seems to like Riordan," I offered.

"The Boss likes the kind of law Riordan practices," Harry said. "He's one of the few good lawyers around town who will take unpopular cases. He's on the Mooney-Billings case, trying to get them out of prison . . . it's been what? . . . five years now since those two went up for a bombing everybody knows they didn't do. And Riordan's been taking on some of the Wobblies who are being prosecuted under the sedition laws. That's why I was surprised to see him with those boys from Sacramento. I didn't think Jimmy would be all that popular with that crowd."

"I recognized two of those men," I told him. "They were Progressives—before reform went out of style, they wielded a lot of power in the state capital."

Harry slapped his forehead. "I forgot you came from

Sacramento—sure you'd know—you'll have to forgive me when I forget . . ."

"I forgive you, Harry," I said as brightly as I could, and he blushed with pleasure.

I wished he weren't so easy to please. I had, after all, pretended not to know those men to see what he could tell me about Riordan. I didn't think that would escape Harry.

By the middle of April I was beginning to feel a small sense of dread. Clive had said he wanted to be in California by the end of April, but there had been no letter from him. When the letter did come, I felt sick at having been right. "Dear Hallie," he wrote, "I'm afraid I must delay my visit. It will be two months, perhaps three, before I can get away."

I had a sinking sensation. The delay, he explained in his precise architect's lettering, was necessary—there were several sets of drawings that needed to be finished at the office, and of course he felt obligated to do them. And Grandmother needed him to accompany her to New York, where she had to appear to take care of some important business. She could not go alone, and there was no one else to go with her.

I sat at the table by the big window in the cottage, looking out into the leafy expanse of a pepper tree. I sat for a long time, watching the light shift as the leaves stirred in the breeze. It was quiet on the hill. A dog barked once. A door rattled. I felt tired, for no reason. How could we have let so many years go by and not even have seen each other? We were all that was left, brother and sister. We should have been together, should have had each other to talk to, to help . . . more than letters. What hadn't I done that I should have done? Why hadn't I tried harder? Fought harder?

All those letters, pouring everything out, but always with the plaintive little plea: "If only we could be together, I know we could figure it out if only we could talk. . . ." My brother, my friend. My only friend. No, Faith had become a friend, but. . . But that was not the same, not the same as your brother. He was the only one who had shared all that had happened, all the hurt, all the long and lonely years.

Would we ever have a chance to be together, to truly get to know one another? Or would we finally meet one day when we were old and dried and everything was behind us. When it wouldn't matter. The time was now, it was almost too late, but now. And I wouldn't let it go, because if I did there would never be another chance. Never.

I scrambled through the desk drawer, pulling out paper and pen, spilling the ink in my determination. Now. Right now was the time.

I wrote: "Clive, listen to me. It has been fifteen years since we last saw each other and that is too long, much too long. All those letters—they kept us together but they were not enough, they were never meant to be enough. I need to see you, to get to know you in person again. We need time to talk, time *together*. You have been kind and dutiful to Grandmother Duer, but now it is time for me. And for you. You have to come, and now. If you don't—if you feel you absolutely can't leave Chicago—then I will come there. It is not the way I would want it—after all, you have a position you need to leave, while I am doing just what I want to be doing—or I will be soon, when they give me the beat they have promised. Even so, if need be I will give it up and come to Chicago. Because the work alone is not enough. Family is important, just as important. And you are all the family I have, except for Grandmother and Grandfather. I refuse to be separated any longer. If we don't take action now, I am convinced we never will. Letters aren't enough anymore, dear brother. I need a friend and I want that friend to be you. Here. Or there. You say which it is to be." I signed it "Your loving sister, Hallie," and posted it to his architectural firm.

I accepted Harry's invitation almost before he offered it. Faith was working late all that week, and a night at the McConaugheys' was just what I needed. I stopped at Eppler's Bakery on the way to the house and picked up a large strawberry-and-cream confection—the first of the season. The boys would, I knew, fight over who got to open the box. It had become a ritual when I went for supper.

"You send them off stuffed and happy and spoiled," Thelma said after supper, when the two of us sat sipping coffee. Harry had taken the boys to a ballgame, and the house was strangely quiet. I did not want to think about Clive; what I wanted was to sit with Thelma and listen to her chatter, to comfort myself in her warmth. I did not want to think about the letter I had posted.

"Harry told me he saw Jimmy Riordan at the fights the other night," Thelma said. "That's a strange, sad story—did Harry tell you?"

I smiled; I had been hoping she would get around to Riordan. I coaxed, "He told me a little—about how you and Mary Margaret were best friends."

"Oh, yes, well. . ." She sighed. "Seeing her now, you'd never know she was such a fun-loving little thing once. We were something, when we were kids—we just did everything together. She was so pert and pretty. The Riordans lived down the block from our house. They were like two peas in a pod, those boys—always together. We were all in love with them—all the girls at St. Brigid's, that is. Mary Margaret used to plot how she would marry one and I'd marry the other." She stopped, shook her head. "I'd tell her, 'Mary, those boys aren't going to stay around. They're going to fly away from all of this, just fly away.' But Mary Margaret had her heart set on Jimmy Riordan. She just didn't know."

"Know?" I asked.

For once Thelma paused. "I don't know what I mean by that," she said. "Sometimes it seems like she didn't know anything. She didn't know how different those boys were, for one thing. Even when they were younger, Jimmy always served Mass and Tom balked. Jimmy seemed to do what people expected, and Tom never did. It was natural, I guess, that Mary would set her cap for Jimmy. When they started keeping company, Tom didn't like it. Not one bit. And when Jimmy married her right after graduation, Tom wouldn't stand up with him. I was her maid of honor, and I know it hurt Jimmy. You could see it. At first Mary felt bad about it, but then Tom always treated her just fine. Some thought Tom was jealous of her, but Harry didn't. He said he talked to Tom about it, and Tom told him he just didn't like to see Jimmy tied down so young, and the babies coming like they did—three of them in a row. But I'm rattling on as usual, more than you want to know, I'm sure."

"Don't be so sure," I confessed. "Actually, I am interested. I met Riordan a few weeks back—the Boss sent me on an errand—and he seemed just, well . . ." I found myself groping for words.

"You don't have to explain to me," Thelma said, leaning across the table and lowering her voice, even though we were alone in the house. "There always was something about those boys—not just their looks, either. Just . . . something," and she laughed like a schoolgirl.

"I remember," she went on, "just before graduation—we girls went to St. Brigid's, you know, and the boys to St. Ignatius—well, Red was already out and working at the paper and he was courting me, so he went along on an outing arranged for both graduating classes. We took a ferry from Sausalito and then we climbed on an old horse-drawn stage to make the trip over the hills to the ocean beach at Willow Camp. The Riordan family had a little fishing cottage right on the beach, and the girls used it to change into swimming costumes. I remember that Mary Margaret and Jimmy and Red and I were all together, but Tom brought a girl from Lowell High School—a tall, pretty blond girl. A Protestant! Heaven forbid!" She laughed her high, trilling laugh and went on, "It was what you expected Tom to do, and of course all the St. Brigid's girls were green with envy, and hated her and then went to confession and spilled it all to the priest. I've always wondered what the priest must have thought of Tom, causing such lust in the minds of all the little graduates . . . I suppose if we had known then what fate had in store for poor Tom . . ." She crossed herself.

"But Jim must have gone to law school," I pointed out.

"Oh yes," Thelma said, "he went because Tom went. We all expected the two of them to go their separate ways—but nobody told Jimmy. And by gosh, they went to law school at St. Ignatius—and they both worked to support Jimmy's family. Tom graduated first in his class and Jimmy came in fourth or fifth, something like that."

"They must have graduated just in time to go off to the war?" I put in.

"Tom was drafted," Thelma answered, frowning, "but Jimmy volunteered. That was the last time Mary Margaret ever talked to me about it. She came the day Jimmy told her he was going. Her face was all swelled up and puffy from the crying. She told me she had begged him not to leave her, not to leave the babies. And she said he was doing it again—choosing his brother over her. She hadn't wanted him to go to law school . . . he'd been away so much, you know. I don't think Mary Margaret had an ounce of an idea what marriage was going to be like—all she had wanted to do was stand up before the altar and take the sacrament. She was unhappy, poor soul. But at least she was among the living. God forgive me, but there are times when I think her life now is an act of contrition. She's over there scrubbing down those filthy steps every morning, and I can't for the life of me figure out why—what she's doing penance for."

Thelma got up to pour another cup of coffee.

"Why do you suppose he came back here after the war?" I asked.

Thelma looked at me, surprised. "He's a decent man, a Catholic.

He knows his responsibilities . . . he's wed to her for life, you know. And the children, too." Then she lowered her voice and said, "He hasn't spent a night with her since he came home. I know that for a fact. I suspect it was the children that brought him back, and that's a blessing, because Mary Margaret gives all she's got to the church. There's no laughter in that house. Her folks used to say she was going to be their nun, and I think that's what she's become, the only way she knows how."

"Do you ever see him?"

"Jimmy? No. I don't know anybody who sees much of him— other than running into him now and again. I know he gives Mary Margaret plenty for the kids and all—though I think she gives most of it to the church. Her boy Colin is a friend of my Bryan's, and Bryan tells me that Colin can ask his dad anytime he needs money for anything. My guess is that Jimmy knows their mother gives most of what he gives her to the church. I'm glad he's found a way around it, because those children need a bit of pleasure."

The more I learned, the more I found myself thinking about Riordan. I tried to imagine the man I had seen that day at the Hall of Justice, and later at the fights, married to a woman who would spend her mornings on her hands and knees in an act of contrition.

The two seemed worlds apart. Why was that? Finally it came to me. His grief, that day, had been immediate and personal. No rituals, no prayer that I could see. Just strong and straight, without apologies either. And at the fights . . . *he knew I was watching, I was sure of it.*

May was a busy month for Faith, and an eventful one for me. Graduation photographs and then wedding portraits kept her in the studio all day. She worked in the darkroom at night, sometimes until one or two in the morning. Faith had become one of the best-known portrait photographers in the city, in part because of the pictures that had appeared in the *Times*. She worked with each subject, arranging with great care, coaxing and talking until she got the expression she wanted. This could take an hour or more, but the result was a large number of satisfied customers, and more calling every day. Often she would curl up on the settee in the reception room and sleep there.

My first major event was a letter from Clive, assuring me that he had made a decision, that he would be coming west. He said he understood how disappointed I must have been at yet another delay, but that this time he would not change his mind. I would not have to go to Chicago. I received the letter with great relief.

Two days later the Boss called me into his office to tell me that with Harry back, I wasn't needed on sports any longer and that I could have the hotel beat if I still wanted it. "However," he said, holding his cigar in the air to stop me from bursting into thank-yous, "first I have a special assignment I want you to take on. I want you to study up on the Marchant case. Agnes Marchant is going to trial very soon and we will need an update, a story that reviews the whole case. This is an important story, and not just in California. Important for the whole country. Lawyers are watching it because they think it is going to set some precedents. You realize that, I am sure. Agnes Marchant is a friend of mine—you should know that as well. I want to give her the most thorough, the very best coverage we possibly can. So get on it right away. Show us what you can do."

I walked back to my desk and sat down, stunned. I was going to get a beat, a real beat, after all the weeks of agitating. But first I was going to cover one of the biggest, most politically important stories in the country. And Clive was coming, and everything was changing. Could this be happening, any of it? All the months of waiting and wanting, and writing letters and recipes and wedding stories. And then: movement, change. A family, and an assignment important enough to change laws, to affect lives.

A copyboy shuffled toward me. "Message from Mr. Curtin," he said, handing me a note.

"Start with her lawyer, Jim Riordan."

EIGHT

SITTING AT THE long table in the *Times*'s library—which we called "the morgue"—with several months of back numbers of the paper spread out before me, I read:

Agnes Marchant, prominent local clubwoman, was arrested last evening after giving a speech at the Hotel Oakland. She will be arraigned on Monday and charged under the state Criminal Syndicalist law, which prohibits advocating the overthrow of the government by violence or being affiliated with an organization that so advocates. Miss Marchant is a member of the American Communist party and has ties to the IWW as well.

I shifted in my chair, trying to ignore the discomfort I felt from sitting for so long. My back ached and the hard oak seat seemed to press into my bones.

I was to see Riordan at three. By noon my stomach was rumbling but I could not take time out to eat; there was too much I needed to know. I turned the pages of the newspapers . . . Mary Miles Minter was playing in *Anne of Green Gables* at the Pantages . . . Fatty Arbuckle's new moving picture, *Crazy to Marry*, was at the New Mission . . . H. Liebes was having a sale on Philippine lingerie—pink silk crepe de chine decorated with tiny figures. I stood and stretched; I was drifting; I would have to concentrate. I checked my notes:

Agnes Marchant, age fifty, librarian. Descendant of five *Mayflower* Pilgrims, father a state senator, uncle a Supreme Court justice appointed by Abraham Lincoln. Graduate of Smith College, worker in settlement houses in New York City, secretary of Associated Charities in Oakland. Lives in family home on shores of Lake Merritt. Joined Socialist party in 1914, active in pacifist causes, opposed U.S. entry into War, defender of Mooney and Billings, member of faction which split off from Socialists to form American Communist party. Prosecution maintains that Communist party, indirectly through Agnes Marchant, sought to overthrow the U.S. government and replace it with the Russian form of communism. Marchant's defense argues that she consistently rejected violence, sabotage or revolutionary terrorism, that her only crime was a keen interest in the welfare of migratory labor, in helping the poorest of the poor, that her whole life attests to this fact.

When Harry heard that I had been given the Marchant story he grinned and said, "Imagine that!" which is what he always says when something good happens. Then he told me, "I suppose you know Agnes Marchant is an old friend of the Boss. He's the one who talked Jimmy Riordan into defending her *pro bono publico*. I hear that about all that's left of the Marchant fortune is the house. If she had to pay lawyer's fees, she'd lose that."

Sanford Curtin was the linchpin once more, I thought. He had handed me one of the biggest political stories of the day, one in which public passions were running high, one in which he had a personal interest. He had not told me how to do it, only that I should put the Marchant case into national perspective, that I should explain the Palmer raids, explain Red purges and Soviet arks and xenophobia.

I took careful notes: A. Mitchel Palmer, attorney general of the United States and a pious Mormon, led the purge against the communists, or Reds, by giving an order to round up thirty-six hundred aliens. They were accused of sedition, and three hundred of them were deported, shipped back "to where they came from" on converted troop ships dubbed "Soviet arks"—back to Lithuania and Estonia and Finland and Italy, cheered on by the "one-hundred-percent Americans" in classic, hysterical xenophobic style.

I went to the dictionary for the definition of "xenophobia" and found: *an unreasonable fear or hatred of foreigners*. And it was raging through the United States, a country settled by immigrants.

"The popular toast 'To Prohibition, fundamentalism and the KKK' gives something of the tenor of the times," I wrote. "Woodrow Wilson says 'a spirit of ruthless brutality' has entered the fiber of American life. The Sedition Acts which were passed as a wartime measure have not yet been repealed, and they have been used to justify the Palmer raids."

I wrote: "Raids were orchestrated by Palmer to take place simultaneously in cities across the land. Agents would sweep into party headquarters, catching those who happened to be there at the time, taking them to holding cells until the citizens could be separated out and held for trial. The rest, the aliens, were simply herded onto the ships and sent away."

A stray thought wandered through my mind: how would they go about sending Agnes Marchant, whose ancestors were on the *Mayflower*, back to "where she came from"?

In one of the clippings, I read where she had told the presiding judge at one of her hearings: "You must remember that I am on trial for an offense punishable by fourteen years' imprisonment. I am an American citizen. I am not asking for sympathy, only justice."

Could they, I wondered, possibly send her to prison for fourteen years for being a member of the Communist party? Yes, I knew, they could. Scores of Wobblies were even now in prison, for nothing more than being members of the IWW. Some, in fact, were pointing out that had not Agnes Marchant been a member of the ruling class, she would already have joined them. Agnes Marchant had agreed, but had added, "None of us is guilty, none should be imprisoned."

It was two o'clock. I made one last note: "The *New Republic* says the issues raised by the Marchant case make it second in importance only to Sacco and Vanzetti." Then I stood, straightened my skirt and went to the washroom to scrub the newsprint from my hands.

I looked closely in the mirror to see if there were any smudges on my face, and decided to take down my hair, brush it and put it up again. I coiled it carefully and caught it with the shell combs. Then I tucked my new waist into my suit skirt. The waist was from H. Liebes, a white *point d'esprit* lace collar on brown China silk. I smoothed my eyebrows with a forefinger, and for some reason, sighed. I checked the time on my mother's gold locket watch. Twenty past two. I put on my hat—which was felt, and soft, and which Faith said made me look "dangerously sophisticated"—and said to the mirror, "Let's go."

The gold letters on the door said "James Francis Riordan, Attorney-at-Law." The secretary glanced up from her typewriter and in a perfunctory way told me to go on in, that he expected me. I tried to ignore the hollow feeling in my stomach. I had been too keyed up about the story; I should have stopped for something to eat.

It was a large room, with a wide view of the inner bay, but it seemed curiously empty. There was a desk with a few stacks of papers, each neatly separated, and several chairs. In the corner was a large leather divan. The only decoration was a painting of a storm at sea, waves crashing on rocks and birds flying into the wind.

He was standing at the window, looking out, one arm propped

on the frame. He was in his shirt sleeves again. I could see the hard creases ironed in by the laundryman. He was taller than I remembered. He did not turn around when I came in.

"Am I early?" I asked.

He turned then and smiled. A careful, guarded smile. "No," he said, "no, not at all. I lost track of time, I suppose—I do that sometimes when the Matson liners are coming in." I joined him at the window and we watched the great white ship make its way into the bay. We spoke in formalities, polite people who had learned the proper phrases that give one time to assess. I had a sense of our words floating about the room, echoing into the far corners. He told me that he liked to welcome whichever of the Matson liners arrived on Friday. Today it was the *Lurline*. We stood there, paying careful attention to the tug that nosed the liner into its berth, all the while trying to get some notion of each other. I had the advantage, I was certain, and it made me uncomfortable. He did not know all that I knew about him from Harry and Thelma. I tried to put it together: this man at the window, the Jimmy Riordan from South of Market, and the man under the stairwell in the Hall of Justice.

I took out my pad and he motioned me to a chair. He did not sit behind the big desk, choosing rather to perch on the edge of it so that the distance between us was not so great.

For a moment I was tempted to blurt out what both of us knew: Defending Agnes Marchant is a hopeless task, so let's begin from there. Instead I said, "With so many successful prosecutions under the Criminal Syndicalist law—and so many people in jail for doing less than Miss Marchant has admitted to doing—how do you plan to defend her?"

He answered carefully, speaking in short, precise sentences. "The Constitution was written by an inspired group of men. It seems to me that it was a miracle that it got written in the first place, and an even greater miracle that the American people came to accept it as a kind of secular Holy Word . . . 'my constitutional rights' is a phrase most people use at one time or another. Unfortunately, few know what those rights are. You can hardly blame them for that particular bit of ignorance when you realize that their lawmakers don't know much more, even though many of them presumably have studied the law. They pass legislation that flies in the face of the Constitution—like the state Criminal Syndicalist law under which Agnes is being prosecuted. It takes awhile to undo this kind of legal mischief."

I looked up at him dubiously. "You are saying that the law under which Agnes is being prosecuted—the law that has already sent scores of Wobblies to jail—is unconstitutional? As a practical matter, that law is on the books and the presiding judge is bound to instruct the jury to abide by it. Chances of its being struck down by a higher court before she goes to trial seem slim, wouldn't you agree? And Miss Marchant has admitted to being a member of the Communist Labor party and that party has advocated the overthrow of the government."

He interrupted to say, "I'm not going to court to defend the Communist Labor party or the IWW. I'm going to be there to defend Agnes Marchant, an American citizen and a member of an illustrious American family. A social worker who has devoted her life to good works."

"Does that mean you are going to portray her as naïve or gullible—even, perhaps, a little dense?"

He studied me now, shifting his weight as he sat. "No, Agnes is none of those. She is stubborn, and she is honest and she does have the courage of her convictions, which are not so complex as some might think. In a strange way, Agnes has something in common with the people who want to see her punished. The people given to action rather than thought. *Good is what works.* The thing is, those other Americans haven't had to spend much time in city slums or in California's migrant labor camps in the Big Valley. Agnes has, and she wants something done about it. Now. It seemed to her that the Socialists offered the best hope for quick change, so she joined them. I don't believe her political theory goes much beyond that."

"Even so," I said, shuffling through my notes, "listen to this," and I read out loud: "'The working class and the employing class have nothing in common. There can be no peace so long as hunger and want are found among millions of working people, and the few who make up the employing class have all the good things of life. Between these two classes a struggle must go on until the workers of the world organize as a class, take possession of the earth and the machinery of production, and abolish the wage system . . . It is the historic mission of the working class to do away with capitalism.'"

He nodded, and for the first time grinned at me. "I doubt," he said, "that Agnes Marchant has ever read the IWW Preamble—that is what you're quoting, isn't it? But if she did, she would have gladly accepted the part about abolishing hunger and want, and ignored the rest—about doing away with capitalism." He leaned forward, as if to share a small side thought. "Besides," he said, "I suppose it comes as a surprise to some, but capitalism is not one of the rights guaranteed by the Constitution."

I threw my hands up, pretending shock. "Do you plan to base your defense of Agnes Marchant on an attack on capitalism?"

He laughed then, outright. "Good Lord, no. Don't you know that Agnes Marchant comes from a long line of capitalists—didn't I point that out to you? My oversight, entirely. Her only weakness, you see, was wanting to help the poor and feed the hungry. . . ."

"So we're back to good little Agnes . . . but what if the jury doesn't see it that way?"

"Look," he said, suddenly quite serious, "Agnes *is* innocent—if not in the narrow sense of a narrow law, in the larger sense. I mean *true* innocence; her goal has been decent and good from the beginning. I think that the words 'Bolshevik' and 'anarchist' throw such fear into men's minds that they cloud the truth, the basic truth of her innocence. But we are going into the courtroom to dispel that fear, to move beyond it to justice."

There was a soft knock on the door, and the secretary popped her head in to say that there was a call from a Mr. Modran. Riordan said to get a number where he could call him back, and turned to me as if impatient at the interruption.

"But the fear *is* there," I said, "and if you read the syndicalist literature you can see why it is there. People are afraid the Reds are going to take over because the Reds say they are going to take over. And it happened in Russia, you know. This new brand of revolution, which the IWW and the American Communist party and the American Communist Labor party all say should be imported—it frightens people. And a lot of men came back from France, and the war, feeling that something *was* wrong at home . . . it's not as if there isn't a basis for that fear."

"Fear is a strange emotion," he answered, frowning. "It is probably always the greatest threat to reason . . . it crowds out thought or any semblance of balance. It makes you forget that there are built-in safeguards, that those inspired men who gave us a constitution seemed to be able to see ahead and know there would be real threats, and answer them . . . But the fear takes over at times, and it is closer to hate than we know . . . and people like Agnes, who for reasons of their own cannot get out of the way, get hurt. But the system of law is there for her, as well as the people she seems to frighten. It is my job to use that law to defend her . . . and that is what I intend to do."

He walked to the window then, and I put my pad and pencil away. It had not been a good interview, not complete, but it was over. "I'd like to talk to Miss Marchant tomorrow, if that is possible," I said.

He nodded. Without turning, he said he would see if it could be arranged, and insisted on being present.

I stood then, feeling awkward, waiting for him to turn around and dismiss me. Instead he said, "That day at the Hall of Justice—"

"Please," I interrupted, "there really is nothing you need to say."

He turned then and looked straight at me. "Yes there is," he went on. "I need to say thank you for the way you told me. It was quite an introduction, wasn't it?"

I looked up at him and nodded.

He turned to look at the painting on the wall. "You must have felt like the storm petrels," he said, explaining, "—the birds that signal a storm at sea."

"Flying against the wind," I said. "Yes. I guess. I didn't like having to be the bearer of such bad news. The Boss hoped I could soften the blow for you, but I don't think there was any way to do that."

He only looked at me, as he had from across the ring, and nodded. For a long moment it seemed there was something more . . . Then he pulled back, businesslike once more, and said, "You can meet Agnes here at eleven tomorrow. When you do meet her, I believe you will understand what I've been trying to explain."

I walked onto Market Street feeling a wild exhilaration. It was an exciting story, one that engaged the most basic conflict in the country. In many ways, it seemed to me, it went to the heart of the matter as even Sacco and Vanzetti did not. Agnes Marchant was, after all, a "one-hundred-percent American." She represented all that was good in the Old Order. That was what Riordan thought. *Riordan.* How long had we talked? I had no idea. An hour, two? And what was it about him? I thought about the storm petrels, and the *Lurline* coming in, and the way he had looked at me. Everything was coming together, from so many different directions. I walked past two sandwich shops before I remembered I needed to eat.

That night I sat up reading back numbers of the *New Republic* and *Solidarity* and the *Industrial Worker*, all of which were reporting on the Marchant case in Oakland, California.

Faith came in at midnight and found me sitting up in bed, the magazines spread on the counterpane. She picked up a copy of *Solidarity*. Her fingernails were browned by chemicals in the developer. "You could be arrested just for reading this," she sighed, sinking down in the chair beside my bed.

"You smell like the darkroom," I said, handing her a bottle of Hind's honey-almond cream. 'Try this on your hands—it'll make you smell nicer."

"I'm so exhausted I don't even care how I smell," she said, yawning. "What's this all about?" she asked then, nodding at the magazines.

I started to tell her about the Marchant case, but her eyes were closing. "Go to bed, Faith," I said. "I'll tell you about it in the morning."

She pushed herself out of the chair, heavy with fatigue. At the door she paused and said, "This Riordan—you've run into him before?"

I reminded her of the day at the Hall of Justice.

"Oh yes, I remember now," she said, adding, "Is he handsome?"

"Very!" I laughed.

"Married?" was the next question.

I knotted a pair of stockings that were close at hand and threw them at her departing back.

"Pity!" she called, waving good night without looking back.

The next morning Faith wandered out of her bedroom just as I was leaving. Groggy with sleep, she was wrapped in a woolen bathrobe with an Indian blanket design.

"Wait a minute," she called after me. "You were going to tell me about that man Riordan."

"Nothing to tell," I called back. "Married, remember?"

She sighed and blew me a kiss that was meant to be consoling.

Walking down the hill, the fog blowing damp against my face, I thought: He *is* a puzzle, and the more I know about him, the more puzzling he becomes. Clearly his personal life is in disarray—his brother dead, he doesn't live with his family. Even his office had seemed stripped of anything that might reveal the man. Except for the storm petrels.

Then I told myself that it would not do to spend any more time pondering on the strange life of Jim Riordan. I was going to have to concentrate on the Marchant case.

They were already in a conference room at Riordan's law firm when I arrived, Agnes Marchant sitting in a chair at the end of a long, highly polished table that caught her reflection quite clearly, and Riordan leaning against the wall nearby, listening to her in that careful way he had. She sat erect, her shoulders squared. She was wearing a soft blouse caught at the neck by a cameo which had the look of an heirloom. She had dressed very carefully; a lace handkerchief was tucked into her sleeve. Her hair was iron gray, her nose long and straight and her eyes—to complete the picture of a strong, resolute woman—should have been sharp and piercing. But they weren't. Agnes Marchant's eyes were soft and gray and afraid.

"Agnes," Riordan said, turning to the older woman, "this is Miss Duer of the *Times*. Miss Duer, Miss Agnes Marchant."

I nodded, and she said wryly, "The defendant."

Riordan laughed, and so did I. Miss Agnes Marchant was afraid, but she still had a sense of humor. I am not sure what I expected; what I had not expected was this kindly-looking woman, a librarian, a lady who sat with her hands folded in her lap, her knees properly together. I could imagine her hands caressing a book, with neat precision pasting in the cards for the lending library, smiling as she handed the book over to a borrower. I could imagine her pouring tea from a Limoges pot or playing a pianoforte that had been brought around the Horn, or working in a rose garden. What I could not imagine was Agnes Marchant delivering a radical speech.

She answered my questions meticulously. "I voted against leaving the Socialist party," she said, "but I was in the minority. I have voted against all measures that in any way would condone violence."

Riordan removed himself; he stood for a time at the window; then he took a chair along the wall, but he was listening. And I was aware of him watching me, studying me. Once I caught his eye and he looked away.

She told me that the speech at the Hotel Oakland had been about conditions in California's migrant-labor camps, and about the plight of the families who traveled up and down the coast harvesting crops, living in rural squalor. The arrest came after someone in the audience asked if she was a member of the Communist party. She had answered truthfully, of course. That was when one Luther Milburn of the Oakland Police Neutrality Squad stepped forward to arrest her.

"Did you know, when the question was asked, that the police were in the audience, ready to arrest you?" I asked.

"Know?" she answered. "No, I didn't know . . . how could I have known?"

"Do you know the name of the man who asked if you were a member of the Communist party?"

"Why, no," she replied. "He was just . . . someone at the lecture, I think."

I looked at Riordan. His expression said, "You see?" I thought: Agnes Marchant will not be found innocent, but she is *an innocent*. And she is, under a thin facade of perfect manners, perfectly terrified. She also, I realized, had a child's faith in justice and the United States Constitution. And, I suspected, in Jim Riordan.

I thanked her, and said good-bye. Riordan excused himself and walked me to the elevator.

We walked down the empty hallway in silence. There was something he wanted to say to me, I was sure of it. About Agnes, and the story? Was he going to ask me to make some point? I hoped not; he had been so careful.

I waited for him to push the call button. When he didn't, I turned to face him. "Is there something?" I asked.

"No," he said. Then, "Yes."

We laughed, and he pressed the button.

"I hope to see you again," he said as the elevator doors began to open.

I stepped in, turned around, and as they closed I said, "I would like that."

That night I heated three large pots of water on the gas rings, dumped them into the bathtub along with lilac salts and just enough cold water to keep from scalding myself. I sank into the warmth and fragrance of the bath and sighed; it was exactly what I needed. There had been too much rush and hurry . . . Agnes Marchant. And Riordan. And Clive, no word in two weeks from Clive. There was too much to think about. I looked at my body, rubbed my hands against my thighs, white in the water, and remembered Riordan in his white shirt, creased by the laundryman's iron. "No," he had said; then, "Yes." I lay back in the warm water and breathed deeply and let the pleasure seep into me.

The telephone rang.

It couldn't be Faith; she had called to say she would be working late. It was past midnight. Who could be calling at this hour? I wouldn't answer it. No. "Call back tomorrow," I said out loud.

Still it rang. Five times, six . . . I did not want to leave the comfort of the water . . . eight times, nine . . .

An emergency? Grandmother? She hadn't been feeling well. I stood, worried now . . . grabbed a robe and wrapped it around me and slipped on the wet floor. I caught myself, it was still ringing . . . eleven times, twelve . . . My heart was pumping. *Don't stop now, please. . . .*

"Yes," I shouted into the receiver. "Yes? Hello?"

There was no sound.

"Who is it?" I said, trying to keep my voice under control. "Who's there?"

"Is this Sutter 128?" a man's voice said.

"Yes," I answered, wary. Something was wrong.

"Faith Moore, does she live there?" The voice was muffled.

"Yes," I said. "Are you calling for Faith? Has something happened to her?"

Silence. Then a click, and the wire went dead.

I was chilled now, wet and cold and worried. I dried myself and pulled on a flannel gown, all the while thinking . . . trying to remember. I called Faith at the studio. She was working in the darkroom; she wondered why I was up so late. I said it was nothing. I sat there then, thinking. Trying to remember. There was something about the voice . . .

Thayer Gerson. It was Thayer Gerson's voice.

The Marchant articles did not come easily. I struggled with the documentation, trying to give all the dry facts new life. I wrote and rewrote my description of Agnes, tracing her gradual move toward the political left, the people she found most concerned with the poor of this land. I wanted to write with enough clarity to make readers understand how the letter of the law was being used to punish many who were innocent. The articles were to carry my byline, so I could express opinions.

That was another thing that troubled me. I wanted to be certain they were my opinions, that I was not swayed by the Boss, or by Riordan. Or by the fact that I had liked Agnes Marchant.

I went over all of my notes, again and again, looking for some contradiction, some warning that I was off track. "This is a modern story," I began, "of how the niece of a United States Supreme Court justice appointed by Abraham Lincoln came to be accused of the crime of sedition."

The words began to come then, to tumble out all at once. I wrote as fast as I could, at times scribbling in shorthand, the ideas were coming so furiously. "How did it happen," I wrote, "that a member of the Oakland police department was in the audience that night, and that someone else rose to ask the damning question?"

I handed the last page of copy to the boy only minutes before the deadline. I hadn't the faintest notion if it was any good.

She said her name but it was not a good connection and I did not hear it. "I hope I am not disturbing you at your work," she went on, "but I did want to let you know how excellent your stories about the case have been. James is pleased, too. You make it all so clear—'a charade, a perversion of justice'—that is exactly right."

Agnes Marchant.

I smiled to myself. She had waited until all three articles appeared, not to seem to try to influence me.

"I've already spoken to Sanford," she went on, "and he told me it was all right to telephone you."

"I'm glad you did, Miss Marchant. And I hope the articles make people understand the issues involved in your case."

"Sometimes I *am* hopeful," she began, then paused. I waited for an awkward moment to see if she would continue. Finally she said, "I'm not at all sure it is appropriate to ask, but I would be very pleased if you could come for tea someday, if you would like, and if I'm not . . ."

"I would like that," I told her, remembering her eyes, ". . . now that I've finished the articles."

We agreed that I would come on Sunday at three. When I put the receiver back in its cradle, I sat wondering at the awful innocence of it: this woman, who was the central figure in a trial of national moment, a trial which could result in her being sent to prison for as many as fourteen years, had just invited me to tea.

On Saturday, a telegraph boy came into the newsroom shouting out, "Hallie Duer." I raised my hand, and he said, "Telegram from Chicago." From Chicago, from Clive. In my haste, I ripped the yellow envelope and part of the telegram. The words pasted on the sheet read: ARRIVE OAKLAND JULY 7 STOP HOPE FIND WORK STOP YOUR BROTHER.

My brother. Dear God, I still had a brother. *And he hoped to find work.* My teeth started to chatter; I was shivering so that I had to wrap my arms around myself and hold tight.

And then Harry's big hand was under my elbow, pushing me out of the office and down Market Street to John's Grill. "We'll get you some coffee and maybe even some brandy in it, before you shake to death."

He didn't ask, but I heard myself telling him . . . about the train station in Chicago, and all the years and all the letters, and how finally I had to do something. I sipped the coffee and felt the brandy warm my stomach, and when I finished talking Harry put his big hand over mine and his eyes glistened. I started to laugh then, and he did too, and John came over to where we were sitting and said, "What's so clucking funny, you ducks?" in his tough, rough style, and we only laughed harder. On the way back to the office I tucked my arm into Harry's and walked, in step. At the door of the *Times* I said, "Thanks." And he said, "For what?"

That evening Faith and I plotted. I would go to Julia Morgan first. She had already offered to help if Clive came out. I would call her for one of our "hard-boiled-egg-at-the-drafting-table" lunches, as she liked to call them. If Julia couldn't offer any encouragement, I would go to Sara. Sara knew every architect in the city. She would help, I was sure of it. But I hoped I didn't have to ask. Too many people came to Sara for favors. I did not want to be one of them. In spite of the differences in our ages, Sara and I had become friends. We saw each other once or twice each month, and spoke on the telephone often. Unlike most women her age, Sara loved to talk on the telephone.

Once, at a band concert in Golden Gate Park, we were stopped by a man who called Sara by name and demanded she give him five hundred dollars. He had invented a cardboard collar which he was certain would revolutionize the men's shirting industry. "Think of all the bachelors with no one to iron their collars!" he had said in deadly earnest. It was ludicrous and pathetic. I was appalled at the man's effrontery, and embarrassed, too, but Sara dispatched him in a practiced, even kindly, manner.

"Does this happen often?" I asked her, and she said, "It's one of the few disadvantages of having money. On the one hand, people give you an inordinate amount of *respect* just for possessing wealth—no matter how you came by it—but on the other hand, the other side of that so-called *respect* is envy, and not a little anger. They despise you for not sharing it. It gives one pause."

"I have heard," I told her, "that you give rather large sums to good causes, and that you go to quite a lot of trouble to conceal your involvement."

"Newspaper people are such gossips," she answered, rapping me lightly on the arm with her folded concert program.

I would ask Sara to help me find a job for Clive only if there was no other way.

My life seemed to be a series of long, somnolent periods interrupted by short bursts of action, after which nothing was ever the same. On Saturday, I knew I had entered such a period, that decisions were being made—by me and by others—that would change everything. I could feel it in my muscles, in my breathing, almost in the way the air seemed to move in the spaces about me. Whenever this happened, I would wake very early in the mornings—at that time when the birds are beginning to stir, making sharp, staccato calls. I would lie in bed in the calm of first light and think . . . about Riordan standing at the window, leaning against the frame, the angle of the light on his face . . . about Clive, telling Grandmother that he was leaving (had he told her yet? did she know?) . . . about the telephone call late in the night, and the voice of Thayer Gerson, the call I had not yet mentioned to Faith . . . about Agnes Marchant and what the day held in store, what new course would be set. . . .

Sunday morning, unable to stay in bed, I got up and dressed. It was not yet seven and I could not bring myself to wake Faith. We had been up late the night before, and she had been working so hard of late. I pulled on a heavy sweater and walking boots and climbed down the hill, walking the steep steps that led down to the wharf. A fine white mist cloaked the waterfront, making it seem snug and private. The city was sleeping, I saw no living being anywhere. I walked and walked, unwilling to turn back, breathing in the damp sweetness of the morning. After a time I found myself at the Matson slip, looking up at the sweeping white prow of the *Lurline*, and I felt exuberant. *Clive was coming* . . . the *Lurline* soared above me . . . *good things were happening* . . .

I decided to take the Model T to Oakland on the car ferry. It would be nice to go early and explore that East Bay city.

Agnes Marchant lived in the Victorian mansion her father had built on the shore of Lake Merritt—a great three-story white confection with a mansard roof, beautifully carved wooden doors, and etched-glass windows. The city had grown up around the Marchant house, but it retained its prominence, set as it was on several acres of green lawn that rolled gently to the edge of the lake. The live oak trees for which the city was named punctuated this grassy expanse, making it seem more a park than a lawn. As I pulled up the drive and parked my machine, I asked myself: *Is this the home of a syndicalist?* The absurdity of it made me laugh. I had come to take tea with a radical, a Red, a Wobbly sympathizer.

"Miss Marchant say you please to wait in parlor," a very small Chinese girl said, adding cheerfully, "She talk now with Luis about fix boat."

The parlor was dark. One by one, the girl pulled open the heavy velvet draperies, raising a stir of dust which swirled in the shafts of sunlight that flooded the room. It seemed to me, for one strange moment, as if a family had walked out of this room one evening thirty years ago, and no one had entered since. I took a seat on a Grecian couch upholstered in stiff horsehair and studied the room. In the corner nearest me, an etagere held small china statuary and seashells, including a chambered nautilus. In the far end of the room was a pianoforte, heavily gilded. (Had it come around the Horn? I would have to remember to ask.) There was a secretary, covered with a thin film of dust. (Who were Agnes Marchant's friends? Surely the Wobblies did not come to tea.) The only evidence of Agnes Marchant's politics was several pamphlets scattered on a side table—*Red Dawn* by Harrison George and the January issue of *One Big Union Monthly*. Had I come here before I wrote the articles on the Marchant case, would I have included that? "In her genteel family home on the shores of Lake Merritt, Agnes Marchant reads syndicalist literature as her capitalist father and DAR mother frown down from their portraits above the mantel."

"I am sorry to have kept you waiting," she said, bustling into the room. "I had meant to meet you at the door and it really is very rude of me not to, your coming all this way. Did you take the streetcar from the ferry?" She did not wait for an answer, but rushed on, "You see, along with this monstrous house I have inherited a yard man who won't take orders because he knew me when I was just a girl, as he continually reminds me. No matter that he was only fifteen when he came to work for my father, and I was eight. I've just spent two weeks trying to convince him to open the old boathouse and make the sailboat seaworthy. He's just now putting the finishing touches on the rigging, and not a moment too soon—James and the children should be here any minute."

James and the children.

"Do you mean James Riordan, your lawyer?" I asked.

She clasped her hands together and gave me a radiant smile. "Yes," she said, as she might have said "amen." She sat down, folded her hands and told me, "I'm afraid Luis has rattled me. Let me catch my breath and explain. Some time ago James mentioned to me that as a boy he was very fond of sailing, and that he felt badly that his children had not had an opportunity to learn. He has a boy, Michael, who is thirteen, a girl, Kathleen, who is twelve, and a younger boy, Colin—I believe he is about ten. I thought about our old sailboat, and it seemed to me that getting it back into the water again was something I might do for James. He has been so very generous with his time and attention, you know. But I won't talk about the case—I'm determined that today is for pleasure. At any rate, Luis did get the boat in surprisingly good repair. I told James, and he called this morning to see if it would be a good day for him to bring the children. I hope you don't mind."

"It's a perfect day," I said, "sunshine and a brisk little wind."

"Perhaps you would like to sail too?" she asked encouragingly.

"I'm afraid I'm a poor sailor," I told her, "but I will like being outdoors, watching from the lawn."

She was sitting opposite me, perched on the edge of a side chair in white muslin and white stockings: a ladies' sailing dress, a bit old-fashioned and very proper. She seemed correct in this setting, safe in the elaborately carved little chair. An automobile stopped in the street outside. Agnes moved to the window. "Here they are," she said. "They've taken a taxi from the ferry." She turned back to me. "How did you come, by the way?"

"I drove. That's my Model T in the front drive."

"How clever of you!" she said, delighted. "Imagine that, driving a machine. Perhaps you can take the Riordans back to the ferry with you? I'm sure they would be ever so pleased."

I waited in the parlor, listening to the introductions. His voice was low, easy, as he introduced the children; then Agnes was herding them into the parlor. "Come and see who is here, James," she said.

Riordan tightened. He recovered enough to greet me politely, at the same time pulling the girl and the smaller of the boys to him in a gesture that was awkwardly protective.

"Miss Duer, Kathleen . . ." He went through the motions of introductions. She was tall and pale, and was wearing a shapeless dress that was faded but freshly laundered and ironed. She could scarcely lift her eyes to mine.

"And Michael," Riordan went on. Michael was tall and dark. He looked more like his father than the others, and would have been handsome except for the stubborn set of his face.

"And this is Colin," Riordan finished.

"I know your friend Bryan McConaughey," I told him.

"How do you know Bryan?" he asked. "He lives in the city."

"So do I," I answered, smiling at the child's big smile, the too-large teeth.

"Miss Duer is a newspaperwoman, Colin," his father broke in. "She works with Bryan's father."

"The Real McCoy!" Colin yelped, and everyone except Michael laughed. Michael had stepped back, separating himself from the group. His eyes wandered around the room.

"Let's be off, there's sailing to do while the sun's out," Agnes announced, ushering us through the hallways of the great house and into a large side porch where tea would be served later. Now there was lemonade and cookies, and a newly cut lawn that smelled of fresh grass, and sun glinting off the water.

The sailboat was tied to a dock, and a small dark man was busying himself beside it. Riordan and Agnes and the boys trailed down to the water's edge, while Kathleen and I spread a tarpaulin in the sundappled shade of a great oak.

I studied the girl as we went about our job. She was slight. Her hair was pulled back in braids that she had, I was sure, plaited herself, since they did not lie neatly on her back, but were pulled forward from an uneven part in the back. I thought of my mother's hands threading through my hair, brushing and gently twining the strands into braids. And then it had been my grandmother's hands, in that same gentle, caressing way, matching ribbons to dresses, blue to go with the blue-and-yellow flowered pinafore, and red to wear with the summer white voile. There were no ribbons in Kathleen Riordan's hair; her braids were tied with bits of string.

I remembered what Thelma had said: *There is no laughter in that house*. I felt an irresistible urge to make this child laugh. We worked together, smoothing the tarpaulin. I was on my knees, reaching for a corner. I turned and looked at her until she looked back. I smiled.

She looked away, but her lips turned up at the corners very slightly. A few delicate blue veins scattered under the transparent skin of her forehead, and there was a very tiny scar above her lip.

"How old are you, Kathleen?" I asked.

"Twelve, ma'am," she whispered, too shy to speak out loud.

"Well, I'm twenty-six, which is more than twice as old as you are, but I'd like it if you would call me Hallie, all the same. All the McConaughey kids do."

I didn't expect an answer, and I didn't get one. We settled on the tarpaulin and studied the scene on the dock. Riordan was wearing white duck trousers and a loose sailing shirt. In spite of his limp, he moved easily about the dock and the boat. He was, clearly, competent in that world. Luis was standing now, talking to Riordan—ignoring Agnes, who stood nearby. After a while Agnes disappeared into the boathouse. Riordan climbed into the sailboat and held it against the dock while Colin scrambled in and then, stiffly, Michael. Michael settled himself as far from his father as he could, his arms at his sides, clearly a passenger.

Riordan pushed off, maneuvering the boat easily into the lake, turning to catch the breeze—the sun lit his face as the sails billowed. I thought of the sweep of the *Lurline*, the grace of the prow, and felt my breath catch.

Kathleen shifted uncomfortably, worried, perhaps, that she should be carrying on a conversation with me.

"Michael didn't want to come sailing today, did he?" I asked.

I caught her by surprise. "How do you know?" she asked, flicking a wary look at me.

"Oh, just the way he is sitting in the sailboat—so polite and stiff and . . ." I stopped myself from saying "unhappy."

"Michael wanted to go to church with Mama," the girl said. "Michael is going to be a priest."

I pulled a clover out of the grassy lawn, careful to trace its long stem before plucking it, so I could tie it to another clover and make a chain. There was nothing to say about Michael. *His wife and now his son.* I looked at the man in the sailboat, deftly turning, bringing it about as the sails luffed. He brought it neatly to the dock, where Michael climbed out. Riordan followed, leaving Colin in the boat, waiting.

Michael walked to the end of the dock and sat down, his back to us. Riordan followed him, leaned down, they spoke for a few minutes. Then Riordan turned, shouted something to Colin and began walking toward us.

"He's going to want me to go sailing now," Kathleen said, a note of panic in her voice.

"Don't you want to go?" I asked.

"No," she said vehemently. "No, I do not."

I turned to look at her. She dropped her eyes. She was shaking.

"If you don't want to go, you don't have to," I said as simply as I could. "I'm certain your father will understand."

"He'll understand," she said, her voice shaking, "but I'll disappoint him. Michael has disappointed him already."

She wanted me to rescue her, to give her an excuse. "Sometimes,"

I said, "it is perfect just to sit in the sun and make clover chains and keep someone else company. I have a feeling that your father loves sailing so much that if he thinks you are content right here, with me, he won't be disappointed."

Her eyes found a point on my shoulder and moved up to my face. "I'm afraid to go," she confessed, quickly lowering her eyes.

Riordan stopped to talk to Agnes, who had just emerged from the boathouse. She went to join Michael on the dock—always the thoughtful hostess—and Riordan came up the lawn toward us.

"Can you keep a secret, Kathleen?" I asked, and when she nodded I told her, "I'm afraid too—of boats and lakes. I could never go out there today, and I would like it if you stayed with me."

She turned now; her eyes held mine. "You aren't just . . ."

"No," I told her, Riordan almost within hearing, "I'm not just saying it. I am very afraid of boats."

"Are you ladies coming sailing?" he called, limping gracefully. "It's a tight craft and there's a dandy breeze." As if to prove him right, the breeze lifted a silk scarf tied loosely around my shoulders, up, and over my face. As I brushed it back, he stood smiling down on us. The sun was behind him; I raised my face, shielded my eyes so that I could see him. I felt the heat of the sun caressing me, felt his eyes on me.

Kathleen spoke in a voice firmer than I thought she could possibly possess. "Not this time, Daddy. We're having such a nice time sitting here, making clover chains and watching you sail—you must sail all you like!"

The words were false-hearty, and clearly planned. Riordan knew; there was a mix of amusement and affection in the way he looked at her. "Are you sure?" he said. "I think you would like it if you would just give it a go . . ."

"We're sure," she said, answering for me again. Protecting me—and thus, herself. Then, as if she couldn't bear not to give him some hope, she said, "Maybe next time."

"Next time for certain," he said to her, only glancing at me.

I grinned up at him, and shrugged. He stood with his hands on his hips. He moved to put his own shadow between me and the sun, so that I was not blinded and could see him clearly.

"I'm glad you're having a nice time, Kathleen," he said, speaking to his daughter but looking at me.

When he left, she said to me, "I don't think he minded too much," and I agreed. For a while I said nothing, so many thoughts were racing through my head. I had never met anyone, it seemed to me, so complex as this man, James Francis, Jimmy, Kathleen's father. He made me feel awkward, off balance, unsure.

Kathleen's question jolted me. "Is it only boats that you're afraid of?"

"And lakes," I added, "but ferryboats don't bother me. This morning I walked down to the docks and got a close view of the *Lurline*, the big white Matson cruise ship. I wondered what it would be like to travel all the way to the Hawaiian Islands on it. I've always wanted to go to the Hawaiian Islands."

She looked at me, no longer shy at meeting my glance. "My father took a trip on a boat when he went to the war."

"Did he?" I asked, pleased that she wanted to talk.

She nodded. "Colin keeps asking him about the soldiers and guns and all, but he doesn't like to talk about it. Daddy told me once that he was scared, though."

He knows how frightened she is, then.

"I think everybody is afraid of something, and if they're honest, they own up to it," I said. "Your father, in the war, had every reason to be afraid."

She was intent on separating blades of grass, pulling them out one by one and laying them in a row on the tarpaulin, where the breeze riffled and scattered them.

"But what if you don't have a reason? What if you're just . . . afraid?"

She lifted her eyes to mine; they were wide, steady. She wanted an answer and she thought I might have one.

"When I was about your age," I told her, "somebody told me that if I was going to be afraid of everything out-of-doors, then I would just have to stay in the house all the time. I think I was afraid of everything that year. I remember at night, the wind would blow a tree outside my window, and a shadow would be cast on the wall opposite my bed. There would be these awful, fearsome shapes moving on the wall." I smiled at her conspiratorially. "That was when I decided that if I could be so scared inside the house, I might as well go out and see the rest of the world."

She was about to say something when Agnes joined us, carrying a tray of lemonade and cookies. "Michael's taking a walk along the lakeshore," she said, handing me the tray as she settled herself on the tarpaulin next to Kathleen. "And it looks to me as if young Colin is going to become the next sailor in the family."

"Kathleen's been nice enough to keep me company," I explained to our hostess. "We're both a little timid about boats and water, if the truth be known."

Agnes busied herself pouring lemonade. "I was always timid about trains. Even streetcars make me nervous, they're so noisy and clattering and all . . . but boats, oh my! I suppose it's because I grew up with them here on the lake—I've spent so much time poking around this lake . . . my, yes." She sighed and looked out to where Riordan and Colin were tacking, the sails taut and white against the blue. She went on: "If you asked me where the safest place in the world was, I would have to say right out there in the middle of that lake in a boat. As a child I spent hours out there—reading and dreaming. Sometimes I would fall asleep, and Father would have to come out with his bullhorn—I can still hear his voice echoing over the water . . . AG . . . NESSS . . ." She laughed and patted Kathleen's stockinged leg and said, "But I am still afraid of those dreadful streetcars."

When Agnes left to see about tea, we sat in silence for a time. I looked at the boat. Colin was at the rudder, his father watching; the wind had picked up and they were moving silently across the wide expanse of the lake.

"Do you really drive a motorcar?" Kathleen asked.

"I do," I told her, "and I'm hoping you'll trust me enough as a driver to let me take you—and your father and brothers—back to the ferry."

She smiled at me with such delight that I knew I had pleased her. "I would trust you," she said, her voice small and intimate.

"Good," I said, but I could not look at her. I could not see her eyes because I knew they would be my own, full of fear and longing, all the tears trapped in a subterranean pool, too deep ever to flow to the surface.

Riordan found me on the upper deck of the ferry, standing at the railing. I knew he was there, behind me, before he said anything. "You've made a conquest of the Riordan children," he began, "even Michael, when you fixed your Model T with that baling wire."

I turned to face him. This time I would not look away. "I've learned to take care of myself," I said firmly. "I drove that machine over more back country roads than I care to remember, and it broke down regularly. As my grandfather told me, 'If you're going to keep company with one of those critters, you'd best tame it.'"

He grinned down at me. "Is that what your grandfather told you?" he teased.

We laughed then. *Oh, Lord*, I thought. What had I said? *Keeping company, keeping company with . . .*

"You tamed it, all right," he added, touching my arm with his fingertips. I had a sudden urge to lean into him, to feel my face against his jacket . . .

"Daddy," Kathleen called, running to us. He pulled her to him; the wind was rising off the water and the child was shivering. She looked up, shy and adoring. "Do you think," she said to him, "that sometime you could take Hallie and me in the sailboat? Maybe not far from the shore, maybe for just a little ride?"

He looked at her. "You and Hallie?" he said, his voice tender. It was the first time he had said my name.

"She said I could call her that," Kathleen told him, burying her face in his coat.

He pulled her close and said, "All you have to do is ask."

NINE

FREDDIE ZEBRA was one of the Boss's Lost Souls. Freddie's name referred to the prison stripes he had worn for thirty-odd years. His aliases were legend; no one knew his real name. When Freddie was released from San Quentin two years before, he went to work doing odd jobs around the paper. Soon he was running errands for the city's hotels. Freddie knew every desk clerk, every bellhop and every garage attendant in town. He also knew every bootlegger and every bookmaker. It was Freddie who volunteered to show me the ropes on the hotel beat. From the hotel manager's office I would get a neatly typed copy of the week's schedule, anemic with society parties and conventions, club meetings and banquets. From Freddie's people I could learn what important actors or actresses were staying under what names, who came to the parties they threw, what politician or famous lawyer or judge was seen coming and going, what showgirl had been invited to what room. Freddie knew most of the showgirls in town—those who performed in theaters and those who didn't. They were a bright, breezy group dressed in the latest short dresses, having forsaken corsets altogether, their hair bobbed and even, sometimes, colored in remarkable hues. Long-legged and invariably laughing, at least when they were in groups. When they came bubbling through hotel lobbies, all the staid businessmen and local ladies in town for lunch would turn and look, and pretend to look away. They did not approve, but they could not resist watching the bright-bauble flow through the lobby.

Each day I stopped first at the Palace, which was closest to the office. Then I made my way over to Union Square and the St. Francis. The cable car took me to the corner of California and Powell, where I would hop off to enter the Fairmont from the garage, and ride the elevator to the entrance on Mason Street, where I could cross over to the Mark Hopkins. That took a good part of the morning; in the afternoon I covered as many of the lesser hotels as I could. One bit of information I picked up my third day on the hotel beat: James Francis Riordan occupied a suite of rooms in the Chancellor.

At first it was fascinating to watch a guest pass a five-dollar bill to a bell captain, utter a few discreet words and presumably get whatever it was he wanted. Liquor was no problem, neither were women or gambling. San Francisco had never been accused of being innocent, as Freddie liked to tell me. He would always add, "You shoulda seen it in the old days." The view from the hotel lobby was enough for me, especially with Freddie Zebra translating.

Soon enough the beat became what every reporter had told me it would be: routine and dull. I would call in my stories, spelling out the names of women's groups and men's fraternal societies and winners of the annual Daughters of the Golden West award. Most of the material Freddie's friends fed me could not be used in the paper, but I always wrote it down anyway. The very act of taking their words and putting them on paper pleased the bellhops and clerks. They seemed not to mind that their words never saw print; after a while I decided they never read the paper. Perhaps they assumed it was all there.

At the end of each day I came back to the city room, wrote

up what I could and, on my way out, stopped to ask Gwen if I had missed any messages. After a while she gave me one of her famous vulture stares and said: "I wish whoever you're waiting for would call and put both our minds at rest."

I was waiting for a call from Riordan. It had been three weeks since the Sunday-afternoon sailing party at Agnes Marchant's. Twice since that day I had been to see Agnes—in part because I liked her, but also because of the contradictions. The Agnes I had met, interviewed, spent a charming afternoon with at her home by the lake was not the historical Agnes, the one who was right now at the center of a raging political storm. That was the Agnes I wanted to discover. I arranged to meet her at the library where she worked. We sat together in a little anteroom off the reading hall.

"I came to believe," she said, her hands folded in her lap, "that many Americans feel disdain for the desperately poor among us. I mean that—disdain. Not sympathy, as one would suppose. But disdain, as if the poor were an affront. And the poor, who have nothing at all, are made to feel that they have no right to live and breathe or even show themselves. That they are worthless. I saw it in the slums of New York, and here in California in the migrant camps.

"Those migrant families do valuable work, of course. Long, hard hours. The children, too, work with their parents in the fields. But again, there was this attitude—that the workers were an affront, that they should be hidden away, out of view. I thought about it a great deal, my dear. And I came to believe that it is the feelings that must be changed before anything can be done. The poor must not be seen as a plague. And they must not be allowed to feel that they are worthless. We must change the way the poor feel about themselves before we can change the conditions they live in. Once I understood, I began to look for a way to take action. The Socialists provided it. I allied myself with the IWW because they had a plan for farm workers which I believed would improve the lot of the migrants. I also believed it was my constitutional right to do this, in the land of the free and the home of the brave." She patted my hand, as if to emphasize the irony. "Does that help you understand what has gone on in this old gray head?"

I came back the following Monday, on Agnes' afternoon off. She was in the rose garden, on her hands and knees. "Did you bring your machine?" she asked. When I said yes, she stood, brushing the dirt from her hands and said, "Good. Would you mind driving me across town to take some cuttings to an old friend? We can talk on the way. And who knows? Perhaps today you will find that revolutionary you've been after."

It was at that moment, I believe, that we became friends.

Friday I called Riordan. When he came on the line I was ready: "I understand there is another delay in the Marchant case—and this time the government is asking for it. Why?"

He didn't answer right away. He wanted to know how I had been, he wanted to tell me how much Kathleen had enjoyed meeting me. He wanted to talk a little first. He was, I was certain, weighing how much he would tell me. Eventually he came back to Agnes. "The reason for the delay," he explained, "is that the government has a couple of 'professional witnesses'—former IWW members who go around the country testifying against Wobblies in trials like Agnes'. These witnesses are tied up just now back East, testifying in another trial, and the government can't get them here in time, so they've asked for a postponement."

"And you agreed?" I asked, surprised. "Wouldn't it have been better to push for a quick trial, so they can't testify at all?"

He paused. "Are we talking now as friends of Agnes Marchant, or are we talking as reporter and defense attorney?"

I hesitated. I would have to be careful. "As friends," I finally said.

"Good," he answered, "because Agnes is going to need all of her friends." He went on to say that he would take every delay he could get, that time was the single best hope. He said that the longer they could keep the case in the courts, the better. "The temper of the country needs to change," he said. "Some very bad laws have to be struck down, and they will be when people come to their senses." Until then, he wanted only to keep Agnes out of jail.

I struggled to think of what to say. "How will she manage?" I started. "It's hard on her now, the not knowing. She needs for it to be over." I heard a pleading note in my voice, and was surprised.

He said, speaking deliberately, "It's better than being locked in a cage, and that's what prisons are. Cages."

I felt sick inside. "Isn't there a chance of acquittal?"

"You're a reporter—that should mean you are also a realist," he answered.

"Riordan," I replied, "she really is an innocent."

"An innocent caught in what amounts to a reign of terror. She has no close relatives, you know. Only a few cousins who seem more interested in the house than in Agnes."

I told him I had seen her twice since the sailing afternoon and that she had, on my last visit, confided some of her fears. He was silent; there was nothing to say.

He cleared his throat as if to signal a change of subject. "There is something I promised Kathleen I would ask you," he began, then hesitated. "I hope you will understand. She is very young, and sometimes she doesn't—"

"She's a lovely child," I interrupted. "I enjoyed being with her."

"Yes, well," he went on, "what I am trying to say—and not doing a very good job of it—is that Kathleen took your remark about wanting to see her again to heart. I've tried to explain how busy you are, how little free time you must have, but she is persistent . . ."

I felt pleased and concerned at once. "I meant it," I told him. "I would like to see Kathleen again sometime."

Sometime. He knew what I meant—not now, but *sometime.* "I'll tell her," he answered, his voice accepting the rebuff.

"Perhaps she might like to meet me at the paper some Saturday," I heard myself saying. "Occasionally I get the afternoon off." It would be complicating, seeing Kathleen. Perhaps it would be better avoided. Then I remembered her question: "What if you don't have a reason, what if you're just afraid?" *As if I had the answer, as if I knew.*

"As a matter of fact, I'm going to be free this Saturday afternoon—tomorrow," I told him. "If that isn't too soon, I would love to see Kathleen."

He was wary now, considering. "I'll have to see," he said. "Is there someplace I could reach you this evening?"

When the telephone rang at about eight, I steeled myself.

Riordan's voice sounded concerned. "Is anything wrong?" he asked.

I tried to laugh. "I always sound angry on the telephone," I told him, "a bad habit I've picked up at the paper."

"It wasn't . . ." he began; then he said, "I've spoken to Kathleen, and she talked to her mother and it is arranged. Kathleen will take the streetcar to your office tomorrow and meet you in the lobby at noon, if that's all right with you. Then you can tell me where to meet you so I can take her home."

I would have to be careful. Don't offer to drive her home, I told myself. Let him make those arrangements. She was his child, his and Mary Margaret's. "I thought we might go to a two-a-day—there's a new Fatty Arbuckle movie at the Granada, with the vaudeville show. Then we could have supper at Leighton's Cafeteria, if that's all right. I haven't been there, but I'm told you take a plate and circle around a table full of food and take what you want." I paused, then added, "Would you like to meet us there?" I asked. "Perhaps you could join us for supper?"

"I'll be waiting outside the theater," he answered.

When I checked the lobby at noon she was there, sitting very straight, her hands gripping the marble bench.

"She's been waiting for twenty minutes," the elevator man whispered, "poor little thing."

Her dress was the same shapeless one she had worn to Agnes's. "Kathleen," I called out to her, "you're here! And we have a beautiful day, and I, for one, am ready for some fun."

She smiled and said, in a voice that cracked, "Me too."

"There is one thing I would like to do first. I'd like to go home to change my dress. If you don't mind, that is. Then I thought we could come back downtown to a moving picture and a show—and your father is going to meet us for some supper."

She nodded and smiled.

"Do you come downtown by yourself very often?" I asked as we walked down Market Street.

"Last week was the first time," she told me. "I came down to Daddy's office on the Judah line. And today again." It was a long speech for Kathleen, but she continued, "Do you remember what Miss Marchant said about being afraid of streetcars?" I said I did. "Well," she went on, "I didn't say so, but I was afraid too. So I asked Daddy if I could come downtown by myself, and he said he'd meet me at the Ferry Building." She paused. "He was right there when I got off, and he brought me a bouquet of daisies."

I took her hand and squeezed it. "He's a nice man, your father." She nodded, and held on to my hand.

I took her to the cottage because we had several hours before the second matinee and because I wanted to change my clothes and brush my hair with more care than I had been able to give it that morning. We stopped at Martinelli's market and had Tony make us two sandwiches. The day was warm enough to sit in the back garden.

Kathleen perched primly on the edge of an old rattan chair, eating her sandwich with precision, all the while letting her eyes roam over the tangled garden. I could almost feel the thoughts that crowded her mind. She wanted to talk to me, I knew that. And I knew she could not find the words to begin, so I gave them to her.

Settling comfortably back into my chair, I began to ask questions. She answered, haltingly at first, telling me about school, about the sisters who taught her—the ones she liked and the ones she didn't. About her friends and her brothers. She did not mention her mother, nor did I. We talked instead about songs, about movies, and the words started to come . . . She loved math and hated sewing, especially embroidery, which was the bane of her current existence. She found history exciting, especially modern history—like the war—but she hated penmanship. She loved French and she loved stickball, when the boys would let her play.

We found we both loved parades, and fresh baked buns and oyster cakes and Fatty Arbuckle and Mabel Normand. And we hated the smell of cabbage cooking, and the look of calf's liver. In a short time she was sitting with her legs tucked under her, one finger distractedly picking up the crumbs left from her sandwich, dreamily talking about her friend Emma, who had never once been on a streetcar all by herself, who could not in a million years imagine how Kathleen could come into the city—all alone—to meet someone and go to a show and to supper.

I changed into my new costume, which I had pressed and made ready the night before: a straight skirt of the shorter length with a loose slipover jumper of knitted jersey wool, and a matching cardigan. The skirt was a soft gray wool, the jumper and cardigan were gray with buff stripes. I had buff shoes to match, with gray lisle stockings. I brushed my hair and tucked it into a tight knot.

"I'm ready," I called to Kathleen, who was examining our little sitting room.

She studied me. "You look beautiful," she said, so solemnly I had to laugh.

"So do you," I told her.

"No, I don't," she came back.

"Are we going to have an argument?" I asked.

The question struck her as funny. She laughed, a lovely bubbling child's laugh. "No," she said.

"Wait," I told her, and disappeared into Faith's room, where I rummaged through her sewing box until I found a length of blue silk ribbon. I cut two pieces.

Her braids had been fastened with twine. I tied the ribbons carefully. "There," I said, "they match the color of your eyes. Which, by the way, are beautiful."

We went swinging down the hill together, Kathleen and I, buoyant with the pleasure of the afternoon that was before us. I could not imagine anyone thinking of her as a sad child.

Wait, something in me warned. Remember, she is Riordan's child, and Mary Margaret's, who scrubs the church steps every morning.

As we cut across Washington Square, I happened to notice the little Antonelli girl, notorious in the neighborhood for her habit of wandering away from home. (Her mother would lean out the window and shout "Ma-ri-a.") We paused long enough to find an older boy to take Maria home to her mother.

"Did you ever do that?" Kathleen asked as we waited for the streetcar.

"Run away from home?" I asked. "No, sometimes I stayed out later than I was supposed to. Once, when I was in high school, I stayed overnight with one of my friends so I could go to a revival tent meeting."

"Didn't you tell your parents?" she asked.

"Yes," I said, "after it was all over. I told my grandparents. I finally felt so badly about not telling them, I thought it would be easier to take my punishment."

I could see that she wanted to ask and that she didn't know if she should. I told her, as briefly as I could, how I had come to live with my grandparents. It wouldn't do to say too much. I did not want her to tell me about her parents, about why her father did not live with them. He would be meeting us soon. I would not want to hear, from her, anything he would not want me to know.

We arrived at Powell and Market with an hour to spare

173

before the matinee. "Let's drop by Faith's studio," I suggested. "It isn't far, and she would like to meet you." The "Closed" sign was in the window. "She's in the darkroom," I explained. "She said she would be there all afternoon. We'll have to ring the bell, but sometimes it takes a few minutes for her to open the door. If she's in the midst of developing or printing, she can't always stop right away." We waited. I rang again, thinking that maybe she hadn't heard. After a few minutes it seemed clear that Faith wasn't in the darkroom after all. I was sorry; I had wanted her to meet Kathleen.

Fatty Arbuckle was her favorite moving-picture actor. "He's not really fat, you know," she told me, "he's just big, and funny. You should see some of the things he can do—jumping and turning somersaults and hanging from buildings. Michael says you really have to be a good athlete to do all of those things."

There was a full orchestra and a vaudeville show that included a dog act, which pleased Kathleen, and then we settled down to see Arbuckle in a new five-reeler called *Brewster's Millions*. The gentle clown, in one scene, was dressed in a baby's nightgown and bonnet and brandished a huge rattle, and he had both of us giggling and gasping for breath.

Coming out of the dark theater, we were blinded by the light. Then I saw Riordan leaning against the wall, waiting for us. Kathleen raced for him and threw her arms around his waist. He was not expecting such a jubilant welcome. He looked at me, and caressed her.

We walked down Market Street, the child between us talking, telling her father about the movie, about the dog act, repeating the funny stories the comedian had told. The shy girl, talking now, at ease with her father and with me.

But he was not at ease and neither was I. He was, however, surprised. I had the feeling that this Kathleen—laughing, animated—was new to him.

"Do you like my hair ribbons?" she asked in a sudden switch

of subjects. "Hallie gave them to me. She says they're the color of my eyes exactly."

"I do like them," he answered, touching her hair, "and Hallie is right. They are the color, exactly."

He looked at me then, and shook his head and smiled to show his amazement, then quickly shifted his attention back to the child.

At the cafeteria we carried our plates around an enormous table filled with food, and chose what we wanted and laughed at the novelty of it. Kathleen positioned herself between us at the table. She was in charge; we waited to follow her lead. In the background an orchestra played Strauss waltzes. It is the only detail I remember. I don't know what I ate, or what the big room looked like except that it had chandeliers which glittered. I don't remember all that Kathleen said, except that she reminded her father he had promised to take us sailing. I only remember being there, with them, knowing I should not like it so much. They walked me to my streetcar, and when it came Riordan put his hand on my arm to help me up, and I could feel the pressure of it—his hand on my arm—all the way home.

When I stepped out of the cottage early the next morning I almost stumbled over the package. It was wrapped roughly in newspaper and tied with butcher's twine. I opened it to find Kathleen's blue hair ribbons, the ones I had given her, crumpled into an ugly wad.

TEN

RIORDAN'S VOICE on the telephone was friendly; he was pleased I had called, which meant he didn't know about the package. I told him as dispassionately as I could, not wanting him to guess how it had shaken me.

"I was away all day yesterday," he said. "I haven't spoken to Kathleen." Then: "Let me get to the bottom of this. I'll call you as soon as I can—but it may be a day or two."

I felt strangely relieved. It was in Riordan's hands now, and he would set things right. *He was a man who could be trusted to set things right.*

I went to the supply cabinet, took out two new pads, sharpened several pencils and was putting on my hat when the Boss stepped out of his office and waved his cigar at me.

"How's the legwoman?" he joked as I moved a stack of galleys so I could sit on the only chair in the room. "Still happy with the hotel beat?"

I made a face and he laughed.

"I know," I said, "you told me so—everybody told me—but I seem to have this need to find things out for myself."

He lit one of his five-cent Owls and a trail of smoke drifted about his head. "Harry's stories will be coming in over the wire starting tomorrow. He's had a week to cover the two training camps. We'll be doing what every other paper in the country will do—cover this fight the week before and the week after until I hope everybody has their fill of it." He stopped to take a few draws on his cigar, which seemed to have gone out. "Ham will be in charge, and he's asked to have you pulled off your beat to help with the rewrite on this Fight of the Century story."

I said I wouldn't mind a bit.

"You know," he went on, pulling still on the stubborn cigar, "Harry brought up the idea of sending you back East too—to do the kind of feminine view of the fights that Sophie Treadwell is doing for the *New York Tribune*."

"And Annie Farrell for the *Examiner*," I put in.

He only nodded and went on, "I wish we could have done it— especially with Dempsey saying you could do a feature. But we had to lease a special wire and hire a telegrapher, and you know what our budget is like."

"I know," I said, trying not to let him see how much I had wanted to go to New Jersey. "I'll go tell Ham I'm signing on to stand by for the fight stories. If I know Harry, we won't have much to do in the way of rewrite. His stories usually go straight from the wire to the pressroom."

I stood, thinking the Boss was finished, but he motioned me to sit down. "There's another feature story I'd like you to think about." He cleared his throat, and seemed to be considering how to start. "In the past year—or the past seven months, maybe . . ." He was stumbling and at the same time trying to light his cigar. "Here, read this," he said, handing me a paper with a story circled in red. I scanned the lead: *Seventeen-year-old Maude Bentmuller died while under anesthetic given preparatory to an attempt to perform a criminal operation, according to Dr. J . D. Hegen, county coroner.*

"Criminal operation" was a euphemism; no newspaper could print the word "abortion."

"It seems to me," the Boss said, regaining his voice, "that I've seen a number of those stories coming out of Modesto, and the Wexford Hotel has figured in more than one of them."

"Do you think Modesto is some sort of a center for these . . ." I hesitated, then said it: "abortions?"

"That's what I would like for you to find out—if you want to."

My mind was racing. "I would have to go as someone who needed an operation, if I expected to get any kind of a story . . . then, if I could promise confidentiality . . ."

"I don't know," he said, frowning. "We are talking about people who are breaking laws that touch on the very essence of life. I'm not certain . . ."

He was beginning to talk himself out of the idea. To stop him I said, "Let me think about it. I'm not sure either, but there may be a way. If you don't feel there is any great hurry . . ."

"Check with me before you do anything. Agreed?"

I agreed, and left for my rounds of hotels. I didn't get to the Fairmont until about two that afternoon. I collected my information and sat on one of the soft plush settees in the vast lobby to make notes. "The Daughters of the Golden West have honored their outgoing president at a luncheon," I began. On the periphery of my vision I noticed Leon Jeevers, the house detective, shuffling purposefully in the direction of the marble staircase. Turning my attention to those stairs, I watched a young woman make her way down them. She was blond, and wore a flowered dress which clung to her, swaying as she swayed. I was on my feet and walking as fast as I could without breaking into a run. The three of us came together at the foot of the staircase.

Just as Leon grabbed her by the arm, I called out, "Miss Conlon, you're late! We've probably lost our reservations."

Leon dropped her arm and turned to look at me. "You know her?" he demanded, confused.

"Yes I do," I said, trying for the right mix of indignation and surprise. "I've been waiting for Miss Conlon here. But you saw me."

We hurried out the door together, Babe Conlon walking so fast that I had to double skip to keep up. She didn't stop until we were halfway down the hill. Then she turned and faced me.

"Okay, thanks," she said, as if it hurt.

"You're welcome," I told her.

"Yeah?" was her reply. "Why's that?"

I laughed outright then, and her face finally cracked into a smile.

"I mean it, kid," she said, "thanks."

"How about lunch?" I asked, "to keep me an honest woman, as it were."

Her look was pure brass and bold. "You buy," she said. "I'm broke."

"How can you be broke?" I wondered.

She didn't even hesitate: "He wrote me a check."

We ate at a minuscule Chinese restaurant tucked away in a basement off Grant Avenue, the kind of place that has about three individual booths, each with a flowered curtain that can be drawn for privacy. It was Babe Conlon's choice.

While she ate, I talked. I told her what had happened to me since I left Sacramento. She nodded and listened as she wielded her chopsticks, popping morsels of pork and green pepper and snow peas into her mouth. I decided not to ask any questions; they would, I felt sure, scare her off. But when she finished she wiped her mouth with a napkin, took a brown cigarette out of her bag, settled back and said: "Old Mason Griffin finally managed to run me out of town. As a going-away present he had one of his baboons give me a couple of shiners. Chipped a tooth, too." She opened her mouth so I could see. "Dirty shit," she added.

"Why did he want you out of town?" I asked.

She shrugged. "You know—good and bad, black and white, foreigner and hundred-percent American. I figure he'll come looking for me before too long." She started to pull on her sweater.

"But why?" I couldn't stop myself from asking.

"Maybe I'm wrong," she said, "maybe he won't." She didn't want to tell me.

Quickly, before she could leave, I scribbled my address and telephone number on a piece of paper. "Or you can always find me at the newspaper—anytime," I said, holding out the paper to her.

She seemed to be debating whether or not to take it. Finally she shoved it into her bag and walked away, shoulders back, the swagger perfection itself. She could still turn and walk away as if nothing had happened, and I felt the same surge of admiration I had felt the first time I ever saw Babe Conlon. Why was it, I asked myself, that she seemed to know something I didn't know?

Faith had wondered what it was about Babe that fascinated me, and I had tried to explain. I told her that it was how Babe lived, or had to live. That it was also, probably, because she was one of the "forbidden" women, the kind "nice" ' women were taught to avoid. And yet, there had been something so *good* about her, the way she stood up for the Mohammedans who were her friends. How she flew in the face of the law—all those Treasury agents with their sawed off shotguns—when she couldn't possibly win. Except, in a way, she had won. But without illusions. I told Faith that Babe had to face fears I couldn't even imagine. And she had faced them, and she could still walk away with a remarkable kind of dignity. Faith said she thought she understood, and that someday she would like to meet Babe to see for herself.

It was eight o'clock by the time I got home. I hurried up the hill, the day's events bouncing about in my head. Faith would be interested that Babe Conlon had surfaced at last, that there was a chance she might get to meet her. On the kitchen table I found a note: "Working at Zev's studio, home late. Call J. Riordan at Sutter 2310."

While I waited for the operator to come onto the line I looked at the scrawled note. Who was Zev? Then I remembered, Zev was an artist with a tiny studio in the Montgomery Building. It was where Faith had been when Kathleen and I had come looking for her at the office.

"I was just about to call you again," Riordan said. "I've spoken to Kathleen. It seems that she did not tell her mother that we had arranged for her to spend the afternoon with you. I believe she felt that she might not be allowed, so she simply avoided telling . . . a sin of omission, you could call it." His voice was strained, tight.

I felt a stab of distress, which quickly turned to anger: "Sin," I said. "You Irish are positively drowning in sin."

Before he could answer I apologized. "I didn't mean that—" I started.

"You're right," he broke in, "and I wish it hadn't happened. You gave Kathleen one of the nicest days of her life—that's the way she put it. I can't remember ever seeing her so lively and happy. Michael was quizzing her when I left, but at the time I thought he was just curious. It seems to have been more than that . . . it was Michael who returned the ribbons."

I felt ill. "She was trying to tell me . . . I don't know how I could have been so thick. She even asked if I had ever run away. It didn't occur to me . . ."

"The Irish may be preoccupied with sin, but you seem to be doing all right in the way of guilt," he said.

"If I had only had my wits about me . . . poor Kathleen!"

His voice was steady now, and serious. "Poor Kathleen is going to be all right," he said, pausing for emphasis. "I'm not sure I could have said that a month ago, but I've discovered there is a tenacious, happy child in there who is going to be all right."

"Will I be able to see her again?" I asked.

"I believe so," he answered. "I'll need to work some things out first."

"Michael?" I probed.

"Yes," he said, clipping off his answer. "It may not be easy. I'm hoping his mother will help."

I wanted to ask him why he always said "his mother"—or

"Kathleen's mother" or "Colin's mother." Never "my wife." But I knew I couldn't, that it was none of my business, that if I intended ever to see Kathleen again I would have to be careful. And I wanted to see her. I was good for Kathleen, I was certain of it. And she was good for me.

"I had an exceptionally nice time with Kathleen," I told him. "I would like to see her again. I hope you will tell her that."

"I will," he promised. "I'm going to be in Marysville all next week on a case, and then I have to travel to Monterey. But when I return, I'll see what I can do. It just needs a little time right now."

I wasn't ready to end the conversation. "Do you suppose," I started, then stumbled over my words. "I mean, when you do return could you . . . ?"

"I'll let you know," he said. "And, Hallie, thank you for being patient with us. I want you to know—"

"I do," I told him.

Harry's first story came clattering in over the wire on Wednesday before the fight, which was scheduled for Saturday, July 2. The sharp staccato brought us all to life. Roy, the telegrapher, had put a Prince Albert can under the receiver so the Morse code was magnified and echoed through the city room. I was stationed at a desk near the telegraph machine. For this major story the paper had leased a special wire direct from ringside, so Harry wouldn't have to wait a turn. We would know what was happening while it was happening.

The fight, which Harry assured me was going to be no fight at all, had captured the imagination of the country. Those who decried boxing as "obscene" and "barbaric" suggested that had the League of Nations received as much press attention, the U.S. would now be a member. The truth was that the people were not as interested in the League as they were in this boxing contest.

No one could satisfy the public passion for news of this fight. The French war hero—tall and elegant and suave—against the roughneck all-American boy. The kid from Main Street USA versus the chap from the Boulevard des Capucines. If those labels were bogus, it didn't matter. What mattered was that this was the "Fight of the Century" and that nobody wanted to miss it.

Harry's first story was datelined "Boyle's Thirty Acres." I watched over his shoulder as Roy decoded the message—Harry's description of the marsh on the outskirts of Jersey City where the fight would be held, of the new wooden arena built to hold ninety thousand.

Hours later another story clattered in over the wire, this one datelined "Manhasset, Long Island, New York." The background story this time was about the French contender's training camp. I had to smile at Harry's description of the French champion's manager: "François Descamps is resplendent in purple sweater, fawn-colored slacks and red Persian slippers." Descamps, Harry went on to say, had become an object of speculation in the international press, with at least one French newspaper claiming he had occult powers. His "evil eye," they declared, would make Dempsey have "an irresistible desire to lie down and quit." When advised of this threat, Harry reported, Dempsey announced a plan to demand that Descamps be forced to wear dark motoring goggles, "through which the malevolent emanation would be unable to pass."

The city room erupted in laughter, Ham's great guffaws sounding over all the rest. The quote was pure Harry McConaughey—The Real McCoy—and everybody in the *Times* newsroom knew it. He would have fed the story to Dempsey, then helped with the reply. And we had it first.

Harry must have been working double time to make it to Atlantic City, where Dempsey was training, and where the temperature—between rainstorms—was in the nineties. Even so, he reported, Dempsey was sparring hard enough to get his eye ripped open. Sprinkled into the hard news was the kind of detail readers hungered for: "When Dempsey isn't training, he sits around the clubroom reading western novels."

An hour later, the wire came alive again, tapping out a small take. "Gentleman" Jim Corbett, former heavyweight champion, had predicted Georges Carpentier the winner. Again, the boys in the sports desks roared with laughter. "Corbett hasn't yet picked a winner," Ham explained. "He's the kiss of death."

It was the last of the day's takes from the East. As I had suspected, Harry's stories required little more than polishing and adding the small words left out for fast transmission over the telegraph wire. The Boss smiled happily. Harry's long association with Dempsey was paying off, we were getting quotes nobody else could get. Our stories were being picked up by other papers, even those with a whole battery of reporters on hand—like the *Chronicle* and the *Examiner*. The fight was scheduled for three on Saturday afternoon, which would be noon on the West Coast. If it didn't last long—and Harry had assured us it wouldn't—we could be on the streets with a first edition without any problem at all, while the two morning papers would have to wait for Sunday's headlines. The Boss was pleased. The *Chronicle* fought back by announcing it would post every detail of the fight in its front window, starting at eleven o'clock. "That's not the same as being on the street in cold type," the Boss crowed, and we knew he was right.

I came into the office early that Saturday to get the rest of my work done so I could be ready to go just as soon as the signals began to come in from ringside. The machine broke its silence at ten o'clock, two hours before the fight was scheduled to begin.

"Hallie," the Boss called out, "come here." The men gathered around the telegrapher moved to make way for me. I read over Roy's shoulder: "Prefer Hallie write lead story, share byline."

I looked at the Boss, amazed. He raised his eyebrows in question. I shrugged, embarrassed by Harry's request. It was Ham's job to assign stories. I couldn't imagine why Harry would ask for such a thing.

"I hope he hasn't fallen off the wagon," Ham said, adding, "You just sit tight and be ready to go, Hallie." I was happy to do just that.

For the next hour Harry's notes came tapping in over the wire, but now they were disjointed, without the usual flow to them. *One o'clock. Sky overcast, rain threatens. Two o'clock . . . arrival of Vanderbilts, Biddles, Rhinelanders, Fords, Astors. Waiting for Al Jolson, George M. Cohan, three Teddy Roosevelt's kids, include Princess Alice. Prelims, Gene Tunney gives Soldier Jones brutal beating, referee calls, Soldier losing too much blood.*

Ham was frowning and chewing the stub of an old cigar. Without a word he handed out the rewrites. I took mine, relieved that Harry's request was being ignored.

At 3:16—12:16 Pacific time—Georges Carpentier climbed into the ring. Half the newsroom had gathered outside the telegrapher's little office. Someone started reading Harry's transmissions out loud: "He is blond and graceful, his face clean-shaven, wearing a robe of gray-and-black silk. Dempsey has three-day stubble of beard and same old black sweater."

The blow-by-blow description of each round followed. *Carpentier is detached, his style classic. Dempsey crouches and moves, glowering, bobbing and weaving, style against force. Carpentier connects with hard right to jaw, Dempsey staggers, crowd roars. Carpentier doesn't follow through and Dempsey recovers . . .* The newsroom was silent, except for the sound of the telegraph, and the*n: Dempsey punishes the Frenchman, wicked short chops to jaw, vicious uppercuts and body punches. Slow, steady, Dempsey is wearing him down.* In the fourth round Dempsey snapped a short right to the jaw and the arena reverberated, quaked with the roar of the crowd, who sensed the end near. Harry writes: *The bankers and the bums are bellowing for blood.* (In the excitement, he is writing again.) *Dempsey hits hard to the heart, Carpentier is down, it is over. Dempsey remains heavyweight champion of the world.* Harry's last transmission is: *It was not a very good fight. That's it. Thanks, Hallie.*

Why is he doing this? I wondered. But Ham was barking out assignments, and there was no time to ponder it.

I didn't lift my eyes from the typewriter until the story I had been assigned was carried off by the copyboy. Then I sat back, stretched and looked around.

The Boss was in his office. I paused in the doorway. "Did Harry say anything to you about covering the fight?" he asked.

"What do you mean, 'covering'?"

"I mean, did you know anything about this shared byline request?"

"No, sir, I did not," I told him tartly, "and I believe I made it clear that I didn't want it."

"Sit down, Hallie," the Boss said, waving me in, "and calm down." He ran his fingers through his thinning hair, and I realized it was Harry he was worried about.

"I don't understand why he would do that," I began. "Harry knew I wanted to cover the fight as the *Times*'s woman on the scene. And you know how much he's helped me. I was disappointed not to get to go, I admit it. But not enough—"

"He's smitten with you, Hallie," the Boss said flatly.

I stared at him. "What?" I asked, not believing I had heard him correctly. He nodded, and said, "That's right."

I was shaking my head. "No," I said, "you're wrong, you don't understand. Harry has helped me tremendously. He knows it isn't easy, a woman covering sports . . . covering any general-news subject, for that matter. He's never once . . ."

When the Boss spoke again his voice was low and soft: "It's one of the real problems, Hallie—being a woman and a reporter. And you are an attractive woman, you know."

"But I haven't done anything to—" I started.

"Sometimes you don't have to," he told me.

I groaned. *It was true.* All the times I had thought he was being sweet because he wanted to help me with the work, but it wasn't just that. It was more.

"The thing is," I said, "Thelma is dear to me, and she and Harry are devoted to each other, I'm certain of that. I thought . . . I felt like one of the family. They treat me that way. The kids, all of them. It just never occurred to me."

"I know it didn't, Hallie. But I saw it coming. I think it has been obvious to some of us." He turned his cigar around in his fingers. "There are so many different kinds of affection in this world," he went on. "Sometimes I am encouraged by that . . . but there are other times when it seems only to add to the confusion."

I felt miserable, and stupid as well. And sad, because everything would be different now. I would have to watch what I said to Harry. I would have to pull back, not go out to the house so often. The old, easy camaraderie would be gone.

"What can I do?" I asked.

"Nothing," the Boss said. "I think Harry will realize what he's done when he sees that we've ignored his byline request. He'll probably be embarrassed, but I doubt he'll bring it up if we don't. And I don't intend to. I suggest you ignore it too."

I nodded and left, feeling empty and tired and suddenly, drained of feeling. Faith wasn't at the cottage when I returned. She seldom ever was these days. We met each other coming and going and our conversations seemed to center on practicalities— shopping and laundry and paying the rent. And now, Harry and Thelma. It wouldn't be the same. It never was, I said to myself. It is always lonely, always.

I opened a can of soup, poured it into a pan, and lit the gas ring. The telephone rang. *Not tonight. I won't answer. No taunting tonight.*

Clive would arrive in four days' time. I could wait four days. After fifteen years, I could wait four more days. For my brother, my family.

The waiting intensified on the Fourth of July, a Monday. While most of San Francisco lined Market Street and Van Ness for the big parade, I was across town at the Marina waiting for the airplane which would deliver the first photographs of the fight. The first relay had left New Jersey as soon after the fight as the film could be developed. That was forty-eight hours ago. The last leg had left Reno at ten-thirty on the morning of the Fourth, and air mail pilot Roy Little had telegraphed: "I am coming."

"Where are you, Roy Little?" I said to myself as I walked the length of Crissy Field. It was almost noon, and a stiff breeze was blowing off the bay. Reporters from the other papers had gathered and were standing in a tight little knot near the airport building. I decided to take another lap of the field rather than join them. I didn't feel up to the effort it took . . . don't be too brash but don't be coy either. Be confident, not arrogant. I was tired of it, tired of working so hard to make them treat me like one of them. Harry had been the only one, that is what I thought. The only one who understood what I was trying to do on the paper. But that was going to be different; now there was no one.

I looked up, scanned the sky to the east. Nothing. Not even a sea gull to mistake for the airplane.

It appeared, dipping over the low white buildings that crowded the city's hills. Soundless, then a sputtering noise as its wings tipped in salute. It was on the ground before I could get back to the pack of reporters, who were scrambling onto the field, pushing for position, wanting to be first to receive the packets. I picked up my skirts and ran. I had been preoccupied, and now I was behind. The pilot pulled himself out of the plane and took off his goggles. He was smiling broadly. "Wait a second, boys," he called as they jostled him. "Just hold on," he shouted as I elbowed through the crowd, pushing, my hands raised to catch his attention.

"What's the matter with you fellows?" the pilot said. "Let the little lady through. Nobody gets any of these until you let her through."

I was first out of the airstrip, and I made it back to the office in good time, considering I had to go the long way around to avoid the Fourth of July parade that clogged Van Ness Avenue. We had a full page of photographs of the fight for the first edition that afternoon, and so did all of the other papers. Getting the pictures first at Crissy Field had made no difference at all.

The stationmaster nodded and consulted his pocket watch, as if it held the answer. "The Overland is going to be one hour late," he said, "though it might make up a little of that out of Sacramento."

Too restless to sit in the waiting room, I walked through the station, reading all of the notices pinned to the walls and listening to the idle chatter of the bootblacks. Then I strolled up and down the platform . . . three, four, five times. I went back into the waiting room, took a seat on one of the highly polished benches and tried to concentrate on Annie Farrell's "A Woman's View of the Fight of the Century." I read the first paragraph twice, and hadn't an idea what it said.

Then the air was filled with sound and motion; the Overland Limited came thundering down the tracks, rocking the platform, smoke pouring, whistles blowing, the sun's late light glinting off the gleaming engine.

I wanted to run, to leave. Clive was coming, and I wanted to run from him. Him. My brother, but a stranger. It was important to remember that he was a stranger. We had been children together, that was all. Was it enough? We had been children, and then we grew up—writing letters, sharing dreams and ideas and hopes. What was missing was the laughter, the arguments, anger and pleasure. We had not shared any of the irrelevant details of living. Was this a mistake? Would I like him? The questions bombarded me as the train pulled slowly into the station, and a crowd suddenly appeared on the platform, waiting too.

I started smiling, I don't know why. Even before I saw him, I could feel myself smiling. The laughter began to bubble up from somewhere inside of me and I had to swallow to keep it from bursting out. I saw him then, standing on the platform, his fine blond hair falling forward over his forehead so that he had to brush it back with his hand. I could hear myself call out to him. He saw me. I remembered then—the look on his face, the way the smile spread up and into his eyes. It was all so slow and sweet and familiar. How could I not have remembered?

The crowd bumped and pushed us along, and all I could do was walk close to him and let them jostle us down the platform. Awkwardly we extricated ourselves from the flow of the crowd and stood, neither of us knowing what to say. He squinted and looked around as if to get his bearings.

"This is Oakland," I said. "We have to take a ferryboat to San Francisco."

There were so many important things to talk about, but all we could manage in those first minutes were the arrangements. He was different, grown up, no longer a boy. But he was the same, too. I could see it in his manner, which was precise, and in the delicate tracery of lines around his eyes when he smiled, and the same small hesitation before speaking.

He tried gamely to laugh. "It's something of a shock," he said. "I mean, I am actually here."

"You are," I said. "You can't begin to know how happy I am that you've come."

He shook his head in disbelief. "It feels like I'm finally home."

ELEVEN

THE PARTY was Faith's idea. She brought it up with a mischievous half-smile which suggested she might just be testing.

"It's August already," she said. "Clive's been here for more than a month and he hasn't met anyone."

"Except Mrs. Giacometti," Clive called from the kitchen to let us know he was listening. The name triggered our laughter. Mrs. Giacometti had appeared at our door two days after Clive's arrival to determine—not very subtly, given her poor command of English—just why he was spending the night in the cottage of two single ladies. Finding him alone, she had demanded, "In whose bed you sleep?" and Clive, far from being embarrassed, had invited her into the cottage to inspect our living arrangements. He took her on a tour, showing her Faith's bedroom, which was perfectly neat, and mine, which was not because Clive's clothes were stored there, on a bracket on the door and stacked on chairs and on my dresser until he could find a place of his own. He demonstrated for her the makeshift bed we had arranged for him in the living room by putting together the settee and a chair. By then the two of them had become conversant in an abbreviated brand of English, so he brought out some of our family pictures to show her our parents and grandparents, and the two of us at various stages in our lives. Faith had entered the cottage at this moment to find, as she liked to put it, "the Italian crone and the fair-haired boy from Chicago, all snug on the settee having a fine time."

"Mrs. Giacometti," Clive said, joining us, "was my first female conquest in San Francisco."

"First and only," Faith shot back.

"So far," he answered, cocking his head to one side so you knew he was teasing too, except maybe he wasn't, maybe he meant it after all. "I could stand to meet someone a little younger, I suppose, and a little slimmer . . . maybe you *should* have a party."

"See?" Faith said, as if I had been arguing against the idea. "You can't keep him to yourself forever."

Clive slipped his arm around my shoulder and gave me a playful tug—we were almost the same height. "You both act," I said, tugging him back, "as if I'm against a party when really I think it's a fine idea. How about the last Sunday of this month? The weather should be good enough so we could be outdoors—we'd never be able to get everybody into the cottage, but we could use the porch and the garden."

"By then I'll be settled in the rooming house and have my things out of your way," Clive put in.

"Thank the Lord for small favors," Faith said. "I thought you were never going to leave." She was smiling; the two had bantered like that almost from the beginning. I had worried that his stay in the cottage might prove to be irritating to Faith, perhaps even to me. But it hadn't. Clive had a talent for fitting in. Faith was away much of the time, and it occurred to me that Clive's arrival relieved her of some responsibility for spending time with me. She had become involved in a kind of art photography—still lifes and outdoor studies of leaves and light, close-ups of ferns or small arrangements of stones. She no longer prowled Chinatown at first light on market day, hoping to make a study of the old people who came to finger lichee nuts and ginger root. When I questioned her about this change of subject, from animate to inanimate, she had shrugged and made some remark about that having been her "social-action" period and that now she was moving into a more formal stage.

Faith had been right about my keeping Clive to myself that first month after his arrival. We had wandered the city together, talking without interruption. He would meet me at the newspaper office and we would take the streetcar all the way out to Ocean Beach and walk and talk and maybe stop at one of the small sandwich houses or go all the way to the end of the beach, to Sutro's Baths, to climb into the gallery and watch the bathers in that great ugly tin building . . . and talk.

The first few days we had been excessively polite to each other, as you are when you want someone to like you. We spent time simply exchanging information—details that had never found their way into our letters, impressions and thoughts. Slowly, very slowly, we moved toward the year when I had been twelve and he fifteen, the summer when our world was destroyed by a sudden storm on a lake and a gunshot in a stand of alders. We would come close and then one or the other of us would shy away. Then we would start over again, slowly inching backward in time, approaching it with caution. And the days passed, and it became a chasm that was growing—or so it seemed to me—and threatening to separate us again. The summer of our parents' death became a splinter lodged in the tender center, festering. It needed lancing.

We were sitting on the hill late one afternoon, Clive and I, watching the fog move back in through the Golden Gate. The last of the children had left, called to supper. It would be cool soon. The fog was rolling in in great white billows, moving steadily, filling the bay. I waited for it to overtake a freighter coming into the harbor; when I could no longer see the ship, I said it: "Tell me what you remember about the day our mother died."

It came then, in a rush: everything. All the hurt and anger and fear he had felt and I had felt. We relived that day and the Thursday after, the fatal decision made in a stand of alders that had sealed our fate, too. Tears welled in my brother's eyes as he told me how he had tried to make himself look at the figure lying on a marble slab in the morgue, but couldn't. His eyes would not open, he had turned his face away and could not look. And Grandmother had come into the room then and looked at our father's body and said, "Yes. That is my son." And what he remembered was the sound of cold metal against cold stone, grating. And the words: *Yes. That is my son,* cold and hard and metallic, ringing in his head.

I was shaking as he told me. I felt dizzy and hot, but all I could do was put my arm in his as we sat side by side on the hill, the fog all around us, soft and white and enveloping. I put my arm in his and leaned my head against his and listened as he wept silently, and knew there was nothing we could not talk about now. We were bound by blood and memories and pain; we were bound by that awful summer and the lake and the stand of alders.

We drove up to the farm, and Grandfather bowed his head at table to say grace. "Thank you, Lord, for sending our grandboy to us. Our hearts sing with joy to see him with his sister at last." Grandmother had said "Amen," and then she had smiled and said the chicken was getting cold and we had better eat, and we passed around the green beans and potatoes and sliced tomatoes ripened on the vine, and were together as I had always dreamed we should be.

On one of those July evenings on the farm, in the long light between sundown and dark, we went for a rambling walk. "Somehow," Clive said as we cut across the pasture, "I never imagined the farm to be this isolated—all this empty country. I always thought of you as surrounded by people."

I had to laugh. "Not much," I said. "Most of the time I felt as if I was suspended somehow, waiting for something to happen. When I was growing up here, it seemed to me that things happened to other people but never to me. I always seemed to be looking on . . . I didn't feel real . . ."

"What do you mean, *real*?" he asked.

"I'm not sure," I answered, a little surprised at myself for putting into words something I had never really thought out. "It just always seemed as if I was practicing."

"For what?" he wanted to know.

"I can't tell you that, either—real laughter, maybe. Real tears. Something like that."

We headed toward the woods, where it promised to be cooler. "Is that why you became a reporter," he probed, "to get closer?"

I took a deep breath. "I think so," I finally said. "I knew I wasn't going to get married. Settling down was the last thing I wanted to do. Teaching school was the next-to-last. There's not much else a woman is expected to do, so I decided I would have to do something unexpected. The first time I saw a woman reporter in action, in the courthouse in Sacramento, I thought: That's it. She was in the middle of the action, she was accepted, she belonged. I suppose I figured that if I was going to take a step out, it might as well be a giant step. About the only people who didn't think me daft were the grandparents—and you, of course."

"And is it what you wanted?" he asked.

We walked in silence while I thought about it. "Sometimes," I said, "the action pulls you in. You will be sitting at ringside with the noise and the shouting and the excitement all around you, and you'll feel a part of it. But most of the time you're looking on, observing. It's what a reporter is supposed to do, of course. Be neutral, detached, not involved. The only story I've covered, so far, that I feel involved in is the Marchant case. You know about it? Well, I've come to know Agnes Marchant, and I am fond of her. Very fond. So what happens to her has become a personal thing. If I cover her trial, it could affect my reporting."

"Aren't reporters allowed to have opinions?" he asked.

"The best newspaperman I know is Sanford Curtin—my boss—and he most certainly has opinions."

We reached the woods, and stopped to sit for a while on a felled tree. "You were lucky," he said, "to be out here, I mean. Grandmother Duer had a conniption when she heard you'd gone into newspapering. If you'd been in Chicago she would have had you arrested for acute humiliation."

I laughed. "Was it that bad?" I said. "I thought she had disowned me ages ago."

"She can't discount you entirely. You look too much like Mother, and Mother was the great tragedy of Grandmother Duer's life, for having the unmitigated gall to marry Father, and worse than that, to make him happy."

I sighed. "You know what I remember best? I remember the four of us in that big upstairs room with the afternoon light pouring in, having tea parties and laughing. I used to put myself to sleep thinking about those times."

"I remember that." He nodded, then added with a trace of bitterness, "And a lot of other things as well."

"Like?" I probed.

"Oh, like once when Mother had a friend visit, someone she had gone to school with I think. When the woman was saying goodbye, Grandmother came out and accused her of taking something, and insisted she look in her bag. Father wasn't at home, and there wasn't anything Mother could do. She cried about it. Until that day I'd never seen Mother cry. Father had a big fuss with Grandmother, and said we were going to move out, as he always did. But we didn't move out. And Mother didn't have any friends over after that."

I looked at Clive. "Do you hate Grandmother Duer?" I asked.

He turned away.

"What did she say when you told her you were leaving?"

"I didn't," he answered. "She doesn't know where I am." He turned back to face me. "She thinks I'm in France, on vacation."

I was astonished. "You mean she doesn't know?"

"You could say I'm a thirty-year-old runaway," he said, trying to grin. "I'm supposed to be back by mid-August." It came in a rush then, as if he couldn't tell me fast enough: How she would have a seizure whenever he talked about coming to California, how the doctor would tell him not to upset her. How he had tried to work up the courage to make a clean break of it, but couldn't. "She insisted on going with me to book passage," he said bitterly. "Lucky for me she's a creature of habit. She always hired the same detective whenever she wanted to check up on me. He wasn't very good. I got to know him, and he was happy to take my money as well as hers. If I don't show up, she'll probably send him out here."

"*If,*" I said, outraged. "What do you mean, *if*? I thought it was settled that you were here to stay. Isn't that what you want? You have interviews. I don't understand. Do you want to stay?"

He was pacing now, his hands shoved into his pockets. "Yes," he said, and then repeated it: "Yes."

"Then you will stay. No *ifs,* Clive. I can be as tough as that old woman."

He looked at me and grinned and said, "I know you can, Hallie. It's me I'm not sure about . . . you don't know her. She always gets her way."

"Not this time," I said. "You *are* strong, Clive. You just haven't had the chance before."

He turned away from me because he didn't want me to see his face. "This must sound pretty silly to you," he said, "but for the first time in my life I know how it feels to be able to come and go. I mean, at the cottage, I can go wherever I want and not have to tell anyone." He held his hand out to me, and we walked together then. "I feel ashamed at times," he said, "for waiting so long."

Something sharp turned in my chest. I tried to explain: "It was easier for me, being here. But you're here too now, and everything is going to be right. I know it is. What you have to do is write her and tell her. Get it over with, so you don't have to dread it anymore."

Clive's first interview was with Julia Morgan. She offered him a position and he accepted, straight off, even though the pay was less than he had been earning. I was stunned that it had been so simple. He liked Miss Morgan, he said, the way she worked and the kind of work she did. He knew, because she told him, that there was little chance for advancement. She explained, too, that she would never take on a partner, if that was his ambition. Clive admired her for her straightforwardness, her determination. And in his own way, I knew, he was as determined not to be a partner as she was not to have one.

"Aren't you worried about saving for your old age?" I chided him, and the question seemed to trigger something. He looked at me, studied me for a time as if he were trying to come to a decision. Then he said, "Neither of us has to worry about our old age. Unless Grandmother Duer decides to live to be a hundred and thirty, which isn't beyond the pale. For as long as I can remember, whenever she wanted me to do something and I balked, she would tell me that I had better watch myself or she would leave me without a penny. She would pull herself up to her full five feet, regal as a queen, and issue this threat. Once she said, 'If you don't listen to me, young man, I'll see that your inheritance is cut off.' That got me to thinking—it was the first time she had intimated that she had to do something to get this 'inheritance' stopped. So I waited until she had aggravated poor old Smithson, her lawyer, to the point where he might tell me. Her way of bouncing him was to call me—the 'man' of the house, you know—to 'see him to the door.' This time the poor guy's face was purple with rage, so bottled that I knew he would blow his cork with the slightest pressure. 'You and your sister have nothing to worry about,' he told me that day. 'Your grandfather set up a trust for your father, whereby the proceeds of his fortune go to your grandmother for as long as she lives, but the principal is held in trust for his child, or in the case of death, for his grandchildren. Your grandfather was a very careful man; the trust is ironclad. Your grandmother cannot break it.'" He stopped and shook his head. "Of course, old Smithson came to see me the next day, when he had cooled down, and begged me not to tell my grandmother that I knew about the trust. I promised that I wouldn't say a word, and I haven't until today. It just seems right that you should know, if I do."

As we made our way down the hill, I told him, "I'll be willing to bet that she finds some way to get around it, to break the trust."

"You may be right," he said. "Do you care?"

I thought about it. "I don't know," I finally said. "Grandfather Duer earned it, and maybe Grandmother had more to do with it than our father. Certainly she had more to do with it than I did. Maybe she should have the right to say what is to become of it."

"The thing that fascinates me," he would tell me later that evening, "is how often people *assume* that money would be the objective, and even when you tell them it isn't, they don't believe you. I suppose at the most basic level, money is synonymous with security—food, a roof over your head. Maybe growing up in that mausoleum in Chicago robbed me of some basic need. I don't know. I just have this empty feeling about the inheritance. Once, I even came close to telling her— when she threatened me—that I would sign a paper relinquishing my share of the principal, that I would gladly sign it over to her if she would just leave me be. But I didn't because I had promised old Smithson, and if she knew I knew, he would be in plenty of trouble."

"Poor miserable old woman," I said.

He took a sip of his hot tea and looked at me over the rim of the cup. "I wish I could pity her," he said, with such hurt in his voice that I felt a sharp pang of regret. Why hadn't I made him come sooner? *Why had I waited so long?*

Early on the Sunday morning of the party, the whole of Telegraph Hill smelled of garlic and herbs, of stewing tomatoes and baking bread. Thin wisps of white smoke issued from those kitchens which used wood-burning stoves. When I mentioned this to Faith, she threw me two more lemons to roll and squeeze and said, "Maybe they're making cookies to bring to the party."

"Garlic cookies?" I asked. "Swell. Garlic cookies and lemonade."

Clive came in carrying a half-dozen baker's boxes balanced under his chin. "You look wonderfully elegant!" Faith told him as she took the boxes. He was wearing a white linen summer suit and a shirt of bold blue and white stripes. "My Chicago duds," he told her. "Not exactly right for a San Francisco summer, but . . ."

"Exotic . . . superior . . . the ladies will swoon," Faith laughed.

"Mrs. Giacometti will adore you," I chimed in, glad for the high spirits, for the growing sense of expectation. We had invited some of our neighbors and I had asked people from the paper. Faith issued what she said was a 'general' invitation to her artist friends. I had sent out a few written invitations—to Julia, Agnes and Sara. And one to Riordan and the children.

I had not heard from Riordan. He was back in town, I knew, because he had made several court appearances for Agnes. But he hadn't called as he said he would. Second thoughts, I suspected. He had decided to let things be. I didn't think he would come, but the invitation seemed a harmless way to let him know I had not forgotten.

"Do you think Julia will come?" I asked Clive.

"No, but she said to thank you for the invitation. She also said to remind you about Thursday. I take it you two have a standing engagement?"

"Hard-boiled eggs—usually at one of her drafting tables, Union Square, weather permitting. First Thursday of the month."

At eleven, right on schedule, the fog lifted and the sun came out, along with what seemed like half the male population of the hill armed with boards and sawhorses, which they quickly fashioned into long tables.

"We make the good party," Mr. D'Agostino called out to us as we stood on the front stoop, amazed. Long tables were being planted in every level space. One end of the street was roped off, and tables were set up where vegetable wagons and the hill's few Fords were usually parked.

"Is there another party going on that we don't know about?" Clive asked.

"I think *we are* the party," Faith answered, her eyes dancing with light. "I think when we invited our neighbors to a 'party' they had a vision that was different from ours."

"How grand," Clive put in, "a real Old World celebration."

And it was. Food suddenly appeared on the long tables—malfatti and cannelloni, polenta casserole and risotto with mushrooms, saltimbocca and frittata and calamari and gnocchi and a score of other dishes I couldn't name. And people began to arrive.

"What shall we do about our lemonade and cookies?" Faith whispered urgently, as if we were caught with an embarrassing problem. We started laughing then, and couldn't stop. It all seemed so wonderfully funny. I ducked into the bedroom to change into the yellow silk chemise I had bought for the occasion. Feeling gay, and a little daring, I looped a long strand of Faith's play pearls around my neck. When I came out, Harry and Thelma were making their way up the hill.

"Some party you girls give," Thelma said as she wrapped her arms around me. Then she held me out to study. "Oh, to have the kind of figure to wear these slim little dresses," she sighed. Harry looked away.

"We had no idea this was going to happen," I whispered to them. "We thought we were having a few friends and neighbors in for lemonade and cookies. Where are the boys?"

"They took off for the hill," Harry said in the studiously detached tone he had affected since his return. "Seems like there is some game going on up there for the kids. There must be two hundred folks out there, Hallie. Do you know them all?"

"No!" I laughed. "But I've decided that doesn't matter. And have you ever seen such food? If I know my neighbor ladies, they'll be watching to make sure we all stuff ourselves."

Gwen arrived with a cousin in tow. She was introduced as Ethel Mayer, a schoolteacher from the Protrero district. She was, I guessed, about twenty-five, pretty with a pink complexion, and plump. Her lavender linen day dress was cut full, in part to camouflage her ample bosom.

"Is this your idea of a private little party to introduce your brother?" Gwen grouched. "I told Ethel here we were visiting some real sophisticated folks."

Everyone laughed but Ethel, who flushed a deep pink at her cousin's crude teasing. They were not, I suspected, very good friends. Clive set things right by explaining to the schoolteacher just what had happened, adding that he found it altogether charming. Then he volunteered to give her a tour of the hill. As they walked off together, Gwen gave me a knowing wink. I guessed, then, why she had brought her cousin. Faith and Clive and I had joked about helping him meet some likely young women, but the reality jarred me.

I turned to Harry and asked him about some minor detail of work, so that Thelma and Gwen would get involved in conversation.

I had seen very little of Harry since his return from New York and the big fight. My preoccupation with Clive was excuse enough, and neither Harry nor I had mentioned his ill-conceived requests over the wire. I hoped that the uneasiness I felt would go away in time.

At that moment a neighbor woman came up carrying a bouquet of marigolds almost as big as chrysanthemums. I thanked her, excused myself and took the flowers into the cottage to find a vase. I was standing at the basin in the kitchen, washing the acrid odor of the marigolds from my fingers, when a small voice said, "Hello, Hallie."

I turned, smiling. "Kathleen! You came—how wonderful."

"You didn't expect us?" her father said, watching me, his eyes flecked with humor at having surprised me.

"I didn't know if you'd come," I answered him. "I hoped you would."

"Colin is here too," Kathleen told me. "He went up the hill to find Bryan."

"Then you saw Harry and Thelma?" I asked, and Riordan nodded.

"I think Kathleen would like to ask you a question," he said, giving the child a slight nudge. She pressed her lips together, too shy to ask.

"I think I know what it is," I told her, and took her by the hand to my room. "They're here, in the drawer. All washed and folded in tissue." I showed her the ribbons. "Whenever you want them, they're here."

She put her arms around me then, and I kissed the top of her head. Riordan watched us through the door. He was looking around the room. I doubted that he missed much. We talked for a while, the three of us, until Sara came to the door with her godson, Porter Reade. I introduced them. It seemed that Porter had been wanting to meet Riordan, and immediately involved him in a conversation about Tom Mooney. Sara chatted comfortably with Kathleen and me, careful to include the child. It was, I realized, another of the things about Sara Hunt that I admired. She knew how to talk to children.

People began to wander in and out of the cottage. Someone would put a hand on my shoulder, and I would turn, smiling. I introduced Sara to Mrs. Gudino, the ancient mother of one of our neighbors, and to my surprise Sara broke into what seemed to be a stream of fluent Italian. Turning back to me, Sara said with obvious pleasure, "She's from Florence, my favorite city in the world next to this one." And the two sat down on the small settee and were lost, at once, in a sea of Italian complete with hand gestures.

Kathleen held on to my hand for a time, smiling up at me whenever I introduced her to someone. After a while she went off to join Colin. Riordan listened to Porter Reade for a few minutes longer, then excused himself and caught my eye. "Do you suppose we could talk for a few minutes?" he asked, adding for the benefit of those within hearing, "I have a message for you."

"Feel like climbing the hill?" I asked. "We can see how the children are doing." He took me by the arm, guiding me through the crowd. I caught a glimpse of Harry and Thelma watching us. As we started up the steep, rough-hewn stairs, his hand moved from my elbow to the small of my back, sending warm, shimmering sensations through me. I guided him to a sheltered space I knew, away from the noise and movement of the children and the party.

"I do have a message for you, in case you were wondering about that subterfuge," he said. "Agnes asked that I give you her regrets. She wasn't up to coming today."

"Is she all right?" I asked, worried.

"I'm not sure. She seems to be managing, but the trial date has finally been set for a week from Thursday. It isn't easy for her."

"I'm going to cover the trial. The Boss assigned me last week, so I'll be there."

"Good. She'll be glad to see a friendly face." He paused, then added, "I don't think it will go more than four, maybe five days."

We could hear the children playing on the other side of the hill. "You brought Colin and Kathleen," I said. "Does that mean you've worked out some of the problems?"

"Some," he said, "and some aren't workable, I'm afraid. But Kathleen can visit, as long as I have time to make arrangements." He paused, smiled down at me. "Thank you for keeping the ribbons for her."

"You knew I would, didn't you?"

The smile widened, moved into his eyes. He looked at me and I could see the thoughts moving, flashing deep. I wanted to know what they were, what he was thinking, all those thoughts, four or five or six moves ahead, as in a chess game.

"You knew," I repeated.

He looked away then, down the Embarcadero, and when he turned back again he wasn't smiling, he was perfectly serious. "I've thought about you these past weeks," he said.

I waited, looking at him; steady, clear.

"I would like to see you again, Hallie," he said.

I nodded. *Yes.* My eyes holding his.

"I'm not sure I should," he went on.

Now I turned away, walked to the edge of the hill, felt a breeze blow my dress against me.

"I think we could be friends," I said. "I would like that." I could feel him behind me, standing close, not touching.

"I would like to meet your brother," he said. "Then I think we should be going."

Harry and Thelma joined us as we walked back to the party. I could see the questions in their faces, the surprise. Riordan filled what might have been an awkward pause with easy talk, about the children and then about people they knew. After he left, Thelma pulled me aside. "When did you get to know Jimmy Riordan?" she said in a low, urgent voice.

"The Agnes Marchant story," I explained, trying to sound off-hand. "He is representing her, and I'm doing the story. I met his children one day at Agnes' house in Oakland."

She looked at me, worried. "You remember what I told you about him?" she asked.

"I remember, Thelma," I said, smiling to try to ease her mind.

"He's a good man," she went on, "but. . ."

"I know, Thelma," I reassured her, squeezing her arm.

A few minutes later, Harry took me aside, cleared his throat, squinted into the sun and started clenching and unclenching his hands. "About Riordan," he finally said, looking away.

"I know, Harry," I said in the softest voice I could command. "Thelma has already warned me. I'm glad you care about me, you and Thelma. Enough to warn me, I mean. I love both of you, I hope you know that."

He looked at me then as if I had said something brilliant. And at that moment, exactly, I knew that I had: of course Harry knew *how* I loved him, he had always known, he had never expected more. And it was enough, it had been enough all along. Why hadn't I seen it?

"Oh, Harry," I said, in the old, easy way, "we are all such foolish people. Truly, truly foolish."

He grinned at me, happy to have our world straight again. And then he said: "I'd never thought about you and Riordan. But just now, seeing you walk down the hill together—I knew I should have."

I wanted to ask him what he had seen, but at that moment Mrs. Altobelli appeared with a covey of relatives from San Jose, "come for the party, my cousin Angelina, my cousin . . ." And Harry, grinning, backed away from the whole noisy, talking, laughing crowd of us.

Out of the corner of my eye I glimpsed Gwen's cousin Ethel sitting on the front stoop of the cottage, and Clive coming out the door and stopping. Had she been waiting for him? I wondered. Had they been together all this time?

I nodded and smiled and talked, as best I could, to the Altobellis, and then I tried to make my way to Mr. Maggiore's shed, where I suspected homemade grappa was being shared. I spotted Faith and managed to whisper to her to join me—but to come alone. In a few minutes she did, and Mr. Maggiore poured each of us a cupful of grappa—a clear homemade brandy—cautioning us to be quiet by putting his gnarled old finger over his lips and saying a rather loud "shhhh."

"Have you ever seen so many people?" Faith asked. "Especially so many you don't know?"

"Everybody seems to be having a fine time," I told her. "It's not so much a party as a celebration." It was true. We stood there looking at the old Italian women in their black dresses, lined up, all in a row on a bench, chattering away. The children darted back and forth, grabbing a biscotto here, a panettone there. The men stood in small clusters while the women moved back and forth about the tables, talking and waving the aprons they had put on to protect their Sunday dresses. Faith's artist friends hovered about the tables too, filling plates for a second or a third time. I watched as a group came together: Porter Reade and one of the artists, a thin bearded fellow, and Clive and the schoolteacher Ethel, and a girl I didn't recognize who turned out to be the eldest daughter of the Langermans, who lived on the corner and owned the grocery.

"It's like looking in one of those machines at the arcade," Faith said. "You know, where the pictures flip so fast it seems as if they're in motion—that's how I feel. People come up to me and say something, and I say something back, and then a moment later it is someone else and I can't remember who I was talking to, and you never have a moment to finish a thought."

"Why is it," I said to her, "that you so very often say out loud what I have been thinking?" I put my hand on her shoulder and she smiled and—I think because we were alone then, and exhilarated by the movement and the sunshine and the wine—told me that she had invited Thayer Gerson to the party. "I don't know if he'll come or not," she said. "Do you mind?"

"Why ask me now?" I answered.

"Because I was afraid to ask before, and he said he wanted to come—he said he thought it was about time he made amends."

"Is that what he said?" I asked, my voice going cold.

She moved away. "Yes, that's what he said," the strain appearing in her voice, too.

It was no use, no use at all. It was inevitable. "Okay," I said, and made myself smile at her. "If that's what you want. Is it?"

"Yes," she said, in a way that told me she had been thinking about it for a long time, and knew.

"Then fine. Amends it is," I answered, and went to find Sara.

"He's making his move," she said, looking about as if she expected to see him. "He'll be charming—and he can be, you know. Do you want me to stay around?"

"Would you?" I asked.

"I would," she answered. "It won't hurt, I think, if he knows we're friends."

"Why is that?" I asked. "Do you have something on him?"

She laughed and said not particularly, but that they did have several friends in common. Friends who were no longer his friends, but hers.

"I wish—" I started.

She interrupted to tell me again that Faith was going to have to make her own mistakes and that all I could do now was to stand by and wait, and be ready if something happened.

"Something will happen, I can feel it coming," I told her, wrapping my arms around myself at the thought of it.

"And so there's nothing to be done," Sara said.

Porter was talking to a group of young Italian men. "They're discussing trade unionism," Sara said. "I can tell. Porter will be well occupied for a time."

"If he's involved with the IWW, he'd better take care," I told her.

"I know," she sighed. "I can see what is coming for Porter, too, and there is no way to stop it. Even if I wanted to—in Porter's case, I'm never sure. I go from one extreme to the other, one minute proud of his strong opinions and staunch support of the workingman, and the other minute scared to death of what might happen to him."

Thayer Gerson arrived, complete with his circle of young admirers. In Europe and on the East Coast, Sara Hunt's portraits were much admired, but here in her hometown, her work was all but unknown. It was the way she wanted it. Thayer Gerson was the opposite exactly; in San Francisco he was lionized, but abroad his reputation was small.

"Sara, dear, what a surprise," he said, gesturing so that the circle opened to include us. Faith stood at his right, her eyes bright, watching me. "And Hallie," he went on, "how good of you to invite me. I've not met your brother yet, but I hope to. I didn't realize that you girls knew the famous Miss Hunt," he said to Faith, patting her hand possessively.

Sara spoke up. "We have you to thank for that, Thayer. Hallie and I met at your Christmas party, but I had to wait awhile to meet Faith."

Gerson made a short speech about the qualities of Sara's work, praising her style and technique and then, quite sincerely, telling us all that Sara was our city's "most prominent" artist, a fact, he said, which "only other artists know."

He held forth then, telling amusing stories, occasionally drawing someone into the talk. I tried to listen as if I had just met him. I could see why he was so often referred to as a "charming" man. He was also attractive, big and well-built like a man who has been at sea a long time, and hard from the physical work.

I entered into the conversation enough, I hoped, to make Faith feel I was making a real effort. But I was glad when someone tapped me on the shoulder to say good-bye and I could excuse myself from the circle.

Sara tucked her arm in mine and left with me. "Well done, Hallie," she said. "Well done."

"Why do I despise him so?" I asked under my breath.

"Because he is despicable," she answered calmly, and then she went on to ask about Kathleen Riordan. "You seem especially fond of her, I noticed."

"I am," I told her. "I would like to see more of her, but . . . well, it's a very complicated story."

"Her father, James Riordan. Porter is highly impressed with him. I think he's the most glorious-looking man I've seen in ages. What do you think?"

I leaned over and kissed her on the cheek, and told her that I thought she was probably the wisest person I had ever met and that I was certainly glad to have her as a friend rather than an enemy, because I figured she could be formidable, in her snug little turbans and matching dresses.

She only gave me a small, pursed-lip smile and told me to extricate Porter from his trade unionists so he could take her home.

By eleven that night the hill was quiet again. It had been, everyone agreed, a *superior* party, a *bellissima* party, a most wonderful meeting of neighbors and friends and relatives. Clive and Faith and I had kicked off our shoes and sunk into the chairs in the living room, tired and excited and full of talk about who had been there and the music and the dancing that had started, spontaneously, as soon as it got dark, when someone turned on a Victrola in an open window.

"And you met yourself a schoolmarm," Faith said to Clive. "I notice she kept you in sight, better watch out."

Clive had laughed and shrugged it off, but he didn't dismiss Miss Ethel Mayer. I started to make a joke about how he had taken the first job offered to him, and I hoped the same wouldn't be true of women—but I thought better of it.

Clive left before midnight. I had thought that Faith might want to talk to me then about Thayer, but she was too weary, she said, to do anything but crawl into bed.

I put on my summer nightgown, which was long and white and cool, and climbed into bed, but I couldn't sleep. Images kept flashing in my head; I felt tense and fretful. I pulled on a sweater and went to sit on the front stoop, hoping to pull things together in my mind . . . Riordan, especially Riordan . . . Harry and Thelma, Kathleen . . . seeing Kathleen again. And Gerson.

I didn't notice the figure making its way up the hill, wavering slightly, holding on to the buildings, until it was upon me.

"I didn't think you'd be waiting up for me," Babe Conlon said, attempting to sound sarcastic even through puffed lips.

"My God, Babe," I asked her, "what happened?" One of her

eyes was swollen shut, her cheek was bruised and there was a cut at the edge of her mouth. She lowered herself tenderly to the stoop. Her dress was torn, and I wondered what other hurts were hidden.

"All I can say is I need a place for tonight. Can you help or not?" she got out, short of breath.

"Yes, of course," I told her, and took over. She let me bathe her cuts and put a cold cloth over her eye. Then I put her in my bed and pulled the quilt up around her, and sat down to keep watch.

"Listen," she said through swollen lips, "I got to get out of town tomorrow. Don't let me sleep too long, I got to get away."

I sat and watched her. I felt calm now and I knew what I was going to do. Tomorrow we would go to Modesto together, Babe Conlon and I. There was a story to be done in Modesto, and Babe could help me get it. That way, she would let me go with her. If she called the shots.

TWELVE

WE HAD BEEN ON the road for two hours, had crossed over the coastal hills and were headed south on the narrow band of road that shot dead center down the valley, and Babe had said no more than a dozen words all that while. She sat high on the passenger seat of my new Franklin with one of my straw hats held in place by a flowing silk scarf patterned with cabbage roses. The scarf had been extracted from the satchel we recovered from a girl named Minnie who met us that morning at the corner of Sansome and Clay.

I had overheard Babe, on the telephone, giving Minnie directions: "Don't tell anybody where you're going and if you see anybody watching the house, don't let them see you leave." She had listened for a moment; then her voice had risen in annoyance: "*Anybody*, Minnie, means anybody you don't know. Anybody could be a tall, mean-looking person or a short and fat and jolly-looking person. Anybody could be anybody."

Now she sat up straight on the seat next to me, her eyes closed as the Franklin moved down the long gravel road, throwing a plume of dust out behind us. I had had to do some fast talking to get Babe to come with me. She had dismissed my idea as not only ridiculous but wrongheaded as well. It had taken longer to talk her into coming with me than it took to convince the Boss to let me go to Modesto to do the abortion story.

The valley stretched out before us, low and flat and open, so vast and so empty that it seemed to swallow any human endeavor. A windrow of eucalyptus trees seemed thin and straggly and temporary, as if the first good wind might blow it away. Here and there a few old wooden houses, weathered by summer dust and winter winds, sat uneasy on their foundations. There were no basements, no storm cellars, and I wondered where farm women stored their watermelon pickles and blackberry jam.

Babe spoke: "Godawful country, isn't it?"

I had to agree.

It was three in the afternoon when we pulled into Modesto, and hot, but nothing in the town offered any relief. I stepped down from the Franklin and made the mistake of putting my hand on the hood. Every surface was hot to the touch; even the sidewalks felt hot through the soles of my shoes. The Wexford Hotel sat at the end of the main street, an ugly gray pile of stone topped by a tin turret. I shaded my eyes to look up and was almost blinded by the sun glinting off the shiny metal.

A fat lady in a dirty flowered wrapper was behind the desk, preoccupied with the peeling and eating of a cucumber. She looked up, chewing methodically, and listened as Babe told her we needed a room.

She spat some cucumber seeds into a wastebasket and said, "One bed or two?"

"Two," Babe answered. The woman looked at me and said, "That'll be three-fifty." I opened my bag before Babe could stop me.

"The sign out front says *two*-fifty," she said, moving in front of me so the woman would have to look at her.

"All the two-fifty rooms are gone." The woman shrugged.

Babe glanced at the keyboard. Only three were missing. "You only got three?" she asked.

"It's all right," I told her, taking out my money purse. As we walked down the dusty corridor that led to our room, I told her I was sorry.

"It's okay," Babe answered. "In fact, it's probably good. She thinks she's got us figured, and that should make it easier."

I asked her to explain.

"She knows you're the one in trouble and that you are paying. One look at you—how you dress, the car you drive, everything— she figures you can afford it. One look at me and she knows I'm familiar with the territory, you could say."

She stood looking in the mirror, which was in need of silvering and so gave back only a dim reflection, which softened the deep purple and red bruises around her eye. She was rubbing her jaw, and for the first time it occurred to me that talking might be painful.

A single bed and a double were crowded into the room, which smelled of dust and age and too many desultory cleanings. Rust marks streaked the porcelain of the single basin in the corner. The window looked over the main street, which was empty in the late-afternoon heat. Across the way was a cafe, the American, its menu lettered on a blackboard in the window. Next to it was a building so long empty there was no longer any trace of what it had been, and I wondered if anybody in town would remember. The town itself seemed so lightly anchored to the earth, its roots so shallow that it seemed it might pull free and go tumbling like some tangle weed, dry and brittle in the wind.

We turned on the fan that was perched on a dresser, took off our dresses and lay down on the beds to rest. The fan turned in long, lazy motions from left to right, stirring the still air and riffling the lace on my underslip each time it passed over me. There was something soothing about the sound of it, the slow lazy motion as it traveled back and forth, back and forth.

I thought about Faith, about how much had gone unsaid between us these last weeks and months, about Thayer Gerson showing up at the party. Yesterday, only yesterday. *Why hadn't she told me he was coming?* No. *Why didn't she ask me if it was all right for him to come?* That was the right question. Was she afraid I would say no? Was that it? I listened to the slow whirring movements of the fan and tried to think how I could ask Faith, how I could break through the barrier of politeness we had built between us. . . .

When I came awake the room was in shadow and Babe was gone. I felt thick, heavy. I did not want to be there in the dusty room. I filled the basin with cold water and splashed my face. I was dressed and brushing my hair when Babe knocked gently on the door and called out, "It's me," before entering.

She was all business. "Everything's set," she said. "Tomorrow morning, at six, we go to a farmhouse about ten miles outside of town. I got directions."

"Not the hotel?" I asked, taking out my notebook.

"Not since that girl died here," she answered.

I looked up at her, ready to write: "Tell me how you arranged it."

That was the deal, after all. I would get her out of town in return for her help in arranging the abortion.

She moved to the window, her back taut. "Let's go over this one more time," she said. "You're not out to nail anybody? Nobody goes to jail because you want to write a story about abortions?"

"That's right," I told her. "I won't use any names, not even the name of this town. I'll be very careful about protecting identities. The idea is to show how easy—or how hard—it is to get an abortion, and what happens when a woman goes looking for one. If I can get the abortionist to talk to me, I hope to find out something about the kinds of women who get them, and what happens to them."

Babe was frowning, or maybe just grimacing from the aches and pains that plagued her. The bruises on her face gave her an angry look. "What about your editor, will he know the names?"

"No. I promise, no one will know but me, and wild horses won't be able to drag them out of me." I tried to laugh, to break the tension.

We ate at a small restaurant called Oleg's which served surprisingly good food. The swarthy man who ran it was expansive and wanted to talk, but Babe was having none of it. (I followed her example, but asked for an explanation.)

"He's got a wife," she explained. "I'd be willing to bet on it, she's out there in the kitchen, and maybe three or four of their kids doing all the dirty work while he sits out here picking his teeth and shining up to the customers. But watch how he talks to the help—that'll give you some idea."

Pretty soon a drab-looking woman pushed backward through the double doors that led to the kitchen. She was carrying a heavy tray of food and almost collided with a table full of dirty dishes. The man barked at her in a language I didn't understand, but the tone was clear. The woman did not answer. It was as if the barrage of angry words were part of the routine, aimed at her bent back. I looked at Babe and raised my eyebrows. For the first time I thought: poor Babe, so knowledgeable about the meannesses that people inflict upon one another.

That night we lay on top of the covers in our separate beds, the heat flat and heavy. Her voice cut through the darkness: "Are you going to tell him you're a reporter?"

"That depends," I answered, feeling my words float out into the thick night air. "If the situation seems at all dangerous, I'll just say I've changed my mind. I'll tell them to keep the money but that I don't want to go through with it after all, and then I'll leave."

My words hung there in the darkness, until it seemed that Babe had nothing more to say and may even have fallen asleep. Then she spoke into the stifling air: "What if it does get dangerous?"

"I don't know," I faltered. "I guess I don't know much about this whole thing—I don't even know anybody who . . ." I stopped myself.

When the words came, they seemed detached, broken: "I had two. When I was a kid."

"Two," I repeated dully.

"Ten, eleven years ago," she said. "I was fifteen the first time."

The silence grew, hung heavy in the air between us. I wanted to say something, anything.

And then Babe told me: "Griffin thinks one of them was his."

I was glad she couldn't see me, glad I could hide my horror in the darkness. And then I was angry with myself because I knew so little, because I had been so stupid. Stupid, Hallie, stupid.

"I was so damn young and so damn dumb." Babe spoke with muffled anger. "He says I murdered it."

Lying there in the heat, I shivered. If I could see her, I guessed she would have the locked-in expression I had seen on her face so often.

She told me then, in a detail that was clinical and detached, how the abortion was done—the packing, how long it took. Never once did she utter the word "me" or "I."

We arrived at the farmhouse ten minutes early. I turned off the engine and we sat outside, the car parked in the dirt ruts that marked the space where wagons had always turned in. It would be hot when the sun came up, but it was pleasant enough now. The air moved about us, carrying the scent of the earth and a lingering ripeness. A rooster crowed to break the morning still. I glanced at Babe. The side of her face was splotched a purple and red. In the softness of the morning it did not look so angry.

The farmhouse huddled under an inadequate cottonwood tree. Chickens scratched around the house and under it as well, since it rested on brick cornerstones. There was no lawn, no green, only a tangled honeysuckle vine across one falling-down bit of gate.

It was time. We picked our way around the chicken droppings.

A dull-eyed girl, barefoot and carrying a baby on her hip, opened the door and made a sound that seemed to indicate we should follow her. She led us through a room that smelled sour, of sleep and torpor and dullness, into another that was starkly different. It would once have been the front parlor, but was now closed off and stripped of all furniture save for a large table covered with a sheet, two straight-backed chairs, a hall tree and a stand with a washbasin. In the corner was a lamp, the kind you sometimes see in doctors' offices.

We sat in silence for a time; my stomach felt dull and empty. I had not wanted to eat, and now I knew I would not be able to eat for a while. I heard the auto stop, brake. From the window I could see a man lower himself, carefully, as if he feared falling, from the driver's seat and take out a black bag.

He was not, I thought, as old as he looked. His suit was too large for him, but I had the feeling that it might once have fit. His eyes were yellow and tired; everything about him suggested an overwhelming weariness.

"I don't want to know your names," he said before we could say anything to him. And then: "Which of you requires the procedure?"

Requires the procedure. I cleared my throat and said it was me. He asked Babe to wait outside. She looked at me and I nodded, as if to say "Nothing to fear."

"Can you tell me how far along you are?" he asked almost before she had closed the door behind her. He was taking off his coat, hanging it meticulously on the hall tree.

"About three months," I answered.

He began to roll up his sleeves, asking questions all the while: my age, my health, any previous pregnancies, any medical problems that I knew about . . . He was precise, careful, efficient. He did not want to waste time, I could see that. In a moment he would ask me to disrobe. I did not have to pretend nervousness when I asked, "Would you mind if I asked you some questions, sir?" (The "sir" had come out automatically, and surprised me.) I rushed on, "Are you a medical doctor?"

He nodded. "I am."

I cleared my throat. "And is that from an accredited medical school?"

He looked at me now, his tired eyes trying to see me. I was a girl in trouble, yet I knew to ask certain questions.

"That's right," he answered, wary now.

"And do you have much experience with these . . . kinds of procedures?" I pushed on.

He let his hands hang loose by his sides and stared at me. "What is it, miss?" he asked. "Are you scared, is that it?"

"I suppose so," I answered. "I mean, I'm not certain about . . ."

His voice seemed to take on new depths of weariness, but there was a certain tenderness there too. "If you're not sure this is the right thing, miss, you should go home and find another way. You don't have to do this, you know."

It was not what I expected, not at all. For an instant I was confused; then I knew what I had to do.

"Doctor, please," I said, talking fast. "My name is Hallie Duer and I'm a reporter for the *San Francisco Times*. I'm going to write a story about what it's like to be pregnant and to get an abortion. That's why I'm here, to do a story. I'm not pregnant."

He backed away from me and seemed to grow smaller and grayer with every step. Finally he bumped into the table with the basin on it and could go no farther.

Anxious to reassure him, I rushed on: "I'm not going to use your name, in fact I won't use any names that could conceivably lead to you. No one will ever know who you are—I don't really want to know about you, but I do want to know about the women who come to you to end pregnancies."

He sat down abruptly, so that for a moment I thought he might tumble over, and folded his hands as a girl might, or a preacher. He was resigned, I could see it—to whatever was going to happen next, to the room, to me. It wasn't so much weariness I had sensed in him as resignation.

"Why?" I prodded him. "Why do you do them?"

He looked down at his hands. "So somebody else won't."

"Somebody?" I probed, as gently as he himself might, in the beginning, pressing here on soft tissues, and pushing there.

"Old Annie over in the Lathrope Hills. Or one of the midwives, or somebody's old aunt, or the Mexicans. They have their own methods, the Mexicans. There's always the risk of infection. Most of the women are malnourished, many are sick to begin with. The risk is high, starting out." He looked as if he were trying to figure how to make his hands work again. "Women get trapped by their bodies," he went on, "so it's kind of like, a kid gets caught in a coon trap. They come to me for help. I'm obliged to give it. There's nobody else in these parts who can do any better. God knows I wish there were. You know . . . you know, the reality is something people don't want to look at. A few days ago a farm woman came to me. She looked to be about fifty, but she was in fact only thirty-two. She already has seven young ones, the oldest twelve. And another on the way. Her man's out of work, they can't feed the ones they've got. It is too much to bear, you can see that . . . too much."

I wanted to interrupt, to ask if he meant it was too much for her to bear or too much for him, but I didn't dare stop him because he had started talking, the words were coming—chances are they had been coming for a long time, and they needed to be out.

"Or a child will come in," he went on, "a little girl, no more than thirteen. Or the ones who are seventeen or so and wanting to get away from home. Bad girls, I guess you'd call them. None of them wants those babies that are growing inside of them. Nobody in God's green earth wants those babies, and outside, here"— he gestured as if to take in the room, the world—"outside, they only say how it's a sin to destroy a fetus, but I tell you, it's sinful to bring babies into a world where they can't hope for anything but ugliness and misery, a world without hope. That's all, just no hope."

He fell silent then. I wrote, wanting to catch every word

because it seemed so simple and yet so eloquent. There was a knock on the door and I realized that Babe must have noticed the sudden silence.

"Everything's fine, Babe," I called to her.

"Babe?" he asked, puzzled.

"My friend," I answered. "That's her name."

He nodded. "I think your friend will know what I'm talking about."

"Why do you say that?" I asked.

"You can tell," he answered. "After a while, you get so you can tell."

I changed the subject. "Can you tell me how many abortions you have performed?" I asked.

He shook himself, as if trying to remember. "How many? I don't know. Many. Maybe a hundred. I've been doing them for two years now. I don't know." He was twisting his hands, wringing them. Suddenly he blurted, "When are they coming?"

"Who?" I asked.

"The police."

I shook my head. "No, no authorities. I meant it when I said I'm a reporter and I'm writing a story. I promise, no police. I won't use your name."

I saw it then: he thought it was all over, that he was out. And he wanted out.

"Why don't you just leave?" I asked. "You haven't been caught, but it seems to me it's only a matter of time. Look how easily I found you! And a girl died in the Wexford Hotel—that's why my editor told me to do this story. Why don't you go someplace else, a town not so poor, where there are other doctors?"

He put his hands over his face and for a moment I thought he was sobbing, but he wasn't. It was only a cough, a dry hacking cough.

"I'll tell you what you want to know," he said, and for the next hour he did.

Babe stood on the street next to the Franklin, her satchel in one hand. I was in the driver's seat, ready to leave for home. "You got everything you need for the story?" she asked.

"Everything," I told her, "thanks to you."

"We're square then," she said, resting her hand on the door. I put mine on top of hers briefly and thanked her and told her to keep in touch.

She said she would, and did not wait for me to leave but walked down the dusty street, satchel in hand, listing gently to one side under the weight of it. She did not say where she was going, and I knew not to ask.

I came into the office just before five, when almost everyone was getting ready to go home. It was seven by the time I finished the story. I sat down at Gwen's switchboard and punched in a line. The telephone rang at the cottage, but there was no answer. I tried Clive's boardinghouse, and a cheerful voice told me that he was out for the evening. I sat there, staring at Gwen's board, trying to think what to do. I was bone-tired and dusty, but I was not ready to go home. Too much was swimming around in my mind; I did not want to be alone.

The telephone rang four times . . . I would hang up on the fifth, I thought, maybe the sixth, it was no use . . . when he answered, absentmindedly, as if he were thinking about something else. "Yes?" he asked.

"Yes?" I repeated, realizing that I needed an explanation for this call. "Riordan, it's Hallie Duer. I didn't think I would reach you—I mean, I didn't think you'd be working so late . . . I called on the off-chance that you might be, and I guess you are . . ."

"What are you trying to say?" he asked, rather sternly I thought. "That you called me but you didn't want to reach me?"

"No!" I said, laughing nervously. "I'm making a mess of this,

Riordan. To be honest, I've just returned from a story—I got back at around five, and finished it, and I thought it would be nice if I could find someone who might like to have a bite of dinner with me, and maybe talk a little, but if you're busy, if . . ." I was beginning to ramble, to jabber on; I couldn't seem to stop.

"So that's it," he said. I had his attention now, I could tell. "You want *someone* to take you out to dinner, is that it?"

"No!" I groaned. "No, please—I was inviting you if you want to, if . . ."

He was laughing. "Make up your mind, woman," he said. "Either you called to have dinner with me or you didn't. Which is it?"

"I did," I sputtered. "I mean, dinner . . . yes."

"Fine," he said, suddenly easy, so I knew he had been playing. I didn't care.

"I'll pick you up in front of your building."

"Give me half an hour to finish."

"Agreed," I said, taking the plug out of the switchboard and smiling to myself.

We sat at a corner table looking out over the water. Across the bay, the lights sparkled, and closer still, red and blue lights moved gently, reflected in the moving water below our window. There were candlelight and white tablecloths, and fresh French bread in a silver basket and small sculptured curls of butter floating in icy water. All the sad, worn-out towns strung along the valley road receded, seemed far away.

"This morning," I began, leaning slightly toward him over the narrow expanse of table, "I was in a ramshackle old farmhouse in the valley . . ." I told him about Babe, and the fat woman in the hotel, and I told him about the abortionist who was not what I had expected, and what I had learned from him, which was not what I had expected, either. I was careful not to mention any names or places; other than that, I told him everything.

He listened, intent on what I was saying, and every now and

then he asked a question. "This doctor—the abortionist—do you feel that he is representative of most abortionists?"

"Not at all," I answered. "That's just the point—I stumbled onto the exception, probably the one man who could show the other side of this issue, the 'reality,' as he called it."

"Hallie," he said, making his fingers into a tent, the tips touching each other, "you can't even use the word 'abortion' in the newspaper, it offends public sensibilities. So how do you think the public is going to receive your news about an abortionist who, if I understand what you are saying, is performing a humanitarian service?"

I bit my lip. "It would have worked—I mean the story would have worked—if I had found some disgusting abortionist who took money from prostitutes only, some low life who trades in sin. That would have appealed to the public prejudices and made for a sensational exclusive. I don't know if that is what the Boss expected when he said there might be a story on abortions. But I do know that if any editor has the courage to run this story, it is Sanford Curtin."

He leaned forward now, his elbows on the table. "Hallie, listen. Courage is one thing; don't confuse it with foolhardiness. Do you think there is even a remote chance of getting a fair hearing on this subject in the current climate? Sanford doesn't shrink from a fight, no. But he also knows you have to pick your fights, and you don't pick one you have no chance of winning."

"Still," I interrupted, "It seems so wrong not to do something to correct the notion . . . that doctor out there and so alone. It isn't right."

"Aren't you making a judgment, Hallie? I mean, on the right and wrong of it? By presenting this doctor as a man who is doing a thankless but necessary job, aren't you taking a moral stand on an issue that goes against the whole of the religious establishment? The Sanctity of Life. You'll have them howling after you—or after Sanford."

"Screaming bloody murder," I said, wincing at the words even as I said them, knowing he was right. The only way I could write about an abortionist was to portray him as a monster.

Changing the subject, Riordan asked me what it was that I liked about Babe. "Her lack of self-pity," I answered. "She has this very clear way of looking at things—not at what she wants them to be, but what is. She's a realist, and yet she's willing to take a stand that goes against reason. Calling someone who could arrest her a 'dumb shit,' for example. I don't know, it seems to me she has real courage."

We talked a little about Agnes then, and a little about Kathleen, and we drank coffee in a comfortable silence, looking at each other over the rims of our cups, studying the reflections of the lights on water.

"Thank you," I finally said. "I needed to talk it out—the story, I mean. I think that must have been why I called you tonight. It seemed as if I was doing it on the spur of the moment, but I wasn't, really. I must have known . . . well, that you would be good enough to hear me out. And maybe I even knew there was a problem with the story, one that I would have to face. So . . . thank you."

He looked at me with a funny small smile on his face, and was about to say something when a large man came lumbering up out of a dark corner of the restaurant.

"Jimmy boy," the man said, breathing hard, as if he had been exerting himself. He clapped a big hand on Riordan's shoulder. "Haven't seen you in a month of Sundays. Your Uncle Ned tells me you work all the time. How's the wife and kiddies?" At this he glanced over at me and made a motion as if to tip his hat, had he been wearing one. The implication was clear. Riordan did not get up. The older man was wheezing; he leaned heavily on the table. "'S funny thing, Jimmy," he said, "but looking at you over here, Paddy and me"—he made a motion, as if to show that Paddy was standing just beyond the circle of light—"we saw you sitting here, and Paddy said, 'If you think about it now, doesn't that make you remember poor Tom'—the pretty lady here, he meant, she's just the kind of girl Tom would bring in, bless him."

Riordan looked at the man with contempt and with unchecked anger. He stood, and for a moment I thought the man was going to simply wither under Riordan's scathing glance. "Get out of here, George," Riordan said. "Tell Paddy I want a check and I want it now."

Outside, he began to walk in long limping strides down the pier until he could go no farther. I was out of breath when I caught up with him. "Riordan," I tried to say, "Riordan, I'm so sorry if I . . ."

He turned on me, his eyes dark and angry. "Why in the hell should you be sorry?" he asked. "Didn't you hear the insulting bastard? Doesn't that bother you?" He was gripping the iron railing, looking out over the black waters of the bay, and I could feel the anger washing over him. I said nothing, afraid that anything I might say would be wrong.

When he turned to look at me again, the anger was under control. In its place was a coldness; all the warmth of the restaurant was gone, he had closed in on himself again. "The thing is," he said, mocking now, "Paddy back there was out of line, but he was right about one thing. You are exactly the kind of girl Tom would want."

I was afraid to say what I wanted to say—that Tom is dead but you aren't. That you're alive but you aren't living. And neither am I, we are alike in that. We are waiting, both of us, involved in others' lives, observers—you in the courtroom, me in the newsroom. We have detached ourselves from the pain of living; we are watching from the sidelines. I held my breath and waited. I had waited for so long, but I would have to wait longer.

As Riordan had predicted, my story did not appear in the pages of the *Times*. The Boss did not make easy excuses. He said quite simply that he did not fault the story, but that people have a way of refusing to look at ugly realities. He said that in a case like this, the public would choose to kill the messenger to avoid bad news. I think he was surprised at how easily I accepted his decision. He had Riordon to thank for that, but I didn't tell him. I only said that the experience had been useful, that I had learned something and that would have to be enough. And he had looked at me in that sad way he had, and nodded, and for an instant I had the uneasy feeling that he knew more than I thought he knew.

"By the way, Hallie," the Boss called after me, "a Treasury agent stopped by yesterday looking for you."

"A Treasury agent?" I echoed.

"A little fellow, short and fat—said his name was Griffin and that he knew you."

"Mason Griffin?" I asked. "What did you tell him?"

"Nothing," the Boss answered. "Not one word."

Sanford Curtin had the kind of instinct that told him when to talk and when not to. Not everybody did.

Somehow Mason Griffin found out that Babe had gone as far as Modesto with me.

THIRTEEN

FREDDIE ZEBRA SCURRIED across the lobby of the St. Francis Hotel, almost knocking over a potted palm in his haste to reach me. He had information, that much I knew. When Freddie side-stepped in that peculiar manner, it meant he had something to tell you that could hardly wait to come rolling off his tongue.

He stuttered it out: "Arbuckle is here—you know, Fatty Arbuckle, the moving-picture actor—with a party of people. A producer, another actor. He drove that big Pierce-Arrow of his up from Los Angeles. Twenty-five thousand dollars—that's what it cost. Has a toilet in it and everything. A regular gasoline palace. They're having a party up there in 1219 right now. It's true—a big party:" He lowered his voice. "And booze. Lots of it. Flowing. What do you think? Should I try to get you invited up?"

I shook my head. "I'm not in the mood for a party, Freddie," I told him, knowing it was highly unlikely that he could get me an invitation anyway. I did sit in the lobby for a time to watch the comings and goings. Every now and then Freddie would hurry by, running his errands, self-importantly going for ice cubes and once for a Victrola that he said Arbuckle himself had ordered so that his guests could dance.

Freddie came back downstairs beaming. "Look at this . . ." He showed me a silver dollar. "He gave me this for a tip. What a heart that man has, sitting up there just as big as life—in his pajamas still. I heard somebody ask him why he didn't get dressed, and he said he burned his backside. That'd be just like him, wouldn't it— Fatty Arbuckle burning his backside?" He cackled, imagining it.

"Who else is up there?" I asked, and he rattled off names of a couple of showgirls. I wrote them down, to please Freddie more than anything, and out of habit, too. Note-taking was becoming second nature.

"Is Arbuckle dancing?" I asked.

"Arbuckle? Naw!" Freddie answered as if the idea itself was ludicrous. "But I can tell you what they're playing—'Second-Hand Rose' and 'Three o'Clock in the Morning' and 'On the Gin Gin Ginny Shore . . .'" That reminded him of the errand he was supposed to be running. "I've got to go over to Gobey's," he said in a stage whisper. "They're drinking orange blossoms up there— crushed ice and orange juice and bootleg gin. Some of those girls are getting a snoutful, I can tell you."

"Sounds pretty dreary to me," I said, and got up to phone in my story: "Roscoe 'Fatty' Arbuckle, the moving-picture actor, arrived in the city on Friday evening, having driven from Los Angeles in his touring car. He was accompanied by director Fred Fischbach and actor Lowell Sherman. Arbuckle recently finished three consecutive films, and the men are on a short holiday." That much the bell captain had given me.

I walked out of the St. Francis and joined a small group that had gathered around the Pierce-Arrow which I knew must belong to Arbuckle. It made my Franklin look like a kiddie car.

Mac, the doorman, caught my eye. "Mr. Arbuckle had it brought around so he could take a friend for a ride. He should be out any minute if you want to wait."

I told him I had heard that Arbuckle was still in his pajamas and it might be a longer wait than anyone expected.

I walked back into the lobby to telephone Faith. "I haven't had lunch, have you?" I asked, and when she wanted to know what time it was I knew she hadn't. "Put the teapot on, then, I'll bring sandwiches," I said.

We spread our lunch on the little table in her waiting room. "A tea party!" Faith chirped. "How lovely."

"Do you realize," I said, measuring my words, "that we've hardly had a meal together in the past three weeks?"

"Who'd you eat with last night?" she asked, shifting the conversation.

"Clive," I said. "And I've seen little enough of him lately, either."

"I'll bet he's been seeing that schoolteacher," she put in, determined to ignore my complaints.

I gave up. "That's right. This weekend he's going to a church social with her."

"A church social?" Faith said, unbelieving. "Poor Clive."

"Actually, he doesn't mind. About the social. He seems really to like her, at least he told me he thinks she is quite nice."

"Is she?" Faith asked in a dubious way.

"I don't know," I answered. "I had very little chance to talk to her at the party, and Gwen hasn't said very much except that her cousin Ethel is 'creeping up on twenty-five' and has some 'big ideas.' When I asked what she meant by 'big ideas' Gwen said something to the effect that Ethel was searching for a suitable husband, a professional man with a 'good' background and 'positive prospects.' Ethel doesn't seem to be very fond of schoolteaching, and would like to have her own family to concentrate on."

Faith frowned into her teacup. "It sounds like grocery shopping," she said.

"I don't know," I answered, trying to sound sincere rather than mocking, "wanting a husband and children, that seems to me to be an understandable goal . . ."

Faith's eyes flashed, and she started to say something, when we heard the door open and close again on the lower landing.

"That's my four-o'clock," she said, dismayed. We hurried to gather up the evidence of our impromptu lunch. She brushed the crumbs from her skirt and smoothed her hair and, just as we heard the customer arrive at the top of the stairs, gave me a quick hug.

I hugged her back and whispered a quick "So long." We were not going to talk about Thayer, not now and probably not ever. A large part of her life was closed to me. It had been for some time, but I hadn't wanted to admit it. I walked back to the office with a strange, sad little pressure that seemed to be lodged beneath my breastbone. It was, I supposed, the residue of acceptance of loss.

The trial of Agnes Marchant began at ten o'clock on the morning of September 8, a bright cloudless Thursday, in the Oakland courtroom of Judge David Wendover, scarcely a mile from the Marchant house on the shores of Lake Merritt.

I felt as I always felt when I entered such a high-ceilinged chamber with its polished wood and shining brass—awed, a little frightened, certain that momentous events were about to take place, that what was to happen was inexorable.

The press bench was full. An additional section was added to accommodate a full contingent of reporters. The *Los Angeles Times* had sent a man and so had the *New York Times*. I was surprised to see Annie Farrell covering for the Hearst papers. It was not her kind of story. This was not a sensational trial, it did not have the emotional impact of Sacco and Vanzetti, the Italian immigrants charged with murder, whom many thought were being tried because they were anarchists. The Marchant case was receiving national attention because it seemed certain to become a test case for the constitutionality of the Criminal Syndicalist laws. No one, except perhaps for Agnes Marchant, believed it would end in this courtroom.

There was a hush as she entered with Riordan. My heart sank at the sight of her, so fragile in her old-fashioned brown suit with its long skirt. When all the eyes in the courtroom turned to her she faltered and blinked, as if blinded by a glare. Riordan grasped her arm and she leaned against him; then she seemed to recover.

I had never seen him in action in the courtroom. In his dark suit with the high white collar, he moved easily through the rituals. In control; at ease; taking his time.

"Quite a handsome fellow," Annie Farrell whispered. "I hear you have an inside track on this story."

I turned my face in her direction and smiled slightly, without looking at her. Later the *New York Times* man stopped me in the hall to ask if I could give him some background on Agnes. When I asked, "Why me?" he answered, "Because I hear you know more about this case than anyone else in town."

"Do you also hear that I have an inside track to Agnes Marchant and her attorney?"

"That too," he said, as if it were a point in my favor.

We talked about the issues of the case, then about the animosity toward the IWW. "Out here," I told him, "most people think it means 'I Won't Work.'" He told me it meant the same back east, that the Wobblies were under attack from all quarters, and given that climate, he didn't think Agnes had a prayer in hell.

Porter Reade—Sara's lanky, intense godson—appeared in the public seats one day, and cornered me in the hallway during a recess. "This is terrible," he said, oblivious of the people surging around us, listening. "What bothers me most," he went on, "is that Mr. Riordan is making everything so clear—I mean, I don't see how anybody can believe that Agnes Marchant plotted to overthrow the government. It's absurd. She's exactly the kind of person we should be applauding—kind and caring about the poor, and willing to put her life on the line. And she's got the best lawyer around—I just think people have taken leave of their senses. I sit there, and hear Mr. Riordan, and look at the jury and I know they aren't listening. They've convicted her already."

I wished Porter would lower his voice. I spoke softly to him, hoping he would take the hint: "Her lawyer has confidence in the system—he doesn't think Agnes will go to jail."

"Maybe not jail," Porter boomed out, "I don't doubt that Mr. Riordan will save her skin, but that's not enough. She's right, and they're wrong—and he can't make them see it. God! They think she's a silly goose or a dangerous Red. Can you understand it?"

"No, Porter, and my job here is to report what happens, not try to justify it." I took him by the arm and ushered him back into the courtroom, where he would have to be quiet. I made a mental note to talk to Sara about Porter. If the boy didn't become more circumspect, he was going to be in trouble, too.

Before I could return to my own place at the press table, Annie Farrell took my arm and said, "The boy's right, Hallie. All Riordan can do is try to keep her out of jail."

I turned to look at her. There was nothing mocking in her eyes, only concern.

"Sometimes I think," I said to her, speaking slowly to get the thought right, "that Agnes is a kind of ritual offering to some unnamed fear, that she is being sacrificed to quiet some vengeful political god."

Annie added: "The maiden lady who has lived a faultless life, ministering to the poor, by example showing the rest of us the way." She patted me on the arm.

In her front-page bylined article the next day, Annie quoted what I had said about unnamed fears and vengeful gods verbatim, attributing it to "a veteran observer." It was, I knew, Annie Farrell's own way of saying "Let the little lady through."

On Friday evening, Freddie Zebra called me at the cottage to say he had heard that one of the girls at the Arbuckle party was dead, and they were saying that Arbuckle did it.

"Did what?" I wanted to know. "Killed her?"

"Raped. Something, I don't know. They said he took her in another room that day at the party and laid on top of her and busted something. Anyway, she's dead."

"That's awful," I told him, repulsed by the idea. "Who is saying all this?"

"People," he mumbled. "I don't know."

"Yes you do, Freddie," I lashed out. "You know who told you and you'd better tell me. I want those names. If this story is true, it's ghastly. And if it isn't true, it's even worse. Roscoe Arbuckle is news, anything he does is news and if he did this it will be the biggest news to hit the papers in a long time. So give me names."

Some strange, strangling sounds came over the wire, as if he were trying to form words. "Maude Delmont, she's one. A friend of the dead girl, she was at the party too. Wearing that other actor's pajamas."

"Where can I find her, and who else have you talked to? I need to check them out."

"I'll find out. Call you right back," he said, and hung up. It was the last anybody heard from Freddie Zebra.

Frannie Bolten answered the telephone. "Sorry to get you out of bed, Frannie," I told her, "but a big story is breaking and I think Gene should meet me in the city room."

He arrived before I did, and called in the police reporters while I scanned my notebooks, looking for the names that I had scribbled last Monday, the names of the showgirls who were in the Arbuckle suite that afternoon. "Here they are!" I shouted, and Gene barked back, "Good girl!"

Zey Preven and Alice Blake. No Prevens were listed in the telephone directory, but there were several Blakes. After three false tries, I found the right one. It was midnight.

"Are you the Alice Blake who was at the Roscoe Arbuckle party at the St. Francis on Monday?"

"What?" she said, groggy and caught off guard.

"They're saying that Arbuckle raped and killed that woman in his bedroom on Monday afternoon. Is that what happened? Virginia Rappé was her name, she's dead."

"Dead?" the woman repeated. "No, listen. It wasn't like that. Please, don't . . . No. That's not right."

"If Arbuckle didn't do it, as you say, then what happened in that room to kill that girl?"

"She was sick, and screaming that she was going to die, but he didn't have anything . . ." She stopped, then said, "I can't talk to you," and hung up.

I sat for a while, thinking about the moving picture I had seen with Kathleen, the big good-natured man with the serious expression that could, in an instant, be transformed by a quizzical little lift of his eyebrows and an impish grin. A funny man, big and innocent. A clown.

"I got him on the phone," Lloyd Garr shouted. "Fatty Arbuckle himself, down in L.A. When I asked him if he'd forced her, or if she was willing, I thought he'd choke to death." He let out a harsh, ugly laugh.

"Did it occur to you that he might not have done it?" I asked sharply. I did not like Lloyd Garr, and now I liked him even less.

"He did it," he said. "That guy's so rich, he can do anything he wants. But they're going to nail him for this—you know why?"

I turned away, not wanting to hear Lloyd Garr's theory, but knowing I would have to. "Because," he said, with a sort of triumph, "the idea is so disgusting—a big fat guy like that laying on top of a girl and busting something inside her . . . that's what people are going to think about."

"Dear God," I said to myself, fearing that he could be right.

The coroner's report said the girl died of peritonitis, the result of a ruptured bladder. That story appeared in the paper, along with an interview with Maude Delmont, the dead girl's friend, who gave a lurid account of the party, and accused Arbuckle of causing Virginia Rappé's death. I was one of six reporters ushered into Maude Delmont's room at the St. Francis. She was propped in bed, looking theatrically wan. Two doctors were in attendance. When the questioning got rough, we were told to leave.

"Do you believe her?" I asked Annie Farrell as we filed out of the room.

"Lousy actress," she answered, "but it's still front-page stuff."

She was right; every paper in the city, including the *Times*, ran four-column headlines repeating Maude Delmont's story, and the police amplified the charges, announcing with self-righteous vigor that Arbuckle would not be able to buy his way out of the crime.

Arbuckle had returned to San Francisco voluntarily, saying he wanted to clear up any misunderstanding, saying he was innocent of the charges, saying that he supposed the reason Maude Delmont was accusing him was that he had asked her to leave the party, and she got sore. But no one else had stepped forward in his defense. When he got to San Francisco, Arbuckle's lawyers insisted he say nothing at all. Everyone, it seemed, had stopped talking. Everyone but Maude Delmont and the district attorney's office, and what they had to say was damning to the movie actor. In a matter of days, all of Fatty Arbuckle's films had been removed from every movie house in America. In a matter of a single week, the man who had symbolized innocent fun had become a satyr, decadent and depraved. Not funny and fat, but disgusting and fat.

On Sunday I located George Glennon, the St. Francis' house detective. He was sitting in the living room of a little house in the Mission, newspapers strewn around him and an empty bottle of home brew on the floor. He was, I figured, about half-drunk. "What do you know about all this?" I asked. "Were you at that party?"

"Listen," he said, "this is all just crazy. Hell. Arbuckle didn't rape her any more than I did. I can't figure why people are listening to that Delmont dame. I talked to the girl—Virginia—and she told me nobody hurt her. She was pretty sick, and at first they thought it was just that she had too much to drink. Delmont was drunk, falling-down drunk. Hell, I sat up with the two of them all that night. And I know that at least two doctors saw the Rappé girl. There were plenty of people at that party, it shouldn't be hard to prove he had nothing to do with that girl's dying. Hell, Arbuckle's no saint, but he shouldn't have to be knocked out by the likes of her."

"Why aren't you at work?" I asked.

He shook his head. "Got canned. For sitting up with the two of them, having a drink or so. Dereliction of duty, the manager said. Hah! Arbuckle paid for everything, and when he left the next morning to go back to Los Angeles on the *Harvard*, they saw him off like he was royalty . . . then when he came back on Saturday to answer questions, they turned him away. Did you know that?"

I said I didn't, and asked if he could give me any leads, any names. He told me to try the hotel doctors. "All kinds of people were up there that day," he repeated.

It was a tangled case, a story with more questions than answers, a sensation. The Hearst papers played it big, concocting doctored photographs—of Virginia Rappé and Arbuckle together, of Arbuckle behind bars. The women's associations were up in arms, demanding that Arbuckle be made to pay for his transgressions, their accusations shrill and angry.

"All they know is what they read in the papers," Harry said to me, "and all they read in the papers makes Arbuckle seem a monster."

When the telephone rang in the cottage before eight the next morning I sat up in bed and tried to shake the sleep away. It would be, I thought, somebody calling on the Arbuckle story. The line crackled so that I had to strain to hear.

"It's me—Babe," a voice said.

"Where are you?" I shouted to make myself heard. "At the South Pole?"

"Almost," she said. "I need you to do me a favor. Could you get a message to Minnie? She's over at 345 Arguello. Tell her to put my things in a box and save them for me. Tell her I'll let her know where to send them as soon as I have a place. And tell her not to let anyone know that she's heard from me. Could you do that?"

"Of course," I said, "but listen, why don't I pick up your things and keep them here until we can get them to you? And, Babe, listen. You should know that Griffin has been asking about you—he came to the newspaper. He knows you went as far as Modesto with me."

"Okay, yeah," she said, and then, "Maybe you better keep my things there. Minnie's not too smart."

"One more thing," I shouted into the phone. "You've read about the Arbuckle story. Do you know anybody who might know two showgirls who were there?"

The line crackled. "Tell Minnie to help you find a girl named Sunny."

"Thanks," I said, and was about to ask how she was feeling, when the line went dead.

On the ferry to Oakland I thought about Agnes Marchant and Roscoe Arbuckle, about how easily they had drifted into the public consciousness as demons, as enemies of the public good. The Arbuckle story had pushed the Marchant case off the front page. Most of the reporters sent to cover the trial had been shifted to the city to track down leads in the more sensational story.

I slipped away early myself that Monday, to make my way to the little house on Arguello where Minnie lived. She sat on the narrow bed in the room that had been Babe's, and watched as I emptied the chifforobe. It didn't take long to collect Babe's possessions. There was a packet of photographs, a journal, a box of jewelry. The only thing that seemed in the least frivolous was a small ceramic dog which sat on a ledge near the window. "She's had that a long time," Minnie told me. "There's some dresses, too." I folded them carefully, recognizing the wrapper she had worn that day in Sacramento when I found her on the back porch after the raid.

Minnie went with me to find Sunny. After several stops, we finally found her sitting in a cafe near Market Street.

"Sunny knows everybody," Minnie had told me. "She's so friendly, you'll see."

I did see. Sunny was one of those people who seem to be in a continual state of high spirits, her speech embroidered with laughter and punctuated with "honeys" and "sweeties."

"Sure I know Zey and Alice, and I know about that party too. Dollie Clark told me about it, she was there later on, after the girl that died had been taken away. Of course, she wasn't dead then. Everybody thought she was just drunk, Dollie said. That's what they told her, anyway. Dollie said that one of the girls who was there told her this Virginia started screaming and ripping off all her clothes and saying she was going to die. And everybody'd had more than a few drinks, of course, and they tried to help her. Put her in a cold bath, things like that."

"You mean she ripped her own clothes off?" I asked, astonished.

"Oh yes," Sunny burbled. "In fact, somebody who knew her said she'd done it before at parties. Whenever she had a few drinks . . . well"—she made a gesture of taking off her dress—"off everything came!" She laughed. "Of course, not everybody at that party was a gentleman," she said. "Dollie was chased around the bedroom by that other actor, Mr. Sherman, and she had to go to Mr. Arbuckle to ask him for help. He told the man to stop it, to leave Dollie alone."

"I don't understand," I said. "If all of this is true, why hasn't anybody gone to the police?"

Sunny's eyes widened. "But they have," she said. "The police know. They've even got Zey and Alice somewhere—*so they'll be sure to tell the truth.*"

I took it to the Boss. "You're right, Hallie. Something is wrong here, and we've got to try to get to the bottom of it. But for now, you stay on the Marchant story. As soon as it's over"—he looked at me then, his eyes sad because he knew it would be over, but not for Agnes—"then you go on the Arbuckle story full-time."

Luis had sat, every day, behind Agnes on the first row of the public benches, wearing a collar that was too large, so that his neck bobbed up and down in it like a turtle's. I thought about the day she had told me about Luis, how he treated her like a little girl because he had worked for her father, how stubborn he was about taking orders. *And how loyal*, I thought.

Agnes sat, her back very straight, her hands folded in her lap, at times twisting her handkerchief, which she otherwise kept tucked into her sleeve. The court sessions had become a very slow, very elegant quadrille: *All rise . . . hear ye, hear ye . . . your honor . . . may it please the court . . .* The stately ritual continued, day after day, until the judge charged the jury and we waited for a verdict.

It took them twenty minutes to find Agnes Marchant guilty as charged.

Agnes closed her eyes and swayed, but Riordan was there. I did not look at her face, but at his—and then quickly away, remembering the day at the Hall of Justice, under the stair. Remembering the despair, the hurt.

When I joined them in an anteroom, Agnes was standing staring out the window and Riordan was sitting in a chair, his elbows propped on the long table that dominated the room.

"Well, the miracle didn't happen," I said in what I hoped was a let's-get-on-with-it tone. "At least the public spectacle is over. Now, I suppose, the real work begins."

Agnes turned to look at me with an expression of amazement. "Begins?" she moaned. "Oh, Hallie, no. It's over."

Slowly Riordan pushed himself out of the chair. "Hallie's right. You are out on appeal, and it's going to be that way for quite a while. I'm sorry, Agnes, but that's the best we can do right now."

Agnes sighed. "You know what I would like?" she said, suddenly wistful. "I'd like to go sit at the seashore and look out at the ocean for a very long time, just to get everything clear in my mind."

Something in her voice made me tremble. "That's probably a very good idea," Riordan said slowly, in a way that made me think he heard it too. "Listen," he went on, "maybe we should all do that—go to the ocean to clear our minds. Why don't the two of you join me at Willow Camp this weekend? There's a fairly nice hotel there for you, and I have a fishing cottage on the beach."

"That sounds very nice," Agnes said. "I think I would like that. Can you go, Hallie?" Her face was full of hope, as if going to the beach would make things right. I could not have denied her, not even if I had wanted to. The Arbuckle story would have to wait; I would have to think up an excuse for missing work on Saturday. I thought about it on the ferry back to the city: how easily I had forfeited my lead on the Arbuckle story to go to the beach.

We were to meet at the Ferry Building in time to catch the nine o'clock ferry to Sausalito. A few minutes before eight, just as I was stuffing a wool sweater into my canvas satchel, the telephone rang. Agnes's voice, strong and clear, rang out: "Hallie, my dear, I'm afraid I can't join you after all for the trip to the beach. My cousin from Seattle has arrived to be with me for a spell, bless her. She has a family and it is hard for her to get away, but she came . . ."

She was obviously pleased about the visit, but I had to be sure. "You've had such a big disappointment, Agnes," I said. "Can you tell me how you feel this morning?"

"I know what you mean," she said, "and I can't say how dear you are to care. But I think I have finally understood what you and James have been trying to explain . . . that patience is what I must learn, that I am going to have to live with this, perhaps for a long time. That's the penalty for being so outspoken." She laughed, and it was a simple laugh—not bitter or angry—and then she asked me to be sure to let "James Francis" know of the change in plans. Calling him James Francis was, for Agnes, a form of endearment.

"Agnes isn't going?" Faith called from the next room. She appeared in the doorway. "What are you going to do, Hal?"

"I'm not sure," I answered, pulling on my coat. "I know one thing, I'm not going to tell him over the telephone."

"Hallie," Faith said, her face full of concern, "listen. Wait. He's married, you know that. And Catholic. You could be hurt." For a moment I thought she was going to try to stop me. But all she did was whisper, "Take care."

I watched him jump off the streetcar and walk, with that long, limping stride, toward me, looking nothing at all like the lawyer I had watched all week. He was wearing a tweed jacket and a cap, and seeing him caused a catch in my throat.

A fine white fog was blowing in, painting the whole of the bay—sky and water alike—a soft white. "Are you ready for a fog-bound sea?" he shouted, dodging between streetcars.

"I am," I called back, trying to control my breathing.

He put his duffel alongside mine and said, "We have a little time before Agnes—"

I raised my hand to stop him. "She isn't coming," I said, and told him why.

He looked at me, studied me. I did not move, did not allow my expression to change. I was here, with my satchel, and I had known that Agnes couldn't come.

He turned to look out over the bay, squinting into the pale light, thinking.

Then he turned back to me. "This changes everything," he said.

I nodded, unable to speak.

"You know that?" he repeated.

I nodded again.

"All right," he said, picking up both our bags and striding down the ramp, onto the swaying deck of the ferryboat *Miranda*.

He walked to the stern, which was empty of passengers, and I followed him, saying nothing. The deckhands cast off and we moved out into the fogbound bay. We stood together, the fog swirling about us, listening to the wailing of the foghorns and the ringing of bells, low over the water. I was shivering, but I was glad for the chill air that blew wisps of my hair from underneath my wool cap. Still he said nothing, only stood looking out over the water. Then a swell from a passing freighter hit the boat broadside and the deck lurched under us. He reached to steady me; his arms were around me and I buried my face in his neck and held hard to him. His lips were close to my ear and he whispered, "I didn't think I could ever want anyone as much as I want you."

A great, flooding rush of warmth went through me, standing there on the stern of the *Miranda*. And as the boat made its way carefully, cautiously through the thickening fog, I said to myself, *he wants me . . .*

We stood, our arms around each other, as the boat rounded Angel Island and moved north. Still I was afraid to speak for fear I would say something wrong, something to make him change his mind. When he asked why I was so silent, I could only think to tell him the truth. He laughed at me then, and leaned to kiss me on my mouth. And then he pulled me hard to him and kissed me again and a warm, moist feeling surged through me.

"Do you know," he told me, "that day at the Hall of Justice—the first day I ever set eyes on you—I watched you, waiting for me at the end of the aisle. I looked at you and I thought, 'My God.' Then when you asked if we could go someplace private—I won't even tell you what I thought."

"Do!" I pleaded, laughing low.

"Later," he promised. "Later."

We sat side by side on the seat of the motorcar that had replaced the horse-drawn stage only a few years ago, for the journey over the Marin hills to the ocean beach. Our legs touched, exerting a fine pressure. A woman and her two small children occupied the seat behind us while the driver sat alone in the front, our extra baggage piled next to him. It was a long ride, I have no idea how long. The road curved close to the ocean for a stretch and, had the fog not obliterated it, the view would have been wonderful. I was told this, and I believed it, but it didn't matter. All that mattered was the man sitting next to me, our legs touching, and the pressure building inside of me, so that I had to breathe in short, careful bursts.

We walked through the willow grove that gave the tiny coastal community its name, and onto the long sandy stretch of ocean beach. It was emptier than I had imagined, and the fishing cottage more isolated, tucked into the sand dunes—themselves camouflaged by great tufts of coarse sea grass.

He fumbled with the door, which had been locked, he said, by Colin, who believed in elaborate security. And then he moved about opening windows to get rid of the stale air, gathering wood for a fire in the stone fireplace at one end of the room.

I stood and watched him and felt quiet. Enormously quiet, perfectly still. I felt something that I could not express: that I was there, finally. No longer an observer, no longer waiting.

When he had finished, when the water was in and the fire lit, he stood and looked at me. He touched my cheek, my ear, my neck. His hand slid under my breast. I lifted my mouth to his.

"Slowly," he whispered, moving his hands to my waist, gently caressing my hips. "I've thought about this moment for so long," he went on, brushing his lips against mine. "Do you understand? I want it to last for a very long time."

We lay on the pallets he had spread before the fire, and I could hear the waves as they rolled in and crested and broke on the shore, I could count the hard rhythm of the sea. His skin was smooth and warm. His hands traced the contours of my body, the cavity between my leg and my thigh. And then there was no sound at all—no ocean, no crackling of the fire—only perfect silence and perfect understanding, the answer to all the years of waiting, all the longing and wanting. Finally, finally I was allowed into a world that was mine. It was as clear and

247

bright as I had wanted it to be . . . and nobody could keep me out, not ever again.

We lay together that afternoon, the fog close about us. We ate and drank and talked and listened to the sound of the sea; the fog closed in, and we became the center of the world.

He found all the soft and secret places and touched them. I traced, with my fingertips, the long scars that striped his back. I wanted to tell him all that I felt, but there were no words. I could only say the obvious: that it was right for me to be with him, that I would break any rule, defy anyone, to stay with him.

We walked the beach at last light, and were up again at dawn, walking barefoot at the tide line so that waves washed over us and wet the bottom of the trousers I wore, which were Michael's and had been left behind. We gathered sand dollars and agates and tiny shells and kicked at the frothy edge of the waves. Then the sun came out for a time and we nestled into the dunes and let it warm and dry us. I sat in the circle of his arms, watching the gulls wheel, and told him how, all of my life, I had not felt *real*—how everything had always seemed rehearsed to me, everything was planned, never *real*. And how, with the first surge of pleasure, I knew—this was real. I was real. We were real.

He caressed the back of my neck, rubbing it, and held me and rocked me gently. He said: "With me, it's as if something that was frozen inside of me has broken loose . . . and I can't be sure . . ."

He stopped then, so I had to ask, "Sure of what?"

When he didn't answer, I said: "Nobody can come between us. Not the woman who is your wife, not your children, not the people who will look at us and talk, nobody. I mean it. I won't allow it, I won't. Nobody is going to stop me from being with you. Not Tom, not anybody."

He sat up: "What made you say Tom?" he asked. "Why Tom?"

I didn't know why, not really, but as soon as I said it I knew I was right. "At the restaurant that night," I said, "when the man told you I looked like 'one of Tom's girls.' It made you so angry, so . . ."

He was looking out to sea now, moving away from me. I had to bring him back. "Tell me about him, about your twin," I said. "If he's going to haunt us, I'd better know what I'm up against."

"My twin," he repeated, taking out one of the long, thin brown cigarettes he smoked. "Do you need to know?" When I nodded, he held the cigarette loosely between his fingers and seemed to study it. "I'll tell you what I can. I'm not sure how much of the truth I understand. I can only try not to tell you lies."

He started talking then, in a voice that was low, with a pained undertone. "Let's say this is a story about brothers—identical twins, the product of a single egg mysteriously split in utero, to produce not one child, as would normally happen, but two. Two who are in every respect identical, one a perfect replica of the other, so that neither is unique. Part of the time the twin feels as if someone has made a grotesque mistake, turning out an extra body . . . and then, of course, that presents a question: Which is the real person, which the copy? Other times, the twin is exhilarated because he can watch himself walking and talking, can glory in there being two of him. Until one dies, or is killed, and the other is left with this terrible sense of loss, as if half of him is dead. And then, after a while—not right away—there is something else, something he doesn't want to admit . . . a sense of relief, as if a correction has been made and at last he is whole. Normal. Not responsible for another, separate body."

A gull flew low above us, its wings outspread so the light shone through them. "Thelma and Harry told me a little about your brother—they said he was something of a maverick."

"Maverick?" he repeated. "I don't know about that—I wouldn't have called him that. He had a future plotted out that was different from most of the kids who grew up South of the Slot, the Irish Catholic kids." His voice registered a certain irony. "Jimmy," he said, using the name his old friends called him, "well, Jimmy didn't figure things out in advance—he left that to Tom. Jimmy married the girl who lived down the street, and began having children, which was what you were expected to do. But he never really thought of himself as separate from Tom, as a person in his own right."

"And Tom?" I asked. "Do you know how Tom thought of himself?"

He shook his head. "I don't, really," he said. "We talked about it enough, but I never figured it out. I think he had tried to separate himself long before I did. And when he went off to war—he never actually admitted this, but I feel pretty certain that it was another way to put some distance between us. I know he wasn't anxious to fight. He hated war and he thought patriotism was one of those convenient emotions that could be used to manipulate."

"Why did you go?" I asked.

He looked out to sea, squinting at the horizon, which had cleared, almost miraculously, so that you could see the dark blue of the Pacific against the lighter blue of the sky. "Don't tell me if it is difficult," I said. "I don't want to do anything to hurt you."

He pulled me back to him and turned my face with his hand, and kissed me very softly on the lips.

"This truth does hurt, Hallie. I was running away, from a marriage, from the responsibility of children. Law school had been a strange experience—Tom made better marks, but I became immersed in it. I was absorbed and excited by all the possibilities. It was one of the happiest times in my life, sitting around and talking cases. Tom had a room near the law school, and I would stay late into the night and talk to him until he would kick me out, tell me to go home. It got so I didn't want to go home, not at all."

He lit the cigarette then. I cupped my hands around the match so the wind wouldn't blow the flame out. When it was lit he went on: "When Tom was drafted and didn't try to get an exemption, I had to go too. Tom was free and I wasn't. It was my own fault, of course. Tom had tried to warn me, but I wouldn't listen. He thought I should stay home with my family."

"He was against your going, then?"

"Yes," he answered. "He teamed up with Mary Margaret to

try to bring me to my senses. But it didn't work. Nothing would have worked, they just didn't know it. I was drowning, and my only hope for survival was the war. As bizarre as that sounds, that's the way it seemed to me at the time."

He sat smoking for a while and I said nothing, waiting. "Do you know how you find out there's going to be a battle the next day?" he finally asked. "The priest comes around to hear confession. But my brother never went; we became each other's confessors."

He took a deep breath. "Tom said I'd made my bed and I was going to have to lie in it. A good stiff Catholic upbringing dies hard, even for a skeptic like Tom. He said divorce was out of the question—for the practical reason that Mary would never agree to it. He just thought I'd have to find some way to meet my obliga- tions—at least financially, and to the children. He said I couldn't quit being a father, and that I'd have to do pretty much what I am doing."

He looked at me then, pain flickering around the depths of the irises in his eyes, and said, "Tom never figured on you."

"I'll just bet he didn't," I said as I rolled over on the sand and kissed him, hard.

FOURTEEN

"ASK HIM TO CALL ME, please, just as soon as he returns," I told Riordan's secretary, who by now recognized my voice.

"Yes, Miss Duer," she answered briskly. "I'll put the message on his desk."

I was disappointed. I had wanted to hear his voice. It had been two days since I had seen him.

"You look moonstruck," Gwen had ventured yesterday. She knew, of course. She had been monitoring our telephone calls, and now she was fishing for details. I smiled and said, "I only howl when the moon is full."

My telephone rang and I grabbed it. "What's happening?" Riordan wanted to know. "The message says you need to speak to me urgently."

"It is urgent, in a way," I told him. "In a small way, actually," I confessed, then explained: "I saw Agnes yesterday, and we discovered that we have the same birthday. October 7. That's next week. I thought that since Agnes didn't get to go to the beach . . ."

"That's right," he said in mock surprise, "she didn't, did she?"

253

Lowering my voice to keep from laughing, I went on, "I was thinking that perhaps we might celebrate together—go over to Willow Camp, a group of us. The seventh is on Friday, but we could go over late Saturday afternoon after work and stay the night."

I waited to give him time to object. When he didn't, I hurried on, "I would like to ask my brother, and Faith. And then I thought we might invite Sara. She has been wanting to meet Agnes, and to see you again too . . ."

"Sara Hunt?" he asked. What he meant was, "Does Sara know about us?"

"Yes," I answered.

He thought about it for a minute; then he said: "That sounds nice. The women can stay in the Dipsea Inn, and Clive and I can bunk in the shack." This last, I was certain, was for Gwen's benefit. "I have to work late tonight," he went on. "How about you?"

"Until eight or so," I answered. "I'm on the Arbuckle case today. I thought I might have dinner at Tadich's."

"About eight-fifteen?" he asked. "Want some company?"

"Always," I told him, knowing the afternoon would pass quickly, now that I had the evening to look forward to.

Our group crowded into Langford & Crane's Sausalito stage to make the long ride over the Marin hills to Willow Camp. Saturday was warm and so clear you could see the faint outline of the Farallon Islands in the distance. The view from the high vantage of the hills was as breathtaking as I had been told, and this time I concentrated on the deep purpled coastline winding to the north. Sara rummaged in the oversized valise she had brought along, and produced two pairs of field glasses, which we passed among us.

The stage was filled; Faith's camera equipment took up one seat and Clive balanced a large bakery box on his knees, which we all pretended not to notice so he could surprise us with the birthday cake. ("For October's Lovely Ladies" it was inscribed.)

We arrived at the two-story Dipsea Inn to find that Riordan had arranged a birthday dinner. The summer people had left, so the large dining room was ours. Mr. Fitzhenry, the proprietor, who seemed fond of Riordan, had gone to great lengths to make the occasion festive. Sara's bulky valise produced several bottles of French champagne, which were quickly put on ice, some red wine for dinner and brandy for "later."

"Sara must have a little French bootlegger hidden away in the basement of the *petit palais*," Faith teased. Even Agnes, who must have been a bit surprised, joined in the laughter.

"I only break selective laws," Sara explained to Agnes.

"So do I," Agnes quipped, and we all laughed.

By the time the champagne was finished, Agnes was feeling sleepy. I saw her to her room and then, feeling a bit giddy, suggested a walk on the beach to the rest of our party.

The air was warm, even for October, and the moon was full, cutting a shimmering path through the sea. We linked arms, the five of us, and walked along the silver shore. In a clear, sweet soprano Faith started singing "By the Light of the Silvery Moon." Clive joined in, and then we were all singing.

When the song was done Sara said what I was feeling: "There are moments when you think, 'All is well. Life is good.' This is one." I slipped my hand into Riordan's, and knew that he felt it, too.

We were on the beach early the next morning. The tide was out and had left a wide shining strip of wet sand that was free of prints, and sea-fresh. Agnes and Sara scoured the high-tide line, looking for jingle shells and agates. Agnes found a fossilized sand dollar and insisted I should have it. "It's not so beautiful as a fresh one, but far more enduring," she said.

Riordan helped Faith carry her cameras to the beach while

Clive and I walked. In the past weeks I had been so absorbed with Riordan and the Arbuckle case that I had seen little of my brother.

"Oh, I've been keeping busy," he told me. "I've been seeing quite a lot of Ethel Mayer. It's strange, you know, to be able to see a girl . . . a woman . . . without Grandmother to contend with. And the strangest thing is that I believe Grandmother would actually approve of Ethel."

I took his arm, and turned to walk into the wind.

"Why is that?" I asked.

"Oh, because Ethel is what you might call an 'old-fashioned' girl, interested in family and home and church, that kind of thing. Traditional."

"I suppose it wouldn't do for you to take up with an untraditional sort?" I chided.

He bent close, as if to speak privately. "Hallie, I can see how you feel about Riordan. And part of me is happy for you, because I've not seen you like this before—so brimming. Riordan's an honorable fellow, I know that. He would never take advantage . . ." He looked away, but I pulled him back. "It's just that," he went on, "his situation, it isn't going to be easy for you and that does worry me. This weekend, here, you're surrounded by people who love and respect you, who are willing to accept. But a lot of people won't. It's going to be hard for you." He hesitated. "Maybe it is possible for you and Riordan to handle it. I don't think I could."

I pressed his arm and pulled him close. "You could if you felt the way I do about Riordan," I told him, "I'm sure of it. But I'm also glad you don't have to. And I'm glad if you've found someone you care for. I'd like to get to know Ethel."

Pleased, he smiled. "She doesn't quite know what to make of you," he said. "I think you scare her—with all the things you do. I've told her that you're not as formidable as all that . . ."

Faith was taking our picture; Riordan, behind her carrying the film box, looked on.

"Come on, Clive," Faith called, "let's go see if we can find those tide pools down by the rocks. You get to carry the film and tripod."

Riordan fell in step beside me and we started walking in the opposite direction, down the sand spit. We passed Agnes and Sara, preoccupied now with the field glasses and seabirds. The sun was rising. I took off my beach wrap and walked in my bathing dress. Riordan watched me, his eyes moving slowly over my body. I did not always know what he was thinking, but now I did. As soon as we were out of sight of the others I put my arms around him and lifted my face to be kissed. He held me close; the sea and the sand and the sky surrounded us. "Do you suppose we could make love in the dunes?" I whispered into his ear.

He looked at me, kissed me again—sweetly, this time—and said, "The thought did occur to me. In fact, that's what I've wanted ever since we got here . . . but we need to talk. We can't go on thinking about making love in the dunes."

"I know," I sighed, "but I want you so much."

"That's why we have to talk," he insisted. "I've been trying to figure a way . . . You know I can't marry you, not yet. I intend to try to find a way, but for now . . .

"It doesn't matter," I told him. He looked surprised, so I repeated it: "The only thing that matters is being with you. Riordan, listen. I never thought I would marry, not ever. But then, I never thought I'd ever feel the way I am feeling about you. If you were free, well . . . But you aren't. I wouldn't quit my work, not even if we could marry. So except for the social difficulties . . . I simply don't see what is to keep us apart."

He didn't say anything for a time. And then he said, "It won't be easy, Hallie. The majority of people will disapprove of us, and that is putting it mildly. It will get mean, hurtful."

"That's just what Clive told me," I sighed.

Riordan stopped and began to dig at a shell embedded in the sand with the toe of his moccasin. "Clive told me that, too," he said.

"In some ways, his attitude surprises me. I thought he would be more disapproving."

"Why would you think that?" I asked, surprised.

"He doesn't seem as independent as you," he answered. "You aren't that much alike."

"Nonsense," I told him. "You don't know Clive. He sees that we are right for each other, he accepts it."

Changing the subject, he asked, "What about Sara?"

I laughed, remembering what Sara had said. "She thinks you have the 'most exquisitely complex' face she has ever seen on a man. She approves of us."

Riordan smiled. "You know, I've been hearing about Sara Hunt for years. I have a friend—a man who grew up in Ireland—who's known Sara a very long time. He's convinced she's one of the Little People."

"She does have a kind of magic about her," I answered. "You know, when I came back from the beach that evening . . . I was just so bursting with everything, I felt so wonderfully alive, and I wanted to tell someone, to show someone how it was. Faith wasn't home, so I called Sara. And she said, 'Come right over.' It was almost as if she had been waiting for me. She listened, and didn't once say I should be careful, or to remember that you were married . . . she just smiled and said that sometimes life gives extraordinary gifts to those who have the courage to accept them."

We walked in silence for a time, until we reached the end of the sand spit. Two egrets were standing in the Bolinas lagoon, their long white bodies reflected in the still water. "What we need," he finally said, "is to find a way to be together while offending as few sensibilities as possible. We can't come over here every time we want to be alone, and if I don't make love to you soon, I'm not going to survive."

"We're going to be married. This Saturday. In the chapel at Grace Cathedral."

Faith stood, hands on her hips, waiting to see what I would say. I said nothing. She had caught me off guard. I knew she had been seeing Thayer, but there had been no hint of marriage. "I'd like for you to be there," she went on, rubbing her elbows now. "I'd like it if you would stand up with me." She laughed nervously.

I only looked at her, stunned at the suddenness of it. She lifted her chin determinedly. "Hallie, I'm going to marry Thayer and I'm going to marry him this Saturday. I know you don't like him, but I'm asking you to accept it, for my sake."

I lashed out: "You're not asking, Faith—you're demanding. You haven't asked me anything, you haven't talked to me about this decision. Have you stopped to ask yourself why he disliked me even before he had met me?"

Faith's face hardened. She turned her back to me and looked out the window. It was raining, a cold and drizzling rain that seemed to seep into the cottage. The warm, sunny October days were behind us now; winter and the rains lay ahead. I couldn't stop myself. "You're making a terrible mistake, Faith."

She turned, the strain showing on her face. "He told me why he dislikes you. He thinks you are hard and domineering and that you want to rule my life. He thinks you are as bad for me as you think he is bad for me. I love you both, and I insist on my right to go on loving you both. Thayer agrees that I have that right, that he will not interfere with my seeing you. I think you might at least do as much, and grant me the right to be with him."

"But why so soon, Faith?" I wailed. "It's only two months or so that you've been seeing him again."

"Longer than that," she said, looking at me solemnly.

"Longer?" I repeated. Then I knew. Of course, she had been seeing him all along—all those times she was at Zev's studio. "Why didn't you tell me? Why did you feel you had to hide it?"

She didn't answer, and it didn't matter. Thayer had had his way, he had made her distrust me.

"It's more than our friendship that's at stake here," I tried to tell her. "I hope we'll always be dear friends. But right now it's you I'm thinking of, your future, your happiness."

She took both of my hands in hers and made me sit down next to her. "Can't I make you understand, Hallie?" she pleaded. "Thayer *does* make me happy. I love being with him, working with him. He thinks my work is important and there is so much he can teach me. He wants what I want—a family, a life together with both of us absorbed in our art. Hallie? Please?"

I looked into her face and wished I could say what she wanted me to say. Instead, I hugged her to me and told her that I hoped to God I was wrong, that more than anything I wanted her to be happy.

She cried a little, and hugged me back and said I would see, that everything was going to be fine. I told her I would go to the wedding, but that I couldn't stand as her witness. She agreed so readily that I felt sure she was relieved. Thayer, I guessed, had not wanted me to be in the wedding party.

It was raining on the first Saturday in November, Faith's wedding day. I sat in the pew between Ethel and Sara, a slow hard knot twisting inside me as the organist played *Lohengrin*'s wedding march. Faith came down the aisle on Clive's arm. She was wearing a mantilla of ivory lace over the shining cap of her hair. Her satin dress, belted low at her hips, fell to mid-calf, and its heavy folds caught the candlelight. She looked exquisite, and my heart ached for her.

Sara's hand moved to touch mine in comfort. At the reception at the Fairmont Hotel, she stood behind me and as we approached the bride and groom, took my arm, as if it was she who needed my support. It was done. They were married, and there was nothing to do but wish them well.

"Come across the street with me for some lunch," Sara said, including Clive and Ethel in her invitation. The four of us walked the short distance to the mansion. Ethel, in a ruffled dress of flowered silk which made her look plumper than she was, stood in the foyer, trying to conceal her awe.

"How perfectly beautiful," she said, her eyes scanning the great curved stair and the walls covered with Sara's private art collection. While Sara showed Ethel to the powder room, Clive and I went into the small parlor, where I sank into a divan.

"Are you feeling as glum as you look?" Clive asked.

"Worse," I answered, glad to drop the pretense. "Much worse."

He nodded sympathetically. "I'm not keen on Thayer myself," he said. "I had this wild idea that I should have grabbed her at the last minute and dragged her out of the church." He grinned; then he was serious. "I guess that in matters of the heart, you have to let people make their own mistakes. And if you care enough about somebody, well . . . you have to just stand by. Don't you agree?"

He was looking at me, his meaning all too clear. "Riordan isn't a mistake, if that's what you're getting at," I snapped. "There is absolutely no doubt in my mind about that."

I watched the smile move into his eyes, coaxing. In another minute I smiled back. He moved behind me and began rubbing my shoulders. "I actually think Riordan is right for you," he told me. "In fact, he's exactly the kind of man who can handle someone like you."

"What do you mean, 'someone like me'?" I challenged, turning to glare at him.

"Don't get so riled, Hallie. I'm not going to fight with you, no matter how mad you are today. 'A modern woman'—a bachelor girl, isn't that what you are?" Keeping his tone light, he went on: "As Ethel says, you are a 'remarkable phenomena.'"

"Someone should tell Ethel that 'phenomena' is the plural, not the feminine form, of 'phenomenon,'" I told him.

Stung, he frowned at me. "I'm sorry," I said. "You're right, I am being spiteful today."

"You should try to remember," he said, still hurt, "that you are different—you and Sara and Faith and Julia. You're out there leading the troops, and that's fine with me. You're not afraid to break the rules, or bend them. But I don't think you should disparage those who choose to live more traditional lives."

"I know," I said. "Clive, I really am sorry." His mention of Julia reminded me of my visit with her, only a day or so before Faith's sudden announcement. It had seemed so important at the time, I was amazed now that I could have forgotten it. "Julia told me about the visit from Grandmother Duer's 'legal representative.' What happened?"

His face darkened. "Nothing. Julia was very nice about it. I got the feeling that she was expecting something."

"She was," I admitted. "I warned her."

"I guess it was a good thing you did," he replied. "I thought my letters to Grandmother would convince her to let it be. Obviously, I was wrong."

"Julia is worried that it is upsetting you. She seems to think you brood over it. I told her you were fine, that she needn't worry."

"It's humiliating," was all he said.

Ethel and Sara were in the hallway; we could hear Ethel asking about the paintings. They would be with us in a few minutes.

I lowered my voice. "Does Ethel know anything about Grandmother Duer?"

He looked up and said defensively, "Some."

"That's good," I told him. "She should be warned, in case someone shows up at her school asking questions."

Clive looked as if he had been slapped. "Grandmother would do that, wouldn't she?" he asked. "Damn her!" It was the first time I had ever heard my brother curse.

All during lunch Ethel's hands caressed the silver and the crystal and the linen and her eyes moved restlessly about the table, the room. She was unsure of herself, and watched us for clues—when to use the fish fork, the finger bowls. Clive, distracted by a new concern, didn't notice. Sara did. But then, Sara noticed everything.

At the door, I stayed behind a few minutes to speak privately with Sara.

"I saw your James Riordan this week," she told me. "He's doing some legal work for me."

I kissed her on the cheek and said, "I know. He told me that I have exquisite taste in friends." And then I added: "But I can't get over the feeling that today I failed one of them."

"No, Hallie," Sara said, "you would only have failed her if you hadn't been there today. Or if you aren't there tomorrow, when she needs you."

Kathleen's fingers flew, twisting the circle of string up and over and down and around until the cat's cradle became a Jacob's ladder. She was sitting in the window seat on the little porch which had been my bedroom and was now a sunporch again.

"Would you say Faith acted *impulsively* or would you say *impromptu*?" she asked.

Kathleen had become fascinated with the shadings of meaning in words. "I would say," I laughed, "that you might start by distinguishing between adverbs and adjectives." The child sat cross-legged, her braids falling forward, her face concentrated. She frowned. I noticed that the string had knotted and said, "Too bad."

"It is," she said. "You must miss her terribly."

Before I could answer, Kathleen lifted her hand for me to listen. "It's Daddy. I can tell the difference now between the sound of your car and his new Star."

"We're late but we think you'll forgive us when you see what we brought," Riordan called out, and Colin added, "Oyster loaf! Still warm. Hurry, let's eat."

"Colin always wants to eat," Kathleen complained as we set the table. Riordan's eyes caught mine. I thought: This is what should be—a father and a mother and two nice youngsters gathering for lunch on a rainy winter Saturday, chattering about nothing much, just happy to be together. I thought: I wish we lived together, all of us. I wish the world would let us, but I knew the world would not. The children had a mother, even if she didn't seem to care for the world and its worries. But they also had a brother who did, and who did not approve of our being together. Michael had made that plain to Riordan. I knew a struggle was under way between them. I also knew that in a while he would take them home, and it would be weeks before the four of us would be together again.

"Tell us about the Arbuckle case, Hallie," Kathleen prompted. "It's all anybody talks about."

"Kids aren't supposed to know about it," Colin put in, "but everybody at school does."

"Do you think Mr. Arbuckle is a *degenerate* or is he *debauched*?" Kathleen asked.

Riordan widened his eyes and waited to see what I would say.

"I often think," I told her, in a gentle parody of the question, "that people are more interested in the *titillating* and *lascivious* details of the trial than in establishing Roscoe Arbuckle's guilt or innocence on the question of manslaughter. A young woman is dead, and the question that must be answered is: was he in any way responsible?"

"What do you think?" Kathleen blurted.

"Young lady," Riordan broke in, "you can read what Hallie has to say about the case in the paper because I have promised to have you home by two. You have to be at church, if I'm not mistaken."

They groaned in concert. As they left, Kathleen called back, "Don't forget—we go sailing Sunday after next. It's all arranged." Riordan followed them out, then returned to retrieve Kathleen's sweater.

"I don't want to go sailing," I whispered, and he gave me a quick, soft kiss and said, "Pray for rain."

The dinner was Clive's idea. He thought that it would "clear the air" to have Ethel meet Riordan and see the two of us together. I had doubts, and so did Riordan, but in the end we decided to trust Clive's intuition.

He had gone to great lengths to choose just the right restaurant—Amadeo's on the wharf—and to reserve an inconspicuous table. It was not, however, inconspicuous enough for Ethel. "I thought we were to have one of the private dining rooms," she complained, loud enough for us to hear.

The bright chatter had disappeared; now she spoke in short, breathless bursts, and she seemed unable to look at Riordan.

It was Ethel who brought up the Arbuckle case. "It's all you hear these days," she said. "In my opinion the man is unspeakable. That poor girl."

As mildly as I could, I pointed out that from the evidence so far it seemed to me as if Arbuckle was not being treated fairly. Ethel acted as if I had attacked her. The anger sputtered out: "He's guilty," she declared. "Make no mistake about that. And the people in this city are not going to abide his flouting of common decency." The word hung in the air: *decency*. Ethel's face flushed a deep pink, and a soft layer of fat beneath her chin began to quiver. I thought for a moment that she was going to burst into tears.

Clive had been wrong, and now he didn't know what to do. Ethel would never be able to accept Riordan and me. Our being together offended her. Was Clive blind, that he hadn't seen that and spared us this debacle? I was angry with them both, and with myself for subjecting Riordan to this scene.

He spoke with careful formality: "Clive, Miss Mayer, Hallie . . . I hope you will understand when I say I will have to leave now. I have an early court appearance tomorrow, and it would be better if I spent the rest of this evening preparing for it."

Ethel sat staring straight ahead, frozen. Clive didn't seem to know what to do. He half-rose, before Riordan grasped him by the arm and told him not to get up, in his manner telling Clive that it was all right.

But it wasn't all right. The anger was rising in my throat, I could taste it. The look on Riordan's face stopped me. *Don't*, he warned. *Play this out.* We had known it could happen, if we were going to be together in public. We would have to be ready to act together, to control our anger, he had said. I closed my eyes for a second, and took a deep breath, and he nodded to me and left.

For the rest of that interminable meal I listened to them and spoke as little as possible. I do not know what I ate, or how it tasted, or how I managed to swallow. It was all I could do to stay and endure the stream of words that flowed around me. Later I would remember Ethel's saying to Clive: "I hope you wrote your Grandmother this week. She must be so terribly lonely." And I remembered how she had smiled and patted my brother's arm, and I knew then why she had agreed to the dinner.

FIFTEEN

"ALL RIGHT," THE BOSS said as Lloyd Garr entered his office. "We're all here now—the team covering the Arbuckle trial—Farlow and Tucker the courts, Lloyd the police and the running story, Hallie the features. The third trial begins next Monday, March 13. That gives us a week."

He paused long enough to introduce a guest, a visiting editor named Downes from some small town in Pennsylvania. It was the Boss's habit to invite visitors to sit in on our meetings. He got right down to business: "We need to see if we can come up with some new angles on covering the trial, something a hundred or so reporters aren't already doing. I'd like to see us make some sense out of this sorry spectacle. Hallie, give us a quick rundown so Downes here will know what's been going on."

"Well," I started, "as you know, Roscoe Arbuckle has had two trials, the first ending in a hung jury—eleven to one for acquittal, the holdout a woman. The second trial was the exact reverse, again a hung jury but this time the holdout was a man. Maude Delmont, the woman who accused Arbuckle of killing her friend Virginia

Rappé, and on whose word much of the district attorney's case was built, was never called to testify. The testimony of the two doctors who saw and treated the dead girl on the day of the party was also blocked by the D.A., as was the testimony of the St. Francis Hotel's house detective, George Glennon. Glennon took his information to the defense when he found out the prosecution wasn't going to call him, but it didn't matter—his testimony was disallowed."

Judd Tucker, who knew everything about San Francisco politics, put in, "Everybody knows that the D.A., Matt Brady, has his eye on the governor's mansion, and he thinks he can get there as the 'man who cleaned up Hollywood.'"

"I shudder to think what would happen if Arbuckle couldn't afford Gavin McNab," the Boss said. "Even so, McNab made a mistake in not putting Arbuckle on the stand for the second trial. He was just so sure he had an acquittal. But what do you think, Hallie? You've watched the whole thing."

"I'm not so sure there is any single answer for why two juries could come to exactly the opposite conclusion," I began. "I believe that everyone in the courtroom knows that Arbuckle did not molest that girl, that in fact of all the men in the hotel suite that day, he was the most thoughtful. But he was the one who gave the party—which means he was also the one who could have stopped it. I remember Freddie Zebra telling me about it at the time, and I said something like, 'It sounds dreadful.'" The city editor interrupted to ask what had happened to Freddie, and the Boss answered with painful brevity that he had disappeared to avoid being implicated in the scandal.

I went on: "Now that we know all that was going on that day, we know it *was* dreadful. When Virginia Rappé started screaming that she was dying and tearing off her clothes, they helped strip her naked and—men and women alike—put her in a tub of ice-cold water. Then one of the men—not Arbuckle—held her upside down because a woman in the room had heard that was a remedy. They were all somewhat drunk, which means they were all breaking the law. It was ghastly, and Arbuckle was party to it. In a way, he is guilty of that—bad company."

Lloyd Garr snorted. "Hell, half the people in this city are guilty of that."

"But they aren't famous," Judd put in, "and they aren't symbols of good, clean fun as Arbuckle is. In a lot of people's minds, that makes him a fraud."

"That's a load of . . ." Lloyd glanced at me, the only woman present, to let me know I was stifling his expression. "Horse manure."

Gene Bolten, the city editor, had been sitting quietly, but now he spoke up. "Maybe we should do some more digging into the backgrounds of some of the women at the party. So far no one has brought out very much about their characters. I've heard the defense purposely didn't want to bring out the real facts about Virginia Rappé, for fear the jury would think they were defaming the dead. But the truth is, that 'loving-and-innocent-girl' picture the prosecution painted was about as far from the truth as you could get. Virginia had a social disease and a life to match."

"Are you trying to say that nice girls don't get gonorrhea?" Lloyd sneered.

I stayed behind to tell the Boss that Riordan was trying to arrange for me to interview McNab.

"Good luck," he said. "That would be quite a coup. McNab hasn't been talking or letting Arbuckle talk. If you could be the first to get to either of them . . . And what you said this morning, about Arbuckle's responsibility, that he could have stopped the party, be sure to put that in one of your stories."

The phone was ringing as I returned to my desk. "He had no trouble at all remembering you from the Dempsey trial," Riordan said without preamble. "He described you as 'pretty and feisty,' and I said, 'That's her.'"

"Will he see me?" I asked, the excitement rising.

"If you behave," he answered.

"Behave—what does that mean?"

"It means," he said, "that you will have to be discreet."

"*Discreet*," I wailed, loud enough for Lloyd to look over at me. "What—?"

But Riordan was laughing now. "Okay," I said, "you've had your fun, now could you just tell me . . ."

I was starting to feel exasperated when he said, "This favor is going to cost you."

"I always pay, don't I?" I answered archly.

There was a pause; I knew he would be smiling. Had I dared to look, I knew Gwen would be smiling too.

"Just tell me where and when," I said, breaking the silence.

"For Gavin," he told me, "tomorrow at the Palace Hotel. He'll meet you at the Garden Court at seven, for breakfast. As for me—"

"You I'll tend to later," I gibed. "But thank you. Thank you, thank you, thank you. I didn't think McNab would see me." I took a deep breath. "I wish I could see you today, but we're really running on this story. Tell me you couldn't see me anyway. Tell me you're in court all day."

"I'm in court all day," he repeated obediently. "Of course, I'll be working late at the office, and if you should happen to be in the neighborhood about six . . ."

"You never know," I said, and hung up.

He did know, though. Several weeks before, when we hadn't been able to see each other for three days in a row, I decided to drop by his office at closing time. I waited until the last secretary had left, then I went into his office, locked the door, leaned against it and announced in as sultry an imitation of Theda Bara as I could: "I have come to ravish you."

We made love on the leather davenport. Afterward, as I was putting up my hair in the little bathroom that adjoined his office, he came up behind me, put his arms around my waist and told me that he could never think of me without wanting me. I looked at him in the mirror and said, "Maybe I should make your office a regular stop on my beat." That was when he told me about buying the place out in the Great Sand Waste.

Gavin McNab was waiting for me at the entrance to the Garden Court, sitting on one of the overstuffed divans. When he saw me, he stood, bowed and said how nice it was to see me outside of a courtroom.

In the weeks of the trials I had come to admire McNab's soft-spoken, eloquent delivery, his patience, his precision. Since he seldom raised his voice, I was surprised when Riordan told me that McNab was seething over the district attorney's tactics. "McNab says it's a 'persecution,' not a 'prosecution,'" Riordan told me.

"I remember you gave Jack Dempsey quite a surprise at the end of his trial," McNab chuckled.

"We patched that up," I told him. "In fact, he even gave me an exclusive interview."

"That's like Jack," McNab said. "He's a mean man in the ring, but not out." His eyes sparkled; then he said, "Jim Riordan said something of the same thing about you."

"He told me he would speak well of me only if I promised to behave and not badger you with questions you couldn't possibly answer," I countered.

"Ask what you please," he told me as the waiter placed a pot of tea and two pieces of toast before him. "I'll answer when I can. I would like to ask you not to take notes, and I will also ask you not to print any of this until after the trial. Is that acceptable?"

I thought for a minute. "If you will agree to talk to me at the end of the trial," I said, "and if I can have an interview with Mr. Arbuckle then, too."

He took a bite of toast, chewed for a while, and then nodded. I stifled the desire to cheer. "At the moment," he began, "the Bill of Rights has been suspended in this city. Roscoe Arbuckle would never have been brought to trial in the first place had it not been for a rapacious woman whose accusation has been refuted by a dozen witnesses, and a district attorney who has allowed his personal ambition to blind him, and lead him into what can only be called a witch hunt. I am a mild man, I believe, but I am outraged by Brady's conduct. He has cleverly confused the public by doing exactly what he has accused Arbuckle of doing—coercing witnesses, blackmailing and terrifying them. He has suppressed testimony, and he has been aided by a pompous, arrogant judge. When this trial is over, I should like to do what I can to get these two men out of public life. Brady is both immoral and indecent. I would like to see that chorus of crones who call themselves 'the women's vigilance committee' take out after Brady." His face was pink with anger. "I suppose you didn't expect quite such a tirade, Miss Duer," he said.

"When this is over," I answered as calmly as I could, "I would like to tell the whole story, from the very beginning through all of the trials. I feel certain that my boss, Sanford Curtin, will agree. Will you give me access to all of the defense material?"

When he didn't answer, I went on, "It seems to me that Dempsey and Arbuckle have some things in common. Both are from poor families, they had to work their way to the top, they knew hard times."

McNab picked up, "Dempsey lived the hobo life and married a prostitute," he said. "Both were born into a social stratum where drinking and womanizing were part of life. It isn't surprising that Dempsey could move into the Hollywood crowd—he and Arbuckle have some mutual friends, did you know that? Then, when they become celebrities, their fans want to pretend—and want them to pretend—that they live a middle-class Methodist life, pure as the driven snow."

He stopped to sip his tea. "The thing is," he went on, "both Dempsey and Arbuckle are strong, silent men who are innately decent. Dempsey's trouble was caused by a divorced wife who was put up to it by a sportswriter. Arbuckle's troubles started with a sad incident, and were compounded by a liar and an ambitious politician who tried to amplify those lies and have them accepted as truth. I suspect both Dempsey and Arbuckle will carry scars from their San Francisco trials to the end of their days."

He looked at his pocket watch. "See me after the trial, Miss Duer. Perhaps we can team up and enlighten the good people of this city."

"It has some of the elements of a Greek tragedy, doesn't it?" I said as we walked out of the elegant dining room, with light streaming through the glass ceiling, "with issues of good and evil, of sin and retribution."

He nodded. "Even a Greek chorus of women who sit there day after day, unwilling to listen to reason or hear truth."

"And throughout the land," I intoned, "the multitudes scream for news of orgies and forbidden pleasures."

He stopped in the front lobby to say good-bye, taking both of my hands in his. "I will be seeing our mutual friend this morning," he told me. "I've known Jim for some time, and I must tell you—I am glad you have come into his life."

I stood there for a time after he had left, and felt whole and full and good. I shook myself. There was work to be done, I couldn't bask in my happiness for too long. I hurried off to a little writing room I knew that was tucked into a corner of the large lobby. There, at a desk, I wrote everything I could remember about the conversation. I would need those notes when it came time to write the story after the trial. I would also have to guard them now. I had promised McNab, and I would have to be careful. Instinctively I glanced up to see if anybody had noticed me . . . and looked into the grinning face of Mason Griffin.

"I thought I recognized you in the dining room, Miss Duer," he said, bouncing across the room on his short legs. "I didn't want to interrupt. You seemed quite absorbed in your note-taking."

I jammed my notebook into my bag and told him, "I'm in a hurry. I have to be—"

"I won't take a minute," he interrupted. "In fact, I suspect we've been working on the same story, you could say. You're involved in the Arbuckle trial, and I'm trying to find out where the liquor came from. My superiors feel it is time that something is done to shut down this town. Your friend Freddie Zebra is cooperating with us."

"What has happened to Freddie?" I asked.

He sighed theatrically. "Poor Freddie is back in prison, I'm afraid. He just couldn't seem to keep away from bad influences."

I did not respond. The silence lay between us, growing with each minute. I was not going to break it, I would not.

"What do you hear from our friend Miss Conlon?" he said.

"Somehow, I didn't think she was a friend of yours," I told him, deflecting the question.

"Where did you get that idea?" he asked, his mouth smiling while his eyes never changed expression. They were cold and hard.

"In Sacramento," I reminded him, "during the raid."

"But you've seen her since," he insisted, "and Minnie tells me you are keeping her things for her, so I suppose you keep in touch."

"You suppose wrong," I lied. "She picked up her things and I haven't heard from her since."

He only looked at me, smiling his fixed smile, and I felt a shiver of fear sparkle through me like heat lightning. In that instant I felt as if the little man standing before me, this ridiculous little man with his short legs and tiny feet encased in spats, with his perpetual smile and cold eyes, was evil incarnate.

"I would like to have a nice long talk with you, Hallie," he said. I cringed at his use of my name; the taste of coffee rose in my throat, bitter.

"We have nothing to talk about," I said, unable to keep the disgust from my voice. "Not Freddie Zebra and not Babe Conlon. Nothing."

"Oh, we have a lot to talk about," he told me in his insinuating high voice. "I could tell you some things, too, about Babe Conlon. Things I am sure you don't know."

"No," I said, louder than I had meant, so that two ladies turned to look. "No. I don't want to know. I haven't seen her and I don't expect to see her. She is gone, I don't know where."

Very slowly, speaking each syllable separately, he said: "She is in Anaheim, California, in a rooming house at 1319 Orchard Street. She will be coming to San Francisco at the end of next month."

The shingled cottage was west of Twin Peaks and south of Golden Gate Park, in an area of dunes and sedge and ice plant that was called, somewhat excessively, "The Great Sand Waste." A few years later, the city moved to overtake these dunes, filling and planting them into neat little suburban streets. But it was then splendidly isolated, with only a few cottages scattered here and there among the dunes. There was a cypress tree in front of the cottage that Riordan bought, an ice plant along the wooden walk that led to it. He bought it from a carpenter who had built it, quite solidly, as a "weekend" home close to the city. The carpenter found it too lonely. It was not too lonely for us; it was where we went to be alone.

When Faith left, I had wanted Riordan to move into the cottage with me but he wouldn't. I knew he couldn't, but for a while I was difficult about it. The few times he did stay the night, we felt as if we had to hide. I went to his hotel rooms only once. The bell captain, who knew me, said, "I always figured Mr. Riordan would go first class." It was supposed to be a compliment. I wanted to strangle him.

We furnished the house in the dunes with wicker chairs and tables, and couches full of soft pillows, and cactus plants which didn't require watering. Riordan's great surprise was a bedstead which must have been built for a giant, on which we put a feather tick so enormous that it seemed as if we were sleeping on a cloud.

"Think what the headlines would say if we should suffocate in the depths of this feather bed," Riordan joked one night as we lay together. "'Local lawyer and sob-sister paramour found dead in well-feathered love nest.'

"Love nest," he repeated, moving his hand under my gown. "Maybe we should add some authenticity."

"Wait," I whispered. "Better make sure this love nest doesn't produce any nestlings."

On the Saturday after my breakfast with Gavin McNab, Riordan picked me up after work and we headed for the Dunes. "What made you change your mind?" he asked. "Why aren't you going to Ethel's for dinner tonight?"

"You," I said, "and Gavin McNab. And Mason Griffin."

"First Ethel," he insisted. "Then Gavin, then Mason Griffin, whoever he is."

"Okay," I said, settling into the comfort of talk, happy knowing we had the whole evening and night and morning ahead of us, luxuriating in it. "First, I decided not to give away one of our Saturday nights because that is what she wanted to take away from me. Clive knows that Saturday is the one night we have together for certain. He knows it is important to me. Still, Ethel insisted that it was the only night I could come to meet her family. I don't particularly want you to have to endure meeting her family, but I am furious that you aren't included. After that disastrous dinner Clive arranged for the four of us— when you were so charming and she was such a rotten snob—I said I'd never subject you to that again. But Clive . . . well . . . He asked me to go and I said I would. And then I met Gavin McNab and he said how glad he was that I had come into your life . . . and that was when I knew I couldn't go to Ethel's. You see, don't you?"

"No," he laughed, touching my cheek with the back of his fingers, "but I'm not going to argue with you. While I really am quite sorry that Clive is having difficulties dealing with our 'situation,' as he calls it, I am glad to have my girl back tonight. Do you want to know what McNab said about you?"

"Tell me!" I demanded.

He swerved to miss a bicyclist. "You do love to hear nice things, don't you?" he teased. "But first, who is this Mason Griffin?"

"First tell me what McNab said, then I'll tell you about Griffin."

"He said he was thunderstruck by you."

"Thunderstruck?" I repeated. "Is that what he said?"

"And that if he were twenty years younger . . ."

"You're lying," I laughed, hoping that he wasn't. I didn't want to talk about Mason Griffin. I wanted to talk about Gavin McNab, and Riordan, and anyone except Mason Griffin.

It wasn't until we had settled before a fire in the dune house with bowls of clam chowder and fresh sourdough bread that I finally started.

When I had finished, Riordan poured me another glass of red wine from the supply I had bought from Mr. Maggiore, and said: "Treasury agents are a strange lot. I was talking to a friend of mine the other day who is on the Chinatown squad, and he got to talking about a Treasury man. He said he is actually perverse—not just a bully, but something of a tormentor. Prohibition seems to give a kind of license to some of these men to practice a personal form of terrorism."

I dipped a chunk of sourdough into my wine. "I think I couldn't stand to have Griffin touch me," I said. "I have this feeling that my skin would be scorched. I know it sounds foolish, but there is something so . . . evil about him. He has this round little belly, and he bounces along laughing all the while like that mechanical lady out at Playland, Laughing Sal, and yet under that fat, smiling little dwarf is a monster."

"Do you think he was responsible for Babe's beating?"

"I'm sure of it," I said. "She didn't tell me that, but I know it."

I paused; then I said what was bothering me: "He wants to talk to me."

Riordan put his soup bowl on the floor in front of the fire. "You don't have to see him; we can do something about that."

"Sure," I answered. "The police are going to laugh me out of town if I complain about this jolly little fellow who only wants to talk to me."

"Do you think he might try to hurt you?" he asked.

"No," I answered without even having to think about it, "he only wants to use me to get to her. The people he hates are people of color and foreigners. And Babe."

Riordan rested his chin on his clasped hands and looked into the fire. "Tell him we will meet with him, you and me. He already knows about us . . ."

"How do you know that?" I asked, surprised.

"Because a man came to our office asking about you. I didn't know who was behind it, so I made some inquiries and came up with Treasury. Now it fits."

"Come in, have a seat." Riordan didn't bother to stand, but remained behind his desk. I was in a chair to his right, which meant that Mason Griffin would have to sit directly in front of the desk. His legs were so short that he had to hop, as a child would, to reach the seat. His perpetual smile was in place.

"Miss Duer," he said, bowing to me. "What a pleasant surprise."

"I don't think it's much of a surprise at all," Riordan told him, wasting no time. "You've been here before, asking about Miss Duer. You know she is a client of mine. And we know you've been to her paper asking questions. You seem to turn up wherever she is."

Griffin's smile was set, but his eyes narrowed. "I'm a Treasury agent, sir. My position requires me to ask questions. And as for running into each other, well, San Francisco is a small enough place, isn't it? As a matter of fact, the two of you seem to run into each other at all kinds of places . . . John's Grill, Willow—"

Riordan cut him off, his voice as angry as I'd ever heard it. "I'm not going to dance with you, Griffin. I am going to give you some good advice. You're right about this being a small town. You may have noticed we have an Irish police chief, Irish judges and your immediate boss—Matt Flynn at Treasury—is Irish too. I grew up with those fellows, and there are some who think we're clannish. Now, I know as well as the next one that a federal agent like yourself has a certain amount of power. And maybe in Sacramento or Elko or any of the other towns you've worked in, the local authorities were willing to look the other way when you went around trampling on citizens' constitutional rights. I can promise you that it isn't going to work that way here, not if you continue harassing Miss Duer or her friend Miss Conlon."

At the mention of Babe's name, the little man's hands gripped the arms of the chair as if he were afraid he might tumble off. And now the smile was gone.

"If you go on with this private little vendetta against these women, you're going to find yourself not only out of a job, you'll find you can't even come into this city without being in danger of breaking some law."

Mason Griffin sat staring at Riordan, his eyes small black pinpoints of rage. He seemed to shudder; then very quickly he hopped down and turned to go. He was going to walk out without saying a word, but Riordan wouldn't let him.

"I want to hear, right now, if you get what I'm telling you," Riordan demanded.

Griffin's hand was on the door, but he turned, his eyes down, and muttered, "Yes, sir."

When he had left, I sat for a few minutes staring at Riordan. "Can you do that?" I asked. "Have him run out of town?"

"If it comes to that," Riordan answered.

"Somehow, I don't think it will. He seemed chastened."

"With someone like Griffin, you never can tell," Riordan answered.

On March 24, in the middle of Roscoe Arbuckle's third trial, Gavin McNab rose at the beginning of the day's proceedings to wish the defendant "happier returns than today" on the occasion of his thirty-fifth birthday. The Scotsman then returned to his excoriation of the district attorney, calling him an "Apache running wild," and of the character of Virginia Rappé, revealing that she had had five abortions between 1908 and 1910, and at the age of sixteen had given birth to an illegitimate daughter. He even turned to the Women's Vigilance Committee, calling them "stony-faced women who haunt the courts, clamoring for blood."

No one escaped his wrath this time. On the stand, he reduced Alice Blake to sobs, but got her to admit that the district attorney had insisted she implicate Arbuckle.

It was ten minutes past five on the afternoon of April 15 when the jury went out. They were back in five minutes. To a packed courtroom, foreman Edward Brown read a statement signed by all of them: "Acquittal is not enough for Roscoe Arbuckle. We feel that a great injustice has been done him. We feel also that it was only our plain duty to give him this exoneration, under the evidence, for there was not the slightest proof adduced to connect him in any way with the commission of a crime. He was manly throughout the case, and told a straightforward story on the witness stand, which we all believed. The happening at the hotel was an unfortunate affair for which Arbuckle, so the evidence shows, was in no way responsible. We wish him success, and hope that the American people will take the judgment of fourteen men and women who have sat listening for thirty-one days to the evidence, that Roscoe Arbuckle is entirely innocent and free from all blame."

There was a long moment of silence, and then a burst of sound:

shouting and clapping, cheering and uproar. In the center was the big man, his face wearing the slap-happy grin so familiar to moviegoers. In the general pandemonium, only the prosecuting team was silent. For the first time since the trials had begun, seven long months before, Matthew Brady, the district attorney, had nothing to say.

I pushed through the crowd, trying to get to McNab when I felt a hand on my arm. I recognized one of McNab's assistants. He drew me aside to say, "Mr. McNab and Mr. Arbuckle will be returning to Los Angeles tonight on the *Lark*. Mr. McNab says to tell you he's very sorry they can't talk to you here in San Francisco, but as you can imagine, Mr. Arbuckle is anxious to be on his way. They suggest you join them for at least part of the trip south, so that they can give you the interviews you were promised."

"I'll be there," I said, trying not to look as pleased as I felt. McNab was a man of his word, and he was about to give me a story that would make front pages all over the country.

Arbuckle sat in a big easy chair in the smoking car of the *Lark*, and talked about the toll the trial had taken. "First I am going to lose forty pounds," he said, patting his large midsection. "Then I'm about due for a comeback, I think." His wife, Minta, walking by, patted him on the back and he grinned up at her, a little-boy grin, full of mischief. She seemed fond of him in a sisterly way. They had been separated for a number of years, but at the first sign of trouble Minta had come running. Arbuckle was easy, relaxed and feeling expansive. He was in a mood to talk, and talk he did about the months of his ordeal. "I figure I've had enough tragedy, I'm ready for some comedy in my life," he joked.

When Arbuckle finished, Gavin McNab joined me and, talking as fast as I could write, spelled out for me how Matthew Brady had abridged Roscoe Arbuckle's "rights to life, liberty and the pursuit of happiness."

I sat up all night writing my story in a room at the Biltmore. At eight o'clock on Friday morning I walked over to the telegraph office and sent it to San Francisco, then I went to the station to book a sleeper for the trip home.

I bought my ticket, and since I had some time I went to the telephone office, where I placed a call to the number in Anaheim that I had written on the back of a photograph of my grandparents.

"What brings you to the Southland?" Babe growled in her husky voice.

"Work," I told her. "And I know this is an emergency number, but I wanted to tell you that Mason Griffin knows where you are—your address, even that you are planning to come to San Francisco next month."

"Hmmm," she said.

I waited, and when she didn't add anything I asked, "Why don't you stay with me at the cottage if you come? I have a feeling he'll leave you alone there."

"How come?" she wanted to know.

"Because," I said, "my attorney friend Jim Riordan and I had a meeting with Griffin. Riordan read him a rather formidable list of consequences, should he decide to go on harassing us. He left with his tail between his legs."

"Hah!" Babe said, unconvinced. "That's just one of his tricks. He's got a whole lot more, but one thing is for sure—he'll never give up."

"Babe," I said, and then I asked: "Was it his?"

For a long while all I could hear over the wire was a low kind of humming sound. Finally she said, "I don't know," and signed off without telling me if she would stay at the cottage.

My story appeared in Saturday's first edition under the title "Arbuckle's Own Story." *Exclusive to the* Times *by Hallie Duer.* The papers were on our desks before the ink was dry. For a few minutes the room was silent while people read; then Harry shouted from across the room, "Good work, Hallie." And a chorus of voices joined in. Even Lloyd Garr came over to say, "This makes you a *bona fide*. A real sob sister."

"Agnes is expecting us, and Kathleen is determined," Riordan said, "so, barring rain or high winds, it looks like we are set to go sailing today."

I sighed and looped one leg over his to keep him from getting out of bed. "Maybe it will snow," I said. "Let's wait and see."

"It hasn't been known to snow in San Francisco in twenty years or more," Riordan laughed, "and you've already postponed this rendezvous twice."

"I've just had an eventful week, one of the most eventful weeks of my life. I don't want to end it with a splash. Do I have to go?"

"No," he said, "but why ask me? This is between you and Kathleen. I don't know why it's so important that the two of you go out in a boat. I'm just the boatman."

I answered my own question: "I have to go. As much as I hate little boats, and I do, a promise is a promise."

Agnes was on the dock, struggling with the sails, when we came around the big house on the lake. Riordan went to help her, and Kathleen and I just stood on the grassy slope watching. My stomach felt empty, my head light.

Kathleen grasped my hand. "We're going to do it," she said, giving herself courage.

"I hope so, sweets," I answered, wanting to overcome a strange, faltering sensation that seemed to affect my knees, making them stiff.

"You look lovely in your middie dresses," Agnes called to us. I tried to smile, but my face would not cooperate.

Riordan held out his hands to receive us, Kathleen first. She stepped in, laughing nervously. The boat rocked as Riordan lifted and settled her in place.

"Now Hallie," he said, his arms out to me. *No. I cannot. Please, no.* The words locked inside of me, I could not say them. The boat swayed under me with a sickening motion. I felt his arms holding me, lowering me into the boat. "Hallie," he said very softly, his eyes filled with concern, "are you sure?" I couldn't speak. *No*, I wanted to say. Instead I nodded.

We were moving gently, turning, tilting from side to side, the sun sparkling bright on the water . . . moving slowly away from the dock. I closed my eyes but I could not close out the sound: water, slapping softly against the boat. Slapping against the rocking boat. *Row row row your boat, gently down the stream* . . . I opened my eyes. A cloud had moved over the sun, it was dark, the water black . . . merrily merrily merrily merrily, life is but a dream . . . A scream gathered deep inside of me, formed and grew, expanding until it cut off my breathing. I had to get up, out, away. *Don't give up, Hallie, love* . . . I stood, the scream rising inside of me, tearing up through my stomach and my chest . . .

"Hallie, sit down." It was Riordan's voice but it was far off and too late, too late.

The water filled my nose and my mouth and my eyes, dark and pulling me down, down, the scream inside of me exploding in the darkness and rising, rising to the surface . . . And then hands were holding me up, firm and tight under my arms, the hands were holding me, my head was above water. They were not my mother's hands, but Riordan's. He was holding me, I could see his face in front of me. "Breathe, Hallie," he was shouting. "Hallie, breathe."

And then the child's arms closed around me, holding me tight, her small hands stroking my face and saying, over and over again. "It's all right now, Hallie. You're safe, everything is all right."

Inside of me, something broke loose and came rushing out small and hard and dry and racking at first. Coughing, gasping, and then the sobs, and a torrent of tears. Real tears, hot and wet and salty, flowing from some hidden well that had been locked and sealed all the years since that summer. My body shook and heaved and the tears gushed out of me. Still the child held me, would not give me up, but rocked me as she would her own child. She told me that everything was going to be all right, and I believed her. She told me we had nothing more to fear, and I knew she was telling the truth.

When I woke in Agnes' big bed, the light outside was dimming. Riordan sat in the half-light, watching me. He leaned close, to see if my eyes had opened, and took my hand and pressed it to his lips. I wanted to smile at him, but my lips were trembling and my eyes filled.

"I can cry," I whispered, "I really can."

"I always knew you could," he told me.

SIXTEEN

FAITH SAT WITH HER hands cupped around her large middle. "I could hardly make it up the hill," she panted. "I don't remember it being so steep."

"You weren't so round when you lived here," I reminded her. "How much longer till baby arrives?"

"Two months," she sighed. "Forever! But at least I've stopped losing my breakfast every time I go into the darkroom. Now that I can abide the smell of the chemicals, I find my legs ache from standing. Having a baby isn't all that much fun, did I tell you?"

"You did," I said, patting her shoulder. "Let me get you some tea. Is it going to be a boy or a girl?"

"I don't care," she said, sharper, I think, than she intended, "but Thayer is mad to have a son since he already has two daughters."

We sat at the kitchen table, the October light streaming in. The window was open and we could hear the dry rustle of the sycamore leaves. "I'd forgotten how nice this is," Faith said, a small ache in her voice. Hearing it, she forced herself to say brightly, "It's lovely to see you looking so happy, Hal."

I poured our tea and told her that I *was* happy. "The other day I was making the sprint across Market Street, trying to keep from being killed by a streetcar, and in the middle of it all I was overcome with this feeling of being totally, gloriously, spilling-over happy," I told her, "and lucky, too—that he wants to be with me. This year has been," I ended in triumph, "almost perfect."

Faith smiled, as if I had done something to make her proud. She reached for my hand and squeezed it. I felt as if I could tell her what I had been wanting to say. "Do you know," I began, "how many people assume I'm not happy because Riordan is married? It's as if we are star-crossed lovers. Even people who know me, who care about me, don't seem to believe me when I say I am happy with things as they are. There is this assumption that marriage is every woman's goal . . ."

Faith shifted uncomfortably in her chair, trying to find the right position, the right words. "I think there is an idea—a feeling, really," she began, "that until you've borne a child you're not wholly a woman. And since marriage is looked on as a precondition—a legal, or moral precondition—to childbearing, when you say you aren't interested in marriage what you are really saying is that you don't want children. And that is heresy." She was holding on to my hand, as if to keep the words flowing. She went on, very softly, "I'm questioning a lot of things these days. The myth of the lady-in-waiting, to begin with. I haven't liked anything about being pregnant, yet I'm frightened about the birth. And I'm even more frightened that I won't like the baby when it gets here."

I was alarmed by the anger in her eyes, and worried by a nagging feeling that she was on edge; there was tension between us and I didn't know why.

"Tell me how I can help," I said.

She pressed my hand hard, and let it go. "Just be here, and talk to me." She was near tears. To fight them she changed the subject abruptly: "How's Clive? He used to come by the studio every now and then, but lately . . ."

"Lately he's spending all of his time either at work or with Ethel. And since Ethel doesn't approve of my 'carrying on,' as she calls it, with Riordan, I don't see very much of them either."

Faith put her fingers to her temple. "It's hard to believe it's been a whole year since we went to the beach—on your birthday last year. You and Riordan and Clive and Agnes and Sara. A year ago this month."

"Just before you got married," I said. "You took pictures, and we built a fire on the beach . . ."

"I was thinking about that the other day," she went on, "about sitting around the fire that day, telling stories about when we were kids, and how we got into trouble. Riordan told that wild tale about him and his brother and the confessional. And then Clive told about the Chicago police catching him when he was sixteen, and accusing him of being a Peeping Tom. Remember?"

I nodded. I remembered. "You mean how he used to roam the neighborhoods at dusk, looking for families sitting around the dinner table?"

Faith went on, "He said he just liked to watch them eating and talking together. It seemed so sad and wistful."

We sat in silence for a few moments. "It's not just women who want marriage and a family to belong to," I said. "Clive wants it, and it seems as if Ethel can give it to him. After falling in love with a married man—something I never considered would ever happen to me—I don't think I can possibly tell anybody else who they should fall in love with and marry."

Faith was shaking her head. "It's not as if you're a home-breaker," she said. "Riordan hasn't lived with his wife for years."

"But I'm not sure if that would make any difference," I told her. "It does make it easier for other people. Harry and Thelma, for example. Still, it is hard for Thelma, particularly. But they continue to see us, and have us out to their house. And Riordan and Harry take their boys out together to a ball game now and then."

"Do they know about your secret hideaway out in the Sand Waste?"

"No," I said. "Only you and Clive know about that."

Faith's portfolio was lying on the table between us, but she had made no move to open it. I began to feel as if the talk was a subterfuge, something to postpone my looking at the photographs. "When do I get to see the new project you told me about . . . what wonderful new photographs have you been doing?"

For a moment it seemed as if she hadn't heard me. Then, nervously, she began to tug at the ties on the portfolio. Her hands, puffy and white, seemed not to be able to work. "I don't know how wonderful you will think they are," she said in a nervous rush of words. "It's something that started almost by accident and turned into a kind of picture story. Something like the essays you and I used to do for the *Times*. At first I was just studying the morning light in the studio—it's quite beautiful through the skylight, as it plays on the marble of the new piece Thayer has been commissioned to do for the city of Portland."

She removed the first of the photographs, a large print, a closeup of Thayer Gerson's powerful hands—big and blunt, gripping a chisel, the focus so sharp you could see the tiny hairs on his fingers. She took out each photograph in turn, fifteen in all, each a strong focus on Gerson's hands, and under them the emerging figure of a dolphin.

When she had finished she looked at me, waiting.

I was repulsed by them; they seemed to me to be nothing like Faith's work.

"They're technically good, of course," I said. "What do you plan to do with them?"

She stumbled over her words: "I wondered if you might want . . . if you would do a story to go with them . . . if maybe the *Times* would want . . ."

I swallowed to keep the anger down. The pictures explained the awkwardness, the tension I had felt. "Was this your idea?" I asked.

"We both thought it would make a good picture story for the Sunday art section," she said.

I tried to measure my words. "Maybe it would," I answered. "But I wish you hadn't asked me to write it because I can't. I won't. And Thayer knew that when he sent you. It's his way of punishing you for seeing me. I'm sorry to be so blunt, and I don't like upsetting you. But I'm not going to make excuses, either."

She sat back in her chair, her shoulders slumped, silent for a time. "All right," she said, more defeated than angry. "I'll try to find somebody else to write it. Do you think the *Times* will buy it?"

"Talk to Gene Bolten," I said. "You know him."

Faith went into the bathroom and stayed for a long while. I could hear the water running, and when she came out her face was splotched and red. She was in command, but only just. And I was in turmoil, fighting anger and guilt.

"I'll walk you down the hill," I said, taking her portfolio. At the corner by the delicatessen we said good-bye in an awkward, perfunctory way. The wall was back; Thayer Gerson had built it himself, with pictures of his strong, blunt, powerful hands.

I loved the city best in the rains; they started blowing in from the Pacific in the first week of November, one storm and then another, with brief respites of sun and bright blue sky. And then the rain again, rivulets of water pouring down the windowpanes and merging, traveling to the gutters and spilling over into the roadways. Raindrops spattered in puddles and glittered on rain slickers. Sometimes in the early evening I would meet Riordan under the canopy of the Western Union office at Market and Drumm, or in the entryway to Old St. Mary's church in Chinatown, and we would walk together, close under his great black umbrella, alone in a sea of umbrellas, to Jack's for dinner.

We had our own table there, reserved for us by an autocratic waiter named Morris who boned our rex sole at table, kept our water glasses filled and protected us. We had become celebrities of a sort. My byline appeared regularly on the front page of the *Times*, and many of my stories were being picked up by the wire services. I continued covering newsworthy court trials, but now and then the Boss would assign me a more political piece. I went to the great Central Valley to write a series of articles about the expansion of the migratory labor force, which had reached the astonishing figure of 120,000. I reported on how these nomadic families lived, hidden away in tents and tar-paper shacks in towns nobody had ever heard about. And then I wrote a series on the initiative campaign for the Water and Power Act, which would bring irrigation to the valley, an act opposed by every private power interest in the state.

At the same time, Riordan was involved in some of the most controversial court cases in the city, most often in defense of an unpopular cause. To people like Porter Reade, Sara's godson, Riordan was a hero. To others he was an apologist for Wobblies and Reds and anarchists. Harding was in the White House, "normalcy" was the catchword, the progressives were out of vogue.

Together, Riordan and I managed a certain notoriety, and now and then a gossip item would appear in one of the competing papers. After the Sandol-Evers fight in Colma, the *News*'s Lady Chatter asked: "What attractive lady reporter was seen with what (married) warhero lawyer at the fights the other night? Everyone at ringside was talking about this twosome." The silliness often got excessive. Another columnist said I was "anything but the frivolous flapper she appears to be." And once, for reasons that escaped me, I was described as "that free spirit who is, nonetheless, the bee's knees."

We avoided appearing in public as much as we could. We made an exception for Harry and Thelma's wedding anniversary on November 18, and took them dinner-dancing at the Rose Bowl in the Palace Hotel. It was one of the city's gayest nightspots, with a full dance orchestra. Thelma had her hair bobbed and permed for the occasion and wore a new short brown satin dress. I chose a rosepink chiffon with a layered skirt and a pointed hemline. With it I wore a tight little matching cloche and waist-length pearls, and Riordan said, in a voice full of innuendo, "*Now* you do look like the bee's knees."

When the band struck up "Carolina in the Morning" Riordan asked, "Do you think you can handle a partner with a bum knee?" We sang along as we glided easily around the gleaming floor . . . and when we came back to the table, Thelma was beaming. "I'd forgotten what marvelous dancers you Riordan boys were—Jimmy won all the contests."

I claimed Harry for the next dance, telling him, "I think your wife wants to take a turn with my partner." Harry was lighter on his feet than I would have thought. We fox-trotted easily, the colored lights playing on the big dance floor. "I'll bet you won a few contests yourself," I told him.

"Not me," he answered, "and if memory serves me, I think it was Tom, not Jimmy, who won all the dance contests. I hope Thelma didn't embarrass him."

"Maybe the bum knee helps," I joked, and then I felt comfortable enough to say what I had been wanting to say: "We are so grateful to you and Thelma for being our friends."

Harry held me out a bit, looking directly into my face, never missing a step, moving and turning easily in time to the music, and he said, "You and Jimmy Riordan belong together. We know that." The music stopped and I looped my arm through his as we threaded our way across the dance floor.

"Thank you, Harry McConaughey," I said. "I will love you for the rest of my life for that."

And Harry said: "What more could a fellow ask?"

That night I rubbed Riordan's back until I could feel his muscles relax. "I wish," I whispered into the curve of his neck, "that you were as satisfied with the way things are as I am."

He turned to look at me, asking, "Is this really what you want? Is it enough?"

I continued massaging his arm. "That's not the right question," I said. "The right question is: Are you happy? And the answer is *yes*. Yes I am, happier than I've ever been in my life. I would be happier if we could wake together every morning, but we can't. And we both do the kind of work we want to do—we're happy in that—which is rare in this world. We aren't pariahs, even if we do get confronted now and then."

"Our friends accept our situation because they know we can't change it," he said. "Maybe it's harder for me than it is for you because I'm the one trapped in a marriage. I'm the one with the children to consider. But sometimes the remarks . . ."

"Shhh," I said. "Don't listen to them. Don't. It doesn't matter what they say."

But it did matter to him and I knew it. It mattered because what they were saying was that Riordan had a nice little deal going—a wife and kids tucked away out in the Sunset and a good-time girl to bed down whenever he wanted. A police lieutenant had said, loud enough for me to hear, "That's one nice piece of ass Riordan's found for himself." I could only imagine what was said to him when I wasn't around.

Perhaps it was why I loved the rain so; it wrapped around us, closed us in, kept us safe from a world that frowned on our being together.

Early in December Faith gave birth to a six-pound, seven-ounce baby girl. I went to the Wakefield Sanatorium, a maternity hospital, to see them.

Faith looked tired and wan, but there was no uneasiness between us now and when she spoke of the baby her eyes came alive.

"Little Emilie is beautiful!" I told her.

"She is, isn't she?" She smiled back.

My gift to Faith was a baby nurse for the two weeks after she left the hospital. She was a solid Irishwoman and came highly recommended by Thelma, who had said, "Katie Gilligan can handle three new babies, and their parents, like nobody you know. She's a marvel."

When Katie Gilligan came to the *Times* office at the end of the two weeks, her mouth was clamped shut.

"How are mother and child doing?" I asked.

"The baby is a fine healthy little girl who sleeps well and eats well, which is a sign of God's grace, because her little mother is going to need a good baby." And then it all came out in a rush: "I'm afraid I spoke out of turn, mum, and I tell you that I'm sorry for it, but it couldn't be helped. I'm certain that Mr. Gerson is an important man, and a famous artist, I don't doubt it. But he is not a considerate man, no. I finally had to tell him that I wasn't there to wait on him or do his bidding. I feel sorry for his wife, I do. There, I've said it. You needn't pay me, miss. I'm afraid I caused something of a stir in the family, and that was not why you sent me, I'm sure." I paid her and gave her a bonus.

On Christmas Day Riordan and I went back to Willow Camp. The beach in the winter was empty, the sea a shimmering gray, the sky luminous. We pulled on heavy sweaters and walked the length of the sand spit, two miles or more, and we talked . . . of politics and people and ideas.

We bought fresh fish from a local fisherman and cooked it over the fire and with it sipped French champagne Riordan had come by. Without ceremony, he gave me a ring—a slim circle of diamonds with a single ruby, designed by Shreve's.

As we lay together in front of the fire that night, he played with a strand of my hair and told me I had diminished his reading time.

"Since you came into my life," he said, "I sleep at night. Used to be I would read until two, sometimes three. And there were long evenings, too—hotel rooms encourage reading."

I had surveyed the books stacked in boxes and on the floor of his hotel rooms. There were a few detective novels, but not many. Quite a few volumes were serious studies of the Great War, like *The Versailles Verdict: The Case for the Central Powers*. He read Aldous Huxley and the Frenchman Jean Cocteau. Grandfather had read everything; Riordan read selectively. His heroes were Abraham Lincoln, John Peter Altgeld and John Stuart Mill. Of the socialists, he much preferred Robert Owen to Karl Marx. Gradually, the books stacked in his hotel rooms came to rest in my cottage on the hill or at the house in the Sand Waste. Now I sat up nights reading, catching up, keeping pace as well as I could.

Babe arrived at the cottage early on New Year's Eve wearing a new fur coat and driving a Packard touring car which seemed as long as a city block. "It looks like a rumrunner," I joked; I was not far from the mark. She wished us a Happy 1923, gave us six bottles of Scotch whiskey and left as abruptly as she had arrived. It was Riordan's first meeting with Babe. They studied each other; then Babe stuck out her hand and they shook. Before she left she asked for his business card, saying, "Who knows when I might need a legal expert?" It was, I knew, her mark of approval.

Later, Riordan's comment was: "You admire tough ladies, don't you?

"Only when they have a generous spirit," I answered.

A few days later Mason Griffin appeared at the newspaper office looking for me. I was out at the time, so the Boss talked to him.

"He's not the same funny little man," he told me. "He seems to have lost his sense of humor. Instead of laughing, he was stuttering, spraying all over the place trying to get it all out. He carried on, I'll tell you—about the bad company you keep, communist lawyers and rumrunning whores and such." Sanford Curtin raised his eyebrows in a classic expression of amused outrage. "According to Mr. Mason Griffin," he went on, "the answer to this country's problems, what will make it great again, is to deport the Jews and the niggers and the wops—his words—and throw in a few Indians and Polacks. I suggested he might like to set up a color scheme—decide on a shade of, say, pale brown . . . closer perhaps to a peach of deep ripeness—and have thousands of cards printed with this precise color dabbed on. Anyone darker would be automatically shipped out on a Soviet ark. At first I suggested it would be quite democratic—after all, everyone would have to abide by this one simple rule. But then I got to thinking about the farmers who work out in the sun all day, and become deeply tanned. So I said that perhaps we could set up some kind of Board for Legitimate Suntans, which would offer reprieves that would go into the winter, when we could see for certain the real color of a man's skin." The Boss paused, and I smiled because I couldn't help it, he was so pleased with himself. He went on, "The little man turned and sputtered out of here spraying spit like one of those little fat wind-up toys you can buy around the holidays."

I would have liked to laugh with him. If Babe hadn't been so nervous during her short visit with us on New Year's Eve, I would have. I knew Babe was not afraid of shadows.

"Incidentally, Hallie," the Boss added, "I talked to someone I know in Treasury about little Mr. Griffin. Mine was not the first complaint—from what I gathered, an inside investigation is under way. They're keeping their eye on him."

The morning light sifted through the moving branches of the sycamore tree, playing patterns on my bedroom ceiling. I lay in bed listening to the clatter of the birds, busy because it was spring and everything was tight and green and alive, about to burst. During the night a mayfly had wandered into my room and was now drifting noiselessly toward the ceiling, trailing its long legs. Mayflies. Grandfather called them "gollywompers." I smiled, thinking of him. We should go to Sacramento this month or next.

I did not want to get up; I wanted to lie there, warm and lazy, and do nothing but study the moving patterns on the ceiling and the mayfly, butting itself against the ceiling now. But I couldn't; I had to catch the noon train to Eureka. I sat up too quickly. The room began to rotate. I closed my eyes and I could feel it moving in a circular pattern. I took a deep breath and put my feet on the floor. After a moment, I got my bearings. It would not do to get sick. I had to cover the Braun-Rozner trial; it was the biggest story to come along in a time. I walked over to the window and took a deep breath of air. The telephone rang.

Steadying myself on pieces of furniture, I made my way to the telephone. "Hallie," Riordan said, "I can't make it this morning— Sid just called and I have to go see the judge right away, while he's in the mood to talk to me. If it wasn't Agnes, I'd say no. I'll try to make it to the train to see you off, but if I can't . . ."

"I know," I said, "it's all right. If I don't see you before I leave, I love you." My eyes filled with tears. I was glad he couldn't see me.

Three hundred women, some of them perched on ladders in the back of the courtroom, crammed into the little courthouse to hear the case of Georgina Braun, who was accused of murdering her lover, a handyman on the Braun farm, named Emmett Rozner. It promised to be a steamy trial. Rozner was known to have dallied with other women, including Mrs. Braun's sister.

While the jury selection was under way, I took notes: "The principals in this trial, in a united front, sit together at the right of the circular desk, Mrs. Braun, the accused, in a blue silk dress and large black hat, her dark hair pulled low over her ears in demure fashion. Her husband, a prosperous man of middle age in a well-tailored suit, sits behind her, his eyes fixed on some middle ground. The sister who had dallied with the handyman sits next to him; now and then the sisters exchange glances and little smiles, as if to show that whatever differences they may have had are now resolved, that they are united in a plea of innocence. The Brauns, who moved here from Seattle two years ago, have closed ranks: they are together now and ready to do battle with the country people who surround them in this little close-knit farm community near the northern border of California. The Rozners sit across from them, the mother and the brothers of the dead man, their faces burned from working in the sun. They are farmers, country people who have worked this land for fifty years. In some way, that is what this trial is all about: city people and country people, two separate worlds with two sets of manners and morals. The Rozners see the Brauns as interlopers, as city people—newcomers—who hired others to work their land, who toyed with the affections of one of their own. Everyone knows how Emmett Rozner came to be lying faceup by the Brauns' chicken coop with three bullet holes in his body. Mrs. Georgina Braun has admitted she put them there. The question that needs answering is one of extenuating circumstances. In this case, those circumstances have to do with the rifle Emmett Rozner was carrying at the time of his death. Will the jury believe the prosecutor when he says Rozner was returning from a hunting foray and had no plan to use the rifle on Georgina Braun? Or will they believe the woman and her sister, both of whom say they saw him raise the gun?"

I paused, feeling suddenly warm. The defendant was wearing a fur coat. "Isn't it terribly hot in here?" I asked the reporter sitting next to me.

"Not particularly," he answered. "Are you all right? Your face is chalk white."

I made my way outside and to the back of the building. A newly plowed field joined the courthouse lawn. I walked toward it, glad for the cold air in my face. I stumbled, caught myself. As I reached the field a wave of nausea overcame me and my stomach convulsed. I leaned over and emptied it into the new plowed earth.

I waited. For the white bedsheets to show a stain, for the slow ache that came each month, for the body's slow routine. I made my way to the courtroom each day that week, one part of me aware of my body, of any signal. *Please*, I would say to myself as a witness recounted yet another version of a love tryst between the accused or her sister and the hired hand. *Oh, please*, I thought as the jury went out and I made my way to the ladies' room. And then the jury came back and set Georgina Braun free, and in the uproar I made my notes, but I knew. The verdict was in: Georgina Braun, who had killed her lover, was innocent. And I was guilty of being with child.

I climbed onto the train and wished I would never have to get off, that I could ride forever through the redwood groves of northern California, that I could stay on the train, rolling and rocking and moving through time, yet separate. I did not want to go back, I did not want to say it out loud. Once the words were said, my world would change; it would never be the same again. I sat by the window, my coat wrapped tight around me, and stared into the passing wilderness. We could come here and build a cabin, and clear the land and be alone. But we couldn't. We were city people and this was a country place. There were no pioneers left, no free land to clear.

Clive met me at the station. "Riordan had to go to Sacramento this morning," he explained as he hefted my valise. "He tried his best to get a delay but he couldn't. He was pretty upset about not being able to meet you." Clive grinned winningly. "I told him I was glad because I've been wanting to talk to you myself." He looked at me closely then and said, "Are you all right, Hal?"

I sank back in the taxi seat and sighed. "I'm just terribly tired, Clive. I've been under the weather some, and all I really want to do is go home, take a warm bath and go over some notes, then to bed." I remembered: "But you said you want to talk to me?"

"It will keep," he answered. "Come on, I'll open a can of soup for you and tuck you in. You look a little green around the gills."

Riordan returned the next day bursting with news. There was so much to talk about—the Eureka trial, his case in Sacramento— and I was so happy to be with him that I waited. We drove out to the house in the Sand Waste and talked some more, and went to bed and made love slowly, sweetly. And still I waited. As soon as it was said, as the words were spoken, everything would be changed, our world would be forever different.

The next morning he was up and had a fire going by the time I opened my eyes. "You've never done that before," he said, "slept long enough for me to make the coffee."

He brought me a cup, then pulled a chair up close to the bed and, cradling his own coffee cup with his hands, said, "Isn't it about time you told me what's on your mind?"

I took a sip of the hot coffee, closing my eyes against the rising steam and the panic. He knew. It was time to tell him, but I wasn't ready. Not yet.

"On my mind?" I repeated, playing for time.

He grinned patiently. "You've been studying me, Hallie."

I nodded. "I guess I have—been studying you, I mean," I started, feeling my way, wanting to find the right words. "I was thinking how strange it would be, if your brother . . . if Tom were still alive . . ."

It was not what I was thinking, but it would work as a diversion. His brother was the only subject that we avoided, the one source of uneasiness between us. There were times when I felt he was waiting for me to ask about it.

He looked into the cup he held in his hand, frowning, his eyes dark and pained.

"I'm sorry," I said, ashamed of myself for the subterfuge. "It's just that sometimes I do wonder," I blundered on, trying to find a way out, "about your brother—why you have such a hard time talking about him. Sometimes I think about what it would be like—what would have happened between us if Tom were . . . I think he wouldn't have . . ." I couldn't seem to stop. I was making matters worse, and I wanted to extricate myself but I didn't know how. Riordan's eyes were on me now, searching my face.

"He wouldn't have what?" he asked in a strained voice.

I shook my head and tried to shrug it off. "Nothing. Really, nothing. I'm being foolish, raising problems which don't even exist. What might have been doesn't matter. Please, forget I brought it up. I am sorry."

But he continued staring at me, the dark lights moving in his eyes. I knew I had to say something so I said: "He wouldn't have approved of me."

He was shaking his head. "Not true," he told me, putting down his coffee and moving to sit close to me on the bed. He smoothed my hair back from my face, his touch so gentle that I could feel tears welling in me. He began to talk then, his voice soft and low, "Remember that night in the restaurant, when an old Irishman said you looked like one of Tom's girls? Remember what I told you then?"

I took a deep breath, wanting to end the charade I had started and not knowing how. Wanting to say what I should say, out loud, and not knowing how to do that, either. "You said that I was the kind of girl Tom would want," I answered.

He looked at me, as if to find something in my face. I heard myself ask him, 'Tom wouldn't have approved of us, would he? He would have tried to talk you out of being with me."

I began to shiver uncontrollably, my teeth to chatter. He pulled the covers close around me and rubbed my arms to warm me. "Hallie," he said in a voice that was strangely hoarse, "I want to talk to you about my brother . . . I need to talk to you about him, about what happened . . . the war and . . ."

"Shh," I said, putting my hand over his mouth and pulling him to me, "don't, please. No more. Not now. We'll talk later. There's time yet . . ."

I wanted to tell him that I didn't care, that his brother was dead, that there was something more important, a new life to consider. I could feel the tears slipping down my cheeks. "Not now, please," I repeated. "Kathleen gets worried when you're late. You'll have to hurry."

He looked away from me, out the window at the long slope of the dunes. And then he pulled me to him and in an exhausted voice said, "Yes. All right."

A flood of relief coursed through me. Our world would not be shattered, not this day.

He left to spend the afternoon with the children. After a while I pulled on an old skirt and one of Riordan's flannel shirts and walked all the way to the ocean. I sat and watched the waves wash in, one and then another. Waves would be washing in next month, next year . . . What would have happened by then, I wondered. To our child, mine and Riordan's. I pulled my knees close to me and tried to imagine how it would be to have this baby. I could go home to Sacramento, to the farm. Give up my job and disappear. Or stay here in the Sand Waste. *Illegitimate. Bastard. Nullius filius—the son of nobody*. Poor little baby, hidden away.

When Riordan returned he was silent in a way that meant he had had some trouble with his family. "It's nothing new," he said when I asked, "Michael is making demands. He tells me Colin is getting into trouble at school, and the nuns are complaining about Kathleen—the usual."

"Is it?" I said. "I didn't know."

"No reason you should," he said. "I've talked to the sisters, and the kinds of complaints they have are the kinds they've been making about kids from the beginning of time—or at least from the beginning of Catholic schools. Kathleen is 'irreverent' and Colin is 'feisty.' It's just something that Michael is using."

"Using for what?" I asked.

Riordan had started gathering up our things and was carrying them to the car. Perhaps he didn't hear me, or perhaps he didn't want to answer. I did not ask again.

The next day I filed my story and left the city room early. I had planned to go to the cottage to do some hand wash—some silk blouses, my *peau d'ange* underthings. Instead, I lay down on the bed and gave myself over to a strange lassitude.

A rapping at the door startled me out of a half-sleep. I groaned. It was probably one of the neighbor children who had seen me come home early. I padded across the floor in my stocking feet. "Who is it?" I called.

"Michael. Michael Riordan," he answered.

He sat stiffly across from me, his hands gripping the arms of the chair, and stared at my shoeless feet. "I'm sorry to disturb you," he said stiffly, avoiding my eyes.

I tucked my feet under me on the divan and told him that I had only been resting, that it was fine for him to come. I said I was glad to see him again.

"Maybe you won't be," he said, "when you hear what I have to say."

I waited.

"I came to ask you to give up my father," he blurted, the muscles in his jaw bulging. He had leaned forward. I could almost see the turmoil inside of him.

I felt very still, still and quiet. It was as if I were drawing in to some place of absolute quiet.

"Michael," I said, "I'm not holding your father against his will. You must know that."

His mouth worked noiselessly for a minute; then he started talking: "They're still kids, Colin and Kathleen. They're young, and they need him. My mother, she needs him too. She's not like other people. She's so close to God. She doesn't know the ways of the world, and my father does. He could show us. I've spoken to Father Demorest about this, and he agrees with me. He knows we need our father at home. But as long as you are here . . ."

"What is it you want me to do, Michael?"

"Send him home to his family. Tell him it is what he should do."

I looked at him steadily; his lip was quavering. "Will you do it?" he asked.

"Your father is free to return to his family anytime he wants," I said. "I would never do anything to stop him, if that is what he decides to do."

He stood, rubbed his hands on his pants leg. It was not the answer he had wanted, but it was more than he had expected. "I wouldn't want him to know I talked to you," he said. I promised I wouldn't tell.

When he had gone, I returned to my bed and drew my knees up to my chest. I could hear the beating of my heart. I wanted to go to sleep and sleep for a long time. I lay there, measuring my breathing, wanting drowsiness to overtake me, to save me. The afternoon light faded, and still I lay awake; the sun played against the leaves of the tree, throwing patterns on the wall. And then there was only shade, and then dark, but sleep would not come. Everything in me seemed to be in motion, to be moving. Flashing, knowing. *There is no way.* I prayed for sleep to save me, to take me away from it . . . the terrible, aching knowing. At first light I stood, holding on to the bed, the door, the wall, and walked to the bathroom, but I could not turn on the light, could not look at my face because I knew what I would see. There is no way. Not for me and Riordan and the baby. I found my handbag and rummaged through it until I found the photograph of Grandmother and Grandfather. And then I sat by the window waiting for it to be light enough to see the telephone number I had written on the back.

Babe's big Packard was parked at the train station in Modesto where she said it would be. She was leaning against the shiny hood, waiting. We drove down the long, straight strip of gravel road and the only sound was the chattering of the tiny stones as they bounced off the fenders of the car. When we stopped in front of the farmhouse she put her hand on my arm and asked, "Are you sure about this?"

The doctor was smaller, grayer than I remembered. I lay on the table, my eyes fixed on a brown water stain on the ceiling. Tears slipped down the sides of my face and into my hair as I felt the cold metal of the forceps move into the soft and warm center of me.

When it was done, Babe gave me some brandy from a flask and patted my hand. She took me back to the hotel to rest. I fell asleep at once, a deep and engulfing sleep that was dreamless, that shut out everything.

Her voice came to me from a long way off. "Hallie. Wake up, talk to me. Hallie." I tried to answer, but I could not. The words that formed in my mind could not find their way out . . . Then, shaking me, pushing me . . . "My God," she said. It was Babe, I knew that. She was pummeling me, pushing and shaking me, making me stand, walk. And then she was shouting at someone. Who? Some man—she was screaming and shouting but I couldn't hear what he was saying to her.

Then we were in the Packard, I was in the back, lying on the backseat. Babe had put blankets around me. I could feel something wet and heavy under me, and I wanted to sleep but the bouncing of the car kept me from it, from the deep velvet sleep . . .

We were driving, and then we would stop. And I could hear the car door close, and Babe's voice. High, shouting, angry. And then we would drive again, for a very long time. I could feel the bouncing and the jostling, and Babe's voice shouting at me, now:

"Hallie. Say something to me. Stay awake." And I would try to say something, but the sound that came out of me was not the words I had meant to say.

Then there were other people: bright lights, voices—soft voices now. Babe's hand tight in mine. Riordan's voice, hard and demanding. Riordan's voice, giving orders. And hands lifting me, gentle hands. And pain, sharp ugly pain tearing at me. Pain and noise and light, bright light. And then dark, and quiet.

When I opened my eyes it was daylight, and a woman sitting in a chair stood and said, as if making a pronouncement, "You're with us again."

The woman was a nurse. She brought in a heavyset man, still young. He told me that his name was Hagen, that he was a doctor and that he had known Jimmy Riordan from way back. He did not smile. When I tried to speak he raised his hand to stop me. "You had a close call, Miss Duer. You're still very weak. Just listen to me now. Before anyone comes to talk to you, I want you to know that we have treated you for a burst appendix. We had to do an emergency operation. It's all there, in the records. The doctor and nurses who were on call last night understand. So do Riordan and the woman who brought you in last night. She's waiting to see you, by the way."

Babe grinned so that her chipped tooth showed. "Don't say anything," she told me. "Just be glad for a man like Riordan." A short, rough laugh broke out of her. "I thought he was going to strangle that fat doctor. He really made the fur fly around here. Riordan told them what they had to do, and they did it. He wasn't going to let you go." She lowered her voice. "He was fierce, I can tell you that."

My eyes filled with tears so that I couldn't see her. She took the edge of the pillowcase and blotted them. "Listen to me now," she said. "Are you listening, Hallie? Because I'm only going to say this once. You need to know this. The only thing that matters to that man is that you're alive. That's all. Now I'm going out to your place in the Sand Waste and sleep for about twenty hours and then I'll be moving on, so I won't see you again for a while. I've called your pal Faith and told her about your appendix busting." She grinned. "She's going to come out and see you."

I held on to her hand. I didn't want her to leave, not until I could say what I needed to say. My eyes filled again with tears. She leaned down and kissed me on the forehead. Then she patted my hand and told me, "So long, kid."

Riordan stayed with me that first week. He fed me, bathed me, carried me from place to place. When he had to go into the office he hired a nurse to be with me. He slept on the little bed on the sun porch, explaining that he didn't want to disturb me. He did not sleep. I would wake in the early-morning hours and see the light. He was gentle, and tender. He dried my tears and held me, and when I tried to tell him, he said to wait, that there was plenty of time, that he wanted me to get stronger.

And then I said it: "If I had told you, what would you have said?"

He took a deep breath, and answered truthfully: "That we would find a way."

"Yes," I said, "I knew you would. But there *was* no way. We had the best we could have, and for me it was enough. It is enough."

He allowed himself the question then: "If I hadn't been married, would you have told me?"

It was not, I said, a question that could be asked. He *was* married. He did have children.

He left the room then. He closed the door behind him and went out where no one could hear him or see him. When he returned he pulled the covers up about me and let his hand linger on my face. I said nothing then; it was not a time to talk.

Faith came on Wednesday with a bowl of fresh-made applesauce and some of the first photographs of Emilie. It was a gray day; the fog hadn't lifted by midafternoon. I sat on the sun porch, wrapped in the new cashmere robe Riordan had bought for me, propped up on the bed with the photographs all around me. The baby was almost six months old now, and it was clear that she had dispelled all of her mother's worst fears. "The pictures are charming—she is charming," I told Faith.

"She makes it all so . . . right," she said, and I was about to ask what she meant when I heard Riordan's car.

"Hallie," he called to me, and something in his voice made me want to hide, want not to hear. His face, the look as he sank back against the doorframe, made something catch in my throat and I could not speak.

"I've got some bad news, some terrible news," he said. Faith rose as if to go, but Riordan motioned for her to stay.

"It's Babe," he said.

My heart started to race. I tried to stand up, to get away. If I could only go, move . . .

Riordan slipped his arm around me and held me. "She's dead, Hallie. Someone got to her at the house in the Sand Waste. . . ."

The wail filled my ears, a long piercing note, a shriek that entered my head. And then, over and over, "My God no, oh please no." I thought it was me; I thought I had made the sound that was echoing through my head. But it wasn't me. It was Faith. She was sitting in the chair with her eyes wide and unseeing, screaming, "Oh please God, no."

SEVENTEEN

WE BURIED BABE in the Laurel Hill Cemetery near the Presidio. When no one came forward to claim her body, I claimed it—or Riordan did, since I was still confined to bed. There was no service, no ceremony. Riordan was there, and Clive, to watch them put her into the earth.

Sara stayed with me and did what I could not do. She retrieved the box from the back of my closet and took out the journal that had belonged to Babe. "Find her real name," I directed, "and the date of her birth, and the names of her parents if you can." I was going to put a marker on her grave. It was all that was left for me to do for Babe, who had saved my life and lost her own.

I watched Sara's face as she scanned the pages of the book, her great dark eyes concentrating. "Here it is," she finally said, and began to read: "'My true name is Dorcas Louisa Conlon. I was born on January 12, 1895, in Angel's Camp, California. My mother, Elsie Conlon, died when I was eleven years old and I went to live with her half-brother and his family, whose name was Sullivan, in the town of Columbia. When I was fourteen the Sullivans moved to another state, but I did not go with them.' "

Sara glanced at me. "Shall I continue?"

"Not out loud," I said. "Please, can you see if there are any names—anybody who might want to know . . .

Sara looked at me and frowned. "I will, but right now I think you need to rest. Too much has happened. You need—"

"I can't rest," I interrupted her, "not until I know—and Riordan won't tell me. But I have to know about Babe . . . It was my fault and—"

"Stop that," Sara said sternly. "It won't help. I'll tell you what I know, and mostly it's from the papers. She was killed in Riordan's house out in the Sand Waste. Her Packard was found abandoned down near Half Moon Bay. The papers say that's a hideout for bootleggers and rumrunners and such, and they seem to feel the killing had to do with clandestine activities. I gather your friend has a record with the local police. Jim has been answering a lot of questions, I know—and asking a lot too. He'll tell you as soon as he feels you're strong enough."

"I know who did it," I said. "Riordan knows too. He must have told them. Mason Griffin killed her. Have they found him yet?"

Sara's face clouded over. "Jim and Sanford have been in contact with the Treasury Department people here in the city and in Washington, but I don't know what they've learned. You'll have to ask them."

"He killed her . . . he did it," I repeated.

Sara raised her voice. "Hallie, stop it. You're going to drive yourself straight back into the hospital. And Riordan is close to exhaustion too. If you can't think about yourself, think about him. The man's not made of iron. I'm going to give you a sleeping powder now so you will rest."

She poured the powder into a glass of water and stirred it. I watched the milky solution whirl. "I'm sorry," I said, drinking it down.

The telephone rang and Sara hurried to get it, glad, I think, for the interruption. I heard her say, "She's still very weak, too weak to talk . . . She's really not quite up to it yet, I'm afraid . . . I know, I know . . . but I think you have to give her time, it's best to let things be for a while." She was kind, and firm.

When she returned I said, "What did Faith want?"

"To explain," she answered.

"There's nothing to explain," I told her, and closed my eyes. "I know what happened. She told Clive and he told me, and it doesn't help. I can't see Faith now. I'm not sure I'll ever be able to see her again."

"Never is a long time," Sara gently chided.

"So is eternity," I answered, unable to keep the bitterness from my voice.

Sara sat with her hands in her lap and studied me.

"Did you know Faith left Thayer?" I asked.

"She's living in her studio with the baby," Sara told me, adding, so I would know, "I've spoken to her a number of times these past weeks."

"Did she tell you how it happened?" I asked.

"You should be feeling drowsy soon," Sara answered, ignoring my question.

"She left him because she finally understood how vicious he could be. But do you know what the knowledge cost? It cost Babe's life!" I turned away, the anger and hurt rising inside me, threatening to start the tears flowing again. I had cried enough. I had to stop.

Sara saw and moved to help. "Hallie, dear," she said, "let me tell you about my visit with Agnes this week. I'll just chatter away, and you listen until you fall asleep . . ."

"No," I said, feeling suddenly stronger. "I want to tell you, because from the very beginning you've been the only one who has known about Thayer, what he's done. What he is capable of doing. Everything." She could see I was determined, and settled back to listen.

"First, Babe called Faith from the hospital because she wanted someone to be with me while Riordan was away at the office. She hadn't slept for days, and she needed to get away, but she didn't want to leave me alone." I paused, looked at Sara. "I didn't have an appendectomy. Did you know that?"

She took my hand in both of hers and began to rub it. "Yes, dear. I knew," she said quietly. "I guessed, really. And when I saw you, and Riordan . . . then I knew."

"So you know why Babe wanted someone to be with me. And Babe knew I trusted Faith, so she trusted her too." I took a deep breath; I could feel that the sleeping powder was beginning to take effect, but I wanted to explain. "So Babe told Faith she was going out to the house in the Sand Waste and sleeping for a long time. But what Babe didn't know, what I didn't know, was that Thayer Gerson knew about the house. Faith had told him. She trusted him enough to tell him. And he told Mason Griffin."

A small sob wrenched out of me. Sara stood, leaned over me with a worried look on her face. "Hallie, please . . ." she pleaded.

"I'm almost done," I told her, "almost done . . . You see, Griffin had come to the studio to question Faith about me and Babe, and Thayer had been there and had wanted to know all about it. Griffin left his calling card behind, with two numbers written on it. Numbers to call if Babe ever showed up."

I took a deep breath. "Faith trusted Thayer, and she shouldn't have. And I trusted Faith, and I shouldn't have. But knowing that doesn't change anything for Babe, does it?"

Sara pulled the quilt up about my shoulders. "How do you know this Griffin didn't already know about the house in the Sand Waste? He seems to have known everything else."

"Maybe he did," I told her, "but he didn't know when Babe would be there alone. And Thayer Gerson told him that. I know he did, because Faith asked him, and he admitted it. Straight out. He told her he was doing his duty, that so far as he knew he was only turning in a rumrunner. That's what Faith told Clive. And I believe her, but I don't want to see her."

When I woke, Riordan was there.

"Did anyone come to the cemetery?" I asked.

"Just a few newspaper reporters," he answered, slumping in the chair beside my bed, "and a few of the curious masses."

"Griffin?"

"No."

"They're not going to get him, are they?" I asked.

Riordan didn't look at me when he said, "I don't know."

May became June, and I lay on the sun porch during the day and tried to read, tried not to think, not to remember. Each time Riordan left to go to the office, I felt a moment of panic. I wanted him to stay, to be with me, and I did not feel easy again until he had returned at night. Grandmother and Grandfather came, and Agnes on her day off from the library, and Thelma and Harry. Riordan brought Kathleen to see me because she was so distressed and worried about me. I could not turn away from any of them, but I didn't want to see them either, not with their sweet faces so filled with sorrow and concern. They didn't know, and I couldn't tell them.

Only Riordan knew, and Clive because I told him, and Sara because she had guessed. Dear Sara, who knew to say, "Can you talk to me, Hallie?"

I told her how empty I felt, how hollow and sad and empty. There had been life within me, and I had been so wrong, and it had cost so much, so terribly much, and I felt so cold and empty. Sara sat on the daybed close to me, my hand in hers, and she said,

"Listen to me now, Hallie. Living requires risk. Mistakes are made, and some are costly. There are people who cannot live with their mistakes," Sara said, "*but you are not one of them*. You are stronger than that. Babe understood about risks, and so must you now. Because if you don't, it will all have been in vain."

And I had said: *But the emptiness, Sara. The terrible emptiness.*

And Sara had said: Yes. *But you will find a way, Hallie. I know you will . . . a way to live with that emptiness.*

When I told Clive that I was beginning to despise the life of an invalid, he took it to mean I was feeling up to a visit from Ethel. I suspected he had delayed as long as he felt he could. After all he had done for me, I was ashamed that I dreaded seeing her.

I napped longer than I had intended, and Ethel arrived early to find me and the cottage in a state of disarray. Her own costume was so carefully selected that the contrast was heightened. When I complimented her on her dress, with its stylish lowered waistline, she was quick to tell me that she had only recently purchased it in the Young Matrons' salon at O'Conner Moffatt. She removed her hat and gloves and stood for a moment, looking for an empty surface to put them on.

"I'm sorry for all the clutter," I apologized, clearing some of Riordan's legal papers from a hall table. "Sara threatened to send the Weatherlees over . . ."

A trilling, girlish laugh poured out of Ethel. "An English butler here, imagine!" she said.

I smiled, and went to put the teakettle on. When I returned, Ethel was ensconced in the living room, ready for a "good chat."

"Clive tells me you've had a very close call, your appendix rupturing and all the complications. It must have left a terrible scar."

For a moment I thought she might ask to see it, but she accepted my assurances that I was well mended, and let me turn the conversation to another subject.

"I suppose I enjoy teaching well enough," she told me, "though I have to admit this year has been difficult. Some of the children are just badly mannered. They misbehave and disrupt the lessons. I speak to their parents, but they refuse to discipline their children. It isn't the way it was when I went to school. Teachers got the respect they deserved then. Now, well . . . the ruffians are taking over, and I'm not sure how much longer I want to contend with it."

The words flowed out of her and into the soft afternoon air. I poured tea and listened, a captive audience. Had her voice been more melodic, I might have been able to doze off, so little was required of me. Now and then she did ask a question about our family, our grandparents for the most part. I was somewhat surprised to learn that she had been corresponding with Grandmother Duer.

I went into the kitchen to refill the cookie tray, and when I returned Ethel occupied herself for a time deciding which of the Italian confections she would select; then she cleared her throat as if to signal a delicate subject. "I want you to know, Hallie," she began, her tone sincere, "that I very much admire women who go out in the world and undertake occupations that once belonged solely to men. I don't have that kind of courage myself," she went on. "I hope that won't keep us from being friends. And I hope that you can understand those of us who don't choose to blaze new trails, but are content with the traditional values—home and hearth and family."

I struggled to find a way to explain that I did understand, that if my own circumstances were different, I too might choose home and hearth, as she put it. Might. I wasn't sure, these past weeks had made me question so much. "Ethel," I began, "I don't think we are so very different, you know. It's not as if . . ." I stopped, then tried to start over. "One thing we definitely have in common is our fondness for Clive."

She changed the subject abruptly. "Did he ever tell you about getting caught peeping into people's houses?" she interrupted breathlessly. "Of course, he was only watching families at the dinner table—he liked seeing them all together, having a happy time." She wanted to know if I didn't think that a bittersweet memory.

I answered, "I think what he said was that he liked to watch them 'in their circle of light.'"

"And isn't that poetic?" she came back. "Isn't that just the most nicely turned phrase?"

I wanted to try to make her understand, so I said very softly, "Everybody wants a circle of light."

Ethel's features settled into a look of triumph. "Do you, Hallie?" she asked. She thought she had been clever; she thought she knew the answer. She thought she had, at last, put me in my place.

"What I want," I told her, "is to get back to work just as soon as I can."

"Pack your bags," the Boss said. "You're going to Shelby, Montana, to cover the Dempsey-Gibbons fight. You finally get to call Dempsey in on that promise of an exclusive."

"That's preposterous," I told him. "The whole thing is preposterous."

"That's right, Hallie, and that's just why we're sending you. It was Harry's idea, and it's a darned good one."

Harry had been watching from the other side of the city room. He ambled over to say, "You don't think I want to go to some godforsaken little cowtown nobody has ever heard of way out in the wilds of Montana, do you?"

"And I should?" I challenged him, hands on my hips.

"Sure you should," the city editor chimed in. "It's your kind of story, Hallie—about how a little two-bit cowtown way up in the middle of Montana decides to put itself on the map by holding a world-championship fight. And they got Dempsey to go along with it. That means the whole doggoned world is going to be reading about Shelby, Montana."

The Boss went on, "Did you know they've built a stadium that will seat forty thousand—in a place where there isn't even a paved road leading into town?"

Still skeptical, I did admit that Tommy Gibbons was a respectable challenger, one of the very few real threats that Dempsey could face.

"It's settled, then," the Boss said. "And Gene is right. The story is the town and the grandiose ideas that make a bunch of country boys think they can put their town on the map with this fight." He stopped, lifted an eyebrow. "Besides, Harry has already wired Dempsey and he says he'll give you all the time you want."

"I get the feeling," I said, looking at the three of them, "that you are trying to get me out of town."

"Of course," the Boss agreed amiably. "We even thought about sending you up to Alaska to cover that part of President Harding's trip, but we decided the wide-open spaces might put the bloom back into your pretty cheeks. Besides which, you'll be back before the President gets to San Francisco—you can cover him here."

I stepped off the train in Shelby, Montana, and stood on the platform and stared. I had never seen a sky so limitless, a land so empty or a town so insignificant. It might have been a setting for a Tom Mix moving picture, the kind that can be pulled down and moved away in a matter of hours. Main Street was wide and dusty and would turn to mud in the first hard rain. Horse troughs still lined the wooden sidewalks. Model T's and horses were in about equal supply.

I left my bag in the home where I had rented a room and wandered around town for a while, past the billiard hall and Aunt Kate's cathouse. There were twenty men to every woman in town, and quite a few of the women resided at Aunt Kate's. There were also two dance halls, the King Tut and the Green Lite. And there was, on the far edge of town, a great open bowl of an arena, set in a land so empty that it seemed as if it belonged in another world.

On July 3, the night before the fight, the temperature stayed in the eighties long after dark. By one o'clock on the day of the fight it was one hundred degrees in the shade.

Clutching a fan I had borrowed from the local funeral parlor and wearing the widest straw hat I had been able to find, I made my way through the press gate and to ringside. Harry Smith and Scoop Gleason were there from the San Francisco papers and Sam Hall had come from the *Los Angeles Examiner.* Sam pointed out Heywood Broun to me, and Damon Runyon and Grantland Rice. "The big boys are all here," Sam said. "They've been asking around about how you got so cozy with Dempsey, him giving you an exclusive and all. Broun says what really made him mad was that you seemed to know what you were writing about."

Seventeen thousand people came into the arena that day, leaving great yawning empty expanses in the cavernous bowl.

The fight started when Dempsey landed a quick left hook. Gibbons came right back with three lefts to the body and a right to the head. Dempsey shook himself, and the crowd cheered. We were going to see a real fight.

"Gibbons is fast," Sam said.

"He's a boxer," I answered. "Dempsey is going to have to wear him down, because I don't think he's going to get the chance to knock him out."

Sam listened, and nodded, and I heard him repeating what I had said later, when it was clear that I had been right.

The bodies of the two fighters glistened in the hundred-degree heat, as the roar of the crowd drifted up and disappeared into the great, empty blue sky.

"I've got a tenner says Gibbons can't go the full fifteen," a New York writer leaned over to say to me, passing a slim flask. It was a challenge. The Western reporters watched me. I took a sip from the flask, wiped my lips as daintily as I could with the back of my hand, and said, "You're on."

I collected my money at the end of the fifteen. Dempsey had won, the hard way. Tommy Gibbons was still on his feet and it looked as if he was still smiling.

Rain clouds had gathered during the last rounds. Almost as soon as the fight ended, the sky darkened, and as we made our way to the telegraph office it began to rain in great silver torrents.

I found a tiny space on the end of a bench in the telegraph office and finished scrawling my story as I waited my turn to send it. It was steamy in the little room and we were packed together so that the smell of damp wool permeated. I took off my hat and was looking for a place to put it when a tall young man in a white summer suit said, "Pardon me, Miss Duer, I'm Jimmy Dawson of the *New York Times*. I wanted to be sure to tell you how much we admired your coverage of the Arbuckle trial. And to tell you that our editors consider the stories you wrote on the Marchant case to be the most accurate available."

"Thank you," I said, and my pleasure must have shown because he smiled at me and added, "If you ever decide to move East, remember you've got some admirers on the *Times*."

My name was called, and I thanked him for his kindness and made my way to the telegrapher thinking: *They are reading my stories in New York City. And they think they are good* . . . I could feel the elation rising in me. I am good at what I do, I am admired . . .

The Boss was right, I did need to get into the field again. There was something vital about sitting front row center, reporting a major event. Something exciting about getting the missing details, about understanding what was happening. "Dempsey is going to have to wear him down," I had said, and my words had been repeated, and I had been right.

And Harry was right, too. Because this wasn't a fight story even though there had been a good fight. This was a story about a town which lusted for recognition as some people lust for money or power. From the beginning, the premise had been ludicrous—that a championship prizefight could bring a place that kind of fame. And that enormous great pine bowl perched on the empty edge of town was a fitting memorial to the foolish dreams of some country boys.

"Have you heard the latest?" one of the reporters called to me as I walked out of the steamy little telegraph office. He was laughing so hard he could scarcely get it out: "Kearns gave an engineer five hundred dollars to hook up a caboose to his engine and take him to Great Falls—and he took their share of the gate with him. Which was everything! Dempsey and Kearns took it all. Gibbons gets nothing, the town gets nothing but bankrupt."

It rained hard for a few minutes, pelting the dusty roads until they turned to mud. Horses and Model T's were churning through the thick ruts, kicking up a mud storm. I finished my wrap-up story on the train out of town, ending with the item about Kearns bribing the engineer. "The champion left town with $257,000," I wrote. "Gibbons left with the satisfaction of having gone fifteen rounds with the great Dempsey. And Shelby stayed—broke now, but, one would hope, wiser for its day in the sun."

That night I stretched out in my Pullman sleeping berth, closed my eyes and let the motion of the train rock me as we rolled through the empty Montana night. Once, when I woke, I lifted the curtain to look out on a desolate landscape in the first gray light of day. I put my hands on my stomach and with my fingertips touched the flatness that might have been full now, but never would be again. I knew that; the doctor didn't have to tell me. I had not told Riordan because it would hurt him, and he had been hurt enough. I could never have a child. A small, aching sadness had come to live inside of me and it would be there, I knew, forever. But I had Riordan, and Kathleen and Colin to help grow up, and work that was important. It had been enough before and it would be enough again, once I learned to live with that small ache.

Montana had been a reprieve. I came home to a world that would have to be arranged again, a world unsettled by bitter memories and losses. The Treasury Department denied that Mason Griffin could have had anything to do with Babe's death. He was, they said, on special duty at the time. They would not comment on his whereabouts, and they refused to produce him.

Riordan was as tender as ever, but something was troubling him, I knew. We no longer had the house at the Sand Waste; we could never go back there again. There was no place where we could be alone and easy. I went to look at a flat in the Noe Valley section of the city, the upper floor of a Victorian which looked east to the hills of Berkeley—and suggested we buy it together. He listened politely, but he was evasive. He lay with me and held me close, but he would not make love to me. I knew why and I knew I could wait. He was afraid—gentle, caressing, but afraid.

We sat on a bench near the Conservatory in Golden Gate Park, watching the cyclists wheel by in numbers. It was a clear, sparkling day, a treat in the middle of the fogbound summer. A display of blue agapanthus brightened the greensward in front of the Conservatory. There was another floral display in honor of the impending visit of the President. The whole city was celebrating; Market Street was strung with banners. The Palace Hotel, where the President and his party would be staying, was covered in red-white-and-blue bunting.

"I have to talk to you," Riordan said. He wasn't looking at me.

I waited, not liking it . . . not wanting him to go on, and not knowing why.

"I have to go home—to the kids," he said. "I have to live with Colin and Kathleen and Michael again."

I stopped breathing.

"Hallie, I'm going back to my family."

I started shaking my head. *No. No.* I turned away from him and tried to get up, but he caught me by my wrists and would not let me go.

"No," I told him, shaking my head, "no."

"Look at me," he said, his voice urgent, "listen. I've made too many mistakes, and one of those mistakes almost cost you your life. I couldn't . . . It's too high a price. The way things are now, the children are suffering and so are you. I've got to do something right—to give you and them a chance at some kind of decent life. I'm going to try to be a father to Colin and Kathleen—and Michael, too, if he'll let me—in the few years of childhood they have left."

I wanted to say no, to scream at him, to cry and plead and beg. I wanted to tell him that I couldn't go on without him, that I didn't care how much time he spent with me or where he lived so long as he didn't push me away . . . I wanted to say all of that but I looked at him and I knew I couldn't. Not to Riordan. And then I remembered Michael. *"Your father is free to return to his family anytime he wants. I would never do anything to stop him."*

Such brave words.

He said very softly, "I've got to do what I promised my brother I would do."

I didn't answer, but only sat there in the sunlight and felt the shadows gather.

EIGHTEEN

THE TELEPHONE RANG and I didn't answer. Clive came to the door and I asked him to leave. Sara sent her car, but I wouldn't go. *Let me be*, I pleaded with them. *Give me time*. I had to find a way to see in the half-light, a way to carry the burden of the cold stone that had settled inside of me.

I tried to read the papers. "PRESIDENT HARDING ARRIVES IN SAN FRANCISCO." "APPEARS GRAY AND WORN." "CANCELS ALL APPOINTMENTS." I could not get beyond the headlines. I could not sleep; I did not want to talk. I wanted only to move, to keep moving. I climbed down the hill to the Embarcadero, walked to Fisherman's Wharf and watched the men on the boats cut and gut their catch and throw the entrails to the gulls. Then I walked over to Aquatic Park and back along Columbus Avenue. I walked until I was too tired to climb the hill; then I climbed it and fell on my bed and slept a troubled sleep, and woke feeling tired and went out again. I drove over to Laurel Hill to Babe's grave, and out to Sutro Forest, and up to Twin Peaks. The city was draped in bunting, red, white and blue for the President, but the President was sick in his suite at the Palace Hotel. He could not see the bunting blowing in the breeze or any of the flags that were flying in his honor or the signs that welcomed him to San Francisco. There would be no parade down Market Street, no bands would play, there would be no marching and no cheering and no laughter. The fun was over before it had ever begun.

I stopped at a grocery on the corner of Alvarado and Noe and asked a woman who was stacking yellow onions if I might use her telephone. It was midday, and I knew he could not be at his hotel, and I had to know. When the operator said, "Mr. Riordan no longer resides here," I felt a sharp sting of pain and made a gasping sound that caused the woman to turn from her onions to look at me.

At first light the next day I was parked across from St. Patrick's, waiting. The streets were empty, the fog made everything gray and damp and chill. I rubbed the windscreen with the heel of my hand so I could see. She came as I imagined she would, out of the fog, wearing a long dress covered by a cotton apron, with a sweater pulled around her for warmth. It was not until she put down her pail and knelt at the steps that I could see the grace in her. I watched in silence as Riordan's wife washed the steps of the old church. There was something delicate, even precise about the way she did it, reaching, swirling in an even, rhythmic motion, bent to the task, neat and methodical and intent. I knew then: I understood perfectly. It was how she had learned to live with the cold stone inside of her.

When I returned to the cottage that morning, a boy who worked at the paper was sitting on the front stoop, waiting. He handed me a note and told me I was supposed to read it right away.

"Hallie," the Boss wrote in a hand so bold it fairly shouted, "Get over to the Rose Bowl at the Palace Hotel for nine-A.M. press briefing. President is seriously ill."

The boy spoke up: "Mr. Curtin says I'm out of a job if I don't bring you back."

"Did he tell you to be sure to say that?" I asked, and when he began to stutter and bluster I put my hand on his shoulder to let him know it was all right, that I was going.

At the Palace Hotel Annie Farrell said, "I wondered when you'd show up. Where've you been?"

"Away," I told her.

"Well, you just made it back in time for the story of the century," she said.

"I thought we did that one last month—or was it last year?" I answered, in the same low, somber tones everybody else was using.

Annie's eyes sparkled, but she managed to stifle a smile.

I caught a glimpse of myself, then, in the mirrored walls of the Rose Bowl, where Riordan and I had danced and laughed together an eternity ago. *A bit pale,* I thought, *a bit too thin, but aside from that she looks the same. She nods, she talks, she even asks the questions she is supposed to ask, and nobody seems to notice what is missing. . . .*

"That's Judson Welliver, the official press representative with the presidential party," Annie filled me in, nodding toward the man who had climbed onto the stage.

He cleared his throat. "The President is suffering from bronchial pneumonia," he told us. "He is being treated by his personal physician, Dr. Charles Sawyer, and by five others as well. We will issue regular bulletins on the state of his health. The President's remaining speeches will be read by members of his staff."

I took a room at the hotel, then called the office to ask that a telephone line be kept open for me. "Do you want somebody to spell you?" the Boss asked.

"I'll call if I do," I told him, and when he said "Good," I knew I'd given the answer he wanted. I was going back to work.

A screen had been placed in the hallway outside of the Presidential Suite, to shield the door from the inquiring eyes of reporters. We set up a kind of camp behind the screen, ignoring

Judson Welliver's bulletin room except for those times when he issued one of his reports.

On Wednesday we were told that the President had spent a "fairly comfortable night," that there was no extension of the pneumonia area and that his heart action was improved. We were given lists of what he had to eat and drink—eggnogs seemed to be his favorite—and were informed that his elimination was improving.

"That's about as much as I care to know about *that*," Annie Farrell whispered, feigning disgust.

We were given quotes from the speeches someone else would deliver . . . about how the President supported a Permanent Court of International Justice, a world court, as a "logical way to prevent war." And how he had said, "I can see Russia only as the supreme tragedy of the world."

Annie Farrell yawned. "He's drinking eggnogs and talking world peace. I think the death watch is over."

By Thursday it seemed she was right. The President, we were informed, was progressing nicely. Some of the local reporters who had been on duty for long hours went home to get some sleep. I did not want to go back to the cottage and I knew I couldn't sleep, even though my eyes burned. It was better here, in the hallway of the Palace Hotel, being Hallie Duer of the *Times*.

At seven that evening, only Steve Early of the Associated Press and I were left outside the Presidential Suite. The others had gone to dinner. Steve was reading the *Saturday Evening Post*. I decided it was time to stretch my legs, and maybe call the office to say that nothing much was going on. Then I heard Mrs. Harding call out.

"What did she say?" I asked Steve. His head was cocked to one side, listening. There had been something in her tone . . . At that moment a Secret Service agent appeared in the hall, not quite running, and slipped into the room.

"Something's happened," Steve said. The agent came out again, but when we tried to stop him he brushed us aside and said, "Nothing, nothing . . ." in a breathless way.

Our eyes met for an instant, confirming each other; then we ran for the telephones. "Stand by," I shouted to Gene Bolten. "Something's happened—it's real trouble, I think. Get ready to run an extra . . ."

Back in the hallway I almost collided with Steve and Judson Welliver and two other reporters. "No news, boys," he was saying. "We can't tell you a thing." We all converged on the Rose Bowl then; something was about to break, you could feel it.

Welliver gave each of us a sheet which began: *President Harding died at 7:30 this evening of an apoplexy stroke . . .*

We looked at each other to see if what we read was right, and then we scattered . . . My lungs almost bursting from the effort, I spoke carefully into the mouthpiece: "The President is dead . . . brain involvement. . . his wife reading to him . . ."

The *Times* had been ready to go, we were first on the street with the news, boys in every neighborhood shouting it out . . . THE PRESIDENT IS DEAD . . . at Lotta's fountain on Market Street, and out in the Richmond . . . PRESIDENT DIES OF STROKE . . . to Russian Hill . . . READ IT IN THE TIMES, PRESIDENT DEAD AT SEVEN-THIRTY TONIGHT . . .

I walked back up Market Street to the office, past people standing, stunned, staring up at the Palace Hotel where the body lay . . . At that moment, the big electric sign on top of the hotel went off, and then lights began to go off in restaurants and theaters all along the great street. There was a hush of disbelief, and then a growing stillness . . . a breeze fluttered and snapped a bit of bunting. In a few hours the gay bunting would be replaced with black crepe, but now the city was trying to absorb the news, to understand the enormity of what had happened. It was as if the stone lodged within me had expanded to fill the whole of the city. And soon, when the news that was even now on the wire, reached cities and towns all over the country, other extras would be brought out and newsboys would shout it out for everyone to hear . . . THE PRESIDENT IS DEAD.

When I got back to the office the Boss wasted no words: "I want you to be on the funeral train when it leaves tomorrow night."

The hearse that carried the President's body moved slowly along New Montgomery and over to Third Street, lined now with somber faces, tear-streaked as the Marine guard moved in slow, even cadence and the Navy Band played Chopin's Funeral March. Stores and banks and schools had been closed. That day the only men working were those who tore down the colorful bunting, as if it were an affront, as if we had had no right to expect to be happy and frivolous. The half-mile route to the Southern Pacific depot, where the funeral train waited to take him home, was lined with veterans and Boy Scouts, and housewives and little girls, their young faces unsure in the early evening light.

We boarded the train in silence. Judson Welliver shepherded the reporters who were to make the trip onto the third of the twelve cars, and spoke to us in hushed tones . . . we would go around the peninsula to Oakland to avoid the ferry crossing, then east along the route of the Overland Limited to Chicago . . . it would be seventy-two hours to Chicago, the funeral train would take precedence over all other rail traffic . . . Mrs. Harding was on board, of course, along with the President's sister, Mrs. Remsberg, and her husband, and General Pershing, and Attorney General Daugherty . . . but we should be circumspect, we should not at this time . . .

Carter Field, a reporter for the New York Tribune who had been traveling with the presidential party on the Western trip, said, "I've been trying to talk to Daugherty for weeks. If this train isn't stopping between here and Chicago I may have a chance." I blinked, and made a mental note to find out why Field wanted to talk to Daugherty . . . and then we were under way, moving east into the night.

At Stockton, fifteen thousand people were standing at the station. As we rolled slowly through, the church bells began to toll. It was one in the morning before we reached Auburn, the little town tucked into the foothills of the Sierra Nevadas, yet three hundred of the townspeople were waiting, their faces lifted in sorrow as the train rolled by. The President's coffin was in the last car, raised so that it could be seen through the windows, lights burning throughout the night, a Marine guard standing watch. Out of the window I could see their faces turn, waiting in silence, fathers lifting children, women covering their mouths as if to stifle any cry, any sound.

We moved up and over the great mountains. In Reno, in the predawn chill, two thousand stood and watched. Only the tolling of the church bells marked our passage.

The crowds gathered in increasing numbers as we moved eastward through the country. They stood at every crossroads, every depot, bearing witness, their heads uncovered in the late-summer heat. At times the crowds would swell to numbers so great the train would move at a crawl, and flowers would be handed up—wreaths of lilies and white roses. It was as if the whole of the country was waiting, sorrowful in the dying summer. In Nebraska, we passed through wheatfields ready for the harvest and in Omaha watched as boys ran in front of the engine to lay coins on the track. There were forty thousand people waiting in Omaha. The only sound was the throbbing of the air pump on the engine and then the slow, mournful tolling of the church bells.

Sometimes a veteran would be standing in the crowd in full uniform, saluting. Or a big-boned farmer, his hat over his heart, baring his white forehead. Their eyes would look into mine, through the glass that separated us. Mile after mile, the soft rolling motion of the train entered my bones. I looked out at them and knew what they knew: the loss, the terrible loss.

It was not Warren Harding they mourned, but the President. The Leader. I watched out the window and listened to the other

reporters talk about Harding. He was openhearted and sentimental, they said. A good fellow. A man who loved order and
normalcy. *Normalcy*, someone said. He invented that word. And
bloviate, someone else said. He invented that word to describe the
long-winded speeches he loved to give. McAdoo, secretary of the
treasury in Wilson's administration, had said Harding's speeches
gave "the impression of an army of pompous phrases moving over
the landscape in search of an idea." Harding was not an able man,
one of the reporters said, but then, the country hadn't wanted an
able man. If he was a secondrater, well—another added—he was
the best of the second-raters. When I asked Carter Field why he
wanted to corner the attorney general, he replied: "To ask him how
he managed to bank seventy-five thousand dollars on a salary of
twelve thousand."

I let the rhythm of the train rock me and comfort me. I
thought of my mother and my father, and I thought of Babe. And
Riordan. And the baby that might have been. I mourned them all
as we moved across the prairie, through fields of wheat riffled by
the warm winds of summer's end. Silently, we passed across the
breadth of the sorrow- sighing land, heavy with harvest, our way
lined by those who had put aside their labors to stand by the tracks,
tears slipping down their cheeks, to bear witness.

When we pulled into the station in Washington, I knew I
would not be returning.

NINETEEN

IN WASHINGTON it was possible to live and work and remain a stranger. It was, in fact, a city of strangers collected from all the corners of the country, there for the short term. Home was some other place.

I did not want to think of home. I did not know if I could, or would, ever go home again. I wanted to live on the surface for a time, to be absorbed by what was happening. Nothing personal, never anything personal. For now I had to be away, to live among strangers. This Southern city, sweltering in the August heat, was as far from San Francisco as I could be.

In Washington the preoccupation was with politics and power. Stories were there, waiting to be written. I found ways to stay on.

Sara Hunt gave me a letter of introduction to Mrs. Nicholas Longworth, Teddy Roosevelt's daughter—the famous "Princess Alice" the press so adored—who is married to one of the most influential members of the House of Representatives. In the attached note Sara commented: "I like Alice well enough but she does lack a certain saving grace—humility. Perhaps you could help her achieve a modicum."

Mrs. Longworth received me on the afternoon of one of the hottest days of the summer. The occasion called for a tailored costume, but the heat was so oppressive I wore, instead, a light gray linen tube dress with an open neck and no sleeves at all. Mrs. Longworth wore a dress of cotton eyelet, with long sleeves and a high collar which seemed to lift her head. She was tall, and she stood so straight that she appeared both imperious and utterly cool. When I made some dull, awkward remark about the heat, she looked at me with those even blue eyes and quite seriously said: "San Franciscans do wilt easily. I believe it's that climate. It has the most debilitating effect. One needs extremes, don't you see. We will sit in the garden." She led the way, walking so rapidly I had to hurry to keep up. In the next hour and a half, I was to discover, she thought as quickly as she walked, and with Alice Longworth one would always have to hurry to keep up.

Before I could ask my first question, she launched several of her own. She wanted to know how Sara and I had met, she wanted me to tell her about the Agnes Marchant case. And she surprised me by mentioning a Duer relation she knew, and by seeming to be familiar with that branch of my family.

Alice Longworth listened well, never interrupting (except, occasionally, to say "Go on," or "Tell me more"). I kept my answers short, and was beginning to feel uncomfortable about the way the interview was going when she suddenly said, "Fine, good. Now tell me what it is you want me to tell you."

"To begin," I said, "tell me what you thought of President Harding."

She sat back in her chair, her arms dropped elegantly so that her hands were hanging loose, and with a calculating half-smile said, "He was a nice-enough man. But he had abysmal taste in friends."

I made a show of pausing, and said breathlessly: "Tell me everything you know."

She erupted in laughter. Not ladylike, pretty laughter, but a loud, barking sound of genuine pleasure.

"My family always told me not to speak to reporters," she said. "They knew I'd get in trouble, and I'm certain that is what you have in mind for me."

We laughed together then, and settled in for a long interview that would cover a whole range of subjects. She spoke in short, animated bursts, laughing often. When I asked her opinion of our new President, she told me, "Coolidge looks as if he had been weaned on a pickle. But I think you'd best not print that. It might offend Mrs. Coolidge, who is quite a nice lady."

My article on Alice Roosevelt Longworth included her father's famous comment that he could manage either the country or his daughter, but not both. It also included some of her more outspoken comments on political figures, though not the Coolidge description. I went into detail to describe her considerable behind-the-scenes efforts to defeat our country's entry into the League of Nations. In all, it was not a totally sympathetic portrait. When the North American Newspaper Alliance picked it up, the story ran in hundreds of papers throughout the country and I supposed that Alice Longworth might be unhappy with me. Famous people, I had learned, often expected glowing articles without even a suggestion of criticism. I knew, too, that Alice Longworth could cause a good many doors in Washington to be closed to me.

The article—which appeared in more than one paper under the headline "AMERICA'S ONLY PRINCESS: ELEGANT BUT TOUGH"—caused quite a stir, and everyone waited to see what Alice would say.

Alice said she thought it a bully story. In a note to me she wrote: "I said you would get me in trouble. Can you come to dinner on the fourteenth?"

I wrote back: "Thank you. Now I know why Sara counts you a friend. I would like to see you again, if we can agree to disagree with as much fun as I had at our first meeting. I am afraid that I cannot, however, come to dinner on the fourteenth. That evening

I will be in New York to cover the Dempsey-Firpo fight." It was, I thought, a just-haughty-enough reply to appeal to her.

New York felt right. I came out of the train station into a burnished afternoon, shafts of autumn light penetrating between the tallest buildings I had ever seen. In Gramercy Park the leaves were rustling dry in the paths and gutters. I had almost forgotten what it was like after the first cold snap; and I breathed it in—the cool, golden air—walking down Fifth Avenue toward midtown, marveling at the sounds and the sights and the movement. Tall gray buildings crowded against wide streets, people walked as if they knew exactly where they were going and couldn't wait to get there, motorcars and buses went every which way, frantically humming, honking and shouting.

By the time I reached Central Park I was tired enough to find a bench to rest for a while. I tried to imagine Dempsey training in this park. The thought made me smile. It was time to think about Dempsey and Luis Firpo, the Argentine fighter who was challenging Dempsey. The man they called "The Bull of the Pampas." Everyone in New York seemed to be talking about the fight.

I arrived early at the Polo Grounds and still had trouble pushing through the crush of people waiting to buy tickets. Jimmy Dawson of the *New York Times* saw me fighting my way to ringside and raised his hands. "Let her through, boys," he shouted, pulling me into the safety of the ringside press section.

"Hallie's here," I heard someone call out, and turning saw Ed Hughes of the *Mail*, and Hype Igoe and Bill McGeehan and Harry Newman and Grantland Rice and Damon Runyon.

"Don't let her looks fool you," Hype called to someone. "She's sparred with Dempsey and won." Suddenly I felt fine. I felt as if I belonged here, at ringside in the Polo Grounds in New York City.

I took my place next to Jack Lawrence of the *New York Tribune* and asked him, "Why all the interest in this fight? I've never seen such a crowd."

Lawrence shrugged. "I don't know," he said. "Nobody thinks Firpo has a prayer. But then, there isn't anybody else good enough to challenge Dempsey. He's got to let somebody have a go at the title. But this big dumb oaf from Argentina—I don't know."

Just then I recognized one of the old boxers who hung around Dempsey's camp; he was checking the ring. I worked my way over to him; he looked up, recognized me and grinned so you could see the missing teeth. "How are things in Dempsey's corner?" I asked.

He shook his head and leaned close, as if to tell me a secret. "I heard Rickard—he's the promoter out here—anyways, I heard Rickard tell the Champ he hoped he wouldn't put the poor dub away with one punch because he'd hate to think of all these nice millionaires out here being sore at the both of them." He stopped, his eyes trying to tell me the secret was coming. "You know what the Champ said?"

I leaned close. "I'll bet it was 'Go to hell.'"

"Right!" he guffawed. "That's it." He poked me in the ribs. "I'll tell the Champ you're here."

I looked out on the rows of people sitting on the benches that had been set up in the infield . . . Lawrence pointed out Babe Ruth and Florenz Ziegfeld, and a Morgan and a Gould and a Rothschild. Two of Alice Longworth's brothers were there, I was told. All the rich and the famous had turned out on this cool, clear night. The women were in furs, and they were as elegant as a first-night crowd on Broadway, Jimmy Dawson told me. I looked up into the cloudless sky and was startled to see a flock of geese flying south.

I had never been in a New York crowd before; it was different from any fight crowd I had ever known. Perhaps that is why I had a feeling of expectation, of tension.

At nine-thirty a Latin band started to play just behind the press section, but even that was hard to hear above the din. A solid mass of bodies filled the Polo Grounds. All the tickets had been sold and then some. There was no room in any aisle. A ripple seemed to run through the crowd, and the two fighters were allowed to come through . . . Dempsey frowning and wearing his usual two-day stubble of beard. Then Firpo, taller and heavier than the champion.

They went through the motions of meeting in the center of the ring to receive instructions: Dempsey and the referee and Firpo and his interpreter. And then they came out, and Firpo was swinging and Dempsey was down. *Ten seconds into the fight and Dempsey had brushed the canvas.* He bounced up, looking nervous and surprised and embarrassed, and the crowd roared. The noise washed up and over, until all you could hear was the animal howl of the packed crowd, swelling and rising into the night.

The fighters fell into a clinch, and I could see the referee's mouth form the word "break"—Firpo seemed to understand, and did what he was told, which was, of course, a mistake. Dempsey let loose a left hook that sent the Latin sprawling.

The noise reached hysterical levels and stayed there. Firpo was on his knees, getting up, but Dempsey was standing over him, waiting, ready to send him sprawling again as soon as he lifted his hands and knees from the canvas . . . circling around, hammering him down . . . four times, five . . . *Stay down, you son of a bitch* someone was screaming into my ear . . . but the Bull of the Pampas didn't stay down, he got up and somehow pulled himself to his feet, lunging, and you could see that Dempsey didn't believe it.

Then Dempsey was flying through the air, his feet floating free as he sailed out of the ring . . . I saw him coming, above us . . . he landed on his back on Jack Lawrence's typewriter. "Get me back in there," he was yelling in that high voice of his. "Get me back . . ." Jack and the Western Union man pushed him off us, heaved him back into the ring. He made it by the count of nine, and he was ready to kill Firpo.

The sound and the fury burst. Great oceans of howls flooded through the stadium, fights broke out behind us as men clawed to see. It was raw and ugly . . . It was how Dempsey had learned to fight in barrooms. For his life. Firpo was trying to get into position to deliver his lethal right. Then Dempsey caught him, hitting him hard enough to lift the challenger up off the ring and send him crashing, sprawled in the form of a crucifix on the canvas.

I was being buffeted from all sides; everybody was moving, trying to get a better look at the sprawled form as the count started . . .

As impossible as it seemed, the Latin roused and looked up and crawled to his knees . . . he was directly in my line of vision. I could see blood spurting from his nose and ears . . . his eyes were not focused. And the champion was there, waiting, crouching and weaving and waiting.

Don't get up, I screamed, but I couldn't even hear myself in the din. It was like happens sometimes in a dream, when you try to scream but nothing comes out. *Don't get up . . . oh please don't get up.* It was over then, and Dempsey strode over to where Firpo was on his hands and knees, and lifted the bigger man up by the waist— sending sprays of blood flying—and carried him to his corner. The crowd went wild.

I stood staring at Jimmy Dawson. He stared back, as shaken, I think, as I at what we had just witnessed. When the noise subsided somewhat and we could make ourselves heard, all he said was, "That was one sweet little four-minute argument."

Grantland Rice thought it "the most sensational fight I've ever seen." The others, stunned by the raw violence, agreed. We filed our stories. Since it was not the kind of fight you could walk away from, I went with the others to Barron's Cabaret in Harlem, where we sat around drinking gin and orange juice and going over the fight, which had lasted a four-minute eternity.

After a while the talk turned to newspapering and stories . . . Sacco and Vanzetti, the kind of president Coolidge would be. They had heard all manner of rumblings about scandals involving the Harding cronies, and they wanted to know what I had been able to turn up. Heywood Broun gave me the name of a friend in the Navy Department he thought might be able to give me some leads. It was good, sitting there with some of New York's finest journalists. I had been able to concentrate, to get the story out, and then I had actually relaxed with a group of men who included me because I was a newspaperwoman.

Jimmy Dawson walked me to a taxi stand and asked if I was planning to stay on the East Coast.

"I'd like to," I answered. "Might as well see if I can make it out here—isn't that what most Westerners need to do, sooner or later?"

He laughed. "You're the first I've heard admit it. Why don't you come over to the paper—I'll be glad to set up a meeting with our editors."

"What makes you think they'll want to meet with me?" I asked.

"Don't be coy, Hallie," he answered. "It doesn't suit you. You're Sanford Curtin's prize reporter, and that means something here. They'll hire you if they can."

Hallie Duer of the *New York Times*. I thought about it. Then I went downtown to my hotel and sat up the rest of the night composing a wire to the Boss.

Before the day was done he wired back: "Would prefer you remain Hallie Duer of the *San Francisco Times*. Can offer monthly retainer for first-look all stories. NANA will syndicate excepting local competition. Come home when can."

Come home when can. He knew, then. I held the yellow sheet in my hand and watched the tears splat onto it in big flat drops.

Then I went back to Washington, rented a small office in the Wyatt Building at F and 14th Street which had a Western Union office on the ground floor, and had calling cards printed which identified me as a correspondent for the *San Francisco Times* and the North American Newspaper Alliance. I had gone national. My stories would appear in every major city in the country. I could stay in Washington and be Hallie Duer of the *San Francisco Times*. I could choose my own stories, most of them, and write them the way I wanted to write them. I could work all day and all night if I pleased. I knew it was the best thing that could have happened to me. I knew I should feel elated.

I moved quickly to settle my affairs in San Francisco; it would not do to hesitate. Letters and wires poured out of my office with an efficiency that masked the pain they caused me. I wrote Clive: "Please tell Faith that I would be pleased if she and Emilie would stay in the cottage, if they wish. I have paid three months' rent in advance, and when that runs out I will be happy to pay half of the rent in exchange for being able to store my things there. It doesn't look as if I will be returning anytime soon, but I don't really want to give up the cottage yet."

Faith wrote back: "Emilie and I are happily ensconced in the cottage and both of us thank you from the bottoms of our hearts. It is ever so much nicer than trying to live at the studio. Emilie loves the sun porch, and she also loves Mr. Maggiore's niece, newly arrived from Palermo, who takes care of her during the day while I am at work. You have been very generous. Someday I will tell you how much it means to us. I believe that in another two months I should be able to pay the whole of the rent. There is so much I want to say to you, Hallie. I hope one day we can be friends again. I should like for you to get to know my Emilie. She calls the cottage 'Halliehome'—all one word—and helps me take good care of your things. We hope that you return before too long." She signed it, "Affectionately, Faith."

I did not answer Faith's letter, not because I didn't want to but because I couldn't think what to say to her. The only sentences I seemed able to form were for the newspaper stories I was turning out prolifically.

I accepted Alice Longworth's invitations because there was no better place to meet people and make connections. Only two months after Harding's death, the rumors of scandal reached epic proportions. "Teapot Dome" and "Elk Hills" became catchwords. Both were huge oil reserves in the West, set aside for the Navy's future needs in case of war. Teapot Dome was in Wyoming, but the bigger reserve—Elk Hills—was in my home state, California. It was too good a story not to pursue.

With an assist from Broun's friend, I spent hours in the Department of the Navy, going through dusty volumes of documents, and days in the Department of the Interior. My digging led to a Los Angeles oilman named Edward Doheny. I was soon to learn that Doheny's lawyer was Gavin McNab. The same Gavin McNab who had defended Dempsey in court that first day I arrived at the *Times*, and who defended Roscoe Arbuckle, and who knew Riordan. I could scarcely believe my good luck.

On the funeral train I had managed to make the acquaintance of the attorney general, Harry Daugherty, who was bound to know what was going on. I requested an interview, reminding him that he had asked me to come see him if I stayed in Washington.

The hawks were circling. You could see it in the way the attorney general paced behind his desk. "What do I think about the rumors of corruption in the Harding administration?" he asked, repeating my opening salvo. "It's not what I think, miss," he said, "it's what I *know*. And what I know, what I am in a position to know, is that the Reds are trying to stir up trouble, to prove corruption to make our government look bad so they can foment a revolution right here in the U.S. of A. That is their plan, my dear. I know that Lenin's collaborator, Grigori Evseevich Zinoviev, has ordered the strikes that are even now taking place in America—in the coal mines, the Reds have bored into the miners' organizations and the railroad unions.

Don't you doubt it for a moment! My department has saved this country from revolution, and we are being attacked for doing our job. I'll even give you the name of the Communist leader in the Senate." He paused for dramatic effect, his eyes flickering back and forth. "It's Burton K. Wheeler of Montana." He chomped on his cigar, satisfied.

But it wasn't going to wash this time; the Harding cronies had been too greedy, too blatant in their greed. Satchels full of cash had been delivered, the Veterans Administration plundered. The scandals went off like timed underground explosions—the sound muffled at first; when word of the devastation reached the surface the people were aghast.

I was in the right place at the right time. Almost every day, I had something new to add to the tale of plunder. My stories were well documented. When it was all over, most of the Harding crowd went either to prison or home in disgrace. The attorney general managed to avoid prison, but his political career was finished. Doheny, who had offered the cash bribes in return for the Elk Hills reserve, went free.

I had breakfast with Doheny's lawyer, Gavin McNab, on the morning of the day he was to leave for California, his work in Washington done.

"Now I know what getting off scot-free means," I said to him. "Doesn't it give you pause?"

He looked at me, his bright eyes darkening. "I did what a lawyer is charged to do—my best for my client."

"Even when you know that client has perverted the system?" I challenged.

He looked at me again, considering. "He didn't quite manage that, now, did he? The Montanans did what they were supposed to do, under the Constitution. And the press did what it was supposed to do, with a good deal of help from you, as a matter of fact. The fact that Mr. Doheny isn't going to prison doesn't mean he has escaped unscathed."

I looked across the elegant hotel dining room, filling now with men in dark suits and high collars, impeccably dressed . . . politicians and lawyers, most of them, going about the business of the country. I turned back and smiled what I hoped was a conciliatory smile. "Do you ever see Roscoe Arbuckle?" I asked.

"Poor Roscoe," he answered. "You know, of course, that after having endured three trials and being totally vindicated, all he wanted to do was go back to work. And they won't let him. Will Hays and the Hollywood big boys have banned him from working in films, at least under his own name. It's a sorry society, isn't it, that thwarts the truth? I am putting together a company to finance pictures for Roscoe to make. He's a wonderful talent, it shouldn't go to waste."

"I wish you luck," I said. "Sometimes . . ." I stopped, appalled to find that my eyes were filling.

Gavin McNab reached across the table and put his hand over mine. Very quietly he said, "I saw our friend Jim Riordan a few weeks back. He told me you were in Washington. I had planned to look you up if you didn't find me first, which I rather expected you would." He paused, as if weighing how much he should say. "Jim is working hard, too hard I suspect. I suppose many of us find solace in our work." He paused again, and I knew I should say something, but I was afraid to trust my voice, afraid I would begin to cry. Seeing my distress, he went on: "It has always seemed to me—in the courtroom and out—that innocence is the most misunderstood of virtues. Society's rules so often run counter to what is truly good. I am sorry, Hallie."

"Thank you," I was able to whisper. We walked out to the lobby together, as we had in San Francisco. When I turned to say goodbye, he kissed me on the forehead as a loving uncle might, and told me to take care. I nodded and walked away as quickly as I could. It wouldn't do to let myself think about Riordan.

Alice Longworth's acerbic gatherings were always a good anti-
dote to emotion; there, I had to be on my toes. Often the hostess
would ask me to stay on after the others left, and we would put
our feet up on the low marble tables and sample a new batch
of her home brew and talk about the most recent revelations
of corruption.

"Harding wasn't a bad man," she said offhandedly, "he was just
a slob."

"You and your Boston friends helped put that slob into the
White House," I reminded her.

She shrugged in the elegant way she had, lifting one shoulder
and an eyebrow, letting her eyelids quaver.

I went on. "You might better have voted for Governor Cox,
who was at least an honest man," I said. "Especially since your rela-
tive was his running mate."

"Franklin?" Alice snorted as if the idea itself was amazing.
"Franklin is a maverick, you know. Not to mention a Democrat.
He really isn't our kind at all. No. As a matter of fact, Franklin
reminds me a great deal of Woodrow Wilson, and you know what
I think of him."

I laughed out loud at her. She looked back at me through lowered lids for a full minute; then her lips turned up and she laughed
too. As Sara had said, Alice Longworth was very good company and
she could laugh at herself.

I arranged to meet Sara in New York that winter, as she was passing
through on her way home from Florence by way of Paris. When
I walked into her suite at the Ritz, she was burrowing through a
large traveling trunk.

"Here they are," was the first thing she said to me, thrusting
some drawings in my face. "As soon as I saw them, I thought of
you." They were sketches of designs by a young Frenchwoman Sara

had met named Gabrielle Chanel. "You have the perfect figure for these very simple, loose-fitting styles. Now all you have to do is find a dressmaker who can run them up for you. And then you must get your hair cut." She was studying me with her artist's eye.

"Hello, Sara," I said, my arms out.

She wrapped her arms around me and kissed me, several times on each cheek.

"Do me a favor," I said, as I felt a lump forming in my throat. "Don't let me cry. Make me laugh . . . shout at me, just don't let me cry."

She held me at arm's length, frowning, and said, "Have you been crying?"

I shook my head. "Only when I see someone from home."

"Ah," she said. "Well, then, I was right. You must concentrate on appearances . . . how you look, how you dress, what you eat. When life is harsh, it is better just to float on the surface for a long time, to breathe the air."

I walked over to the window and looked down at the people hurrying by. "Surfaces," I said, "I suppose."

Sara seemed to shake herself then. She stood up abruptly and said, "Let's go to a musical show. And then let's have an extravagant dinner someplace and go to one of those private clubs where you have to knock on the door and say something and they serve rotten gin. Do we need an escort?"

"Why ever would we?" I laughed.

"That's what I thought you would say," she said, her eyes sparkling.

Clive and Ethel were married at Grace Cathedral in the spring of 1924, Ethel having converted from Methodist to Episcopal. (I was surprised to learn that our father had been baptized in the Episcopal church.) When I suggested giving them a wedding trip as their gift, they accepted. They would come east to Niagara Falls, and spend some time with me in Washington.

That winter I moved into an apartment at Connecticut Avenue and Kalorama Road. It was bright and airy and spacious. I had planned to have it furnished by the time the newlyweds arrived, but I seemed not to be able to get much beyond the basic necessities—a bed, some chairs, a desk. After three unproductive shopping trips, I admitted that I simply did not want to collect any furniture; I did not want to turn this apartment into a home. I was incapable of putting a picture on a wall. I could hardly bring myself to put my books into the bookcases. I did not want to be permanent, I didn't want to collect objects. They became weights, excess baggage. Even so, three days before Clive and Ethel were to arrive, I purchased a divan and a rug and a table and some chairs. At least, I said to myself when they were in place, I've gotten rid of the echo.

Ethel was brimming with news . . . about the wedding and how each pew had been decorated with tiny bouquets of cornflowers and baby's breath . . . about the gifts they had received, the most spectacular of which was a silver tea service from Sara which must have cost a fortune and which, she said, glancing at Clive, she would like to exchange for something more practical . . . about how they had stopped off in Chicago for a few days to visit Grandmother Duer, and what a nice lady she had turned out to be and how gracious in that magnificent big house. . . .

Clive did not look at me when Ethel said they had seen Grandmother. I had not known the stop was on their itinerary. I wanted to talk to Clive about it, but decided to wait until we were alone. Instead, I made the mistake of asking about Julia Morgan.

Ethel answered angrily. "Did you know that Miss Morgan refuses to even consider taking a partner?" she asked, her voice so irate that I thought it best to follow Clive's lead, and change the subject.

The following day Ethel wanted to have her hair done at a beauty salon she had read about. I made the appointment for her, then suggested that I show Clive my office while we waited for her. It was not a plan that appealed to Ethel. She preferred I stay with her and that Clive run some errands. She said she didn't want to miss a thing in Washington, and especially she didn't want to miss a "tour" of my office.

I had given them my bedroom and had moved a cot into the room I used as an office at home. Unable to sleep, I was at my desk in the early-morning hours, going over some notes on a routine story I would need to file in the following three or four days. The knock on the door was light, Clive's voice low, not to disturb his sleeping wife.

The smile moved into his eyes, and I grinned back in the old way and said, "Come on in, sit down, talk to me." At that moment I realized how much I had missed him, and how I longed for one of our rambling talk sessions. There was so much I wanted to ask, so much I needed to know, and it was so good just to see him again.

He sank into the one comfortable chair in the small room, and I put my elbows on the desk to let him know I was ready to talk. I tried to sort out all the questions that were flying around in my mind, trying to find the right place to begin.

Clive started: "You look good, Hal, you really do. A little thin, but better than I expected."

"What did you expect?" I asked, amused.

He shook his head. "Well, when you left . . . we were all worried about you . . . Sara and Agnes and Faith. And Riordan."

Riordan. Yes. I wanted to ask about Riordan, but I would need a little time. I couldn't rush into a conversation about Riordan, so I asked, "What happened in Chicago?"

The smile was gone now. A shock of fine blond hair fell forward, and he brushed it back in the familiar gesture. "Grandmother," he said, in a voice that seemed weary and resigned, "Grandmother never changes. It's hard to explain, and I'm not certain I can explain—not to you, Hallie—but . . ."

The sound traveled down the hallway and through the closed door.

"Clive," Ethel called.

I waited. Clive looked at me, and then he looked away.

Again: "Clive!" The tone was urgent.

"She is a little nervous, being away from home," he said, not looking at me. "I'd better go."

They were to stay for two weeks. I had planned to go into the office for an hour each day, and spend the remainder of the time with them, showing them around Washington. At the end of the first week, a story came in over the wire datelined Aiken, South Carolina. A masked mob of 150 had lynched three Negroes. The three had been tried and found guilty of murdering the sheriff of the town, but a higher court had overturned the decision, and had even released one of the three. The others were to have stood trial again. It was the kind of story that had been coming over the wire with a disturbing frequency in the past year, and I had determined to do a probing story on one of these cases. It was the excuse I needed.

"I'm afraid duty calls," I told my brother and sister-in-law. "I hope you'll stay on and enjoy yourselves in Washington." Seeing the set look on Ethel's face, I added, "I would feel badly leaving like this if you weren't on your wedding trip. Three is a crowd, after all."

For the first time, Ethel had nothing to say.

I left that same night for South Carolina. The next day I found my way down a dirt road in the scrub woods outside of Aiken, and in a tar-paper shack I talked to the mother and the sister of the boy who had been set free by the courts, only to be murdered by a mob. I looked into their great sorrowing eyes and watched as they sat, dumb, rocking back and forth in their grief. When it was time for me to leave, the sister walked back down the dirt road with me, and stood there for an awkward moment, and finally she said: "When you put it down, say that he were a good boy."

By the time I returned to Washington, Ethel and Clive had left and the apartment seemed mockingly empty. It had not been a good visit, yet it had stirred in me sharp memories of San Francisco that I had, until then, managed to stifle. All I had to sustain me now were the letters—letters from home. One was waiting from Agnes, her elegant handwriting covering page after page of thick cream-colored paper.

June 1, 1924

Dear Hallie,

For some reason lost in the vagaries of memory, I have always celebrated (in a very small, very private way) the first day of June. I suppose because it signals, for me, the beginning of the sweetest part of summer. At any rate, it seemed a perfect occasion to treat myself to the writing of this letter. (Did you know I look forward to writing to you? I've actually made quite a ritual of it—tea before the fireplace, with a fire therein if it is cool enough—and then settling in at Father's old secretary to scribble off these notes.)

By now you will have heard all about Clive and Ethel's quite lovely wedding. Faith and I went together; Sara was out of town, visiting friends in southern California, so we were deprived of her good company. There were quite a lot of people there, though the only ones I happened to be acquainted with were your nice friends Harry and Thelma. Faith and I did have a lovely long chat about a project which I am encouraging her to undertake, and that is the photographing of migrant farm laborers in the Central Valley. Their conditions remain as thoroughly miserable as they were a decade ago, and more. But I continue to pray that something can be done for these poorest of creatures on God's earth. I am thinking of asking for a leave of absence from the library so that I might accompany Faith. Perhaps I could help with dear little Emilie, and be something of a guide.

I suppose, also, I want to leave Oakland for a time. Do you know it will soon be five years—five very long years—since I was caught up in Mr. Palmer's big Red scare and found guilty of five counts of criminal syndicalism? I remember thinking, at the time, that it was rather amusing to be called a "parlor Bolshevik." I am no longer amused, to paraphrase the good Queen Victoria.

I suppose it was inevitable that it would be my case that would become the California *cause célèbre*. The Oakland "clubwoman." (Why did the newspapers always call me that? The only club I've ever belonged to was the Librarians' Circle.) Officer Bradley came into the library the other day. He is the member of the Police Neutrality Squad who arrested me after the speech at the Civic League. He made an elaborate show of borrowing a book, and of speaking to me. I suppose he wants to make certain I am available, when they come to get me. And yet, why not? Last year seventy-two people were in prison for the crime of belonging to the IWW. I did join. I did believe that the Industrial Workers of the World might be able to help California's poor migrant workers. Do you suppose the Learned Men of the high court will see the folly of it all—a librarian joining the IWW to help the migrants? But you know all of this, so why do I bore you, and myself, by repeating it? Perhaps I am getting old.

I do sometimes think that, had I just thrown it all in and gone to prison when they found me guilty, I would have only seven years to serve! But enough.

You cannot imagine my delight at your wicked description of Teddy Roosevelt's girl. I know that you find her "great fun" as you say, and that Sara likes her quite a lot, but I find it difficult to forgive her the mischief she made in regard to the League of Nations. She did play a role in its defeat, you know. I met her father on a number of occasions, and I admit to a certain fondness for him. I didn't approve of his military excursions, of course. But I did like Teddy the reformer, the conservationist, the outdoorsman. I wish he had taken a hand with that girl of his, either seeing to her education or convincing her to stay out of politics.

And now, I hope you will forgive me if I intrude into some area that you may wish to remain sacrosanct. But I feel I must ask your direction in a personal matter, which is this: I should have had to be blind not to see the affection between James and yourself. And dense not to know that your continued absence must have something to do with it. I am not asking for an explanation, nor do I feel I should have one. What I do wish to be free of is the strain I feel when I speak (or write) to either of you about the other. I do not know how much to say, what to tell you . . . what to tell James, when I hear from you. It makes me feel quite alone, the two of you having been such mainstays in my long struggle. I was reminded of this dichotomy again at the wedding, when Harry asked me some question that involved the two of you, and I felt constrained to avoid a direct reply. Can you help me?

I hope all goes well with your work, dear girl. It is such a pleasure to read your stories; I marvel at your ability to move about the country so, and we are proud of you, all of us who love you.

> With much affection,
> Agnes

I read the letter through, twice. That night I lay awake composing my reply to Agnes, couched in words as careful as her own: *Both you and Riordan are as dear to me as ever you were; you may, of course, repeat anything that I tell you. I miss both of you terribly, and San Francisco, and all of my friends....*

All of my friends ...

The next morning I woke, suddenly, at first light, thinking of Faith, remembering how she laughed, and how she and Clive had harmonized on the beach at Willow Camp ... "By the Light of the Silvery Moon" ... Tears welled. I wiped them away, turned on the light and went to my desk to write to Faith.

> *Telegraph Hill,*
> *San Francisco*
> *June 20, 1924*

Dear, sweet Hallie,

Your lovely big long letter came today and I am already making elaborate plans to answer it with a ten-pound reply which I will probably start immediately upon posting this brief note, which I am determined will be on its way this very day so that you will know how much your letter means to me.

To answer your first question: Yes! Yes! Yes! I want to talk to you again—not just exchange information, but talk as we once did, by letter for now but in person before too long, I hope.

There are so many things I want to say to you, and so much I want to ask. (Tell me what you think about the new styles, about the Dawes Plan, about life and love and the hereafter . . . all those things we once discussed with an ease and an intensity I've never found with anyone else.)

I have missed you, Hallie.

You will have to hear about Emilie, of course. Prepare yourself. And we must talk about marriage and what it means and what it doesn't mean (I have a great deal to say about that), and about art and work. I want to tell you about the photographs I am doing, about which I am greatly excited. Agnes has been urging me to go out to the valley to visit some of the migrant farm-labor camps. She and Emilie and I will go together this summer, at the height of the harvest season. I am to be driver-photographer and Agnes will be guide and mother's helper. Sara's godson, Porter Reade, may go with us. He is interested in all forms of labor exploitation, he says.

It is not possible to combine full devotion to work with motherhood. There are times when I want desperately to take my cameras and go out early in the morning when the light is good, but I cannot. And yet I will not allow myself to think of my Emilie as a distraction or a deterrent. It is Emilie who gives me my most direct, most joyous contact with life. With my cameras I can transfer life to an image on paper, I can freeze the moment. Is this an attempt at immortality, I wonder? And if I spend all of my time and all of my energy in the pursuit of my work, am I removing myself from my own mortality? Is it the same for writers—do you ever feel so intent on getting the moment down on paper that you are removed from life itself? I don't know, I don't know. (How many times have we ended long discussions that way?)

I do know that before I go to sleep tonight, I will tiptoe

into my child's room to watch her sleep, and my heart will swell with wonder and with joy.

I have not seen Riordan since you left, but I read about him in the papers often enough. He is called "the West Coast Clarence Darrow" but Porter claims he is much more than that because he takes not only the hopeless cases, but he has a better-conceived social conscience. He defends more and more labor agitators. (Porter among them.)

You asked if Thayer sees Emilie. The answer is no. It was his choice, made with an ease that stupefied me—but for which I am grateful.

Do you remember saying to me once, in what seems another age—but was in fact only two years ago—that you felt the ability to forgive was the most transcendent of the graces, and the most difficult to attain. I thank whatever gods are in attendance that you have, as you said in your letter, come better to understand certain weaknesses of the heart.

I am sorry for Clive, Hallie. For a time after you left, he visited me regularly and even confided in me and sought my counsel, which I gave and which he proceeded to ignore. I can only suppose that is why he stopped coming. And I can only tell you that he had his own doubts, but did not listen to them.

This was to have been a quick note, but can you see how much I have bottled up? I will stop now, and soon you will receive a much longer, better-organized letter.

More, more, more, more to come.

With love from me and kisses from Emilie.

Yours,
Faith

TWENTY

ALL THAT WINTER and into the spring I moved between New York and Washington with a regularity that was almost routine. The room clerks at the Algonquin knew I preferred a room on the south side of the building, the waiters at 21 greeted me familiarly, and so did some of the salesladies at Lord & Taylor.

If I was never completely happy, I was not morose. My writing was improving. I felt I was progressing, and the Boss confirmed it in a handwritten letter which I carried in my bag for weeks, and read so often that it began to fall apart at the folds. He wrote: "Your most recent piece on the peculiar American madness for fads—mahjongg and flagpole sitting and marathon dancing—is going to become a classic. You have grown considerably in your craft. I believe you to have made the important leap from dependable observer to innovative interpreter. From the very beginning I knew you were quick. What I could not have known was if you would be able to acquire that second sense only the best reporters possess: the ability to absorb the whole and draw from it interesting and important conclusions. You now have, I do believe, that rare sense of balance which some might call wisdom. I hesitate to use that word, suspecting it will make you cringe. At any rate, Hallie my girl, you are growing as a writer, and I sense there are reservoirs within you, yet to be tapped."

Alice Longworth was right about the seasons. Ice storms and hundred-degree heat tended to toughen. But then, as if in recompense, there would be moments of a sweet and piercing beauty, unlike anything I had ever known.

One day late in February a gentle snow fell on New York until by nightfall a soft, white hush lay over the city. The only colors were the muted gray of the buildings and winter-bare trees against a perfect mantle of fresh snow.

Wrapped warm in my fur coat, I walked slowly through Central Park in the early evening, raising my face to watch the great white flakes floating to earth, feeling them catch in my eyelashes and cling to the fur close to my face. It was as if I had entered a world of white; snow mounded on the branches of trees and filled in the delicate traceries of iron fences, and the only sound was the crunch of snow under my boots. I was alone in this glistening world, and it felt full and pure and joyful.

In New York I became acquainted with a group of magazine writers and editors—from *Variety* and *Cosmopolitan* and *Collier's*—who invited me to join them on their evening excursions into what they liked to call "the uncharted city." One evening I went along with them to Harlem, to one of the colored jazz clubs that were becoming popular.

Our guide on these forays was a tall, coltish boy named Asa Rosenblum, called Rosie, who worked as an editorial assistant on *Variety* and was crazy for colored music. It was Rosie who asked if I would like to hear what he called "real" jazz, the kind you never hear in the white clubs, he said. The two of us went to a dingy little basement speak where I heard Bessie Smith sing the blues, putting into pure and throbbing sound all that I felt. After that, whenever I was in New York, Rosie and I would make the rounds of the Harlem clubs, coming out of the smoky depths to breathe in the cold early-morning air. We would walk then, sometimes all the way to the Hudson River to stand and watch the boats move in the first morning light. Sometimes Rosie would sing a phrase from one of the songs, repeating it over and over again—humming and scatting—as we walked.

In Washington, it was March and the countryside was brown and wet and ugly, with leftover patches of dirty snow. The rain mixed with sleet, my gloves got wet and my hands became red and rough, and then the first yellow spray of forsythia appeared against a hillside of winter brush. The new green came next, everywhere a pale and perfect color against the light, then a whole spectrum burst of greens. Gardeners appeared along Pennsylvania Avenue and on the grounds of the White House and around the Smithsonian. You could smell the earth, you could actually feel all the green rising to the surface.

During that first year in the East, it seemed as if I was spending more time waiting on drafty train platforms or rolling through the countryside than I did writing stories. More than once I wished we were back in the good old days of long skirts and high-topped boots. Then, at least, my knees wouldn't have chafed, or cold air wouldn't have blown up under my short skirts. I bought woolly underwear and flannels and galoshes and learned how to circumvent snowbanks in my Packard runabout. Like every other working reporter, I kept a flask of brandy hidden in the luggage compartment—for emergencies.

In Washington, social life was part of the job. The capital was a Southern city, and conservative. As a female newspaper reporter, I would not have been considered appropriate for most guest lists had not Alice Longworth given me her stamp of approval. Alice was a force of hurricane magnitude in social Washington. After dinner one evening, when the men repaired to the library to smoke cigars and drink brandy and we women were expected to take ourselves to the hostess's upstairs sitting room, one of the ladies mentioned that I seemed to be having a lively conversation with the senator from Louisiana, a famous bore. Alice popped up with, "Hallie can talk pig when she has to." The remark made the rounds, and I found myself with more invitations than I cared to have.

Often I found myself partnered at dinner with a bachelor Alice thought to be a "suitable suitor," a junior senator or rising young diplomat or military career officer. Most were serious and ambitious and narrow. A few were charming, and I would see them again, and it would be pleasant for a while. Until the moment came when he would move to touch me—a simple gesture, putting his hand on the small of my back as we stood in a receiving line, or tucking my arm in his as we walked down the street together. I would flinch. Everything in me would shrink from the contact. And finally I would have to say "I'm sorry." He would be hurt at first, then annoyed. A few demanded an explanation, intimating that I had wasted their time. I could never give one. I could never tell them that I was as chagrined as they.

I suppose I should not have been surprised when a reporter— angry because I had beat him on a story he thought he had locked up—called me a "frigid bitch."

I didn't want it to be true, I didn't want to feel frozen inside or to believe that what had happened to me in Modesto had left me scraped of all desire.

Late that spring, the editors of *Cosmopolitan* magazine asked me to go to Death Valley to interview the film director Erich Von Stroheim, who was shooting the last scenes of his epic *Greed* on location. I went because I had seen the desert once before in the springtime, and I would be in California again. Not home, but close.

I was met at the station in Beatty by a man who looked as if he might have stepped out of a movie set. He was wearing jodhpurs and a white shirt that blinded in the noon light; his skin was the palest of browns and his eyes were dark and hypnotic. He introduced himself, in heavy French accents, as Jacques Tournier, an assistant to Von Stroheim, and explained that he had been given "the delightful assignment" of transferring me to the set.

We set off in a truck, traveling on a narrow roadway blown over with sand. I shaded my eyes to get a clear view of this barren landscape—dunes, stretching in long, billowing waves, a breeze catching and lifting the top layer of sand and blowing it free. No tree anywhere, only an occasional bush.

I glanced at my driver. He was of an age to have been in the war. He must have recognized the question because he said, "I was born and live always in Indochina. I have been in France since only three years."

I wondered how often he had had to make that admission. Would he, like Dempsey, have been considered a "slacker"—especially in France, where so many of his generation had perished? Where Tom Riordan had perished.

"I am here to study the film techniques. Then I go back," he said, as if I had asked. And then, "Duer—is French?"

I had started to make notes on the terrain, the great, open emptiness and the grandeur, so I answered absentmindedly, "The name is, yes. But like most Americans, I'm a mixture."

He swung around a long, low bend and the encampment lay ahead—large tents and a jumble of equipment, trucks and dollies and platforms. It looked like some strange copy of an oasis, picked up in Los Angeles and dropped here in the middle of Death Valley.

The Frenchman took me to the guest tent, hefting my satchel and walking in ahead of me, turning to show with pride that it was quite large enough to stand in. There were, in fact, three cots and several bits of Moroccan furniture. The walls were draped with striped awnings, and Oriental carpets covered the ground. I laughed out loud.

His face registered surprise, then dismay. "Is not good?"

"No, no," I answered, recovering, "it's just that it looks like something you would see in a Valentino movie—you know, *The Sheik*?"

He relaxed. "You are nice when you laugh . . . somewhat French, I think, but more American. A mixture, as you say."

For three days I observed Von Stroheim at work on the film, and interviewed him whenever I could—a total of no more than an hour. He was imperious, polite and removed. Whenever I would ask a question he didn't want to answer—about the rumors that his backers were threatening to take the film away from him for cutting—Jacques would suddenly appear, and the director would announce the end of our session.

One evening most of the cast and crew piled into motorcars and trucks and drove all the way to Furnace Creek, which boasted a general store, a cafe and a well-stocked bootlegger. The party lasted past midnight, with dancing and singing and plenty of drinking and cutting up. I could imagine Roscoe Arbuckle in this crowd—hardworking, hard-playing. Yet they were up and ready to go before sunrise the next morning.

The night before my departure another expedition into town was organized but this time I begged off. I waved good-bye to the group, which included almost everybody in camp, and then I decided to take a short walk to see the dunes in the last purple light of day.

I walked to a point which looked out over a sea of color—red from the fading sun's rays, and shades of gray, and a pure, fine purple where the shadows deepened. How could anyone think the desert to be dead? I wondered. One had only to look carefully to see all of the life—at my feet, tiny panamint daisies and pen-stamen and miniature desert lilies . . . nothing bright and garish, only subtle, tiny flowers . . . delicate, but perfect, in the palest shades of lavender and ivory and gold.

It was not so hot now; the day's heat, unbearable at noon, was almost pleasant in the evening. I returned to the tent to pack, raising the flap to let some of the hot trapped air out. No one was about; whoever was left in camp, I decided, would be in the food tent, eating supper. I took off my cotton-drill skirt and my blouse and packed them at the bottom of my bag with the other dirty clothes. I stood for a moment in my camisole and underpants, thinking what I should pack next. . . .

I could feel his eyes on me before I turned. He was standing in the tent opening, a bottle in one hand and two glasses in the other, looking at me.

Don't hurry, I told myself, reaching for my kimono. I tied the sash as casually as I could and said, "I thought you went into town with the others."

He did not answer at once, but allowed the silence to thicken. Finally he said, "I changed my mind."

"Why?" I asked, as if it didn't really matter but I might as well make conversation.

"You leave tomorrow?" he asked.

I continued packing. The Frenchman had been given the job of keeping me happy, presumably to make certain I wrote a glowing story about the master. I didn't like it; it made me angry and it made me sad.

My silence disturbed him, because his next words were awkward. "You must forgive me, please, for looking so at you."

"Is that bottle for me?" I interrupted, ignoring his apology.

He looked down as if he hadn't seen it before. "Calvados," he said, "apple brandy, I think you say."

"Good!" I said with bravado, sitting on the carpet in front of one of the shiny Moroccan tables. "Let's try it."

I caught him off guard. He hesitated, but when I motioned him to sit next to me, he did. I took the bottle from him and poured both of us a drink, lifted my glass and said, "Now you can report to the Great One that you plied me with brandy and sent me home ecstatically happy."

He studied me for a long moment, not certain if I was making fun, not sure if he understood the implications.

"You might like the calvados," he said tentatively, without any of the undertones I had expected.

I took another long, smooth sip of the liquor and asked, "What will you tell Von Stroheim?"

He swallowed, pressed his lips together as if to hold in the taste and then he said, "I will say to him that you are not a silly girl, I will say that. And then," he went on, lights appearing in the dark eyes, "then I will tell him that you have a beautiful body—small breasts, firm, slim hips . . . the American girl's beautiful long legs."

I shook my head and laughed. "I expect that is exactly what you will say."

"Why not?" He grinned, pouring me another.

"To better Franco-American relations," I toasted, letting the liquor slip slowly down my throat, warming me.

He drank, then looked as if he had something to say that was serious. I hoped he wouldn't ruin the tone, the mocking cheerfulness I wanted to establish.

"You think it is an act, I know," he said, "but what is true is that you are beautiful—not like the girls in the film, all round and puffy pretty. But sleek and beautiful, like a woman."

"Thank you," I said, bending forward to touch the side of my glass to his face. I laughed then and began to hum "Bye Bye Blackbird." He smiled, and a delicate little flicker of warmth stirred inside of me.

I waited. He had a questioning look on his face, as if he was trying to understand. Carefully, very lightly, he grazed the soft inside of my arm with his fingertips, scarcely touching my skin, moving up and down my arm, sending small electric surges through me.

I was afraid to breathe. It was so small and fragile, the feeling rising inside, so small and fragile, like the anemones in the sand, and I feared crushing it. He leaned to brush his lips against mine, lightly. Very lightly.

I felt a surge then, strong and sure, hot and moist. His lips moved to my neck. I closed my eyes, lifted my head. He slipped his hand under my robe and a shower of warmth splashed inside of me. *Oh God, I am still alive, I can feel, I am not barren.* The thoughts crowded in as tears slipped down my face.

And then he stopped. I opened my eyes to see his on me, dark and full of concern. He pulled me close to him, comfortably close, and held me and whispered, "Do you feel how beautiful you are now? How smooth your skin, how it wants?" His voice was low and urgent, and lulling, too. "I want you very much, but I think we do not make love. Because . . . because . . ."

I turned to look into his face; now it was my turn to question.

He smiled, and kissed the tip end of my nose, and went on: "Because I am arrogant, I confess it. I want you, but it is not me that you want. And because of the hurt, and all the sadness. And because it is enough, no? to sit close together like this, and drink calvados, and feel the warmth."

I could only manage to press my wet face against his and whisper, "It is enough, yes." And then, my voice catching, "Thank you."

A copy of a magazine someone had left behind lay on the train seat, and as I rolled through the Maryland countryside I turned the pages idly. A page of poems by Edna St. Vincent Millay—every magazine had to have one or two—presented itself. Distractedly I began to read . . . and then I found myself impaled on a poem titled "Eel-grass."

> *No matter what I say,*
> *All that I really love*
> *Is the rain that flattens on the bay.*
> *And the eel-grass in the cove;*
> *The jingle-shells that lie and bleach*
> *At the tide-line, and the trace*
> *Of higher-tides along the beach:*
> *Nothing in this place.*

I looked out of the window into the backyards of strange houses, seeing and not seeing. I read it again, two times . . . three . . . I looked out the window once more, down the back streets of Baltimore with their lines of white marble steps, and I thought: *Nothing in this place.*

I tore the page from the magazine and took it with me. In the apartment in Washington I smoothed it and placed it next to the photograph Faith had taken at Willow Camp, of Clive and me talking, our heads close together . . . and out of the picture but there, always there for me on the beach that day, Riordan, waiting in the dunes. *All that I really love . . .*

"Lots of letters from home," Paula called out to me over the clattering of the new teletypewriter machines. I gathered up the accumulation of mail that was waiting for me in the Western Union offices on the ground floor and struggled up the stairs to my office. While reaching into my bag to get my keys, I tilted the package of mail so that it spilled all over the floor. Gathering it up, I saw a thick packet from Faith—more pictures of Emilie, I was sure—and fat letters from both Agnes and Thelma, who had proved to be the best of the letter writers from home. There was a note from Sara—probably to tell me she was coming east. Sara only wrote when there was information to impart. Grandfather had sent an envelope big enough to hold half a pound of clippings—he had taken to cutting every story he thought I should read—and Grandmother would tell me what fruits she planned to put up this summer. *Letters from home* . . . the sweetest part of my exile.

Business before pleasure, I said to myself, opening the envelope from Sanford Curtin. It would be the response to my request not to go to Chicago to cover the Bobby Franks murder trial. ("I'll think about it and write you," he had shouted over the long-distance lines when I called from Nevada.)

He wrote: "Hallie, dear girl. I understand and even sympathize with your disillusionment with the manner in which murder trials are being reported, especially in the tabloids. I agree with you that it has become an especially crude form of public entertainment. And yes, the Chicago trial does have all the elements that would lend themselves to a press orgy—two young men who admit to having kidnapped and killed young Bobby for the thrill of it. Arrogant, cold—not to mention rich—young men. But as you know, my friend Clarence Darrow has agreed to conduct the defense. It is a hopeless case, of course. But that is not the only reason Darrow is taking it on, as some would have you believe. The reason, I know, is that Darrow is as much an opponent of the death penalty as I am. He sees in this case a chance to make a strong stand against that most heinous of practices—killing a man in the name of justice. All he wants to do is save those two—who are, after all, only nineteen years of age—from the gas chamber. That is why I want you to be there, so that at least one news reporter can look at the mechanics of this case, especially the new psychoanalytic theories that Darrow plans to bring forth, and report them rationally. Nathan Leopold and Richard Loeb are cold, heartless murderers and they must forfeit their freedom, but never their lives. I believe, as does Darrow, that no man has the right to take the life of another and call it just.

"I hope I have convinced you, Hallie. On the same awful subject of crime and punishment, I am enclosing a clipping from the paper that I believe you would want to see. I've attached Judd's background notes, to give you all the information we have."

The clipping, dated June 1, read:

The body of Mason Griffin, 51, was found in an abandoned building in South Park yesterday. Although the body was in a decomposed state, police say they suspect foul play.

Griffin was known to local authorities as a Treasury agent. A spokesman for that department says he was dismissed three years ago, and has not been seen since.

Judd's notes added: "The circumstances surrounding this death are too sordid to appear in print. The body was mutilated. Griffin appears to have been a deviant, involved in the worst kinds of physical perversion. He was a suspect in several cases involving the sexual abuse of young boys. One police detective told me the killing was the kind they see when somebody has a score to settle. He said, 'The little bastard got what he deserved.' He doubts there will be any arrests in the case, since police regard it as a falling-out among thieves."

I walked to the window and stood looking down on the street, on people walking and motorcars pushing their way through the traffic, on the shadow thrown by the leafy sycamores on the sidewalk. I thought: *The Boss is right, it doesn't help.* Babe was gone and she was good, and now her murderer is dead . . . and it doesn't help. I watched as the movement of air stirred the leaves and sent patterns of sunlight and shadow on the pavement, sunlight and sorrows.

Very carefully, I placed the letters from home in a satchel. I would read them later, but not now.

I did not want to go to Chicago, but I went. I was in the courtroom when Clarence Darrow stood to plead the two young murderers guilty. In his deceptively simple, country-boy delivery he set forth a passionately enlightened case against capital punishment. The two young killers, he said, should never go free. But they should not be put to death, he went on to plead, because they were so emotionally disturbed that they could not be held responsible for the terrible deed they had done. He did not convince either the public or the press, who, with a few exceptions, would happily have lynched Darrow along with Leopold and Loeb. He did convince the court, who sent the two to prison for life.

I had not wanted to go to Chicago for another reason. Grandmother Duer was there, in the big house on the lake. And the boathouse, and the dark expanse of Lake Michigan. I had the taxi driver go by, slowly. And back again. And then I sent a note saying that I would like to see her. The reply was written by someone who identified herself as "Nurse-companion to Mrs. Simon Duer." She said: "Your grandmother asks me to inform you that she is unable to receive you."

I sat in the backseat of the taxi, looking at the buildings, looking at Chicago. It was just another city, after all. At Union Station I stood on the platform, remembering. And it didn't hurt. It was over, I was free.

I wanted to talk to Clive, to tell him how easy it had been after all this time. One last gesture, one last rejection. Done.

What I did not know, could not have known, was that even then the web was being wound ever tighter around my brother, that Clive would not escape.

The news came to me in a letter from home, waiting for me when I returned from Tennessee, where I had gone to cover the Scopes trial in the summer of 1925.

August 5, 1925

Dear Hallie,

It is quite a treat to be able to follow one's sister's peregrinations in the public prints. From your stories on the "Monkey Trial" I get the feeling that the hot air in Dayton, Tennessee, was not only atmospheric. I also got the distinct impression that you were disappointed with Mr. Darrow and dismayed by Mr. Bryan. It seems to me that the Bible Belt, as Mr. Mencken calls it, is the least congenial place in which to hold an argument on the issue of teaching the biblical theory of creation versus Darwinian evolution. I am very glad that your story stressed that the trial changed nothing—the law remains, Mr. Scopes was found guilty and made to pay a small fine. Still in all, I envy you for being there, for seeing this passion play acted out.

I have some news of my own. As I'm certain you've guessed by now, opening my own architectural office has not proved as good an idea as we had hoped. Miss Morgan has been kind, but I cannot support my family with the few jobs she is able to send to me. Simon is three months old now, and sturdy, so we feel he is able to make the move to Chicago. Grandmother's health is failing, and she has asked us to make our home with her. Ethel is agreeable, she and Grandmother get on quite well. I feel sure I can get a position with my old firm.

I think it is the right thing to do, Hallie. I hope that it also means I will be able to see you more often, Chicago being a good deal closer to you than San Francisco.

Faith has taken Simon's first portraits, and you will have one soon.

Ethel sends you her love, and so do I.

As ever,
Clive

He had said, "I will be able to see you more often." Poor Clive, poor dear, sweet Clive. Could he possibly believe that he would be allowed to see me? Didn't he remember? He had his own family now, and Grandmother was part of it and I was not. Perhaps he didn't know, perhaps that is how he could manage.

It wouldn't do to cry, I told myself. It was too late to cry, too late to help, too late.

TWENTY-ONE

AFTER THE HARDING SCANDALS played out, a reporter had to scratch for stories in Washington. President Coolidge continued giving weekly press conferences—in his own manner. All questions would be submitted in advance, he would thumb through the stack until he came upon one he liked, and then he would hold forth on it for twenty minutes. Once during the annual flower show, he spoke at length on the chrysanthemum. The President was making his point: when things were going well, as they seemed to be, the less said the better.

The big stories seemed always to be happening elsewhere, and that is where I was most of the time. I never managed to get draperies in my apartment, and the refrigerator seemed always to hold a bottle of sour milk. "This place has the look of being permanently temporary," Sara said on one of her trips through town. Sara knew.

Dempsey hadn't fought a title match since Firpo, three years before. And yet he was almost constantly on the sports pages. The public couldn't seem to get enough of him; everything he did was news.

He had his nose reconstructed and made movies which made both money and news. He married the movie star Estelle Taylor and they made movies together and that made news. It didn't matter that he was a terrible actor, people seemed only to want to see him.

I met the new Mrs. Dempsey in New York, not long after their marriage. Dempsey introduced me as "a classy dame who likes the fight game." He whispered, "See what you can do for me, Hallie."

I did what I could for him, which was not very much. Estelle hated boxing and the fights and the kinds of people it attracted. She was also pretty and funny, and she loved Dempsey, whom she called "Ginsberg."

I don't quite know what I expected of the two of them. A mismatch, probably. The pug and the beauty. But it wasn't like that. She was light and quick and seemed to draw out a whimsy in Dempsey I didn't realize he had.

I saw them off when they sailed for Europe; I kissed them both good-bye, and wished them a happy time and stood on the dock until the *Berengaria* pulled away. I wondered then how much time they would have together, how long it would be. I knew that Estelle wanted him to quit, and I knew he couldn't. It wasn't the right time, not for either of them.

The title bout was set for September 23, 1926, in Philadelphia. With Gene Tunney, the "Fighting Marine." He wasn't in Dempsey's class, of course—nobody thought he was. But somebody had to be given a shot at the title; it had been three long years.

Harry was coming to Philadelphia to cover the fight for the *Times*, and I would meet him there.

Harry came ambling down the platform in Philadelphia, his suit as baggy as ever, his shirt as rumpled, his grin as lopsided. I ran to meet him, my arms out, and he picked me up and hugged me and let me kiss him on both cheeks.

"I am so glad to see you," I told him. "You look wonderful to me."

"You don't look so bad yourself, kiddo," he answered. "Sara told me how snazzy you look, but I didn't expect this."

I laughed, and held on to his arm and felt as excited as I had for a very long time, seeing someone from home.

We talked—or rather, I asked questions and Harry talked. Whenever he wanted to know something of what I had been doing, I put him off. I kept him so busy talking he scarcely had a chance to eat his dinner. "I want to know everything about everybody," I had started, and Harry obliged, filling in all the bits and pieces that I had somehow missed in the letters from home.

. . . Gwen had been fired from her job as telephone operator, for telling Laddy Dugan's wife he was stepping out on her. And Faith's little Emilie had been adopted by Thelma and the boys, and by Harry himself, who couldn't imagine a brighter, more adorable little girl.

"Sara told me that Julia Morgan was pretty upset about Clive's leaving, did you know that?" Harry asked. I told him I did, and that I was pretty certain that Clive was just as upset.

"Ethel?" he asked, and I said yes, and Harry shook his head knowingly.

"How are they doing in Chicago?" he asked.

"Clive asked me to write him at his office," I told him. "That should give you some idea of my standing in the family."

The conversation skipped to Agnes and the continuing court case. "I've been keeping close watch on it," I told him. "I think it will reach the U.S. Supreme Court sometime next year."

"When you think of it," Harry said, "it's been going on for about as long as the Sacco and Vanzetti case. What do you think will happen there?"

"I don't know. I've never seen such a hue and cry, and I can't really believe they'll be put to death. I don't want to believe it."

"At least Agnes doesn't have a death sentence hanging over her," Harry said.

"Doesn't she?" I asked. "She's in her mid-fifties now—fifteen years in jail will be the same as a death sentence. Especially for Agnes . . ."

We sat thinking about it in silence, Harry gloomily stirring his coffee. "Jimmy doesn't think it will happen—jail, I mean." He frowned. "You know he lives out there in a back room of the Sunset district house—Michael's old room. Michael's in seminary in Santa Clara, but you know that. Mary Margaret spends as much time as they'll let her at St. Anne's Convent, keeping house and cooking. She wants to move in, Thelma tells me—Thelma heard it from one of the sisters. She wants to be a housekeeper full time in exchange for room and board and all the praying she can do. The only reason she goes home at all is that the sisters tell her it's her duty to her family."

"What about Kathleen and Colin?" I asked.

"Kathleen is as pretty as a picture—she looks a lot like her dad. And Colin is fine. Jimmy's turned into a doting father. He watches over their schoolwork, and goes to all the activities with them. They call themselves 'the Three Musketeers.'"

"Riordan said he wanted to do something right—it sounds as if he is."

"I've always wondered why you call him that," Harry interrupted. "Riordan, I mean."

"I guess 'Jimmy' didn't seem quite right for me—I didn't grow up with him like you and Thelma. And I didn't know him when he had a twin, so for me there's only been one Riordan. I've really never thought about it, though."

"I've spent a good bit of time with him since you left," Harry said. "We take the boys to games, things like that. Sometimes we catch a bite to eat and go to the fights together."

There was something more he wanted to say, but I wasn't sure he would. He started hesitantly. "You know how contained Jimmy is, how he's always in control. At least, that's the way I feel about him. Like there's some sort of screen that he keeps up, and there's something going on in his head but you can never quite figure out what it is . . . do you know what I mean?"

"I'm not sure," I said. "Maybe . . . there were always dimensions, depths to him . . . complexities that I could never fully fathom."

We had finished two cups of coffee and the restaurant was emptying. "Let's walk," Harry said. "I feel like I've been sitting forever."

The light was dimming; in another half-hour it would be dark. We walked along the brick sidewalks, too engrossed in the conversation to notice where we were, even. "You know he figured you'd meet somebody in Washington," Harry told me.

"I know," I said, "but you were talking about his self-control— the screen, I think you called it, that you think he keeps."

"Something happened one night not too long ago, and it made me think," he began. "But let me start at the start. The diocese raised some money to build a new gymnasium for the high school, and nothing would do but that they name it the Thomas J. Riordan Memorial Gymnasium. Jimmy thought it was a terrible idea, and said so, and you would think that would have ended it, but no. One of the big money raisers doesn't like the kinds of cases Jimmy takes on—working for Mooney and the Reds—and I think when he found out how opposed Jimmy was, he decided to push it. The priests backed him, and all of a sudden Jimmy had lots of folks— the mayor included—putting the squeeze on. They even got Colin and Kathleen into the act, and Jimmy doesn't like to say no to them. Funny thing, though, Mary Margaret spoke up and said that she agreed with Jimmy, that Tom wouldn't have wanted it. But everybody figured that was sour grapes—that she never did like Tom too much."

"He's told me about Tom," I said. "I can imagine how grotesque it must seem, what a terrible dilemma."

"Anyway," Harry went on, "Jimmy finally caved in. He even

agreed to give the speech. I went over to cover it for the paper—I'd written a column on it, agreeing with Jimmy, and I got so much hate mail from that one column that I figured he could use my support."

"What was the gist of your column?" I asked.

"I put it politely, but what I said was that Tom would have hated it. He didn't believe in the church, and he sure as hell didn't believe in war, and the idea of turning into some sort of patriot would have bothered the hell out of him. That's what got people so riled, me putting words in a dead man's mouth. Anyway, Thelma reminded me that I had some journals packed away upstairs. She had them all wrapped in oilcloth, and I went through them to see if Tom had ever said anything to me that I could quote directly. We used to talk about things like war and patriotism in those early days—before anybody thought there'd be a war we would get into."

He stopped, a little embarrassed. "I fancied myself a Jack London back then, writing down everything that seemed important. Just about everything did. I was hanging around with Tom quite a bit, and we talked about Life. With a capital L. You know how you do when the sap is rising. Anyway, I thought I might find something to support Jimmy."

"Did you?" I asked.

"No," Harry answered. "I was surprised at all the things we did manage to talk about, and of course there was a lot of other crazy stuff."

"Crazy how?" I prodded.

"Kid things, like the time we drove Tooney Cavanaugh's father's Model T out on Ocean Beach, and then went wandering off for some reason, and when we came back the tide had come in and the T was floating out to sea."

I laughed. "Was Riordan there—Jim I mean?"

"He says he wasn't. Doesn't remember a thing about it—he says that Tom didn't always tell him everything, and that's probably so. Anyway, to get to the point of all of this . . ."

We were at my hotel now, having walked any number of blocks, and the air was chill but I guided him to a park bench across the way to finish his story.

"I found enough oblique kinds of things in those journals to give me an uneasy feeling . . . I mean, I'd forgotten how intense Tom could be, how many ideas he had, how he felt on so many different subjects. I think if he were alive, he'd be one of your political rebels—off looking at how the Bolshies are doing it, probably."

"In other words, the good Catholic burghers insisted he be made to represent something he would have opposed with a passion. And Jim made the speech? What did he say?"

"It was as good as it could be, short of blasphemy. Short. Terse. Honest. I think the kids were satisfied, but nobody else was. The Irish like a good cry, you know. They were expecting something hypocritical and maudlin."

"What then?" I prompted.

"Then I went to the paper to file my story, and something told me I had better go out to the house to see how Jimmy was doing. I found him sitting in that little back room, still wearing his suit but with the collar loosened, and he'd managed to polish off half a bottle of good Scotch. Told me it was a gift from a satisfied client. At first I thought he was cold sober, but when he started talking I knew things were askew . . . it was all pretty jumbled, and I didn't understand everything he said . . . but by the time he finished the bottle, he was ready to kill his brother. In fact, he stood up and took aim and threw the bottle at the mirror. Smashed it to smithereens and woke up the kids. I calmed them down, then I sat up with him until I figured he was okay. As you know, I've had some experience with drunks."

I put my hand on his arm so he would know I was glad he had told me. "I miss him, Harry," was all I could think to say.

Harry said, "I know you do, kiddo. I know you do."

The next night we made our way to ringside in the Sesquicentennial Stadium. It was a cool forty degrees, and rain clouds had begun to gather. Even so, the place was packed.

Dempsey came out to a cascade of boos. "What's that all about?" I asked, and Runyon answered, "He hasn't defended in three years, that's all. They're just letting him know they don't like it."

For Tunney, the crowd cheered. He was good-looking, clean-cut, and he was wearing a robe that had "U.S. Marines" in script across the back.

"What's wrong with Dempsey?" I asked, and Harry answered, "He's been sick for a couple of days. Looks like some kind of food poisoning."

"Then why's he fighting?"

Harry only shrugged. "Says he has to." And then he added, "I'm not sure it makes any difference. I don't think he can pull it off this time."

I looked into the ring; the referee was giving instructions, the two fighters were looking at the floor. Suddenly, sheets of rain began to pour down on them, and the fight was on.

At the end of the second round, Harry said, "Dempsey's finished."

A drip of rainwater fell off the end of my nose, and suddenly I felt angry. It was so obvious. Harry was right. Tunney was boxing—precisely, carefully, taking as few blows as possible. And Dempsey was charging—his usual wild, raging charges, going for it all, the knockout. The fury was bottled up in him and in the ring he could let it out, but it didn't matter anymore. Tunney wasn't playing that game. It was over for Dempsey, and he didn't know it, and he wouldn't stop.

He wouldn't give in.

By the end of the eighth round, one of Dempsey's eyes was closed. By the tenth, his cheeks were badly bruised and he was bleeding from the mouth. The rain washing over him gave him a ghastly appearance. But he wouldn't stop, he took everything Tunney gave him and kept his feet. He didn't take a single round, not one. At the end of the fifteenth, he couldn't see at all when the referee raised Tunney's hand and proclaimed him the new Heavyweight Champion of the World.

The crowds cheered for the new champion, but I didn't cheer, and neither did Harry. We sat there, our eyes on Dempsey. He couldn't see, could scarcely stand. His eyes were swollen shut, he was as badly battered as I had seen him. He was hanging on to his seconds, telling them something . . . and then they helped him, guided him to Tunney. Everybody's eyes were on them now, the old champion and the new. Dempsey making his way to say something to Tunney.

And then the chanting started. Softly at first . . . Dempsey . . . Dempsey . . . and it gained momentum, the crowd chanting his name . . . DEMPSEY . . . DEMPSEY . . . He stopped, lifted his head into the rain as if to help him hear . . . 120,000 voices raised in the night . . . DEMPSEY . . . DEMPSEY . . . He was climbing down near us, and suddenly I had to get to him, had to tell him . . . Harry saw, and came to help me push my way through . . . we were almost there, almost within touching distance, I could see his face . . . DEMPSEY, the crowd roared, and again, DEMPSEY . . . I was shouting, too, I had to let him know . . . I could see his face, battered and bruised, and the tears were streaming down it, Jack Dempsey in defeat was crying because he understood, finally, why the crowd was chanting his name . . . There was a surge, we were pushed back, we couldn't reach him, but it was all right. I had seen his face, I didn't have to tell him, he already knew.

I returned from Philadelphia to find my birthday letter from Agnes waiting.

> *Oakland, California*
> *October 7, 1926*
>
> Hallie, my dear,
>
> I am sitting by my fire, wrapped in the beautiful cashmere shawl you sent for my birthday, feeling both cozy

and elegant. I cannot remember when a gift so lifted my spirits, reminding me that life is filled with soft things to wrap oneself in. And of course cashmere is practical for this climate. I shall wear it into the city next week for yet another of the interminable court appearances, after which our friend James Francis has been kind enough to invite me to join him and Kathleen for dinner and the symphony. I will accept, in part because it may be a very long time before I am able to hear a symphony again. After six years of appeals, even with the help of a legal magician like James, time is running out for me. It looks now as if the Supreme Court of the United States of America will decide what is to become of me. Do you remember the day when James said, "We'll take it to the Supreme Court if we have to"? Oh yes, well. It is grand in a way, isn't it? I wonder what my good uncle would think, were he still sitting on that august court? Probably that he had always known his niece to be a silly goose, to get caught up in the great Red scare.

By now you will have received the trinket I sent you, hand-delivered by our good friend Harry in Philadelphia. The necklace belonged to my Aunt Charlotte. I felt it would look especially nice with the dark green silk velvet I saw you wear once. Happy Birthday, Hallie dear.

Do you know, I realize that I am almost twice your age. I hope you will understand what I mean when I say that it has never seemed to me that so many years separate us. Often, with younger people, the barrier of years is there. But not with you, and I am hard put to explain why. Whatever the reason, in my thoughts you are not my contemporary but my peer. (That is how I look at it; perhaps I overstate my position.) What I am trying to say, badly I fear, is that I value you dearly as a friend. There have been times when, had it not been for you and James, I should not have been able to continue. I wish I were as brave as you. When I said this to James, he told me, "I think Hallie would tell you, 'It was brave to take the position you took, and to hold to it in spite of the fear.'"

If I seem unduly nostalgic today, count it to our shared birthday and an unexpected visit from Harry. He wanted to tell me all about his visit with you, which he did, and which made me feel ever so good. I found myself telling Harry about our first meeting—the time you came to James's office to interview me. I had to laugh, remembering. It seems that James had met you once before, and believed you would write a story that was sympathetic to my position—a hard order at a time when "Red" and "Bolshevik" and "anarchist" were flung at anyone who joined the IWW. You proceeded to ask such probing questions that, when you left, we wondered what we had done. (I remember James saying that he hadn't counted on having a tiger by the tail!) I was quailing when I opened the *Times* the next day, and then exhilarated to read a story which put it all so clearly, the explanation I had been trying to give all along. In this whole terrible time, that was one of the best moments.

I do carry on so! To return to Aunt Charlotte's necklace, Harry said that you were pleased with it. (His words were quite a bit more lavish, actually, and of course that pleases me.) The next time you find yourself at a party with Mrs. Longworth, please do wear Aunt Charlotte's necklace and tell her it was a gift from a parlor Bolshevik of your acquaintance. From what you tell me of her, she should be delighted.

I detected a note of weariness in your last letter, and I must say that for several days I puzzled over your comment that you had found yourself "in the center of events, and the center is often hollow." It has made me think that, once we become acquainted with someone to the point where we are allowed to know something about them, we are only at the beginning. The complexities multiply . . . I think of the child's toy called a kaleidoscope, which you put to your eye and turn, and bits of colored paper form endless patterns, never repeating.

To answer your question, dear child—yes, I am filled with fears of prison, not the least of which is the idea of being locked in a cage. In my dreams, keys turn and I cannot breathe. There are nights when I do not allow myself to sleep, for fear I will dream. There are nights when I am tempted to row out into the middle of the lake, where I can be safe.

But such dreary thoughts for a birthday! I have rattled on quite a long time now; the light is dimming, my fire is almost out. The sky is lovely as it nears last light. Where you are, at this hour, it will already be dark. I shall pull my beautiful shawl about me and read for a while. I am fast into Elinor Wylie's *The Venetian Glass Nephew*, which is, I am afraid, enjoyable nonsense "laid," as the advertisements like to say, "in the tapestried green-lagooned Venice of 1782." Naturally I dare not be seen reading it at the library, where we all agree it is not literature. My *public* reading is Mr. Santayana's *Dialogues in Limbo*. A wise choice, should Mr. Holmes and Mr. Brandeis and their brothers on the court find me "a clear and imminent danger of some substantive evil."

I long to see you. Perhaps you will come home again. I can only hope that I will be here when you do.

Yours affectionately,
Agnes

I had been monitoring Agnes' case all along. It looked now as if it would reach the Supreme Court sometime next year. California was one of the few states actively pursuing the syndicalist cases. I thought the High Court would surely reverse the decision and free Agnes. Holmes and Brandeis, I believed, would not let us down.

November came and went without my usual letter from Thelma, so I opened the December letter the moment it arrived.

San Francisco
December 13, 1926

Dear Hallie,

All the McConaugheys wish you the happiest of holiday seasons! Forgive me for missing last month's letter—I was determined not to let December slip by without sending the news hereabouts.

Generally, we are all well and happy. Faith and Emilie will join us on Christmas Day. The boys make such a fuss over that darling child, and I have to admit, so do I. We have all of us been invited to tea on Christmas Sunday at Agnes'. It will be a grand outing for the youngsters. Harry tells me he feels sure it is Agnes' way of saying good-bye to us all, but I won't believe that our Lord will take her from among us and let her be sent to prison. Mr. Curtin is to be there, and so, too, is your friend Sara Hunt. And Jimmy and Colin and Kathleen, of course. I said to Harry that only Hallie will be missing, and Harry said what is the truth: Hallie will be sorely missed. We had all so hoped that you might come back this year to be with us.

Kathleen has become quite a beauty. She is seventeen now, and ever so grown-up. Since Mary Margaret left to live at the convent of St. Anne's, Jimmy and the children have decided to move out of the Sunset house. Colin was over yesterday and said that it looks like they've found a duplex out in the Noe Valley district, I believe. One of those lovely old Victorians with a view to the East Bay. Kathleen will stay home and keep house for her father and brother so long as Colin is in school, but that is only another year. I suppose Jimmy is looking to the time when they will be gone, and he won't need such a big place.

Speaking of Jimmy . . . and Harry, too. The reason I didn't find time to write you last month was that my Harry lost his way, and we have had quite a time of it. I don't even know all of the details myself, or what happened, and to be honest with you, I'm just so glad that it is all over and done with that I don't want to stir it up. Somehow, it had to do with another old school chum of ours—Arthur Hagen, who is a doctor now, and who used to run with the boys. Something happened between Arthur and Harry, and then dear Jimmy got involved in it, and I'm ashamed to admit it, but Harry took out after Jimmy and somehow the police got into it. They wanted Jimmy to swear out a warrant or some such thing, but he wouldn't. In fact, it was Jimmy who got Harry out of jail and fixed things up. Jimmy told me Harry only fell off the wagon this once, and he knew it wouldn't happen again. But Jimmy wouldn't tell me what it was all about. And Arthur Hagen doesn't want to have anything to do with his old South of Market friends. (He wishes we would all evaporate, Harry says.) Anyway, it is all over and done with and no harm done, Jimmy assures me. And you know how there is just something about Jimmy that you always know what he says is so.

I have a new washing machine! It is an early Christmas present from Harry and the boys, to make my chores a good deal easier. We all read your stories, Hallie. You are our "famous" friend, and the boys never tire of bragging about you. But we do long to see you, and even though

Clive and his family have moved back to Chicago, we hope you think of this as home, and that you will come home to us soon.

> All our love,
> from Thelma

The letter began to shake in my hand. *Arthur Hagen.* The doctor who had been there that terrible night. Questions flew at me, questions I could not ask.

TWENTY-TWO

AT SOME POINT in every assignment, things fall into place. I get the time sequence down, detailing the order in which events happened. I discover which were planned and which could not have been, I collect all of the facts, including those that conflict, and put them together. There are always digressions, side issues that must be taken into account. But at some point everything comes together and I can write the story.

Most of these stories center on dramatic events: murders, deaths, scandals. Many involve court trials, which give both structure and dignity to events that are, more often than not, sordid. Emotions run high, lives and reputations are at stake, the drama is real and often raw. And I am there as the observer, the witness, the teller of the tale.

What I have learned in my years of covering these news events is that nothing is ever as it first seems. The concerned reporter questions everything, because true innocence is as rare as true guilt, and absolute good is as commonplace as absolute evil. And I have learned that the ways man has devised to judge those extremes are crude; justice, no matter the trappings, is elusive.

I have also come to believe that it is the unplanned action, the unexpected, on which most stories turn.

Sara came through Washington that spring. I tried to find out if she knew about Harry's binge, but if she did, she wasn't saying. I didn't press it. One never did with Sara.

Lindbergh flew the Atlantic in his *Spirit of St. Louis* that May. On a tip from a friend of his father's, who had served in the Senate, I went up to Long Island to see the young pilot off. Lindbergh had no idea, then, that he would become a hero. He was making the flight to collect the prize money that was waiting for the first man to fly solo to Paris. He didn't think it was going to be all that difficult.

I stood in a storm of shredded paper in the crowd at City Hall in New York to welcome back the new hero. When he arrived in an open car, waving now and then, not at all comfortable in the role of hero, I felt the same electric thrill that seemed to run through the thousands that gathered. We needed a hero, and Lindbergh was the perfect candidate.

In August I did what I had dreaded having to do, and went to Charlestown State Prison in Massachusetts to the electrocution of Nicola Sacco and Bartolomeo Vanzetti. I recorded the time of their deaths: Sacco, 12:19. Vanzetti, 12:26. And the amps and the voltage, and the last words of both men . . . spoken from the death chamber. "*Viva l'anarchia,*" Sacco said. "Farewell, my wife and child and all my friends. A good evening, gentlemen. Farewell, Mother." And Vanzetti, the fishmonger and poet, the dreamer Vanzetti: "I wish to tell you that I am innocent and never committed any crime, but sometimes some sins. I am an innocent man." I recorded that he wore a blue striped denim shirt and gray trousers and gray socks and black slippers, and that the trousers were slit to the knee. And that Dr. George Burgess Magrath pronounced him dead.

As 1927 moved from summer into autumn, I had the curious feeling that other things were falling into place, that soon there would be a coming together and I would begin to understand what I had not understood before.

Dempsey was going to fight Tunney again, though he had said he wouldn't. The date was set: September 22, in Chicago. And the Supreme Court, at last, would decide Agnes Marchant's fate.

I thought I would not go to Chicago. I did not want to be witness to a final Dempsey defeat. I had hoped he would do as Estelle begged, and quit the ring. But the gorge was still rising in him, as Runyon put it, and he couldn't quit, not yet. Not even if it meant the end of his marriage, which I felt sure it did.

Then the unexpected happened, and I changed my mind about Chicago. On September 1, Clive wired that Grandmother Duer had died, and asked me to come to the funeral. I wired back to say that it would be hypocritical of me to come for the funeral, but that I would arrive on September 20 for the Dempsey fight and that I was looking forward to meeting my nephew and niece for the first time.

Ethel had given birth to a daughter early that year. So long as Grandmother lived, I had not been welcome in Chicago. Now I was going to get to meet the children and see Clive again.

My brother had gained in girth in the three years since I had last seen him, and his hair had thinned so that it no longer fell forward, but his smile still moved into his eyes when he saw me. "You look like a prosperous Chicago professional," I told him.

"And you look like a beautiful and famous star newspaper reporter. *Very tres chic* as Ethel will say. She will never forgive you."

"How are Ethel and the children?" I asked.

"The children are fine," he answered, grinning a little sheepishly at his omission. "The baby reminds me of her Aunt Hallie. She will look you straight in the eye and refuse to smile on command. It drives her mother wild."

I ignored the gibes at Ethel and asked, "Tell me about Simon."

We settled in the back of a Pierce-Arrow, and after Clive directed the chauffeur he said, "Simon. Well, he is small for his age, and timid. He minds well, sometimes I think too well. He does have an aptitude for games. And he likes music."

"Maybe we'll have a musician in the family," I laughed.

"Or another architect," he said sardonically.

"How *is* your work?" I asked.

He looked out of the window, and I had begun to think he wasn't going to answer when he said dully, "I haven't been back since the funeral."

Before I could question him, we pulled into the drive and the prospect of entering this house, after so many years, silenced me. Clive, too, seemed to stiffen as we went through the heavy doors.

Ethel, in mourning black, was waiting for us. I tried not to show my surprise at the change in her appearance. She had ballooned in size, until her face looked like a caricature of the prettily plump bride I remembered.

"Don't you look very *tres chic*," she said. "You mustn't look at me. Babies ruin the figure!"

"Where are those babies?" I asked. "I can hardly wait—"

"This is their nap time," Ethel cut in. "I thought we would have tea in the front drawing room first. Nurse will bring them down after a bit."

Ethel chattered on, and part of me listened while another part took in the large room that had figured in so many of my bad dreams. Clive took a seat at the far end of the tulipwood couch and said nothing at all. My childhood memory was of a large room filled with dark furniture. Since then, I had been in enough grand homes to recognize the quality of the pieces Grandmother had collected.

"As soon as a proper mourning period is over," Ethel was saying, "we intend to get rid of this dreadful dark old furniture and get something more modern. Don't we, dear?"

Clive hadn't been listening. Ethel waited, looking at him so he would know she expected an answer.

"What?" he finally said; then, "Oh yes, this old furniture. I do think we should throw out the Chippendale secretary, certainly. And that japanned table, too. Need any old furniture, Hallie?" I wondered if Ethel recognized the sarcasm. She shot him a reproving glance, and was about to go on, when the sound of the children distracted her.

"Here they are," Clive said, rising and smiling for the first time since we had entered the house. "Simon, come meet your Auntie Hallie. And Nora, bring Phoebe to me. Ah," he said as he took the baby, "there's my girl. Come look at your niece, Hallie."

I smiled at Simon, who was small and pale, with his father's fine blond hair, but he could only look at his shoes. "Shall we have a look at your baby sister, Simon?" I asked, but he couldn't find the courage to look up.

Phoebe, the baby, stared directly at me, as Clive had said she would. Her great blue eyes never once wavered. And then, without coaxing, she broke into a smile.

"You've won her over!" Clive announced, delighted. "The very first time and you get a smile. That's something, Hal." It was the first time he had called me Hal.

"Don't be silly, Clive," Ethel snapped. "You'll make Hallie think the baby doesn't smile at all. Give her back to Nurse, and sit down. Simon has something to say."

Clive did as he was told, and I did too. The nurse, a solid girl, took the baby, and Clive and I took our seats.

All eyes turned to the little boy who could not seem to lift his eyes from the floor. "All right, Simon," his mother said, as if demanding recitation of a stubborn student, "we're waiting."

The child spoke in a whisper so low as to be barely audible, and he ran all the words together: "Thank you for all the presents and for coming to see us."

"Louder," Ethel said, "and speak slowly."

I interrupted to say that I had heard every word, and that Simon was very welcome. I wanted him to look at me, so that I could smile and show him it was all right, but he couldn't.

Ethel wouldn't have it. "If you can't speak up, Simon, then you must leave and come back when you can." She turned to the nurse and said, "Take them upstairs."

I waited for Clive to protest, to come to the boy's rescue, but he only sat with his legs crossed, his lips tight. Was it always like this between them? I wondered. Or had my appearance caused the anger? Ethel poured another cup of tea into one of Grandmother's porcelain cups. It was lukewarm. I thought of teatime at Alice Longworth's, with the piping-hot glasses of Earl Grey served in heavy Russian silver holders. I wished I were there, at Alice's tea table, with the talk bubbling all around.

I shook myself. I had wanted to hold Phoebe and look into those inscrutable baby eyes. I had wanted time with Simon, when he wasn't afraid.

"I sent the children away," Ethel surprised me by saying, "because Clive has something he wants to discuss with you."

Clive sat bolt upright and gave her such a scathing look that I thought for a moment he was going to shout, but when he spoke, his voice was even and tight: "This is not the time, Ethel. You know that." The rancor has been there all along, I thought; my presence might have exacerbated it, but I hadn't caused it.

Ethel tried to laugh; her swollen hands fluttered around the tea table. Suddenly I felt tired. "I think Clive's right," I said, determined to end this scene. "I have to get over to my hotel and settle in, there are press credentials to arrange for the fight, and—"

"Aren't you staying here?" Clive asked.

"I need to be downtown," I told him, "near the telegraph office. Would you like to go to the fight with me?"

"Your grandmother would absolutely turn in her grave," Ethel broke in. "She was apoplectic about your even writing about the fights, Hallie." She laughed condescendingly. "Grandmother kept saying how offensive it was to see the family name in the public papers."

"Good," I told her. "Why don't I try to get two extra tickets,

Ethel, so you can go with us. Then Grandmother can *spin* in her grave."

Ethel's face settled into layers of disapproving fat. "I don't believe that's a very respectful way to speak of someone who has passed from us so recently," she said, "and especially to say it in her house."

I lost my patience then. "Ethel," I said, "I did not like Grandmother Duer. I didn't respect her, and I do not mourn her. As you said, I offended her. And she offended me, greatly. As for this house, it isn't hers anymore, is it?"

"You are quite correct," Ethel said, clipping off the words. "The house is ours. And now I understand why she left everything else to us in her will."

I looked at Clive, and wished I hadn't. He looked stricken. His mouth opened as if he wanted to say something, but nothing came out. For a moment I thought he might fly into a rage, break something, hit out . . . scream or cry. But he only stood there, unable to speak, as Ethel chattered on. "Actually, I was wrong to say she left it all to us. The estate is left in trust to our children, though she did give Clive and me a generous living allowance and the house, so long as we live in it. And Clive is earning a handsome salary as well, looking after the family holdings. The only proviso is that he not return to his drafting job. And she didn't exactly forget you, after all. You've been left quite a beautiful ring—it was your mother's, I believe. I brought it down this evening, so we could give it to you first thing. It's in the secretary, in the third drawer—would you fetch it please, Clive?"

All of this was said in her normal voice, ignoring her husband. I watched, first in horror and then in dismay, as Clive did as he was told, and fetched.

"I'm sure you know, Hallie," Ethel said in what were meant to be conciliatory tones, "that we had nothing at all to do with the will, and were quite surprised by it. Shocked, really. Clive had thought everything would be divided equally, and of course that is what we would have wished—had we had a voice in the matter. But we didn't—"

"I'm sure you didn't, Ethel," I told her. "I am going to say good-bye to you now. But I want a few minutes alone with my brother before I go."

"If this has to do with the will, I think I—"

"It has nothing to do with anything except my brother and me," I told her, holding the door for her and closing it after her.

Clive was sitting on a rosewood settee, the Peacock's jewelry box trembling in his hands. I sat next to him, took the box and opened it to find an exquisite topaz, surrounded by a cluster of diamonds, nestling in the white velvet lining which had yellowed with age. I slipped it on the ring finger of my left hand and said, in a voice as low and coaxing as I could make it, "It's a beautiful ring."

A small sob broke out of him. "That's it, your inheritance. All of it," he managed to say.

I put my arm around him then, and held him as tightly as I could. "Listen to me now, Clive, please," I said. "It doesn't matter, the will. I told you a long time ago that she would find a way to break it—"

"Which *she* do you mean?" he snapped, angry and impotent.

"It doesn't much matter, does it?" I replied, as gently as I could.

He looked at me then, his eyes rimmed in red. "You're right," he answered, beaten. "And here I am, right back where I started, and I did it all myself, didn't I?"

We sat in silence for a few moments; then he said in a voice so low I had to strain to hear: "I'm sorry, Hal. I wanted to change, but I couldn't. I just couldn't. I tried, but I couldn't . . . and I'm sorry, so damned sorry. You're right to be disappointed in me."

"Shh," I told him, rubbing his arm now, hurting for him and knowing there was nothing I could do, nothing I could ever have done. "It's all right, Clive," I said. "Really it is. I know you couldn't help what happened. Not from the beginning. I know that now. You're my brother, you always will be and I will always love you."

I touched my forehead to his, and we sat like that for a long minute. "I love you," I repeated, "and nobody—not Grandmother Duer, not Ethel—will ever be able to change that."

He walked me to the car, holding tight to my hand. The last thing I said to him was, "Kiss the babies for me, will you do that?"

And Clive, unable to speak, only clung hard to me for a long moment, then finally released me and nodded.

I returned to my hotel with a heavy, if resigned, heart, and found a certain comfort in routine. I made calls to confirm my credentials for the fight, and calls to send the wires I needed to send, and to set up interviews and arrange transportation and get directions to Soldier's Field. I went about all of this mechanically, listening to my voice, surprised at how businesslike I sounded. I was preparing to go to a fight I didn't want to see, preparing to visit Dempsey's wife, Estelle, who would be tearful and angry and afraid. I didn't want to see Dempsey because he would be able to tell that I felt he would lose. Most of all, I wanted to leave this place, this city, the scene of my brother's defeat.

As I was crossing the wide expanse of lobby a bellboy called in a nasal singsong: "Wire for Miss Duer. Paging Miss Hallie Duer."

I ripped open the yellow envelope. It was from Paula at the Western Union office in Washington and it said, "Supreme Court let stand Marchant decision."

Guilty. Agnes was to have no reprieve. Holmes and Brandeis had been our last hope, and they had found her "a clear and present danger of some substantive evil."

No. I stood there in the middle of the marble lobby, not wanting to believe it. There must have been some mistake. Not Agnes, no. Paula must have it wrong.

I began to tremble. Paula wouldn't get it wrong. She knew how much it meant. Someone passed by and called out to me, and when

I didn't answer, he came back and asked me if anything was wrong.

I shook my head and made my way to a chair and sank into it, reading the wire again. *Guilty.* They were going to send Agnes to prison. Oh God.

I looked up at the chandelier and it seemed to dim for a long moment. When the lights came up again I found I could stand. Then I went to my room, packed my bags and took a taxi to Union Station. A redcap carried my bags, and at the bottom of the long flight of stairs he turned, waiting for me, and asked, "Where to, miss?"

I looked at him.

He repeated his question.

The ticket in my bag was to Washington.

"Home," I told him, "I'm going home."

"And where's that, miss?"

"California," I heard myself say. "San Francisco."

TWENTY-THREE

IN OMAHA I GOT OFF the train long enough to buy a newspaper and attempt a long-distance telephone call to Oakland. "DEMPSEY LOSES" the headline said. Not "TUNNEY WINS," but "DEMPSEY LOSES." *In the annals of boxing,* the story began, *this fight will go down as one of the greatest of them all.*

"Luis?" I shouted over the crackling noises on the telephone line. "It's Hallie. Agnes—how is she?" But all I could catch were a few scattered words: "... all night ... boat ... sick ... doctor."

I climbed back onto the train with a gathering sense of dread. *"There are nights when I am tempted to row out into the middle of the lake,"* Agnes had written. I allowed myself to fall into the lull of the rolling motion of the train as it moved westward, going home. Over and over again, I thought as I let myself be rocked gently sideways . . . going home, I am going home . . . I was moving, but now I was moving in the right direction. Home.

In Oakland I climbed down and stood for a long time and looked at the familiar dusty palm trees and the September sun hazy on the brown hills. I looked at a pile of purple bougainvillea spilling over a white stucco wall, and breathed in the scent of eucalyptus. I knew where I was, knew every turn and place, and I would have been spilling over with pleasure had I not been so afraid of what I would find in the big house on the lake.

Luis saw my taxi pull up and ran down the stairs to meet me, his hands pumping up and down as if he were trying to talk with them; he was smiling and making funny little laughing sounds, to show his surprise and his pleasure. "Oh yes you've come," he kept repeating, moving his hands up and down. "Oh yes, you've come."

"Is she . . . ?" I asked.

"She be all right now," he said between giggles. "She plenty mad at me for finding her, but I say sure I find you—you think I don't know all your hiding places, little girl? I know she go out on lake in boat . . . you know she did that? All night long on lake! But I find her, and bring her in and make the girl give her warm bath. Doctor say she be all right now. But she plenty mad at me."

My relief must have shown in my face, because he started patting me on the arm and telling me not to worry, not to worry. "You go on up, she sleeping some time, but you go on up. Good medicine, you've come!"

Luis, I thought, who had worked for her father, and who has loved her all these years . . . and I wondered: What do we know of love, really, any of us?

I came into the room quietly, not to startle her. She was lying with her face to the window, away from me, and her eyes were closed. She turned, saw me, and for a moment she didn't seem to understand. Then: "Hallie? Is it you?"

I leaned over to kiss her, and she gripped my hand tightly, with a strength I didn't know she possessed.

She said, sighing, "Hallie. You've come. I am so glad."

I stayed with Agnes, talking to her and reading to her and sitting by her bed. When she fell asleep, I wandered through the big house, through all the dusty rooms, then out into the park that surrounded the house, and down to the lake. I did not call anyone to say I had returned. I was home again, but I needed time to feel the sun, to get used to being back, and time to help Agnes control the fears that threatened to consume her.

On the fourth day I was walking at the back of the house, near the lake, when I heard a car on the front drive. I caught only a glimpse, but it was enough: tall, limping, hurrying up the stairs. Riordan, in a great rush.

I stood frozen, unable to move. The house seemed far away, I hadn't the energy to climb the grassy slope. I stepped forward, in a slow motion, everything in me wanting to run, but I was not able. It would take all the energy, every ounce I could summon, to make it to the back door, through the hallway, to the stairs.

I stood at the bottom of the stairwell, listening to their voices. Riordan's, low and excited. And Agnes: animated, with a life to it I hadn't heard since my return. I wanted to know why he was here, what had happened, but I couldn't seem to lift my foot to climb the stairs. I could only hold on to the wide newel post, which was round and smooth under my hands, and wait.

He was standing at the top of the stairway, looking down at me. Only looking. I held tight to the post. He started down the stairs then, not taking his eyes from my face, moving slowly. And then he said, his breath coming in short bursts, "A pardon . . . the governor has pardoned Agnes . . . a full pardon . . . it's over . . . she's free."

"Free?" I whispered, not believing. "Free?"

And then his arms were around me, holding me, repeating over and over again, "Yes. Free. It's all over, all over."

Sara insisted we must have a party at her house on Nob Hill to celebrate Agnes' pardon and my return, as well as our birthdays—Agnes' and mine—which was that Friday.

"If ever there was reason to celebrate," she said, "this is it." Agnes was feeling well enough to come. Everybody I had longed to see during all those years of exile was there: Sanford Curtin, Harry and Thelma and their boys, Faith and Emilie, and Kathleen and Colin, and some of my old friends from the paper, and some of Agnes'. Even Luis was coaxed into coming.

I stood in the foyer of Sara's *petit palais*, close to tears as I welcomed old friends, and knew that I was home again.

Kathleen wrapped her arms around me and kissed me and then she said, "I was so afraid you wouldn't be as beautiful as I remembered, but you are!"

I took her face in my hands and told her, "Ah, but look at you, Kathleen Riordan—just look at you."

She flushed with pleasure and stood with me, holding my hand tight, and Riordan watched us.

We had been circling each other, Riordan and I. There was so much to say that we seemed unable to begin. After he explained how he had convinced the governor to grant Agnes the pardon—"so she wouldn't become a martyr"—a silence had fallen over us that we had not been able to break. He watched me; I could feel his eyes on me, and I was trying to find a way to begin . . .

Faith came in, causing a great stir of warmth and excitement—I had forgotten how she exuded pleasure. She threw her arms around me, hugging me so hard my ring scratched her. She inspected my mother's ring, and said, "It's almost as beautiful as having you home."

I laughed and held her tightly and then I told her that it was time I made a new friend. Emilie had been studying me all this time; she had her mother's great dark eyes, and she said, quite seriously, that, yes, she would like to be my friend.

The noise and excitement of being back, of seeing everyone, swirled about me. Now and then I would glance up, locate Riordan, make certain he was still there. There was time now, I told myself. Time for everything.

As if in response to my thought, the Boss took me aside. "Have you thought about working on this coast, Hallie?" he said.

I told him, "That is just what I was thinking. Could you tell?"

He chuckled and began the familiar chore of trying to light one of his cigars. "Something has come up," he began. "I won't go into detail now. But I thought I'd let you know . . . A group of six West Coast newspapers, including ours, has decided to send a correspondent to Europe and Soviet Russia on special assignment. To report on conditions there, political and economic. To interview the leaders of the major countries, and the people. The war will have been over ten years next year, and people want to know what's happening in Europe. It would mean being over there two, maybe three months. If you are willing, I would like to put you up for it. There isn't a reporter on any of the other papers with the kind of background you've got for this assignment."

"Even if I am a woman?" I asked.

"Even if you are a woman," he answered, grinning. "Let's talk about it more next week. It'll be nice to have you back in the newsroom, Hallie."

I told him it was nice to be back, and wondered when I had made the decision.

I think I have never felt so adored as on that evening of my thirty-third birthday. I would have liked for it never to end, but I saw Riordan's hand on Kathleen's elbow, and I knew it was a signal.

Then Harry was talking to Riordan, and Thelma and the boys came to say good-bye with Colin and Kathleen, and when they left, Riordan and Harry stayed behind. Agnes had to go to work the next day, so the party broke up rather quickly, until only Harry and Riordan, Sara and I were left. I had decided to stay with Sara for a time; she had plenty of room, and she wanted me, and it was more convenient to be in the city.

Sara shepherded us into the front drawing room. When a maid came to clear away the ashtrays and clutter, Sara asked that she leave, and added that we should not be disturbed.

Suddenly the air was charged; something was about to happen, I could feel it. I looked at Riordan. He didn't know, I could see that.

"Have a seat," Sara said, perching on a little lacquered Chinese stool. I sat down on the settee, facing Harry, but Riordan moved to the window and stood looking down on California Street; his back was tense. I could hear a cable car go by, ringing its bell to signal the crossing.

Harry squirmed in his seat and twisted his hands. Sara offered a nightcap, which Riordan and I refused. "I won't offer our friend Harry one," Sara said purposefully, "or he might go off on another binge, hurling accusations."

Riordan made a half-turn, frowning. He glanced at me, then away.

"I suppose I'd better get on with this," Harry said awkwardly. "I've been thinking about it for a long time, and I think it's the right thing to do . . . the only person I've talked to is Sara here, and she thinks so too. . . ."

"That's right, Harry," Sara agreed, pushing him to go on. Riordan turned back to the street, as if he were watching something.

"Hallie doesn't know about my big drunk," Harry proceeded. "It happened near the end of last year, after I got back from Philadelphia. I don't know what I expected to find when I saw you there, Hallie. But I came away feeling sad. I mean, it seemed to me like something was missing, and I didn't know . . ." His voice trailed off; he didn't finish.

"So I got to thinking," he went on, "and putting things together, and asking a few questions. And I managed to jump to the wrong conclusions, right off. And in a big way, as Jim will tell you. I got to talking to a doctor that Jim and I grew up with, about the appendectomy he performed on you, Hallie." He winced, looking at me. I had been expecting it, so I looked back steadily. "I found out that it wasn't really an appendectomy, and I found out how close you came to . . . dying . . . and somehow I got the idea that Jimmy had been responsible for it, so I got myself roaring drunk and went barreling into his office and made an ass of myself, swinging at Jim here, who was good at ducking, thank God." He tried to smile, but the mood wasn't right. "Somebody—not Jim—heard the ruckus and called the police, and I ended up in the drunk tank."

Riordan turned around, his face set in the hard lines I had seen before, in the courtroom, when he was being pressed. "I don't think you need to go into any of this, Harry. Hallie knows what happened in the hospital, and so does Sara. So why do this?"

Harry wagged his head. "I'm sorry, I really am, but I don't know any other way to do it—what I have to do. Because Hallie came home, Jim. And I need to tell her how it all came about."

"How what came about?" Riordan asked.

"You told me you'd hear me out," Harry reminded him, "and I told you it's important to Hallie that you do."

Riordan glanced at me again, worried, and turned back to the window as if he couldn't quite manage to sit down and face us.

"I was wrong," Harry picked up again. "I got the crazy idea that Jim had arranged the whole thing, and that he had forced you to do what you did—so I came like a bull and all Riordan did was bail me out of jail and refuse to press charges. Well, Sara got wind of what had happened, so she came after me and straightened me out in no uncertain terms." He smiled wryly at Sara. "And Sara told me what trouble a fool with wrong information could make.

"I nursed my wounds for a while then," Harry went on. "I kept muddling it around in my head, and thinking that if I had only been a little bit smarter I would have seen it sooner . . . after the appendectomy, how upset you were, how Jim took care of you, how Babe's death caused you such terrible pain. And all the while I had the feeling there was something more, something that just didn't square. And I started putting it all together. You see, I had kept these old journals . . . and when I thought I knew what I was getting at, I came to Sara and told her, and she got busy and did the real detective work. When we were both sure, well . . . we didn't know what we should do with it. Until you came home, Hallie. Until now."

Riordan was staring at Harry, his face white. I had seen him like that only once before, the first time that I met him . . . the shock and hurt and all the dark angles.

"I don't understand—" I started to say, but Sara lifted her hand to quiet me.

"Wait," she told me, "be patient."

Harry heaved himself up and started to pace on the opposite side of the room from Riordan, whose mouth was tight and grim.

Suddenly Harry said, "Hallie, do you remember when I asked you, back in Philadelphia, why you always called Jimmy 'Riordan'? You said you didn't know, that 'Jimmy' just didn't seem right to you." He paused. "Well, it wasn't right. It never was. Jimmy died in France. Tom came home. Isn't that right, Tom?"

Riordan was staring at Harry. The two stood looking at each other, and silence filled the room, swelling and swelling, growing and pressing against me until I could hear every sound: Sara's taffeta dress rustling as she shifted on the little stool. . . Harry's breathing, heavy short gasps . . . a motorcar starting down the hill on California, its brakes grating . . . a cold shiver ran up my arms, goose flesh appeared . . . I felt the words struggling to form, to rise . . . echoes of other words. I looked at him, waiting now. His face, all dark angles braced against the storm . . . waiting now, waiting for me.

I looked at him, remembering all the echoes. I tried to get up.

Harry moved to help me, but Sara stopped him. "No," Sara said, "give her time, give her time."

"Tom?" I said, looking up at him, then pulling myself up. "Is that right?"

I lost my balance and he reached to steady me, giving me his hand, looking at me, hurt and worried.

"Yes," I said, "of course it's right." I searched his face, and it was there. He closed his eyes and held tight to my hand. "How could I not have known?" I asked, my voice quavering. "How could I possibly not have known?"

Sara, on her little stool, wrapped her arms around her knees and watched us with relief. Harry began to talk then, his voice calm and melodious.

"I think I know what a shock it must be, Hallie. It seemed so obvious to me, too, when I put it all together. I kept wondering why nobody else had suspected. But then I realized that most of us knew Jimmy wanted out of the marriage, that he was running away to war, so it didn't make sense that Tom would take his place. The other way around would make sense. The first time it ever crossed my mind was when the four of us went dancing that time, on our anniversary—Thelma's and mine. Thelma said something about what a great dancer Jimmy was—but I remembered that it wasn't Jimmy, it was Tom who was the dancer, even with a bum knee. And the kind of law you came back to practice—Tom was the radical. I dug out my journals, and there was a lot of stuff in there that Tom had said. I figured he was a lot closer to the radicals than Jimmy ever was.

"I started to test you," Harry went on, looking at Riordan. "Little things kept coming up, like the time we drove the car out onto Ocean Beach and the tide came in and caught it. You told me you couldn't remember, that Tom didn't tell you everything. But it was right there in my journals—Jimmy talking about that episode. It was his kind of escapade, not Tom's. There were other things too." Harry sighed.

"And most of all there was the gymnasium—God, I could see what a terrible thing that would be to have to do. Give a speech in honor of your own memorial. Then I remembered that Mary Margaret had backed you on that one, much to everybody's surprise, and I figured that maybe she knew."

Riordan sat down then, next to me, but leaning forward with his head in his hands, listening. Harry went on, "I couldn't believe she would come out with it so easy, but she did. She told me that as far as she was concerned, the man she married never did come home from the war, and that was why she kept scrubbing those damned steps every day. I asked her if she knew for sure, and she said there never would be a way anybody could know for sure. But in her mind, you were Tom. She figured that you must have worked it out between you, that if Jimmy got hurt or killed, Tom would take care of his family. She believes that God sent you to provide for them. It seemed perfectly logical to Mary. She never said anything, she told me, because people would have said she was crazy, and because she thought it would be good for the children to have a father who looked exactly like their own. Mary Margaret has this very practical streak." He grimaced in an attempt at humor.

Sara had been watching me through all of this, her great brown eyes filled with worry. Feelings were flooding through me. I had to try to grasp what it meant, to remember, to translate . . . It should have been so clear to me, I should have known, I kept thinking. And now everything was suddenly upside down, changed. Forever changed.

I turned to Riordan and forced myself to ask, "Why? Why didn't you tell me?"

He leaned back on the couch, throwing his head back with his eyes closed, trying to catch hold, I knew. I looked at his face and felt a sharp, clear catch in my chest. *Tom. Always Tom.*

In a voice straining to be normal, he tried to answer: "I didn't think . . . I couldn't allow . . . It was never . . ."

Sara stepped in. "That is a question you will have to answer,

Riordan. I am assuming you will stay on tonight, after Harry leaves and I turn in. You and Hallie have a great deal to talk about, that much is clear. But right now, for our benefit if you will—Harry's and mine as well as Hallie's—could you tell us *why* you did it? Mary Margaret might have thought it a noble Catholic gesture—sacrificing one's own future for a twin. But the Tom that Harry has described, and the Riordan I've come to know, wouldn't make that kind of maudlin sacrificial decision."

Sara's abrasive speech seemed to give Riordan strength. He sat up straight, and when I put my hand out to him, he took it and held it in both of his own.

"It wasn't a decision at all, really," he finally said. "Nothing was planned, I could never have known that what happened would happen. Never. I've gone over it in my mind a thousand times, trying to think it through—to see where I made the critical mistake." He stood and brushed his hair back as if to help him think. Then he started to speak, haltingly at first, until the words began to come of their own accord. Kept in too long, they came spilling out:

"On the night of July 14 we were holding a sector of the Marne. The priests came that night to hear confession. That meant there was going to be a battle the next day, you knew that. Some of the boys called the priests the 'blackbirds of death.'" He stopped, leaned forward and pressed his fingers into his eyes. "Jimmy went to confession that night. It was the only time he ever did . . . over there, I mean. We were in a wheatfield. You could smell the grain. And you could smell the fear. What the Germans didn't know, and we didn't either, was how understrength our division was.

"There were fifteen hundred of us. When it was all over, four hundred were still alive. Just about midnight, the German artillery cut loose with poison-gas shells and shrapnel, getting us ready. They started coming across the Marne about two-thirty that morning, at a narrows in the river. They were using pontoons, and we were hiding in the wheatfields, waiting. Our orders were to let them get to within thirty feet, and then to fire."

Riordan stopped. We waited, knowing the effort he was making. "Everything was smoldering, we met the Germans at the riverbank and it was hand-to-hand with grenades and bayonets and trench knives . . . it was the most ghastly thing I've ever seen or ever imagined. It went on forever . . . the dead, piled by the water, and the sound of the crying . . ."

He shook himself. "We were in the rear at first, but as the men began to fall, we moved up . . . and then I heard Jimmy cry out. He was just sitting there, and he looked all right. I shook him, but he was making this sound . . . this awful sound . . . and he told me he'd been hit."

He stopped, took a deep breath, and went on, "I couldn't see that anything was wrong with him, but the smoke was thick, it was hard with all the smoke. Then he told me he was going to die. A German was coming at us, and . . . I killed him . . . and Jimmy was crying. He said he had committed a mortal sin; he kept saying it over and over again. A sin, and that his immortal soul would be damned, and that I had to go back in his place."

He sat in silence for a while. "I managed to drag him back, in the middle of hell, and he was pulling at my tags . . ." I watched the tears squeeze out of his eyes, and I wanted to put my hand out to him, but I stopped myself. He went on, "He was so scared, he kept saying that I had to give him my tags, and he was grabbing at me so I couldn't move him. And all I wanted to do was get him out of there, to one of the corpsmen, so I pulled off my tags and gave them to him to quiet him down. I don't know what he did with his. I started dragging him back, and the smoke was so thick. My eyes were watering . . . but he wasn't fighting me anymore . . . and then there was a burst of light, and I thought my leg had been blown off . . ."

He took another deep breath, and squeezed the point between his eyes with his fingers, as if to massage it. When he continued, his voice was hoarse. "I woke in a hospital tent. They told me my brother was dead and that my knee was pretty well mangled but that I'd probably be able to walk well enough to go home to my wife and kids."

He cried then, very softly. I could see his back shaking but I could not hear him. We sat, Harry and Sara and I, and we waited. It was all we could do. Finally he took out his handkerchief, wiped his eyes and moved to the window, wanting to regain his composure. He was not moving away from us, only wanting to get through it.

When he spoke again, his voice was in control. "That was when the real insanity began. Because I thought they were right. I thought I was Jimmy, that Tom really was dead. It didn't seem to hurt so much, that way. Thinking that Tom was dead. I know they were giving me morphine to deaden the pain, and I would sleep and wake up and know that one of us was dead, but I didn't know which one. And they told me I was Jimmy, and that seemed to hurt less—thinking it was Tom that was dead. I know this doesn't make any sense at all, but that is what happened. One of us was dead, but I didn't know which one, and I didn't remember about the identification tags. I didn't remember that for a long time, and by the time I did, it was too late. Or maybe it was too late the minute I gave him mine. I kept thinking about that. I hadn't thought Jimmy was hurt so badly. I didn't believe he was going to die. I gave him the tags to keep him quiet so I could get him away from the danger."

He shook his head. "Maybe if I had said right away what had happened, they would have believed me. But for weeks I answered to the name of Riordan, J. F., instead of Riordan, T. J. I even signed my name on papers 'James Francis.' And when men in our outfit came to see me, and said how sorry they were about Tom, I didn't say anything. But I remember thinking: you don't have to cry about Tom. I don't know, maybe I pretended to be Jimmy because I couldn't accept his death."

"Jesus, Riordan," Harry broke in, his voice husky. "You don't have to say any more, Jesus . . ."

"No," Riordan said, "let me get it out, I suppose I've needed to for a long time. You deserve to know it all. I guess it was on the boat on the way back that I finally figured out who I was and what had happened. I know I felt an awful weight inside me, and a terrible loss. As if I were only half-alive. I suppose that was when I made myself face up to his death. My brother . . . I thought about him all the way home. On the ship, and then in the hospital again. I would lie there for hours, remembering how terrified he had been at the idea of dying, of losing his immortal soul."

"And you couldn't allow it, could you?" Sara said very softly.

Riordan looked at her, his face haggard. He shook his head, and he whispered, "No. I know it doesn't make any sense, but I had to do what he asked. I knew it then, and I know it now. I had to take my brother's place . . . because he asked me to."

Harry cleared his throat. "And none of us except Mary Margaret suspected. People who had known you all your life, and nobody suspected."

Riordan shrugged. "There really was no way to tell us apart. Even our dental records are similar. It all came down to my word, and so I came back and did what I had told Jimmy he should do— provide for his family, even if he didn't live with them. And be a father to his children. It was a great relief, of course, that Mary seemed to know, but we never talked about it. I thought that she would accept it as God's will."

He looked at me then, and said: "But then I met you, and everything was changed."

"I have just one thing to add," Sara put in, "before we leave the two of you. That is about my trip to Washington this spring. I didn't tell you at the time, Hallie, because we weren't certain what we should do—Harry and I—but I poked around the Veterans Administration and managed to find a young man named Shoup who fought with your regiment in France, Riordan. He lives in West Virginia now, and has his own scars to show for that July battle. The story he told me in a general way corroborates the one you just told. He was amazed to find out it was Tom who died, because he heard Jimmy calling out to you by name, begging you to give him something. He heard your brother say he was dying, and he heard you tell him he wasn't."

Harry stood and hitched up his pants. "That's in case you should want to try to set the record straight," he said, "there is corroborating evidence."

Riordan leaned back, exhausted now, and sighed. "Even if I could, Harry . . . even if I thought that might be a way out, it wouldn't work. It won't go."

"Why not?" Harry wanted to know. "We believe it, Sara and Hallie and me. Why shouldn't everybody else?"

"Setting aside all other things—setting aside Colin and Kathleen and Michael—if I had told you this, had just come out and said, 'Look, there was a mistake and I'm not Jimmy Riordan after all, I'm Tom,' what would you have said?"

When Harry didn't answer, he went on: "You would have doubted it, to begin with. For one thing, you know how I feel about Hallie, and you know I want to marry her. It would be a way out of an impossible marriage. It's a fanciful tale, at best. And what would my law partners think? And the people I represent? The papers would have a good time with it, the tabloids. And there is no proof, none that will stand up in a court of law. The Shoup boy in West Virginia—I could shatter his testimony myself. I know how impossible it was to see or hear anything clearly that day. And Jimmy and I *sounded* alike, remember? The same voice inflections."

I moved close to him and put my hand on his arm. He touched my face, and with an expression of sweet sorrow told me, "The only thing that is changed is that you know, you and Sara and Harry." There were flickering points of pain lighting his eyes. "I know how much this charade has cost, Hallie. You asked why I didn't tell you. I wanted to. God knows, I wanted to. There were times when I thought I had to, but I didn't. I didn't because if I told you, there would never be a way to let you go. If you knew that we had an absolute right to be together, you would stay, no matter how much it cost you. And it almost cost your life. That was when I knew I had to make you go—I thought you would find something more than I could give . . ."

Harry was standing, and Sara too. They were ready to leave us; we stood close together, the four of us. Sara had her hand on my back, rubbing it gently. Riordan put his hand out to Harry, and instead Harry embraced him, and the two men clapped each other softly on the back. Tears were in Sara's eyes as Riordan bent to kiss her. She put her hands on his face and shook her head in sympathy and love and understanding. And then she said, "It is our secret, and it is safe with us."

Sara told us that she would be leaving early the next day, that the house was ours for as long as we liked. That she would see us when she returned.

When they left, I turned to Riordan; we stood facing each other. He waited, and I reached to put my arms around him. "You said nothing had changed," I whispered, my mouth close to his. "But that isn't true, everything has changed. Everything."

We talked into the night, Riordan and I. We lay together in the canopied bed in Sara's guestroom, his arms about me, touching me with great sweetness, and my body yearned for him. I studied his face, traced the lines of his mouth and I remembered. "That time in the restaurant, soon after I had met you. A man called Paddy said that I looked 'like one of Tom's girls.' And you got so angry—I had to chase you down the pier, and when I caught up all you would say was, 'He's right. You are Tom's girl.'"

Echoes of other conversations came back to me as I lay there on the big bed in his arms. "That time on the beach," I began, "when I asked you to tell me about your twin . . . you said something I couldn't forget. I thought about it for days after, and I think I even wrote it down. You said, 'I'll tell you what I can,' and then you said you didn't know how much of the truth you understood, but that you would try not to tell me lies."

He pulled me close, and I could feel the want in him, too, but there was so much to say first, so much to clear away.

"You talked to me about how it was, being a twin, about feeling that one of you was a copy but you didn't know which, about how you had mourned your brother, and then the relief you had felt . . ."

"You remember too much," he said, kissing the nape of my neck, and I felt my body yearning, reaching.

"I said that I needed to know if Tom was going to haunt us . . ." I went on, and he smiled and kissed me softly on the mouth. "And you were Tom. You were always Tom, and you were always mine."

"I had been waiting for you all my life, Hallie," he said. "I knew that, I still know that. I had never known until I met you what it could be, what could exist between two people. When you left, I thought . . . I had been alive, and it was over. God . . ."

I ran my hand over his chest, Tom's chest, and felt everything in me rising, full and flowing. . . .

"I think I am going to die if you don't make love to me. But I have to tell you this first, I must. I have to tell you, and you have to listen and hear what I am saying, and believe me. Believe me as I believe you. I don't need a marriage ceremony to be married to you. I have been tied to you, to your body and your heart and the whole of you, for all these years, and I have longed for you and wanted you. And now I have you, and I do not need to be married, I do not need children to be complete. I never wanted a conventional marriage. I told you that, but you didn't believe me. Sometimes now I think you wanted it so much that you wouldn't hear me. You talked about your work, how you took pleasure in it, the importance of it. What you are doing is important. Agnes is witness to that. But what I do is important too. I want the freedom to be able to come and go, I need that. If the Boss gets me the special assignment to go to Europe, I want to go. I would like it if you could go with me, at least for part of the trip. I would like it if we could sail on the *Ile de France* as 'Mr. and Mrs. Thomas Riordan' and go to the American cemetery at Romagne-sous-Montfaucon, where Jimmy is buried, and make peace of a kind. I would like it if we could find a way to live together. Or if not together, a way that we can be together. I'm willing to do whatever we have to do to make it possible, just as long as I can stay in San Francisco and be with you."

"The subterfuge, Hallie? The hiding, the pretending?"

"Every marriage has its subterfuges," I answered. "Some have a great deal more devastating subterfuges than we will ever have. Ours will be a matter of form, not of substance."

"Will it be enough for you?" he asked.

I kissed him, pressing hard and long into his mouth, and then I asked, "Will it be enough for you?"

He pulled me to him, and I came to him, *and it was all that I ever wanted.*

www.ingramcontent.com/pod-product-compliance
Lightning Source LLC
Chambersburg PA
CBHW030547020726
47494CB00005B/1518